12/04

I0397276

THE CITY TRILOGY

Modern Chinese Literature from Taiwan

THE CITY TRILOGY

FIVE JADE DISKS

DEFENDERS OF THE DRAGON CITY

TALE OF A FEATHER

CHANG HSI-KUO

Translated from the Chinese by John Balcom

COLUMBIA UNIVERSITY PRESS / NEW YORK

Columbia University Press wishes to express its appreciation for
assistance given by the Chiang Ching-kuo Foundation for
International Scholarly Exchange in the preparation of the
translation and in the publication of this series.

Columbia University Press
Publishers Since 1893
New York
Chichester, West Sussex

Library of Congress Cataloging-in-Publication Data
Chang, S. K. (Shi Kuo), 1944–   [Cheng. English]
The city trilogy : Five jade disks, defenders of the Dragon City,
Tale of a feather / Chang Ksi-kuo ; translated from the Chinese by John Balcom.
    p.   cm. — (Modern Chinese literature from Taiwan)
ISBN 0–231–12852–5
1. Chang, S. K. (Shi Kuo), 1944–   — Translations into English.
I. Balcom, John. II. Title. III. Series.
PL2837.H68 C4613 2003
895.1'352—dc21   2002073709

Columbia University Press books
are printed on permanent and durable acid-free paper.
Printed in the United States of America
c 10 9 8 7 6 5 4 3 2

CONTENTS

CHANG HSI-KUO AND SCIENCE FICTION IN TAIWAN

Chang Hsi-kuo (b. 1944) is considered the father of science fiction in Taiwan, and *The City Trilogy* is his magnum opus in the genre. It has been said that no other modern Chinese novel is like *The City Trilogy*.[1] It is a unique blend of East and West, as if *Star Wars* met the worlds contained in classical Chinese chivalric and fantastic fiction and historical romance. But except for a few specialists in the West, few English-speaking readers are even aware that science fiction is written in Chinese, and few know anything about Chang Hsi-kuo, a highly acclaimed writer in the Chinese-speaking world.

Chang is both a prolific author and a noted scientist. As an author, he is justly famous for his works of realist fiction as well as his science fiction. He has published 28 novels and several volumes of short stories and essays. The thematic range, the variety of genres he has tried, and the stylistic virtuosity of his work are sufficient to make him the envy of any professional writer. Dr. Chang earned his Ph.D. in electrical engineering from the University of California at Berkeley. He is a professor in the computer science department at the University of Pittsburgh and director of the Center for Parallel, Distributed, and Intelligent Systems there. He has authored more than 225 scientific papers and authored or edited numerous scientific and technical books.

Chang Hsi-kuo's emergence as a writer of both realist and science fiction coincided with the rise of the postwar modernist movement in Taiwan literature. This movement, which had a significant impact on literature in Taiwan and fundamentally transformed artistic assumptions of writers and readers for generations to come, was launched by a group of Taiwan University students in their journal *Modern Literature* (*Xiandai wenxue*) (1960–1973). The young editors of the magazine agreed that the grand tradition of realism in Chinese literature was in decline, and to remedy that situation they proposed to assimilate western modernism. The magazine undertook a program of introducing major western authors as well as publishing the exciting new works of young authors.[2] The appropriation of western literary modernism became the focus of Taiwan's young iconoclastic writers. They toyed with existentialism, nihilism, and the romantic exaltation of the artist. Exploration of language and voice, violation of formal conventions, and linguistic hermeticism all came to characterize the experimental literature of Taiwan modernism.

It was in this vibrant atmosphere that Chang's first novel, *Reverend Pi*, was published in 1963 and his first work of science fiction, the short story "Biography of a Superman," was published in 1969. But unlike most of his young contemporaries, Chang Hsi-kuo began his writing career as a realist obsessed with China and contemporary issues. His realistic stories and novels, concerned about the human condition, inevitably contain a message and express a set of ideals. Life and social change in Taiwan constitute the matter of this fiction,[3] which includes such important works published in the 1970s as the novel *The Chess Champion* and the collection of short stories *Banana Boat*. Indeed, his obsession with China and the events of the day set Chang apart from the majority of the island's modernists, who tended to be more interested in psychological exploration.

Although Chang continued to write in the realist mode, he was growing dissatisfied, feeling that it was too constraining and inadequate for expressing himself. An avid reader of science fiction, Chang sought to introduce the genre to Chinese readers and writers by translating western science fiction stories and by writing his own stories and novels. Among his favorite authors are Arthur C. Clarke, Isaac Asimov, Philip K. Dick, and Robert A. Heinlein, but he asserts that the work of Borges also has been important to him.[4] The subculture of science fiction that Chang encountered as a graduate student in the United States appealed to him immediately. During the McCarthy period and after, writers' expression of radicalism and veiled critiques of contemporary society in the States were largely confined to this genre.[5] Its obvious fictitiousness allowed them to question reality and examine larger truths unimpeded by political considerations. Paradoxically, Chang has come to feel that science fiction is more effective for exploring the truth and can be more "real" than realist fiction.[6] Clearly the genre was ideally suited to his own concerns as a serious writer; the same truth-seeking impulse and obsessions that inform Chang's realist works also inform his science fiction. In a sense his interest in science fiction can be seen as a continuation of the program of artistic appropriation initiated by the modernists as well as a logical trajectory for his own writing career.

There are two histories of science fiction in China: the first includes the precursors of the genre that were published in the late Qing dynasty;[7] the second begins in postwar Taiwan with the appropriation, interpretation, and transformation of the genre by Taiwan writers. The postwar history is of primary concern to us here. The first science fiction of the postwar period was published in Taiwan in the 1950s and included several translations that appeared in magazines for young adults. In the late 1950s, Zhao Zifan (b. 1924) published a trilogy of sci-fi novels (*Flying Saucers Journey Through Space*, 1956; *A Record of Travels in Space*, 1958; *The Earth Seen from the Moon*, 1959) that sold amazingly well and went into multiple print runs. However, it was not until the late 1960s that the genre really took off. In 1966, Chang Hsi-kuo wrote his first sci-fi short story; in 1968, the *China Times* published Zhang Xiaofeng's science fiction; and in 1969 Huang Hai (b. 1943) published a collection of sci-fi stories titled *The Year 1010*. The genre continued to grow and develop throughout the coming decades.[8]

Established writers such as Huang Hai and Chang Hsi-kuo continued to write. Other authors of science fiction such as Ye Yandu (b. 1949) began publishing. In the 1970s, Chang Hsi-kuo, using the pen name Xing Shi, began a column in the *United Daily News* devoted to introducing works of western science fiction in translation. He also edited an anthology of science fiction in translation titled *Death of the Sea* (1978).

The 1980s saw critical recognition of the genre. In 1981, Huang Fan's (b. 1950) novella *Zero* was awarded the *United Daily News* literary award for a novella, the first time any major award was given to a work of science fiction. In 1982, the Chinese Literature and Art Association gave its award for fiction to Huang Hai, again recognizing the genre. More anthologies appeared with more and more writers trying their hand at science fiction. Chang published a collection of short stories entitled *The Nebula Suite* in 1980. In 1989 he founded *Mirage*, a sci-fi magazine. *Five Jade Disks*, the first volume of *The City Trilogy*, was published in 1984 after being serialized in the *China Times*; the second volume of the trilogy, *Defenders of the Dragon City*, appeared in 1986; and *Tale of a Feather*, the third and final volume, in 1991. The genre remains robust in Taiwan, and Chang continues to be a dynamic promoter. In the 1990s, he published two more collections of science fiction short stories: *The Golden Gown* (1994) and *Glassworld* (1999).

Chang Hsi-kuo has been concerned with the creation of a distinctly Chinese science fiction. But what does that mean? Interestingly, much of the critical discussion of the genre in the West has focused on the problem of definition. The now-standard definition is that proposed by Darko Suvin in his *Metamorphoses of Science Fiction*: "a literary genre whose necessary and sufficient conditions are the presence and interaction of estrangement and cognition, and whose main formal device is an imaginative framework alternative to the author's empirical environment."[9] Estrangement is achieved through the creation of an imaginative fictional world that, when juxtaposed with the mundane world, allows for the critical examination of the latter. Cognition ensures the critical examination that accounts rationally for the imagined world and for its connections and differences with the mundane world.[10]

This interaction of estrangement and cognition is axiomatic for all science fiction, including Chang's. What differentiates his work from western examples is an invigorating blend of science fiction and features of traditional Chinese fictional genres and history. For Chang, Chinese science fiction is inevitably intertwined with Chinese history (fictional or real). Looking at the future sheds light on the past and vice versa. It is this obsession with history that sets Chinese science fiction apart from American science fiction. Chang himself says that the "models" for his own work came less from western examples of the genre than from history, of which he has always been a voracious reader.[11] However, some critics see parallels between Chang's search for the truth and a moralizing and didactic purpose in traditional fiction to awaken readers to the truth.[12] The fantastic elements in science fiction also have classical precursors—one only need recall such classics as *Journey to the West* and *The Investiture of the Gods*.

The City Trilogy is Chang Hsi-kuo's most sustained work in the science fiction genre to date and took approximately ten years to complete. It grew out of Chang's story "City of the Bronze Statue," which was published in the literary supplement of the *United Daily News* on August 18, 1980. The story was incorporated as the prologue of the trilogy itself. According to Chang, the story is about the true nature of human society in general and Chinese society in particular. As Chang elaborated upon it, he added a host of well-defined characters, worldviews, and philosophies for all the various peoples, and even a language—the written characters of the Huhui language in the novel are his creation. Chang's imaginary world is one of the most fully realized in all Chinese science fiction. Its scope and complexity will remind readers of J.R.R. Tolkien's fantasy classic *Lord of the Rings*. But the trilogy also warrants comparison with the classics of Chinese fiction and martial arts fiction. The interest in history and military strategy are reminiscent of the *Romance of the Three Kingdoms*; the attention to characterization recalls *Outlaws of the Marsh*. The warrior brotherhoods, the political intrigue, the martial arts, and the sense of justice manifested by the protagonists are all features one commonly encounters in martial arts fiction, both classical and contemporary.

Like all good sci-fi, Chang's trilogy entertains as it compels the reader to ponder more profound issues. Chang believes that the most basic concern of science fiction is the examination of the human condition. Thematically, the trilogy is concerned with historical determinism.[13] Symbolically, the Bronze Statue can be said to represent history—how it is remade and revised, but also how it can determine the fate of a people.[14] The contemplation of the fate of Sunlon City and the Huhui people in Chang's tale provides ample food for thought regarding the world today. But as Chang points out, the story of Sunlon City—like the story of humanity—can really never be finished.[15] So stay tuned for the next installment.

J.B.

Paris / Monterey / Vancouver, 2002

NOTES

1. David Der-wei Wang, *Fin-de-siècle Splendor: Repressed Modernities of Late Qing Fiction, 1849–1911* (Stanford: Stanford University Press, 1997), 339.

2. Sung-sheng Yvonne Chang, *Modernism and the Nativist Resistance: Contemporary Fiction from Taiwan* (Durham: Duke University Press, 1993), 1–22 and Leo Ou-fan Lee, "Modernism and Romanticism in Taiwan Literature" in Jeannette L. Faurot, ed., *Chinese Fiction from Taiwan: Critical Perspectives* (Bloomington: Indiana University Press, 1980), 6–30.

3. Joseph S.M. Lau, "Obsession with Taiwan: The Fiction of Chang Hsi-kuo," in Jeannette L. Faurot, ed., *Chinese Fiction from Taiwan: Critical Perspectives*, 148–65.

4. Chang Hsi-kuo, unpublished interview with the translator, 25 July 2002.

5. David Meltzer, ed., "Interview with Kenneth Rexroth," in *Golden Gate: Interviews with 5 San Francisco Poets* (San Francisco: Wingbow Press, 1976), 31.

6. Chang Hsi-kuo, interview, 25 July 2002.

7. For a detailed discussion of some of these precursors, see David Der-wei Wang's *Fin-de-siècle Splendor*, especially the chapter titled "Confused Horizons: Science Fantasy," 252–312.

8. The brief overview of the development of science fiction in this introduction was derived from Huang Zhongtian, et al., *A General Survey of Taiwan's New Literature* (*Taiwan xinwenxue gaiguan*) (Taipei: Daohe chubanshe, 1992), especially chapter 10, section 2, 543–55, as well as the 25 July 2002 interview with Chang Hsi-kuo.

9. Darko Suvin, *Metamorphoses of Science Fiction* (New Haven: Yale University Press, 1979), 7–8.

10. See Carl Freedman, *Critical Theory and Science Fiction* (Hanover: Wesleyan University Press, 2000), 17–18.

11. Chang Hsi-kuo, interview, 25 July 2002.

12. See for example Wang Yijia, "Science Fiction and Literary Sketches" (*Kehuan xiaoshuo yu biji xiaoshuo*), in *Mirage* (*Huanxiang*) inaugural issue (Taipei, 1989): 59–66. Also see Leo Ou-fan Lee's comments in "Brief Discussion of Nebula Suite" (*Xingyun zuqu jianlun*), his preface to Chang Hsi-kuo's *The Nebula Suite* (*Xingyun zuqu*) (Taipei: Zhishi xitong chuban youxian gongsi, 1980).

13. See Chang Hsi-kuo's afterword to *Tale of a feather* (*Yiyu mao*) (Taipei: Zhishi xitong chuban youxian gongsi, 1991) 203–4.

14. See Wang Jianyuan, "Commentary" (*Pingzhu*), appended to Chang's "City of the Bronze Statue" (*Tongxiang Cheng*) as it appeared in Chang Hsi-kuo, ed., *Anthology of Contemporary Science Fiction* (*Dangdai kehuan xiaoshuoxuan*) (Taipei: Zhishi xitong chuban youxian gongsi, 1983), 113–15.

15. Chang Hsi-kuo, afterword to *Tale of a Feather*, 204.

ACKNOWLEDGMENTS

The translation of Chang Hsi-kuo's trilogy took approximately eighteen months to complete, mostly with time snatched on weekends, during vacations, or after work. Rendering Professor Chang's wonderful novel into English was as challenging as it was enjoyable. I can't say that I have been entirely successful in capturing all the nuances of the original, especially the puns and wordplay that the author so revels in, but I have striven to capture the verve, humor, and intelligence of the original. If I have managed to covey even a fraction of the pleasure I have found in the novel, then I must count the translation a success.

As in any project of this scope, many individuals have made contributions in one way or another. I would like to thank David Der-wei Wang for introducing me to Chang Hsi-kuo's science fiction, for allowing me to translate *The City Trilogy* for Columbia University's Taiwan literature series, and for his enthusiastic support for Taiwan literature and its translation. Professor Chang Hsi-kuo has also been supportive and helpful at all stages. A word of thanks is due Jennifer Crewe, editorial director at Columbia, for seeing this book through production and working to overcome all difficulties. My sincere thanks to Howard Goldblatt, *il miglior fabbro*, for his example and encouragement over the years and for his kind words for this project. A tip of the hat to Robert Hegel, friend and mentor, for Han dynasty official titles. I am grateful to Leslie Kriesel, my editor at Columbia, for yet another fine job—this translation has benefited from her keen eye and attention to detail. In addition, I would like to express my gratitude to the Chiang Ching-kuo Foundation for International Scholarly Exchange for supporting the translation. And special thanks must, as always, go to my wife Yingtsih, herself a translator, who read and commented on the entire manuscript. This translation is dedicated to her.

THE CITY TRILOGY

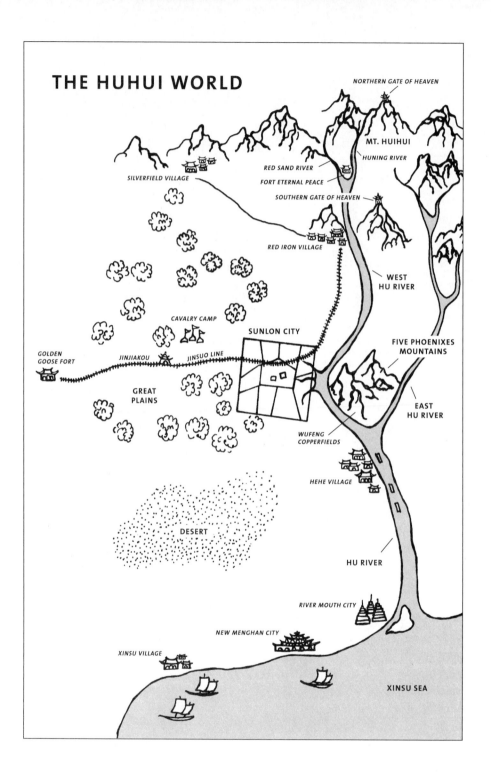

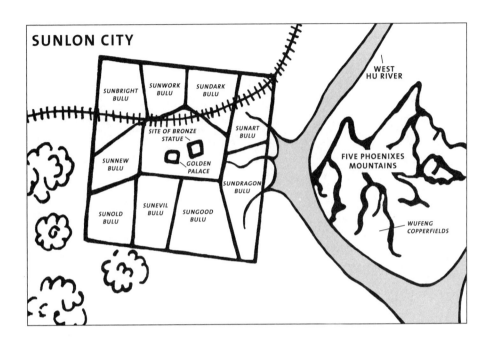

SUNLON CITY

SUNBRIGHT BULU

SUNWORK BULU

SUNDARK BULU

SUNART BULU

SITE OF BRONZE STATUE

GOLDEN PALACE

SUNNEW BULU

SUNDRAGON BULU

SUNOLD BULU

SUNEVIL BULU

SUNGOOD BULU

WEST HU RIVER

FIVE PHOENIXES MOUNTAINS

WUFENG COPPERFIELDS

ONE

FIVE JADE DISKS

PROLOGUE

The bronze statue towered more than 330 meters above the city center and covered an area in excess of 6,700 square meters. The city stood on a vast grassy plain, but all that could be seen from 80 kilometers away was the huge statue, shining under the purple sun of the Huhui planet. According to travelers in those days, the most notable feature of the planet visible from a spaceship was the Bronze Statue of Sunlon[1] City. It was more magnificent even than the Golden Palace of the capital, and was unique not only on the Huhui planet but also in the universe.

There are a number of legends concerning the origin of the Bronze Statue. According to Huhui historical records, the first Bronze Statue was erected in memory of the earliest group of settlers. But most agree that the statue was of the city's first leader. Others have suggested that it was taken as spoils in the Third Interstellar War; but all later historians agree that it existed in Sunlon City by the time of that war. At first the statue, which

---

[1] On the origins of the name "Sunlon City": Historians believe that the name is a compound formed from the words *sun* and *Babylon*. The first group of settlers from Earth named the city "Sunlon" in honor of their sun and solar system and in hopes that the city might one day become as prosperous and renowned as Babylon. Linguists, however, emphasize the sibilant nature of the language of the Serpent people (*sun*) and the palatal nature of the language of the Leopard people (*lon*) in the name. The words *sun* and *lon* in the languages of these people have the same meaning—"to eat people, to cannibalize." Thus the name of the city can be translated as "the man-eating city." This is, of course, merely a hypothesis.

was considered large in its day, was only 33 meters in height, nothing compared to the colossus it later became.

Twenty years after the end of the Third Interstellar War, the Huhui king, who had disappeared in the chaos of the war, suddenly returned to Sunlon City. The king's younger brother, who had succeeded him, was unwilling to step down in his favor. Both sides resorted to arms. With the secret assistance of the old ministers, the old king captured the capital, and the new king fled to the grassy plains. After being restored to power, the old king exterminated everyone in the new king's faction. In addition to displaying the 1,000-plus heads on the city wall, he had the Bronze Statue melted down along with the arms of the defeated faction and recast in a statue in his own likeness. The old king died soon thereafter, and since the heir was still young, the king's brother, with the help of the Leopard people, retook Sunlon City. After the new king was restored, he likewise killed all the members of the old king's faction, melted down the Bronze Statue, and had it recast in his own image. As luck would have it, the young heir managed to escape to the plains, and 12 years later he led a force against the city. The war between the old and new factions continued for more than 1,000 years. According to Huhui historical records, Sunlon City changed hands 31 times. The upheaval of those days is apparent in the name given to it by historians: the "Thousand-Year War."

The Thousand-Year War was in fact a civil war between the old and new factions and made no positive contribution during the Anliu Era of Huhui civilization, except perhaps the progress made in bronze metallurgy. For regardless of which faction took the city, the first thing they did was to put the losing faction to the sword and melt down their armor along with the Bronze Statue and recast it anew. Each time, greater numbers of people died and there was a concomitant increase in the size of the statue. The seventeenth time Sunlon City changed hands, the statue was already 99 meters high. Regardless of how metallurgic techniques progressed, smelting the bronze for such a huge statue was a long and arduous job. Each time the victorious faction cast a new statue, the nation's resources were exhausted and the people impoverished. Complaints were rampant. Often, as soon as the statue was recast the losing faction was again attacking the city, and work would soon have to recommence on the statue.

But the statue had to be recast, for it had become the nightmare of all those who ruled the city. A poet expressed it best when he wrote:

All the world's eyes
Are fixed on the bronze image
Growing larger by the day.

The nineteenth time that Sunlon City changed hands, the victors ordered that the statue be destroyed and never recast. But in one night the brave prince of the new faction became the object of contempt and was forsaken, and on the following day he was stabbed to death in his bath by his subordinates. Sunlon City changed hands for the twentieth time. After such a frightful lesson, no ruler of the city ever dared go against tradition again. The Bronze Statue had to be recast regardless of how arduous the task or how it drained the state coffers.

The rulers of Sunlon City were ambivalent in their attitude toward the statue: they risked their lives if they failed to recast it, but doing so would also ruin the state. Having to make such a difficult choice was enough to turn the hair of the wisest king white from worry. The people of Sunlon City were no less ambivalent. They hated the statue because so many fathers and sons, along with their armor, ended up incorporated in it. Some lost their footing and fell into the molten metal in the bronze-casting cauldron; others died crushed beneath falling pieces of the statue as it was demolished; and still others fell dead from exhaustion on the roadside as they helped move the statue. Consequently, there were many bitter memories associated with the statue. But the symbol of Sunlon City also was a great source of pride. The city's greatness was founded on the very existence of the statue; it was the reason the city's glorious deeds were on everybody's lips. Never was there a Huhui poet who didn't write a poem cursing the statue; nor was there ever one who didn't praise it. On account of this, even today, when young Huhui people find that the course of love does not run smooth, they always allude to an unreciprocating lover as the "Bronze Statue of Sunlon City" in their love letters.

When the city changed hands for the twenty-ninth time, the statue was a huge 165 meters in height. The mere sight of it would leave anyone who contemplated melting it down utterly terror stricken. Once, after the old king's faction gained the upper hand, the general arrogantly entered the city. His subordinates led him to the statue and after a mere glance at it, he fell from his horse and lay in a coma for three days. On the third night, someone saw him, barefoot with his hands behind his back, pacing back and forth, mumbling to himself on the square in front of the palace. In the morning, the sentries discovered him—he had hanged himself in the palace. Some said that he had committed suicide; others claimed that he had lost his mind; others said that the souls in the statue had possessed him and forced him to take his own life.

Whatever the truth of the matter, in the 37 years after the general hanged himself, neither army would enter—Sunlon City existed in a power vacuum. The leaders of both sides realized that whoever dared to enter the city would have to recast the statue, a deed for which they all lacked sufficient courage. The city was simply left to its own devices. It was the will of heaven, no doubt. That 37-year period saw the beginnings of the democratic tradition of Huhui civilization. Since Sunlon City was avoided by both factions and was without a leader, chaos reigned for many years. Later, an old pedant urged the residents, in accordance with the ancient laws of Earth, to form the first republican government, now termed the "First Republic" by historians. The city changed hands for the thirtieth time.

After the founding of the republic, prosperity gradually returned to the city. The people lived and worked in peace and contentment, and industry and commerce developed rapidly. When the senior statesmen of the republic grew conceited, some people felt it was time to recast the statue. They pointed out that it was in the image of the last king of the new faction and as such was no longer worthy of respect and veneration. After all, the successes of the republic had long since surpassed those of the old kings, and naturally this called for a new statue. But everyone differed on whose likeness it should bear. There was no consensus. Some people suggested that many small statues should be made to honor the city's founders, but others thought that the statue should honor the city's first ruler. Although they could not say so publicly, the senior statesmen of the republic, of course, all secretly hoped that the statue would be remade in their image.

Many were opposed to recasting the statue. They pointed out that the kings of old had ended up destroying the nation and themselves on account of the statue, and that a republican government should not be given to such vanities. The cavalries of the old and new factions continued to appear on the plains outside Sunlon City, as a reminder that they could enter at any time. It was felt that wasting all available manpower and materials on the statue was tantamount to foolishly inviting self-destruction. Besides, the statue was already 165 meters high and weighed more than 100 tons. The last time it was recast, the process took 10 years. Was it possible that the republican government would ignore the opposition of the city residents and insist on doing things its own way?

The power of those in favor of and those against the statue was great, and neither side would yield. But in the end, it was the old pedant who had suggested a republican form of government who came up with a way out of the impasse. The old man was more than 90 years old, but he was sharper than many young people. His solution was unprecedented in Huhui history and had a tremendous impact on future generations. He was of the opinion that there was no need to recast the statue; they could simply add another layer of bronze. In that way, not only would the new statue be larger than the old, but there would be no need to destroy the old statue and manpower and materials would be saved. But more important, future rulers would never speak lightly of tearing down the statue. At most, they would add another layer of bronze, because the old statue remained intact inside the new.

The old pedant's idea was quickly and unanimously adopted by the senate of the republican government. The merchants and common people of the city were gladdened and greatly relieved. It was a brilliant plan that satisfied both sides! The people felt a great deal of gratitude to the old pedant, and in recognition of his meritorious service in having initated the republic, the new statue would be made in his likeness. But little did anyone know that this would cost the old pedant his life and bring the First Republic to an end.

News of the republic's new statue spread rapidly over the plains, rousing the anger of the leaders of the old and new factions alike. Once they realized that it was not so hard to redo the statue, they burned with ambition and, giving up their former differences, organized a combined force and besieged Sunlon City. The republican government fought valiantly for three years but could not hold out forever. The day the city fell, every last senior statesman was in the senate, where, rather than flee, they set themselves afire to die for their country. The republican forces defending the city fought to the last man. Not one surrendered. The tragic end of the First Republic was lamented by Huhui poets in song that stirred the hearts of countless later freedom fighters. The combined army entered the city and the subsequent slaughter lasted three days, during which the old pedant and the 35 members of his family were all put to the sword. It was ordered that his head and those of his family be hung on the city wall and never taken down. Only 124 years later, after the success of the democratic revolution and the founding of the Second Republic, were the heads removed, at which time the Bronze Statue was remade in the old pendant's likeness.

After the triumph of the combined army, the prince of the new faction and the princess of the old faction were united as king and queen. And thus, the Thousand-Year-War between the factions came to an end, and a new layer of bronze was quickly added to the republic's statue. Huhui history entered a new era, marking the end of fighting between the old and new factions but the beginning of war between the Royalist party and the Democratic party. In the following 2,000 years, there were 27 republican revolutions and 27 restorations. The leopard was the symbol of the Royalists and the green snake that of the Democratic force. Hence, the historians' term the "Snake and Leopard War." The last time the two sides reached a détente, Huhui history entered a period of constitutional monarchy, and the Anliu Era of Huhui culture saw the birth of a golden age.

In the 2,000 years of the Snake and Leopard War, 54 layers of bronze were added to the statue, making it a majestic colossus nearly 330 meters in height. The early years of the constitutional monarchy produced several generals and ministers of great talent and bold vision who redid the statue several times. But adding just one new layer to the colossal statue in itself became a feat of engineering. The last time a layer of bronze was added, it cost millions and brought down the cabinet. After that, no minister ever tried to add another layer of metal to the statue.

The Bronze Statue itself gradually began to change. The many layers of bronze that were added over time were originally in the likenesses of various historical figures. It is unclear whether time or the influence of gravity was to blame for the statue gradually taking on a new appearance. The face was no longer identifiable as that of any one historical figure, but rather seemed a composite of many. When the residents of Sunlon City or the tourists looked at the statue, they all had the strange feeling that they were looking at a living being rather than hundreds of tons of metal. Some said that when they looked at the statue it seemed as if the whole of Huhui history was looking back at them. Others said that the face of the Bronze Statue was not that of an ordinary person. Various myths about the statue gradually spread far and wide. Some swore that when they passed it at night they could hear its heavy breathing. The residents in several lanes near it claimed to have heard the sounds of weeping and sighing coming from inside. These rumors, though denied by the government, spread like wildfire. But on the other hand, the government thought the appearance of various myths was not so strange given all the wronged souls buried by the statue. Only after the Bronze Statue Cult emerged and people began worshipping the statue as the one true god did the government, in a fit of panic, adopt severe measures prohibiting the new cult from preaching and holding religious services.

Huhui civilization at that time reached its zenith, like the noonday sun. Advances in art, culture, commerce, industry, technology, and defense placed the Huhui far ahead of any other galaxies in the vicinity of the Milky Way. Therefore, the Huhui planet became the leader of eighteen nearby galaxies. Later historians found it difficult to explain the appearance of the primitive Bronze Statue cult in the capital of Sunlon City given the advances during the Anliu Era of Huhui civilization.

The magical powers of the statue grew day by day. Despite the fact that the city government added no new layers of bronze, the statue continued to grow. Some people wondered if the cult followers were working on the statue in secret, which was highly unlikely, because, first of all, although the followers knelt before the statue to worship it, they dared not touch the statue since they considered it an act of profanation. Second, even if they did want to refurbish the statue, it would have been difficult for them to go undetected by the guards posted there. There was another more scientific theory that postulated that as a result of the sinking of the geological strata beneath the city, a fissure appeared beneath the statue through which molten magma was forced into the statue, making it swell much like a balloon. This also explained why at times the statue appeared to be sweating or weeping. But regardless of the theories, the ever-growing statue did instill fear in the general populace. In the silence of the night, it could be heard to pant; the sound was clearly audible to all, even those who didn't believe in the cult. The statue's expression grew ferocious and terrifying. When the newly arrived ambassador from another country first laid eyes on the statue, he blurted out, "It's the face of the devil!"

Over the next 100-plus years, the statue continued to increase in size, reaching 396 meters in height. It also expanded, spreading to occupy the square in which it stood as well as 4 or 5 residential blocks. The number of believers increased as the statue grew, and despite vigorous attempts by the government to control the cult, its power continued to grow. Masses of children sporting Bronze Statue buttons marched through the City. Women who wore pendants inlaid with images of the Bronze Statue came to pray for favors. Philosophers wrote long theses on whether the statue was the one and only true god of the universe. Doctrinal differences emerged between cult sects, often resulting in bloody conflicts. The bodies of the followers who died for their faith were piled before the statue.

But the statue was apparently unmoved by these incidents and seemed intent only on continuing to grow. The Bronze Statue Cult, which initially had been suppressed by the authorities, became the state religion when the prime minister and the cabinet members joined. The Huhui planet was the leader of an alliance of 18 galaxies and asked all other members to convert to the cult. Due to Huhui military threats, 13 did as requested, while the other 5 withdrew from the alliance. Fanatical cult members on the Huhui planet organized a crusade against the recreant members. The armed conflicts led to intervention by neighboring superpower galaxies. A series of unfortunate incidents ensued and, like a chain reaction, led to the Fourth Interstellar War.

The Fourth Interstellar War lasted 250 years and had a devastating impact on all of the civilizations in the Milky Way galaxy. The facts are recorded in great detail in *The Complete History of the Fourth Interstellar War* and need not be repeated here. Shortly after an armistice was signed, the chief instigator of the war was punished. The fleet from the G Supergalaxy surrounded the small Huhui planet. A fearless imperial outer space fleet appeared in the sky above Sunlon City, and in a matter of 20 minutes vaporized the Bronze Statue, leaving an empty patch of scorched earth in the city center.

But the myths about the Bronze Statue survived even after it was vaporized. It was said that the day before the statue was destroyed it wept unceasingly and its facial expression showed a rare kindness. One believer later recalled that when he saw the statue crying he realized that the statue was the very soul of the city. Another said that the vaporized statue had not disappeared into the atmosphere but had reappeared in the mountains near the upper reaches of the Hu River. Others said that they believed the statue would rematerialize in the city center to lead the Huhui heroes in a Fifth Interstellar War to restore the fame and influence of the cult. These legends are still current in the Huhui world.

But one thing was certain—the fate of the statue was closely linked to that of the city. After the statue disappeared, the Anliu Era of Huhui civilization was on the road to collapse. Twenty-five years after the statue was vaporized, the city was attacked by the Serpent people and ended up in ruins. Shortly thereafter, the Serpent people of the Hu River Valley became extinct. The exact nature of the relationship between this bizarre history and the Bronze Statue remains to be verified by later historians.

—from *The Visitor's Guide to Ancient Sunlon City*

1

Dusk in Sunlon City.

The sun setting on the Huhui planet cast a purple light over the tightly clustered houses of the capital. The enormous purple sun occupied one tenth of the sky; as the huge disk gradually set, the entire city seemed to be shrouded in its halo, and to sink with it. In the days when the statue still stood, it seemed to be the only thing in the city of comparable magnitude to the sun. Even today the old people still take great delight in telling how at sunset the head of the statue glowed with a strange light and how the statue resembled some huge ancient Buddha from time immemorial, inspiring awe as it faced the dying purple sun of the Huhui planet. But the Bronze Statue had long since disappeared. Without it, Sunlon City seemed unable to resist the purple sun's strong gravitational pull. Each building, tree, and pedestrian appeared to be permeated with the purple light, unable to extricate themselves. Even their shadows were tinged purple by the sun. The moment the huge disk set, all shadows seemed to stretch off endlessly in the opposite direction as if to escape the purple sun's grasp. But the effort was futile because even at night, purple clouds still filled the sky like sentinels of that huge sun standing guard over the planet.

A bluish gray interstellar warship sat on the square at the center of Sunlon City, the patch of scorched earth that was the former site of the Bronze Statue. Sentries had been posted all around the vessel. As soon as the sun set, a fierce wind driving sand blew over the plains to assail the city. As the wild, gritty wind whipped through the square, it raised the scarlet capes of the sentries, scouring their faces and bodies with sand. But the Shan warriors, who had great endurance and who had undergone a long period of training, stood impassive even in the most trying conditions. As the wind passed, they raised their guns and shouted in unison to demonstrate to the Huhui planet and to remind the residents of Sunlon City that they were the masters.

The residents of the city did their best to ignore the existence of the Shan occupying force. Regardless of how brilliantly the Shan sentries deported themselves, not one of the Huhui people coming out of the buildings around the square even looked at them. At the end of the workday, the government employees, workers, and students all quickly disappeared down the gritty, windy streets. The warship, the sentries, and the howling wind were the only things that remained on the square.

But the nightlife in the nine *bulu*, or municipal districts, of Sunlon City was just beginning. Upon passing through the gates of their bulu, the people relaxed and talked naturally, as evinced by their expressions and loud voices. Soon the narrow lanes were filled with people. The Huhui liked a noisy and lively atmosphere, and were fond of nightlife. Snack shops did a brisk business, selling quick-fried centipedes, deep-fried fish balls, and a thick snake soup. The customers ate with relish, paying no attention to the sand that the wind might deposit in their bowls. A small Feathered person performed on the stones while a 180-centimeter Serpent person, coiled up in the shadows, sold Serpent wonder drugs. Light flickered in the wind lamps in front of the shops. And amid the dusty wind, people talked loudly and stopped now and then to listen to the soft, entrancing song of a soul toucher,[1] drifting from a tavern.

In addition to the city center, there were nine bulu that surrounded the Golden Palace. It is said that Sunlon City was founded by nine houses of interstellar immigrants, which today formed the nine bulu. During the time of the Snake and Leopard War, the lords of the bulu had such immense wealth that they could decide the rise and fall of the Huhui Empire. With the coming of the constitutional monarchy, the government undertook to reduce the power of these lords. They were prohibited from retaining ministers and soldiers and from holding positions in the government. This led to the Uprising of Golden Goose Fort, the final war of restoration in which seven of the nine bulu lords took part. After it failed,

---

[1] Soul toucher is the Huhui term for "songstress."

the lords were sentenced to death, a setback from which the individual bulu governments never recovered. But the residents of the city were all proud of their own bulu. Each had its own ball team, and the annual championship match was an event of great importance that often led to violence. At the time of the Fourth Interstellar War, the Huhui Empire dispatched an expeditionary fleet of warships. On each ship was painted the insignia of a particular bulu. Frequently the forces from one bulu would stand by and not lift a finger to assist the forces of another during battle. Even the fanatical members of the Bronze Statue Cult were powerless to change these traditions. After the occupation forces took control of the city, the Shan commander had a plan to break up the bulu, and ordered that the populations be moved and integrated. His goal, of course, was to facilitate rule of the city. But unexpectedly, all he accomplished was to stir up Huhui resistance. Not long thereafter, Sunlon City exploded in a large-scale armed revolt and, although it was quickly suppressed, the Shan commander was forced to relinquish his plan. And thus bulu traditions continued to be handed down. A short time later, an internal disturbance occurred in the G Supergalaxy. Over time, most of the Shan occupation force was transferred home, leaving only a small, symbolic contingent to guard the city center. Small patrols were sent out into the bulu only during daylight. Nightfall saw them concentrated around the interstellar warship, where they could defend themselves with the vessel's superior firepower. Although the Huhui people soon saw through the empty-city stratagem of the Shan occupation forces, the underground revolutionary organization was reluctant to act rashly. Although there was just one warship, it had enough firepower to destroy the entire city more than nine times over.

This tense and unstable situation lasted for five years. On the surface, the city remained calm and peaceful in spite of the occasional Shan soldier being killed and revolutionary being captured and vaporized. Under the purple sun, life went on as usual. But as soon as night fell and the sand-carrying wind whipped up on the plains, the revolutionaries would become active in the bulu. Therefore, it should come as no surprise that the Shan occupation forces would not enter the bulu at night.

It was a special night in the Sungood bulu. There were twice as many Huhui people on the streets as usual. Although some just seemed to be wandering around, others were filled with expectations as if waiting for something to happen. In the middle of the night the wind increased, and the fine powdery sand rained down. The Huhui people called this sand rain "late rain." When the late rain began to fall, the shops started closing up. People were unhappy about this and grumbled, but they all left and returned home. By the time a centimeter of sand had accumulated on the streets, the number of people had gradually dwindled. The sand wouldn't be swept up until the following morning when the shopkeepers opened for business. Day and night, this was the regular rhythm of life in Sunlon City.

The Sungood bulu night market was closed; the streets were empty. But the lights were still bright on the second floor of a tavern that had already put up a CLOSED sign. In the main room on the second floor, three Huhui people were having a heated argument. Their faces were gray and their ears black.[2] The leader was a big, tall Huhui man, his face tinged a light purple and his beard golden. He wore the green robe of a Sungood warrior, on the back and front of which were embroidered three green snakes. At his waist was a short sword with a hilt carved in the shape of a snake with its mouth open. The other two were dressed in the same fashion, the only difference being that their robes were embroidered with only one green snake insignia each. They too carried short swords with hilts carved like snakes at their waists.

One of them, who had a pockmarked face, pounded on the table and shouted. "Brother, the Sungood people have never cowered on the eve of battle. All the warriors are waiting for you to give the signal to attack with your snake whistle. Everything is ready, but now you are hesitating. Many are ready to die and have already taken their ultimate loyalty pills. You know that they have only three days to live. If we don't make our move now, they will have sacrificed themselves for nothing. What will you tell their families?"

"Our Great Lord ordered us to take up arms, but he ordered no one to take a loyalty pill," the man with the golden beard replied coldly. "Those who have done so have disobeyed orders and should die. They are not to be pitied."

"Nonsense!" shouted the man with the pockmarked face, trembling with rage. "The Death Commandos are the Sungood bulu's best. If they all die, then how will you deal with the Shan?"

"Brother Yu Fang, what Yu Kui says is true," said the short warrior. "There are only around ninety or so Death Commandos in the bulu.

---

[2] When they are angry, the faces of Huhui people turn black, and not red like the people of Earth. This is probably related to the water quality in Sunlon City and to the fact that, starting from childhood, the Huhui people eat insects.

We'd never be able to train their likes again. If you let them die for nothing, of course, they will have sought and obtained their lofty ideal of death. But even if they have no regrets, others will tremble with fear and from then on, no one will ever respond to an order from our Great Lord."

The man with the golden beard fixed his eyes on the short warrior and gripped his sword with his right hand. "Are you second-guessing our Great Lord? You dare betray him?" he asked in a deep voice.

In fear, the short warrior stepped back a few paces. He wanted to argue but changed his mind.

But the warrior with the pockmarked face would not back down. He also gripped his sword. "There is no need to obey an ill-conceived order. You issued the order that will kill our best men without our Great Lord's authorization. It's you who will pay."

In a rage, the man with the golden beard threw back his head and roared with laughter. The two men knew his temper and cautiously readied themselves. The man with the golden beard suddenly restrained his laughter. "Yesterday, we went to see the Great Lord and he ordered us to take up arms. You heard everything he said. You both know that putting on battle dress is the first step in a large-scale uprising. The Death Commandos of our bulu are to take their loyalty pills and fight to the end only after the loyalty order has been given. The Great Lord did not issue such an order yesterday, and the very tone of his voice indicated that he hadn't entirely made up his mind. You clearly heard what he said. How could anyone take a loyalty pill under those circumstances? I didn't learn about this until today. Without such an order, loyal Death Commandos would never take their own lives. No one else but the three of us met with the Great Lord yesterday. Which one of you mistakenly issued the loyalty order?"

As he lightly tapped the snake-head hilt of his short sword with his right hand, the eyes of the man with the golden beard shone as he shifted his gaze from one warrior to the other.

The man with the pockmarked face could not control his anger and shot back, "Who mistakenly issued the loyalty order? You are the only one with the loyalty order flag. Even if we wanted to issue the order, we couldn't do it without the flag. But those who took the pills today all claimed that they had seen the flag. How do you explain that?"

"You're right, I do have the flag," said the man with the golden beard. "I swear on the purple sun above that I let no one see or touch it. So how could they have seen it? Who showed it to them?"

The pockmarked warrior and the short warrior looked at each other.

"Brother," said the short warrior, "we asked several of the Death Commandos, and they all said that a masked warrior of about your height made the rounds with the flag. We thought you had conveyed our lord's order. We were all very excited and quite ready to die. We never expected that there would be no uprising tonight. If we don't rebel within the next three days, we'll lose ninety warriors."

"I know, I know," said the warrior with the golden beard, his right hand still on the hilt of his sword. "One of us intentionally issued the order, and that makes him a danger. If we don't fight, then nearly one hundred Death Commandos will be sent to their graves for nothing. But if we revolt just because we don't want to see our Death Commandos die for nothing, then we might be walking into a Shan trap and be annihilated with one stroke! The spy is treacherous. Who is it? It's not me, so it must be one of you."

The two warriors looked at each other in dismay.

The short warrior couldn't help laughing. "Brother, your reasoning is impeccable. First of all, the masked warrior with the command flag was a big man. Neither of us has the flag, so how could one of us be the spy?"

"I'm not the spy, it has to be one of you two. It's my guess that the spy will never confess, so I may as well slay the both of you. First I'll kill the traitor among us; then I'll ask the Great Lord to do with me as he will. We have been like brothers, but I can't consider that when disposing of a traitor. Prepare to die!"

In a flash, his sword was out of its scabbard. Immediately, the room was filled with a green light. The two warriors had no choice but to unsheathe their swords as well. The warrior with the pockmarked face withdrew to one corner, and the short warrior stepped to one side. Seeing the situation, the warrior with the golden beard sneered and made ready to fight in close quarters.

"Brother, if you kill us, the Great Lord will assume that you are the spy," said the short warrior hastily, "and that you killed us to eliminate witnesses. You have the command flag for the loyalty order, which makes you the prime suspect. If you kill us you'll never be able to prove your innocence."

The warrior with the golden beard hesitated.

"Brother, this is no time to act impulsively," said the short warrior, taking advantage of his hesitation. "The way I see it, someone else secretly issued the loyalty order. He posed as you so as to sow discord among us. Fortunately, we still have three days to investigate and question the warriors who took the loyalty pills. If we can uncover the spy among us and kill him, we can placate everyone. And if we can secure an antidote in three days, we might be able to save the hundred Death Commandos."

The man with the golden beard nodded his head in response, then shook his head. "There is no antidote for the ultimate loyalty pills, otherwise they wouldn't bear such a name. But what you say is true. If we do nothing, the Death Commandos will not be able to depart in peace. You two investigate; I must go see our Great Lord and inform him of the situation. If our Great Lord finds me at fault, I will pay with my life. But the two of you must get to the bottom of this, otherwise I won't be able to die in peace."

With nothing else to say, the warrior with the golden beard pushed open the window and leaped out. Seeing him leave, the short warrior returned his sword to its scabbard.

"What a temper!" said the warrior. "He's always so rash in making decisions, even when he doesn't entirely understand the situation. I urged him not to listen to the Old Do-Gooder's rubbish, because it would put him in a difficult position. But he wouldn't listen to me. Not only is there going to be a bad end to a good start, but someone was able to steal the command flag. If this gets out, we'll be the laughingstock of all the other bulu."

"Brother Yu Fang always believes everything the Old Do-Gooder says," said the warrior with the pockmarked face angrily. "The Old Do-Gooder has done a lot of harm. He's a bulu lord who can't lead, and one I just can't follow. Every time he says we're going to rebel, he's the first to have second thoughts. That's not so bad, but for the Death Commandos to die for such an unworthy lord is unfortunate. I'd rather fight it out with the Shan once and for all. If the Death Commandos die, how could we, as members of the Green Snake Brotherhood, go on living in the Sungood bulu?"

As the warrior with the pockmarked face spoke, a young soul toucher entered carrying a wooden tray. On it were three bowls of snake soup. The girl had long eyebrows and whiter skin than the average Huhui person. Her eyes indicated that she was a clever, artful girl. To her surprise, there were only two people left in the room.

"Has Brother Yu Fang left? All of you were so noisy just a moment ago. How could he disappear just like that?"

"That's the way he is," joked the warrior with the pockmarked face.

"He's very impulsive. I should be going too. Yu Jin, it looks like the three bowls of snake soup are yours."

"Have something to eat before you leave," hurriedly replied the soul toucher.

Yu Kui forced a smile and shook his head. He leaped out the window the warrior with the golden beard had just used. The short warrior rushed to the window in time to see only a shadow vanish down the lane. The sandstorm had ended and not a single star shone in the pitch-black sky, but innumerable spike-shaped purple clouds hung down like a bed of iron nails. Night on the Huhui planet was like a huge gulag for imprisoning one small planet in the universe. Looking at the sky, the short warrior was assailed by an inexplicable feeling of depression. He had seen the starry night of the other world. So many stars that shone like gemstones, enticing one into the bosom of the spirit of the night. At that time he was a captain in the Imperial Expeditionary Fleet. He was a young man looking for adventure even amid the cruel atrocities of an interstellar war. He remembered how he had stared at that watery blue planet and the stars shining brightly all around it when the Imperial Fleet had set down on the moon of the old world to wait for the counterattacking starships to appear in the vault of heaven.

"Brother Yu Jin, what are you thinking?" He had not noticed the girl put down the tray and approach him. Her soft hand touched his as it rest on the hilt of his sword. "You look like you're ready for a fight. What were you arguing about?"

"Nothing, Miss Qi. Go to bed. I should be leaving."

Hearing that he was about to go, she pouted. "You never come here. Why are you in such a hurry to leave? I've been waiting for you all night. Let's have a talk."

"Not tonight, my good girl. I'll come back and see you in two days, okay?" The short warrior couldn't help but gently touch her soft cheek.

"No. The uprising has already been called off. So what is so urgent? I've missed you. Don't go."

The short warrior was startled. "How do you know it was called off? I know nothing about an uprising. Who told you?"

"Don't lie to me. Everyone in the Sungood bulu knows that the Old Do-Gooder has been busily preparing for action but doesn't have the guts to go through with it. A moment ago, when you were all up here talking, a customer downstairs told me that the uprising had been postponed again, and that it was all just a drill."

"Which customer? Where is he?"

"He left a long time ago. He didn't belong to our bulu. He looked like a Gaiwenese. Very tall. Right! He was a Gaiwenese here on business." Miss Qi wrapped her arms around the short warrior's neck, like ivy twined around a tree. "You see, even people from other planets know about it. So why keep it a secret from me?"

The short warrior responded perfunctorily to the affectionate young soul toucher as he pondered what she had told him. It was a total fiasco if even the Gaiwenese knew about it. They were the gypsies of the universe. After their planet was vaporized, the Gaiwenese, without a land they could call home, spread to the farthest corners of the universe. They were good at business, very practical, and would sell you out for the meagerest profit. About a hundred of them lived in Sunlon City, and many of them spied for the Shan. If the Gaiwenese knew about the uprising, then the Shan must have learned of it a long time ago. The Old Do-Gooder was indeed despicable.

The short warrior forcibly extricated himself from Miss Qi's embrace and tried to comfort her with a few words. "I have to go, my girl. I really have to go."

Just as Miss Qi was about to speak, the short warrior bolted and jumped out the window. As soon as she was certain he was long gone, she clapped her hands three times. The door opened and a man appeared. He had no face, and in place of a head was a smooth ball of flesh without ears, eyes, nose, or mouth. But strangely, he could speak, and his voice was high-pitched like that of a young girl.

"Have the three fine Yu heroes gone?"

Miss Qi showed no fear of the man. She smiled and pointed to the three bowls of snake soup. "They're gone. They didn't eat a thing. It's all yours."

He sat down without being asked twice and proceeded to lower his head and slurp down a bowl of soup. His eyes, nose, ears, and mouth were all on top of his head. When he lowered his head, he looked like a normal person straight on, but in profile it was altogether a different matter. Miss Qi sat down and watched him practically inhale the three bowls of soup.

"Yu Fang went to see the Old Do-Gooder. The other two went to investigate a spy who issued the loyalty pill order. They argued all night with no other result than to make a bigger mess of things. It was really funny."

"They're all fools." Polishing off the soup, he raised his head. He took out a hankie and wiped his little mouth on top of his head. "Sometimes, you really wonder about these jerks in the Green Snake Brotherhood. The only thing Yu Fang understands is loyalty. Yu Kui is an uncultured fellow and a boor. The Old Do-Gooder is weak and indecisive. The Shan are here to stay if we have to rely on the likes of them to do anything."

"It's too bad that the Death Commandos have to die," said Miss Qi. "Ah 占 (chu), is there an antidote for the loyalty pills?"

Ah 占 (chu) looked up, as was normal for him, and after a long pause replied, "You can say that there is and that there isn't."

Miss Qi laughed. "Don't kid around. Is there or is there not an antidote?"

As usual, Ah 占 (chu) blinked (dust was always falling in the poor guy's eyes) as he replied. "The Old Do-Gooder has an antidote, but he doesn't know it, so it's the same as not having one at all."

"How can that be? He might be an old fool, but how could he not know that he has the antidote?"

"It is strange. The antidote can be found in a painting in the old guy's private quarters. Not only is he unaware of it, but none of the leaders of the Green Snake Brotherhood knows about it."

"How do *you* know about it?"

Ah 占 (chu) laughed heartily. "Who in the nine bulu doesn't know that the Serpent people talk the most, the Leopard people are the most deceitful, the Feathered people the most able, and the 占 (chu) people the wisest? Is there anything that can escape my notice?"

She knew that what he said was not an empty boast. As far back as she could remember, this short, fat 占 (chu) person with his eyes on top of his head had been with her and taught her many things. And though he was gluttonous, lazy, proud, and conceited, he was very learned. It was said that all 占 (chu) people had photographic memories and that they were telepathic. Many of the Huhui historians were 占 (chu) people. For a time, Ah 占 (chu) had worked as a historian in the Municipal History Office. After the Shan began to rule the city, he was approached several times and asked to return to work, but always he had declined. In this way he had lost his pension, and thanks to this he had become a kindermann[3] to the Qi family.

"Since you know where it is, help me get it."

Ah 占 (chu) remained silent as he listened to Miss Qi. After a long pause, he replied, "Why do you want the antidote?"

---

[3] A kindermann is a private household tutor. The Huhui are accustomed to hiring kindermann for their children. They are also responsible for protecting the child.

"That's the only way that the Death Commandos can be saved. Can you bear to watch them die for nothing?" asked Miss Qi, somewhat perplexed. "Our very survival is bound up with them and we can't just stand by and do nothing, regardless of how foolish the Old Do-Gooder is or how incompetent the Green Snake Brotherhood might be."

"But that's not what your *dada*[4] thinks," snorted Ah 出 (chu). "It would be best if we didn't get involved."

Miss Qi frowned. She hated to be contradicted, especially once her mind was made up. Nor was she willing to give up this opportunity.

"Dada said not to help the Old Do-Gooder; he never said anything about not helping the bulu avoid extermination. Ah 出 (chu), you think of a way to get the antidote, and I'll find a use for it."

Ah 出 (chu) knew how stubborn the young girl could be. Once she had made up her mind, no one could dissuade her from her purpose. He regretted having opened his mouth. Now all he could do was try to scare her. "I'd have to enter the Old Do-Gooder's private quarters for the antidote," said Ah 出 (chu), "an offense punishable by death."

"If you're afraid, I'll do it myself."

So saying, Miss Qi took a long sword from where it hung on the wall, and holding the hilt and point, flexed the blade. She then buckled it to her waist. "Are you coming or not?"

"I'm coming, I'm coming," said Ah 出 (chu), unable to make any other reply.

Although Ah 出 (chu) had committed himself in word, he didn't take a step. Miss Qi took no notice of him, went straight to a cabinet and fetched a very strange-looking helmet, and unceremoniously placed it on his head. In the top of the helmet was a periscope. With a 叮叮 (lu-mu) helmet[5] in place, 出 (chu) people could use the periscope to scope out the area in front of them. Beneath the helmet was affixed a mask of a human face. This enabled the 出 (chu) people to look and act like anyone else.

Miss Qi helped Ah 出 (chu) with the helmet. She then gave it a sharp rap and asked, "Are you coming or not?"

Ah 出 (chu) knew there was no backing out. He leaped out the window with Miss Qi.

---

[4] *Dada* is Huhui for "father."

[5] 叮叮, pronounced "lu-mu." Huhui for "look around" or "size up." It also means "to watch and wait/skulk." Therefore, "What are you 叮叮 for?" means roughly "What are you watching and waiting for like a thief?" A 叮叮 helmet is a special helmet used by 出 (chu) people.

It was the dead of night in Sunlon City. The purple clouds that hung like spikes had spread, forming a purple carpet. Everything was completely covered with a layer of yellow sand. Shafts of bluish light stood between the purple empyrean and the yellow earth. Even the most romantic of poets would have been left speechless by the spectacular night of the Huhui planet. When a troubadour from the old world first saw the purple heavens, yellow earth, and colonnade of bluish shafts of light, he sighed and said, "I always thought man was the lord of the universe. But after coming to Sunlon City I believe that man is no more than a slave of the universe." Night in Sunlon City left most people so depressed that few would venture outside. In the dead of night the city was a ghost town, with only that strange bluish light lingering over the streets.

Ah 凸 (chu) followed Miss Qi's attractive figure up and down over the low roofs of the Sungood bulu. She stopped before the palace walls and Ah 凸 (chu) caught up with her.

"Miss, it sounds like someone in the palace is still awake. Let's come back tomorrow."

"There are always sentries," she said, pouting. "If we can't get inside tonight, it'll be the same tomorrow. Let's go."

She unsheathed the sword at her waist. Ah 凸 (chu) hurriedly stopped her. "If you have to have the antidote, I'll steal it for you."

A smile spread over her face. She had been waiting for Ah 凸 (chu) to volunteer.

"Then you agree. No regrets!"

"When did you ever hear Ah 凸 (chu) go back on his word? Okay, Miss, you go back. As for the antidote, leave it to me. I'll have it within three days, no matter what."

"Within three days! I need it tonight."

"I agreed to steal the antidote, and I'll do it. If I can't get it tonight, I'll get it tomorrow. You have to let me try, right? Now go back."

"I'll go back when you steal the antidote from the palace."

Ah 凸 (chu) could do nothing but leap the wall in one bound. He quickly hid under the nearest eaves. Grasping a beam with his feet, he hung upside down, listening carefully. He heard the sound of Miss Qi's footsteps gradually fading away outside the wall. Ah 凸 (chu) couldn't help but heave a sigh. It was his misfortune to have such a stubborn young mistress. But it was his own fault—she had become like this because he spoiled her, consenting to her every request. He could guess why she wanted the antidote. Even such a young girl had her own schemes. He hoped that Yu Jin wouldn't spurn her affections; otherwise, she would be impossible to handle. Preoccupied with his thoughts, Ah 凸 nearly forgot he was hanging under the eaves. Suddenly he heard someone speaking loudly inside. Startled, he collected himself and listened intently to what was being said.

2

Although Ah 出 (chu) couldn't see what was going on inside, his naturally sharp ears could recognize Yu Fang's voice. He sounded quite agitated. Another person "uh-huh"ed, and would occasionally interject a few unrelated and insignificant comments. Ah 出 (chu) recognized the voice as that of the lord of the Sungood bulu.

"M'Lord, it is only fitting that I pay for my crime with my life. It was my fault that the Death Commandos took the loyalty pills. Given the present circumstances, I offer my life in atonement. As the Death Commandos have but three days to live, I would lead them into a battle to end all battles with the Shan, to repay the benevolence of m'Lord's confidence."

"Well, well, well," replied the Old Do-Gooder. Ah 出 (chu) couldn't help but snicker. Yu Fang really was incorrigibly stubborn and persistent. After having served the Old Do-Gooder for so many years, he still lacked the slightest understanding of his temperament. He actually believed that he would let him lead the Death Commandos in a large-scale uprising.

"M'Lord," answered Yu Fang, "perhaps it is the will of heaven that I seize this opportunity to lead the uprising. Over the years many Sungood martyrs have given their lives for the cause of overthrowing the Shan empire. If Shan rule is to be toppled today, all Huhui people look to the Sungood people to be the vanguard. M'Lord, if we fail to act this time, the demise of the Death Commandos will be of little consequence, but we will be made a universal laughingstock. M'Lord, please make a decision."

Ah 出 (chu) couldn't believe his ears, and expected the worst. How could Yu Fang speak of overthrowing the Shan empire to the imposing head of a bulu? Since the Shan invasion, the Royalists and the Republicans had no choice but to join forces to battle the foreigners, but that did not mean that the Royalists had entirely given up the idea of a restoration.

"Yu Fang," replied the Old Do-Gooder, "I understand what you are saying. Go home. I have my own thoughts on the matter."

But Yu Fang wouldn't give up. "M'Lord," he replied in an admonishing tone, "there is no time to delay. Issue the order, and I will lead the men into battle tomorrow morning."

"Yu Fang!" shouted the old lord so angrily that even Ah 出 (chu), who was hanging from the eaves, gasped in fear, "you lost the command flag through carelessness. I know you as loyal and devoted and see no need for you to be punished. But what kind of nonsense are you talking now? The Shan warship is still in the city, so how am I to fight them? I will not hear another word about it."

"But the Death Commandos . . ."

"I am aware of the situation. Say no more."

Then the room was silent. Ah 出 (chu), who was still hanging from the eaves, waited for what seemed a long time, thinking. After he was certain everyone had left the room, and just as he was on the point of dropping from the eaves, he heard something that sounded like the buzzing of a mosquito.

"What's a fat bat like you thinking?" the voice asked.

Ah 出 (chu) was frightened out of his wits. He didn't stir.

"Hanging there without moving is not a solution," continued the voice. "Did you ever hear the expression 'a silkworm trapped in its own cocoon'? Hanging there like that, you really look like a big worm caught in its own cocoon, waiting for someone to come along and pluck it."

Everything went black, and Ah 出 (chu) knew that someone had covered the periscope on his 口口 (lu-mu) helmet. He considered putting up a struggle but found himself held fast. Someone had him by the ankles and picked him up. He flapped around a bit and then fell head first to the ground. His fall left his face bruised and swollen. He dared not make a sound. Then someone unmasked him. Laughter greeted Ah 出 (chu)'s cry of pain.

"I was right: you are a 出 (chu) person."

Ah 出 (chu) twisted around to get a look at his assailant. He saw a man dressed entirely in black. He also wore a black mask, and a small Bronze

Statue hung at his breast. Seeing the image of the Bronze Statue on the chest of the stranger in black, Ah 出 (chu) began to tremble and collapsed on the ground.

"A follower of the Bronze Statue, the Supreme One!"

The Stranger in Black laughed loudly. "Right you are. So you recognized me. No wonder people say 出 (chu) people are smart. How did you know that I am the supreme leader?"

"By the Bronze Statue you wear," stammered Ah 出 (chu). "There are fifty rings and fifty folds, each denoting status. If you are not the Supreme One, then who is?"

"Right again." The Stranger in Black seemed quite pleased, but then he sighed. "Unfortunately, there are few people these days who can recognize my true stature. You 出 (chu) people are in charge of the histories, and therefore you are of course knowledgeable. How many common Huhui people understand the true magnitude of my authority?"

"But you're not the real Supreme One. You're bogus."

"Nonsense!" the Stranger in Black said, flying into a rage. He pressed his foot into Ah 出 (chu)'s neck, making him cry out in pain. "Who dares to say that I'm a fake?"

"There is only one Supreme One, and he is the high priest. When the Bronze Statue was vaporized, he chose self-immolation for his faith by hurling himself into the molten metal. The Bronze Statue he wore was also vaporized. All members of the cult died in battle or died as martyrs for their religion, save for a very few who managed to flee the city. After the catastrophe, the cult was no longer a force to contend with. A phoney like you might be able to fool most people, but not me!"

The Stranger in Black removed his foot from Ah 出 (chu)'s neck. Ah 出 (chu) lay gasping on the ground while looking for a way to escape. Miss Qi had talked him into sneaking into the palace. He had planned just to reconnoiter the place and return later to steal the antidote. He never expected to be caught, much less by a cult member, and the highest ranking one at that! In addition to his being a phoney, there was something else strange about that person: a moment ago he had been shouting, but the palace sentries had never sounded the alarm. The more Ah 出 (chu) thought about it, the stranger it all seemed.

"Everyone believes that the Bronze Statue Cult has collapsed," said the Stranger in Black. "Even the Shan think that we have vanished and don't give us a second thought. They are afraid that the Royalists and the Republicans will one day join forces and rise up. But the rabble that make up the Green Snake Brotherhood are really of no concern, and what's left of the feudal Leopard Brotherhood should all be resting in peace by now. The only people really capable of leading the Huhui people to throw off the yoke of Shan rule are the followers of the Bronze Statue Cult. And though fruit and flowers must fall, scattered by the wind, Sunlon City will be reborn!"

High-spirited, the Stranger in Black sonorously and forcefully recited those lines of poetry. Ah 凵 (chu), who was still lying on the ground, couldn't help being moved. True, though the city was at its nadir, it would one day recover its greatness. Nor was the cult follower the only one who harbored such thoughts. The strangely shaped 凵 (chu) person and the Stranger in Black standing beside him seemed to understand each other, even if only for a moment.

Almost immediately, Ah 凵 (chu) was aware of the awkwardness of his situation. "Since you call yourself the Supreme One," said Ah 凵 (chu) loudly, "what is it that brings you to Sungood bulu? Though our bulu is small, can we allow you to behave so audaciously?"

"What a cunning 凵 (chu) person," said the Stranger in Black, giving a queer laugh. "Here you are at your lord's quarters in the middle of the night and you're questioning me. What are you up to? Tell me, should I turn you over to the palace sentries so that they can interrogate you and torture you?"

The Stranger in Black then kicked Ah 凵 (chu) in the belly, causing him a great deal of pain. "Consider yourself lucky that I have no interest in helping the Old Do-Gooder," said the Stranger in Black. "I saw something amiss and caught a fat hanging bat, never thinking it was a 凵 (chu) person, and a thief at that! Isn't that strange? You must be an odd one. Don't worry, as I said, I have no intention of helping the Old Do-Gooder. But since I have you, you can be of use to me. Let's go."

So saying, the Stranger in Black picked up hefty Ah 凵 (chu) as if he were as light as a string of dumplings. To Ah 凵 (chu) it seemed that he flew over the palace wall and over rows of houses to a small, open square. He felt oppressed by the cold. Stealing a glance, he noticed that a shaft of blue light fell in the very center of the square.

Suddenly he understood what the Stranger in Black had in mind and shouted, "Manipulating time and space! You really are the Supreme One!"

"The twenty-seventh. Paramita Hare Krishna Holy Holy Holy Law of Moses, Below the Honored Bronze Statue Never Sinking Dharmapala Mountain God 7113218. In you go!"

The Stranger in Black threw Ah凸(chu) into the very center of the shaft of blue light. Terrified, he shouted, "Impossible, I can't . . ."

"Sure you can," said the Stranger in Black as he leaped into the shaft of blue light himself. His black robe shone with a dazzling purple light. He had become a Stranger in Purple. "Give it to me. I know you凸(chu) people all have spells. Recite it!"

"No, I can't. . . ."

"Enough already," said the Stranger in Purple sternly. He then raised his arms toward the sky, and gradually the shaft of blue light changed color and luster, and what looked like flames sprang up all around them. "Spill the spell, or it will soon be too late."

Ah凸(chu) suddenly felt cold all over and figured that the Stranger in Purple wasn't bluffing. He began to mumble, reciting the "Song of the 凸(chu)"[1]:

凸呷 *(chu-ru)*

凸呷 *(chu-ru)*

-ロ⊢-ロ⊢ *(lu-mu) (lu-mu)*

⊢-ロ⊢-⊣ *(mu-lu) (mu-lu)*

⊡ □ *(du-wu)*

⊡ □ *(du-wu)*

凸呷 *(chu-ru)*

凸呷 *(chu-ru)*

As Ah凸(chu) was reciting the spell, the shaft of light gradually turned red, and what appeared to be flames danced above and below, flooding the center of the shaft. The light then became pure gold in color, and the two human forms within began to emit a blinding white light. Then a sound like silk being torn was heard and the shaft of light began to rise off the ground, quickly receding into the sky along with the two human shapes, only to disappear without a trace into the purple clouds. With one shaft of light gone, the others began slowly to shift positions, as if to form a colonnade and close off a rift in space and time in the Huhui world. Tranquility returned once again to the night.

After a long while, the distant mountains seemed to tremble, and the first ray of light from the purple sun shot over the peaks. Wherever the

---

[1] The first stanza of the *Song of Chu*. For a commentary on the song, see *Fifty Thousand Huhui Folk Songs*, published by the Committee for the Compilation of Ancient Huhui Culture.

light fell, the shafts of blue light suddenly vanished. By the time the purple sun had risen above the mountains, the shafts of light had all but disappeared and the clouds had reverted to their original spikelike forms. The Huhui planet was freed from the prison of night, and the land was allowed a breathing spell. The purple sun, huge beyond compare, once again reasserted its awe-inspiring reign over Sunlon City. The residents awoke, and the shopkeepers swept away the accumulated sand. Laborers, students, office workers surged out of countless small lanes of the bulu toward the gates. The greedy mouths of the skyscrapers in the center of the city swallowed the antlike files of people. The Shan guards were relieved by their vigorous replacements. So began another day on the Huhui planet.

A young girl with a worried look on her face sat waiting by the window on the second floor of a tavern in a narrow alley in the Sungood bulu. She hadn't slept all night and her tender young face, unadorned with makeup, looked thin and wan. She sat upright and entirely motionless, and unwillingly stepped away from the window only after being called repeatedly by someone.

"I'm coming, Dada."

Miss Qi stepped into an inner room where a man with silver whiskers sat cross-legged on a wooden bed, rolling wisdom beads[2] between his fingers. The walls in the dark room were covered with wisdom bead charts. Hearing Miss Qi enter, the old man broke into a childlike smile and his eyes widened.

"Child, I have thought of yet another calculation that can be performed on the wisdom beads. I am certain that no one ever thought of it before. Hurry up and go get Ah 出 (chu). I want him to find out if such a calculation has ever been noted."

Miss Qi began to massage the old man's shoulders ever so gently, and in a half-scolding, half-coaxing tone said, "Dada, why bother troubling yourself about such calculations so early in the morning? If you don't behave, I'll hide your beads, and then we'll see where that leaves you."

"You don't understand," said the old man, tightly grasping his beads, fearful lest Miss Qi actually make good on her word. "These days, the

---

[2] The Huhui use them to count, to perform mathematical calculations, and to make deductions. The beads are forty-nine in number, and are all different sizes. Operations can be done either serially or synchronously. Huhui people who are proficient in the use of the beads are called "the wise." They are the Huhui intellectuals.

magic of the beads is understood by very few young people, and few are willing to modestly apply themselves to studying them. It's not important for girls to understand them, but what will happen now that boys know just as little? Child, when it comes time to finding a match to 🔲 (qia),[3] the only thing that I require is that the young man have a knowledge of the beads. If he knows nothing of the beads, he can give up all thought to 🔲 (qia) my daughter."

"Dada, you're at it again." Embarrassed, Miss Qi tapped her father. "As long as Dada is still alive I will not 🔲 (qia)."

"Silly child. Can you spend your whole life with your dada? I asked Ah 🔲 (chu) to diligently seek out all young men in the bulu who understand the beads. They need not know more than me; they need not be intellectual; but you must he happy and feel that it is someone you can 🔲 (qia), then your dada will have peace of mind. Actually . . ." Old man Qi paused for a moment before continuing decisively, "Actually, all that matters is that he understand the wisdom beads. Even if he is from another bulu, your dada won't care."

Miss Qi laughed. She knew her father, and he did not speak lightly. He disliked people from other bulu. But if it were a choice between someone from another bulu and someone who didn't understand the wisdom beads, he would certainly choose the former, all things considered. She couldn't help thinking of Yu Jin of the Green Snake Brotherhood. His swordsmanship was good, but did he know anything about the wisdom beads? Never had she had the chance to ask him. But most men knew nothing about them. If he knew nothing, what would her dada think? It was a concern. But then, she didn't even know if he liked her. What was the point of worrying so much? Thinking about this, she couldn't help feeling a bit sad.

Without knowing what she was thinking, her father continued, "Ah 🔲 (chu) is very learned when it comes to the beads, but he isn't as knowledgeable as me. No man he chooses could be wrong. But what about Ah 🔲 (chu)? Ask him to come here. I'd like him to look over this new calculation of mine."

Startled, Miss Qi smiled. What if Ah 🔲 (chu) hadn't come back? Her dada would become suspicious. Where had he gone? If he had managed to steal the antidote, he should have come back right away. Could it be

---

[3] 🔲, pronounced "qia." Huhui for "to take a husband or wife." It means the "proper" or "right" person, Huhui for "sweetheart." When "two people 🔲" means "two people are deeply in love."

that he had pulled it off? Or had he been captured by the Old Do-Gooder's sentries? Miss Qi was somewhat ㅂㅁ (chu-ru).[4] She had to deceive her dada. "Ah ㅂ (chu) went to buy groceries for me. He'll be back soon."

The old man snorted. "That's too bad. Next time don't ask Ah ㅂ (chu) to buy the groceries. After all, he isn't our servant. I asked him to be your kindermann but never said anything about odd jobs. You should ask Ah Wen to do such things. And Ah Wen? Why didn't you ask Ah Wen to go?"

Rolling her eyes, Miss Qi hastily replied, "Ah Wen hasn't arrived yet. I asked Ah ㅂ (chu) to go early because the market has fresh sea serpent fin, your favorite. If you scold me, next time I won't buy any goodies like that for you."

The silver-whiskered old man smiled and closed his eyes. Miss Qi knew that he was again contemplating wisdom bead calculations. Before he could ask any more questions, she hurriedly left the room and flew down the stairs. Ah Wen had just arrived and was in the kitchen washing vegetables. The door to Ah ㅂ (chu)'s small room behind the kitchen was unlocked. Although she knew it was too soon for Ah ㅂ (chu) to have returned, Miss Qi couldn't help opening his door for a peek. The room was neat and orderly with everything in its place. Even the books on his shelf were arranged alphabetically from ㅂ (chu) to ■ (woo). She noticed three thick volumes titled *A Comprehensive Guide to the Latest Wisdom Bead Calculations*. Ah ㅂ (chu) had so many things in common with her father. No wonder they were on such close, friendly terms. She thumbed through the books and then replaced them on the shelf. She was getting upset wondering what was keeping him. As Miss Qi slipped out of his room, she was noticed by Ah Wen, who was dumping the water she had used to wash the vegetables.

Smiling, the fat servant woman said, "You are up early, child. Are your dada and Ah ㅂ (chu) up? Are they playing with the beads again? Should I take breakfast up to them?"

Ah Wen always referred to wisdom bead calculations as "playing with the beads." Regardless of how often Miss Qi corrected her, she never changed. Miss Qi was not in the mood to try again. "Dada hasn't eaten yet," she told her. "Please prepare breakfast for him. I asked Ah ㅂ (chu) to

---

[4] ㅂㅁ, pronounced "chu-ru." Huhui for "apprehensive." The solemn ceremony in which the Huhui worship the gods is also known as ㅂㅁ.

buy some groceries. I'm going out too. If Dada asks for me, tell him I'll be back around noon. Understand?"

"Won't you have breakfast first, child? How many bowls of snake soup should I prepare today?"

"The same as usual—three hundred." Fearing that Ah Wen would detain her longer, Miss Qi hurriedly left the house. The lane was quiet; everyone going to work was probably already in the central district of Sunlon City. At the mouth of the lane, she looked at the various slogans pasted on the wall. One read:

> *One man and one woman is just right,*
> *⊡ (duan) and it means the end of the line,*
> *⊡ (luan) and everything's a mess,*
> *⊕ (san) and everything will fall apart,*
> *⊕ (man) and everything will be out of control!*[5]

Beneath the slogan for the new marriage system advocated by the occupying Shan people was a slogan that had been pasted up by the ⊡ (luan) rights movement:

> *A man can ⊡ (qia) a man,*
> *Why can't a woman ⊡ (qia) a woman?*
> *Huhui women*
> *Fight to the end for equal rights!*

In addition to the ⊡ (luan) rights movement slogan, there were slogans from the various political factions, large and small, of Sunlon City, among which a very small one immediately attracted Miss Qi's notice. It was yellowed and had clearly been there for some time. In a bold cursive script was written:

---

[5] Among the Huhui people, men outnumber women 1.72:1, which has produced a complicated system of marriages. There are generally four types of marriage recognized by society: 1) ⊡, pronounced "qia," which is a marriage of one man and one woman; 2) ⊡, pronounced "duan," which is a marriage of two men; 3) ⊕, pronounced "san," which is a marriage of two men and one woman; 4) ⊕, pronounced "man," which is the marriage of three men and one woman. Marriage between women, which is not recognized by society, is known as ⊡, pronounced "luan." After the morally conservative Shan entered Sunlon City, they encouraged the Huhui to practice a one man–one woman form of marriage. They put up slogans all over town. For more on Huhui marriage practices, cf. *An Investigation of the Huhui Marital System*, by Ichikawa Yasuo, published by the Research Institute for Huhui Civilization, Kyoto University, Japan.

A great wind rises;
Valiant soldiers gather;
The general gives his orders;
Orders solely to be obeyed.

In the lower left-hand corner of the slogan was a lifelike drawing of a leopard. Miss Qi knew that the leopard was the insignia of the Leopard Brotherhood of the Royalist faction. The general mentioned in the third line was an obvious reference to General Shi, the leader of the Royalist faction. General Shi was an enigmatic figure: no one had ever seen his face, but everyone knew that he was a descendant of the Lord of Golden Goose Fort and that from his youth he was valiant above all others. He had led the entire Leopard Brotherhood in an ambush of the occupying Shan forces. And though he had won the undying enmity of the Shan, they had been unable to apprehend him. Ah 出 (chu) had narrated General Shi's deeds to her ever since she was a child. And although she had been born in Sungood bulu—the heart of democracy—she couldn't help feeling that the Royalist fighters stood head and shoulders above the rustic warriors for democracy. The only exception was Yu Jin. A strange feeling came over her as she looked at the Leopard Brotherhood slogan. Sungood bulu had always been the territory of the democratic forces; the Royalists had never been active there. Where had the slogan come from? Pondering, she reached out to touch the lifelike drawing of the leopard. As she did so, someone took tight hold of her arm.

"Freeze! So you're the one that's been putting up rebellious slogans. I've got you at last."

Startled, Miss Qi struggled with all her might but was unable to free herself from the Shan officer's strong grip. She knew it was pointless to resist. Her eyes burned with hate as she fixed her gaze on him. But when she ceased to struggle, he unexpectedly let go of her.

"Miss, no one would expect that someone of your tender years could possibly be a Royalist. Sorry, but I must ask you to step inside for a talk."

Miss Qi looked the Shan officer up and down, sizing him up. As a rule, the Shan were much bigger and taller than the Huhui, and this one was three heads taller than she. His skin was brown, as were his eyes. The fierce look in his eyes and his straight nose made him look especially dignified. Miss Qi glanced at him, blushed, and lowered her head. The Shan officer motioned to her.

"Miss," he said, "I am not going to ▣ (du)[6] you. Please come along quietly and you will not be harmed." He spoke Huhui quite well.

"I didn't put up any slogans," said Miss Qi softly. "The Sungood people will not be ruled by the Shan forever, but we won't be used by the Royalists either!"

So saying, she proudly thrust her chest forward, to the amusement of the Shan officer.

"Okay, I believe you. You're not a Royalist, but still I must ask you to step inside for a talk. The situation the last few days has been somewhat . . . odd. After you, Miss."

Miss Qi realized that it was pointless to argue. She followed the officer down an alleyway. Soon she saw a Shan patrol car parked in the center of a small square. Several fully armed Shan warriors stood guard. She bit her lip, wondering how she could have been so careless as to insist on leaving the house at the hour of the Shan morning patrols. If she had left a little later she would have missed the patrol. Just as she was thinking about how foolish she had been, she heard the high-pitched sound of a whistle.

It was a snake whistle! Instinctively, she squatted. There was a flash of white light and the patrol car was engulfed in orange flames; it exploded almost immediately, sending up a column of thick smoke. The orange flames also reduced the warriors standing guard around the car to heaps of cinders, but they never let out a cry. The Shan officer by Miss Qi's side had pulled out his gun, but he had been hemmed in by a ring of yellow light. He was frozen fast, and grimaced in pain. The yellow light vanished in a matter of seconds, and the officer fell to the ground paralyzed. Miss Qi then saw five Sungood warriors clad in green rushing toward her. The short warrior in the lead had a short sword in the shape of a snake buckled at his waist. She recognized him at once.

"Yu Jin!"

It was Yu Jin, one of the three remarkable Yu brothers. But he didn't seem at all pleased to see her.

"Miss Qi," he said as if to rebuke her, "is this any time to be running around on the streets? Fortunately we found you; otherwise, you would have been locked up by these Shan bastards, and that might have proved too much for you."

"I . . ." she said, "because Ah 出 (chu) . . ."

Yu Jin cut her off before she could finish.

---

[6] ▣, pronounced "du," which means "to fetter" or "shackle."

"We'll talk later. Let's get out of here. We'll be in a tight spot if any more Shan patrol cars show up."

He took out his snake whistle and blew three times, rapidly. The four other Sungood warriors picked up the wounded and unconscious Shan officer and sped down an alley adjoining the square. They leaped a low wall and passed through some bushes, until they came to the door of a wooden house. An old man had the door open in a flash and they ducked in. Miss Qi could detect the smell of saltpeter in the air. She seemed to faintly hear a snake whistle being blown. Overcome with excitement, she asked Yu Jin, who was squatting beside the door, "Is the uprising really beginning?"

Yu Jin snorted. "It should have begun a long time ago, then we wouldn't be in the mess we're in now."

Miss Qi thought about pursuing the matter, but when she saw the anger and exhaustion filling the short warrior's face, she thought better of the idea. Seeing as how Yu Jin hadn't yet said a considerate word to her, she felt quite upset. But he had launched a surprise attack on the Shan patrol to rescue her. Evidently he did care about her. Or was it merely a coincidence? Had he been planning the attack all along? She felt 忐忑 (chu-ru).

The Shan officer who was lying on the floor gradually regained consciousness. He moved his feet and hands, and moaned. Yu Jin nodded to one of the warriors, who took out a hypodermic and packet of medicine. He gave the officer a shot, and the dark-skinned man gave a jerk and passed out again.

Miss Qi couldn't bear the sight. "Yu Jin, why don't you just kill him and be done with it?"

"Did you see the insignia on his sleeve?" asked Yu Jin. "He is a field officer in the occupying army. There are only six of them, and we captured one of them alive today. Perhaps the bastard can supply us with some invaluable intelligence. I think the order to take the loyalty pills was a Shan trick to rouse the Sungood bulu to action so as to crush us as a warning to the other bulu. If through their deadly trap the Shan were to prevail, then their rule would meet with no resistance and they could expect smooth sailing."

Suddenly Miss Qi recalled the Leopard slogan she had seen on the wall, and related it to Yu Jin in detail.

After thinking about it, Yu Jin replied, "That really is strange. To the best of my knowledge, General Shi is still raising an army at Golden Goose Fort and his main force is still gathered on the grassy plains. General Shi hasn't entered the city yet, so how could his orders appear? It's probably another part of the Shan strategy. We should inform the Leopard Brotherhood as soon as possible, so that they can avoid being taken in."

The short warrior smiled at Miss Qi as he spoke. "I never guessed you were so attentive to details. Thank you."

As praise from Yu Jin was rare, Miss Qi was elated. But almost at once Yu Jin fell deep into thought and seemed to have completely forgotten that she even existed. She feared seeing him in this mood, and didn't have a clue as to what he was thinking. His being so thoughtful was what had initially attracted her to this young member of the Green Snake Brotherhood. Unlike other warriors, he didn't seem the least bit interested in talking about fighting. Nor did he like to get drunk. When others were in high spirits, he sat to one side drinking quietly. She had seen him use a sword and his swordsmanship was exceptional, but he made no sound and was like a swift, silent leopard. He was in fact more like a Royalist swordsman. Although she had never seen one, she imagined that they would be just that haughty, cold, and pensive. No wonder she always felt he was different from other Green Snake Brotherhood warriors. It was a mere accident of birth that he was not a Royalist swordsman. She wondered if he had any regrets on that score.

As the affectionate soul toucher was feeling sorry for Yu Jin, the short warrior seemed to emerge from his deep thought.

"Turn on the skyvision," he said to the old man of the house.

As instructed, the old man turned it on. He adjusted a few knobs, and the small square they had left earlier appeared on the screen. The patrol car in the center of the square was still burning, but three others were parked nearby. Yu Jin knew that the image on the screen was coming from the transmitted brain waves of a comrade equipped with skyvision who was keeping watch from a window near the square. He was pleased to know that the underground organization that the Green Snake Brotherhood had spent ten years building was functioning. Regardless of their firepower, the Shan would never be able to entirely subjugate Sunlon City short of vaporizing it.

The Shan warriors on the skyvision screen were busy questioning the residents and shop owners around the square. Yu Jin couldn't help but smile broadly. They would learn nothing. Even if they shot all the Huhui people on the scene, they still wouldn't be able to learn anything. Besides, each time the Shan executed one Huhui they would add three members to the underground organization. The more people who died, the stronger grew the Huhui will to resist. Were the occupying forces oblivious to this? Certainly they understood it, but they had no other choice. They were doomed to play the butcher's role just as Yu Jin was destined to play the part of the underground hero. Although both sides knew where they stood, there was no other way.

Yu Jin noticed a tall, blue-skinned fellow standing beside a patrol car. As he scrutinized him, he knew it had to be a Gaiwenese. So the Shan were paying the Gaiwenese to spy. The Gaiwenese person's back was to the screen and Yu Jin couldn't see his face. After considering the situation for a moment, he ordered the old man to have a look-see.

At first, the old man didn't understand what Yu Jin wanted. Once he understood, he looked panic-stricken. But he knew he had to follow orders and he closed his eyes. Yu Jin knew that he was communicating telepathically with the comrade hiding near the square. After a while, the image on the screen changed. The comrade in hiding had left the building and was walking toward the center of the square. The Shan patrol car on the screen was growing larger, and all the Shan soldiers next to the car looked out from the screen. The Gaiwenese also turned to look, an expression of surprise on his face. Two Shan soldiers lifted their guns. Suddenly a red light flashed over the screen and then turned a leaden-ash color.

"Did you get a good look at that Gaiwenese pig's ugly mug?" said Yu Jin to his four subordinates.

In all seriousness, the four nodded. "Remember it well," he said, gnashing his teeth. "I want him taken alive. I want that Gaiwenese pig captured alive so that I can question him." As he finished speaking, he noticed that tears were streaming down the old man's face.

"Who was he?" asked Yu Jin warmly.

"He was my grandson. He was only twelve. . . ." The old man sobbed and said nothing more. During the skyvision transmission, Miss Qi had not uttered a word. Suddenly she leaped to her feet.

"Yu Jin, how could you do such a thing?"

"I wanted to see that Gaiwenese pig's face," replied Yu Jin calmly. "There was no other way."

"But he was only twelve. How could you bear to let him die that way? You . . . you're so heartless!"

She struck Yu Jin. Yu Jin bore the blow, neither resisting nor trying to explain. It was the tearful old man who interceded to stop her.

"Miss, don't hit him. Fifth Master was right. It was the only way we could catch the Gaiwenese. He didn't die unjustly, not in the least. . . ."

The old man choked back his sobs; Miss Qi wept aloud. Yu Jin sighed.

"I had no other choice," said Yu Jin. "But we must all be prepared to sacrifice ourselves for ultimate victory. Since the Death Commandos took the loyalty pills yesterday, the very survival of the Sungood bulu has reached a critical juncture. Today, a number of the Death Commandos have undertaken suicide missions on their own. They have all been wiped out by the Shan patrols. Yu Fang and Yu Kui have been running here and there to calm the Death Commandos. At this point, it looks as if the situation is under control. The Shan know that the Death Commandos are unwilling to sacrifice themselves for nothing and that they'll start a fight only to leave themselves open to destruction. Once the Death Commando groups have been decimated, the Sungood bulu will be carved up by the Shan. But the Shan plan doesn't stop there. They might be using similar strategies to deal with the Royalists and the Bronze Statue Cult, and the other bulu. Whatever it takes, we must find out what their overall plan is to prevent them from annihilating the Huhui revolutionary armed forces."

"If we are to prevent them from destroying the Sungood bulu," said Miss Qi, wiping her tears away, "then we first have to save the Death Commandos. There is an antidote. I left the house to find Ah 出 (chu) because he knows where it can be found. . . ."

"Ah 出 (chu) knows of an antidote!" said Yu Jin, startled. "Where is it? And where is Ah 出 (chu)?"

"I haven't seen him. I asked him to obtain the antidote last night, but he hasn't returned. But he did tell me that it could be found in a painting in the Old Do-Gooder's quarters."

Hearing this, Yu Jin mumbled to himself. "So the antidote is in a painting in the Old Do-Gooder's quarters. The antidote in a painting . . . the Old Do-Gooder's . . ."

"Okay, let's go," said Yu Jin to Miss Qi and the four warriors after a lengthy pause.

3

The purple sun of the Huhui planet reached its zenith and seemed to pause, stopping directly above the Golden Palace. Its color changed from purple to a golden yellow. Only at noon did that huge ancient sun begin to shine fiercely, regaining a little of the majesty it had possessed aeons before. The people all stepped indoors to avoid the heat that scorched men, beasts, and plants alike. Unable to endure it, many of the Shan sentries standing guard around the interstellar warship fainted. But shortly after noon, the sun seemed to have spent itself and, as if someone had shut off the switch, became its purple, gloomy self again. It also seemed to increase in size, filling up a disproportionately large part of the Huhui sky.

As the noon light[1] was fading, several explosions tore through parts of the Sungood bulu, sending up columns of thick smoke that were visible for kilometers around. The Huhui people working in the high-rises downtown thronged to the windows to see what was happening. No one dared utter a word because all the buildings had been fitted by the Shan with skyvision monitors. But as they looked at one another, they couldn't conceal the expectation and excitement they felt. The Sungood bulu, known throughout the Huhui planet for its bravery and fighting ability, had finally made its move.

Shortly, groups of Shan patrol cars were seen leaving the city center and speeding off toward the Sungood bulu, where they were deployed at gates

---

[1] The light of the purple sun at noon is referred to as "*zehui*" in Huhui.

and roads. The interstellar warship in the square at the city center was slowly lifting off, its huge gun turrets turning, seeking out key targets within the city. The Huhui people in the skyscrapers trembled. The older ones remembered how the Shan dragon-class dreadnought had vaporized the Bronze Statue. Although the young people had not experienced the destruction at the end of the Fourth Interstellar War, the stories of their parents' generation were enough to set them trembling.

All eyes of the Huhui people were fixed on that gigantic, ominous thing in the air above the city. It hovered, no longer rising or changing position. It seemed to have temporarily taken the purple sun's place; its bluish gray hull shone. It ruled over the city majestically, exuding destructiveness. The Huhui people in the high-rises lowered their heads in shame. They knew that their bodies of flesh and blood were no match for an attack by the huge metal monstrosity.

But things were different in Sungood bulu. Although there were Shan patrol cars at all the gates and fortified points in the roads, it seemed as though countless eyes gazed with hate from every hidden corner, watching every move the Shan made. Every Shan soldier knew that war was imminent. They stood uneasily beside their patrol cars, ready at any time to meet an enemy attack. Frequently they turned their eyes to the sky, secretly hoping that the warship's firepower would be adequate to ensure their safe retreat.

The seventy-plus Death Commandos and the suicide squads they led spied on the Shan from the shadows. They used skyvision to pass information back and forth. All underground bases had joined together as one, ready to launch a massive suicidal assault at any time. The underground organization headquarters was located beneath a warehouse in the center of the Sungood bulu. The leaders of the Green Snake Brotherhood—Yu Fang, Yu Kui, and Yu Jin—were all there. Yu Fang anxiously paced back and forth, and Yu Jin was strenuously advising him.

"Yu Fang, we can't delay any longer. Since last night more that twenty Death Commandos have already given their lives, and more than ten bases have been destroyed by the enemy. How much longer can we continue to pacify the Death Commandos? Just a short while ago, the fourth suicide squad launched an attack on its own. And although they did manage to destroy three patrol cars, the entire squad was lost. Intermittently throwing troops into battle this way goes against all military sense. Either we give the order for a full-scale attack or we hurry up and find the antidote."

"Yu Jin," angrily replied the man with golden whiskers, "our lord has already ordered that there be no attack. I called on him last night and he said he had his reasons. So why do you go on like this?"

"The matter has come to a head," said Yu Jin, smiling coldly, "and the Old Do-Gooder is still so indecisive. Okay, so he doesn't agree to an attack, but he can't oppose us searching for an antidote for the loyalty pills. Can there be any love lost when you've seen with your own eyes how our crack troops are being destroyed piecemeal by the Shan?"

"These men have been our comrades for many years," said the big man with golden whiskers, sighing. "How can I not be affected? But you say the antidote is hidden in a painting in our lord's quarters, which is very strange. How can I broach this with our lord? Can we just go in and search the palace without authorization?"

"We have no choice," said the pockmarked warrior, stamping his foot, "and you still want to argue about it. Yu Jin is right, together we should attack the Shan with all we have. Even if we are defeated, a worthy death and glory will be ours. I can't stand this being picked off one by one. Since the Old Do-Gooder is known to be the most benevolent person in Sun-lon City, how can he stand by and watch as his own soldiers die? I think we should just go to the palace and see him. If he consents to a search of the palace, that will be the end of the matter; if he does not consent, I'll kill him on the spot. . . ."

"You've gone too far!" Yu Fang slapped him in the face and sent him reeling and falling, sprawled on the ground.

"As long as I live," said Yu Fang, his hand on the hilt of his sword, "I will permit no rebellion against our master. That is not the way of the Green Snake Brotherhood."

"You're right," said the man with the pockmarked face as he sat on the ground, "that is not the way of the Green Snake Brotherhood. But it has only been in the last two hundred years that we have looked up to the head of the Sungood bulu as our lord and master. The overriding aim of the forces of democracy has been the overthrow of the monarchy. Before that time, when the Bronze Statue Cult waxed strong, intimidating both the Democratic and the Royalist forces, we lacked support in all bulu. Only the head of the Sungood bulu offered us complete protection. It was at that time, when the survival of our brotherhood was at stake, that our brothers decided to take the head of the Sungood bulu as their lord. The circumstances today are completely different. The Bronze Statue Cult is finished; now our enemy is the Shan occupation force. If the Old Do-Gooder is of one mind with us to fight the enemy, then we will continue to call him lord and master. If he wishes to hold us back, then we must break with him. Yu Fang, you cannot be so closed minded."

"The Green Snake Brotherhood and the Sungood people," said Yu Fang, stroking his yellow whiskers, "are now inseparable. Who among us is not a Sungood person? Since we all are Sungood people, we cannot rebel against our lord."

Hearing Yu Fang, the warrior with the pockmarked face was infuriated and leaped to his feet. Then, pointing at Yu Fang, he began to revile him: "And you have the nerve to call yourself a member of the Democratic faction. How can you be so dense? The monarchy can be overthrown, so why not the head of the bulu?"

Yu Jin could see that the arguing was getting worse, and if it continued it would lead nowhere. He was just about to speak when Miss Qi, who had been sitting on the sidelines listening to the argument, suddenly tittered softly.

"And here I always thought that the three exceptional Yu brothers were heroes to 凸 (chu) heaven and 凹 (ru) earth.[2] I never thought that all you can do is argue among yourselves. It's a fight of earth-shaking proportions outside, and you guys can't decide anything. How disappointing!"

Hearing her speak, the two stopped arguing. Yu Fang looked embarrassed and stammered, "What Miss Qi says is right. I'm not qualified to lead the Green Snake Brotherhood. Miss Qi, in your opinion, what should be done?"

"As Ah 凸 (chu) said," replied Miss Qi, laughing, "the Old Do-Gooder is unaware that the antidote is hidden in a painting in his quarters. Since he doesn't know about it, why don't you go and plead with him? Perhaps he'll hand over the painting once he knows the stakes. If he refuses, then argue about it. There is still time."

Hearing this, Yu Fang and Yu Kui had nothing to say. Yu Jin was laughing to himself, for he had had the same thought. But having been uttered by Miss Qi, the words had a different significance.

"Miss Qi is right," said Yu Jin, seizing the opportunity. "Let's first go talk to the Old Do-Gooder. If he refuses, then we'll decide on our next step. This morning, I captured a Shan field officer alive. If nothing else works, we can force him to lead us into the Shan Command, where we can catch them off guard. It wouldn't be a general uprising, so the Old Do-Gooder wouldn't oppose us. If we can catch their commander, we can

[2] The expression 凸 heaven 凹 earth means "to be of colossal stature or indomitable spirit" in Huhui.

force him to order the warship to leave Sunlon City. If we can't catch him, then we'll kill as many of the enemy as possible."

Saying all he had to say in one breath, Yu Jin himself knew that there was really not much hope for his plan to succeed. But there was nothing else that they could do. Without even an acknowledging nod, Yu Fang drew out his sword and shouted: "Okay, let's do it! I've let down the brotherhood and should have paid the ultimate price for my crimes. Death means nothing! Though fruit and flowers must fall, scattered by the wind, Sunlon City will be reborn! We'll each make our own way to the palace, where we will reassemble."

Yu Fang then opened the revolving door to the underground head-quarters and was gone in the blink of an eye. Yu Kui laughed and likewise □ ■ (wu-woo).[3] Yu Jin was about to leave when Miss Qi grabbed him by the sleeve and said in a sweet, girlish voice, "I'll go with you, Yu Jin."

"Miss Qi," replied Yu Jin hurriedly, "you should go home as quickly as you can. This is an internal matter for the Green Snake Brotherhood alone. You needn't concern yourself."

Miss Qi would have none of it and, pretending to be angry, replied, "When something involves the survival of the Sungood bulu, how can you say that it is an internal matter for the Green Snake Brotherhood? Also, Ah 凸 (chu) disappeared in the Old Do-Gooder's palace last night. I should go and ask him if he saw him or not."

Finding himself instantly ensnared by the young soul toucher, Yu Jin frowned, but a scheme came to mind. He continued, "You stay at head-quarters and keep an eye on that Shan prisoner."

"No way. You want me to stay here? What happens if by some chance the Shan attack?" She leaned toward him, something the short warrior feared. Although he did like the passionate young girl, he knew that he would never fall in love again. In his mind's eye all he could see was the heavy fighting sixteen years earlier at the fall of the Huhui empire. After organized resistance in Sunlon City had collapsed, he was wounded and fled back to the Sungood bulu. He found that his home had been razed and his lovely wife and daughter were gone. He swore to have revenge and fight the Shan to the end. Miss Qi was young and could 凸 (qia) someone else. She didn't have to 凸 (qia) a middle-aged warrior past his prime.

Yu Jin pushed Miss Qi away and said, "Okay. Wait till I've ▣ (du) that Shan bastard in a torture device, and then we'll leave."

---

[3] □ ■ is pronounced "wu-woo" and means "to disappear."

The Shan officer was still unconscious. Yu Jin shoved him into a steel cage. He then turned a round wheel on the cage, reducing it in size. Only when the officer had been squeezed into a ball and it sounded as if his bones were cracking did Yu Jin stop tightening the ⊡ (du) cage.[4] Turning her head away, Miss Qi asked, "Must you torture him?"

"He won't die. These Shan bastards might not be good for much, but they sure can take pain. If I don't turn the ⊡ (du) cage down tight, he might try something."

Yu Jin could feel that Miss Qi felt sorry for the officer, which made him a little jealous. He gave the wheel another turn, squeezing the big officer into an unrecognizable mass. Unable to take it any longer, Miss Qi said, "Okay, that's enough."

The short warrior stopped turning the wheel, but Miss Qi could see that his eyes burned with hate. She remembered how Yu Jin had calmly sent that twelve-year-old boy to his death that morning by ordering him to take a peek at the Gaiwenese. Without a doubt he knew that the boy would be killed. Normally he was so quiet and well-mannered, but as soon as he encountered a Shan, he seemed to become a killing machine. At that moment she couldn't decide if she really liked this cold-blooded killer. He must have loved his wife and daughter deeply to harbor such hatred for the Shan. She pitied him. But she couldn't understand how such great hate and such great love could exist simultaneously within one person's heart.

Once Yu Jin had ⊡ (du) the prisoner, he opened the mechanical revolving door to the underground headquarters, and Miss Qi followed him into the elevator. They rapidly ascended to the ground floor of the warehouse and opened a secret door amid piles of wooden crates. From the side door of the warehouse, Yu Jin quickly led Miss Qi down an alleyway. Although it was just past noon, that huge purple sun was already dimming. Yu Jin had seen the suns of many worlds, but only the purple sun of this world made him feel so depressed. But it also kept their activities from being detected by the Shan. The two ran down the twisting alley and shortly reached the palace wall. Grasping Miss Qi's hand, Yu Jin leaped, and the two of them found themselves inside the front courtyard.

The palace of the leader of the Sungood bulu had been one of Sunlon City's eight beautiful sights. But the main palace had been completely destroyed in the Fourth Interstellar War, and all that remained was a pile

---

[4] ⊡ is pronounced "du" and is a Huhui implement of torture.

of rubble. It had never been rebuilt. Jin Zhong'an, the head of the Sungood bulu, was a charitable soul; nine years before, when a great famine had hit Sunlon City, he had opened the granaries to help the people and thus saved countless numbers and earned for himself the sobriquet "Old Do-Gooder." It was said that there was no money to repair the palace because he was so enthusiastic about doing good works. His admirers praised him by saying that he loved the people as himself. His detractors criticized him by saying that his favors sprang from baser motives, that he was actually greedy and cruel by nature, and that he was pretending to be poor so as not to have to spend any money to fix the palace. But regardless of how his opponents reviled him, his fame spread far and wide, and of the nine great bulu lords, he was second only to He He, head of the Sundragon bulu.

Yu Jin and Miss Qi walked up the steps at the side of the palace. Yu Fang and Yu Kui were already standing respectfully, hands at their sides, next to the Old Do-Gooder. The head of the Sungood bulu was about sixty years old and had white hair. His mouth was especially wide and seemed to divide his square face in two. His extremely small dark eyes were fixed on Yu Jin and Miss Qi. Somewhat against his will, Yu Jin knelt and said, "Yu Jin to see his Excellency." Miss Qi also knelt. The Old Do-Gooder smiled and said, "Well, well. Arise, stand up. Well, isn't this Miss Qi? My, how you have grown. Your father and I are old friends. I saw you ten years ago when you were nothing but a child, and now you're a young lady. Well, well. How is your father?"

Somewhat surprised, Miss Qi wasn't sure how to respond. She had never heard her father mention the head of the bulu; nor had Ah 凸 (chu) ever said anything about him. Without waiting for her to answer, the Old Do-Gooder raised his hands in a □ (wu) gesture.

"I hope all is well with him. 凸-冂 冂卜 (chu-lu-ru-mu).[5] Well, well. We all need the blessings of our ancestors. The developments of the last few days have been unfavorable to us. The fearless warship of the Shan has already lifted off and is ready at any moment to vaporize our bulu. I cannot control the Death Commandos—they are blindly wreaking havoc. If this continues it will lead to genocide."

"I must report, m'Lord," said Yu Jin, seizing his chance, "that the Death Commandos are ignoring orders because they have already taken

---

[5] 凸-冂 冂卜 is pronounced "chu-lu-ru-mu," and is a Huhui expression meaning "health and happiness."

their loyalty pills. They have no alternative but to fight because they all will die. If we find an antidote, there is a chance that they can be stopped, and we can avoid paying the ultimate price."

The Old Do-Gooder nodded his head and replied in a kindly voice, "That makes sense. The Death Commandos are faithful and true, and this is a great comfort to me. But loyalty alone is not enough. Yu Fang just told me that there might be an antidote and that it might be in a painting in my quarters. Is that true, Miss Qi?"

Miss Qi immediately repeated what Ah 出 (chu) had told her, but made no mention of their plan to check his room during the night. The Old Do-Gooder stroked his beard as he listened to her. Then he muttered, "If it's in the palace, how is it that I know nothing about it? But Ah 出 (chu) is very knowledgeable. Perhaps he has learned something from the secret books of previous dynasties. Okay. Come with me and we will look for it together. I'm willing to turn the palace upside down if it means saving my loyal Death Commandos!"

No one had expected that the Old Do-Gooder would have agreed with such alacrity to a search of the palace; they were overjoyed. Yu Fang could scarcely hide the gratitude he felt and nearly fell to his knees. Even Yu Kui mumbled to himself, swearing that henceforward he would be entirely loyal to the Old Do-Gooder. With the old man leading the way, they all trooped off to his private quarters.

His quarters were located in one of two treasure palaces. After the main palace was burned down, the Old Do-Gooder repaired the side palace to serve as the new main palace and had another one built for his residence. It was constructed out of black wood from the headwaters of the Hu River. Each log was 66 meters long and 1 1/2 meters square. At the end of each of the eaves was carved a snake or strange beast, each decorated with a copper head. There were 500 pairs of snakes and strange beasts on the roof ridge.

Once inside the palace, everyone relaxed. The walls were covered with 300 or 400 paintings, large and small. Feasting his eyes on them, the pock-marked warrior slowed his pace and whispered to Yu Jin, "We've been fooled by the Old Do-Gooder. How are we going to find the painting containing the antidote Ah 出 (chu) mentioned? We can't tear up all of them. I think he's having fun with us."

As he spoke, he became increasingly emotional and was on the point of drawing his sword when Yu Jin hurriedly stopped him.

"Don't be rash, Yu Kui; wait a moment."

Standing in the middle of the palace, the Old Do-Gooder smiled and said, "This is where I keep my collection of famous paintings. All right, this is all of them. Miss Qi, which painting was it that Ah 出 (chu) mentioned to you? Was there anything special about it?"

Miss Qi glanced surreptitiously at Yu Jin and said, "He didn't say. I don't know which one he had in mind. What a mess, and Ah 出 (chu) has disappeared. But it's hard to say if we could find it even if he were here. Unfortunately, no one knows his whereabouts."

The Old Do-Gooder sighed several times. "Well," he said, "that's the fate of our bulu. My poor Death Commandos. That they should be sacrificed one by one like this really is a pity, a real pity."

Listening to him, the three Yu brothers remained silent. Miss Qi rolled her eyes and said, "M'Lord, how many paintings are there in this room?"

The old man seemed stunned; then, smiling, he replied, "Beats me! They are all national treasures that have been handed down through the ages. I'm not sure exactly how many. Perhaps three or four hundred."

"Since they are national treasures, there should be a detailed list." Miss Qi refused to let the matter rest. "M'Lord, can you ask the chamberlain to locate the catalogue?"

The Old Do-Gooder's dark eyes narrowed to two small slits, 目目 (lu-mu), and after a while he ordered the chamberlain to fetch the list of paintings, which he took from a wooden cabinet in the corner of the room. Yu Jin took up position behind the man to have a look. The man seemed a bit nervous as he flipped through the list.

"M'Lord, I must report that there are 372 paintings."

"Wrong!" said Miss Qi. "There are only 371 paintings hanging here. One is missing."

"Well, well," replied the Old Do-Gooder, laughing. "Miss Qi has good eyes. Having just entered the palace, how is it that you know there are 371 paintings hanging here?"

"When I say there are 371 paintings here, I mean there are 371 paintings," said Miss Qi. "If you don't believe me, count them yourself."

As she finished speaking, Yu Fang and Yu Kui had already rushed to count the paintings. Yu Jin remained standing behind the chamberlain holding the list. The man trembled slightly and then said, "M'Lord, I must report that the room is short one painting."

Hearing this, the Old Do-Gooder angrily replied, "Short one painting! How is it that I was not informed? Where is it?"

"M'Lord, I must report that yesterday when the room was being cleaned, one painting was carelessly knocked to the ground where its frame was cracked. It was taken to a carpenter to be repaired."

"Nonsense! Go and get it this instant."

The chamberlain immediately kowtowed and was gone in a flash. Yu Fang and Yu Kui stopped counting, and the room grew silent. Yu Jin tightly gripped the sword at his waist.

The Old Do-Gooder didn't look at them but simply mumbled to himself with his hands behind his back. "Nonsense. What a bunch of nonsense. You can't take your eyes off these scoundrels for one minute, or they get up to all sorts of mischief. They must be taught a lesson."

Miss Qi chuckled derisively, knowing that the old man's words were intended for the ears of the three Yu brothers. Although he heard Miss Qi laugh to herself, he kept his composure. Shortly, the chamberlain returned at a run with the painting. Everyone gathered around for a look. They all gasped and stared blankly.

The painting depicted a palatial hall in which three people, dressed in ancient costume, were seated. A colorless disk rested on top of each of their heads. On the long table before the three people were placed five jade disks, three of which were blue and two of which were green. An old man with a long beard was peeking at them from the doorway.

Everyone examined the painting, but no one understood what it meant. "What sort of painting is this?" asked Yu Kui, the frankest member of the group. "This is a national treasure? I don't get it."

Yu Fang glared at his brother. Then he spoke to the Old Do-Gooder. "M'Lord, what are the origins of this painting? Why is it so odd looking?"

"Well, well," replied the Old Do-Gooder, smiling, "so I'm a collector and not a connoisseur. I don't know the origins of each and every painting. Lai Fu, check the list and see what it says."

The chamberlain whose name was Lai Fu took a long time to search through the list.

"The painting is titled *Five Jade Disks*," he said. "It was taken as booty from Tai Nan during the Third Interstellar War."

Everyone was still in the dark. The Old Do-Gooder stroked his beard and muttered, "Well, we've got the painting. But is it the one containing the antidote? If so, then where is it hidden?"

The three Yu brothers looked at one another. Suddenly, Yu Kui reached out, snatched the painting out of Lai Fu's hands, and smashed the frame. It had already been broken and fell apart in his hands. He tossed the painting aside and proceeded to break the frame into smaller pieces. Soon the ground was littered with small bits, but he did not find the antidote. In a rage he roared strangely, clutched the bits and pieces, grinding them to bits. Yu Kui was about to tear up the painting, but Yu Fang shouted to him to stop.

"Yu Kui, control yourself!"

"Where is the antidote? The antidote has to he here. Where is it?" said Yu Kui as he searched among the pieces of wood. "Where can the antidote be?"

Witnessing Yu Kui's nearly insane behavior, the Old Do-Gooder sighed and said, "You've done all that you could do to find an antidote for the loyalty pills. It's a pity that no one knows in which painting it can be found nor how it is concealed. I'm deeply touched by your loyalty. Well, well. You'd all best go home. I'll handle the matter of the Death Commandos."

The three Yu brothers were extremely disappointed. Yu Fang pulled Yu Kui to his feet and motioned to everyone that they should take their leave of the old man. Miss Qi looked at the *Five Jade Disks* painting on the ground and, smiling sweetly, said to the Old Do-Gooder, "M'Lord, although we haven't been able to locate the antidote, could you loan us this canvas? Perhaps when Ah 出 (chu) returns he'll he able to give us the key to the painting."

There was a slight change in the Old Do-Gooder's expression, and then he smiled and said, "Miss Qi, you are very prudent; it's clear you come from a family of scholars. Is your father still fond of the wisdom beads? Well, well. Take the painting. You can return it in a few days, that will be plenty of time."

"In a few days the Death Commandos will all be dead. How can you say there is plenty of time?" asked Yu Kui angrily, his voice quavering with rage. Yu Fang quickly covered his brother's mouth. The Old Do-Gooder acted as if he had heard nothing, and then ordered Lai Fu to see them out of the palace.

Once outside the Old Do-Gooder's black wood palace, Yu Kui began to curse.

"We've been played for fools by the Old Do-Gooder. If it hadn't been for Miss Qi's sharp eyes, who knows where he would have hidden the painting? Who knows what he's up to? He may already have removed the antidote. I say we return immediately to the palace and beat the truth out of him."

"Yu Kui," said Yu Fang, admonishing his brother, "his Excellency himself escorted us to search for the painting, and he generously loaned us this one as well. Why so suspicious? Is he no less concerned than we are about saving the Death Commandos?"

Yu Jin snorted contemptuously. He had no desire to argue with Yu Fang, so he changed the topic.

"In any case, I believe that this *Five Jade Disks* is the painting that contains the antidote that Ah 出 (chu) spoke of. It's a strange painting, and I fear that only one who has mastered Tai Nan history will comprehend its profound mysteries. It's unfortunate that Ah 出 (chu) has disappeared."

"Shall we ask my dada to look at it?" asked Miss Qi suddenly. "If Dada is willing to help us, I'm sure he would he able to solve the riddle of *Five Jade Disks.*"

After some consideration, the three Yu brothers decided it was the only option. They knew that Miss Qi's father was one of the few sages in the Sungood bulu who understood the wisdom beads. He was also highly esteemed by one and all.

"Your father strongly dislikes the Old Do-Gooder," said Yu Jin, still uncertain. "Do you think he will help us?"

"If he refuses, I have ways to make him help us." So saying, Miss Qi turned and set off. Yu Jin followed at once while his two brothers drew their swords to protect them. The four of them turned a bend in the twisting alley and disappeared from sight.

At about the same time Miss Qi and the Yu brothers disappeared, someone peeked over the palace wall. It was none other than Lai Fu, the chamberlain who had retrieved the *Five Jade Disks* painting. As he paused to look, someone behind him seemed to be giving him orders. Lai Fu nodded, went over the wall, darted down the alley, and quickly disappeared.

The purple sun of the Huhui planet was gradually setting. That huge bluish gray interstellar warship hovered, haloed by the sun's light as if it were but an ornament of the sun. There was a white flash, and another violent explosion rocked the Sungood bulu. It seemed to send tremors through the purple sun. The warship proceeded to directly above the site of the explosion, its gun turrets never ceasing to turn, but without firing. After a while, it began a slow descent to the square at the city center. The Shan patrols that had been dispatched to keep order in the various bulu also returned to the square. The Huhui people all breathed a sigh of relief. They poured out of the high-rises around the square and headed home. The strong, sandy wind from the plains once again blew over Sunlon City. And night gradually fell over the Huhui planet.

The fires that had been started by the explosions had all been extinguished. Snake lamps were lit in all the houses under the shroud of purple clouds. Small bluish-green flames rose from the mouths of the copper-colored lamps. Each time a revolutionary made the ultimate sacrifice, it was the custom among the Sungood people to light their snake lamps as a show of mourning for the deceased. It was also a form of silent protest against the Shan. In every window on every street, without exception, the small bluish-green flames could be seen. As usual, the narrow streets were filled with people. But amid the mass of Huhui people went a tall, blue-skinned fellow, hunched over in an attempt to conceal his true size. He pushed his way through the crowds, eavesdropping. He hesitated for a moment in the vicinity of a tavern from which the familiar song of the soul toucher drifted. A smile floated over the Gaiwenese person's face. After 叮咛 (lu-mu) for a while to make sure that no Huhui person noticed him, he raised the door curtain and entered the tavern.

4

In spite of the series of explosions that had occurred in Sunlon City that day, business was better than usual at the Qi family tavern. Perhaps because the situation was unstable, a powder keg ready to explode, people were out in numbers in search of news, and it just so happened that everyone seemed to end up in the restaurant district of the Sungood bulu. Miss Qi had instructed Ah Wen and two of her husbands, Ah Two and Ah Three, to go out and busy themselves serving the customers. Ah Wen's other husband, Ah Four, served as cook in the tavern kitchen. Originally, Ah Two had been scheduled to work that night and Ah Four and Ah Three were to have the night off; now, for whatever reason, they began to argue. Then, grabbing each other by the hair, they went to see Miss Qi's father to ask him to settle the dispute. They continued their squabble in the old man's room. At first Ah Wen and Ah Two tried to mediate, but they ended up being drawn into the fracas as well. In the brawl, Ah Wen was punched in her right eye. She cried and cried. She served customers for a while, then ran over to complain to Miss Qi.

"A ⇧ (man) marriage is hard on a person, child. When you ⊡ (qia), ⊡ (qia) just one person. Whatever you do, don't be like me and bring trouble on yourself by ⇧⇧ (man-man)! Two people will certainly have their troubles, but nothing like the jealous quarrels of three men. Men are petty and like to argue about their place in the pecking order. They're all rotten."

Miss Qi knew that Ah Wen complained just to be complaining. Inwardly, she was quite happy to see her husbands fighting over her. Ah

Wen had married a butcher, a driver, and a cook and called them respectively Ah Two, Ah Three, and Ah Four. There was no Ah One. Ah Wen had deliberately left the top position open to be filled by her ideal spouse. However, women were not allowed by Huhui law to have more than three husbands; thus her dream had gone unrealized, and instead she had more than her share of headaches. All three of her husbands were after the coveted top place, and argued incessantly about it day in and day out. Miss Qi marveled at how fat and ugly Ah Wen had managed to 口 (qia) three men and enjoy such bountiful good fortune. But she herself could never do such a thing. She was quite willing to wait a lifetime if necessary for the right person.

Customers continued pouring in, and the downstairs had long since been filled. Upstairs, aside from a small room used by her father and the three Yu brothers, there were no seats either. In a sweat, Ah Wen, Ah Two and Ah Three bustled between floors. Each time hefty Ah Two took another order of snake soup up the stairs, he first would heave a great sigh to let Ah Wen know how hard he was working. But Ah Three, the skinny driver, never complained; occasionally he would disappear to the toilet or some other place to take an elation pill. Ah Wen could not count the times she had fought with Ah Three over his addiction. She even threatened to ■ (woo) him,[1] but Ah Three was unable to break his bad habit. All drivers in Sunlon City were wealthy, which perhaps had something to do with all the wind and sand that made travel on foot unpleasant. Ah

---

[1] ■ is pronounced "woo" and means to divorce a husband. According to Huhui custom, if a wife says to her husband, "I don't love you" nine successive times, then she can ■ him. But if a husband replies 99 successive times, "I still love you," then the divorce is nullified. The next time, a wife must repeat the words "I don't love you" 999 successive times to divorce her husband. Each time divorce is attempted, there is an increase in the number of times the words must be repeated. By the same token, if a husband wishes to ■ his wife, he must perform the same procedure. Thus a great effort is required for the Huhui to divorce or preserve a marriage. The mouth tiring is less a problem than keeping an accurate count. For if a mistake is made in counting, the person must start again from the very beginning. It is quite common to see a Huhui standing at the door of a house repeating rapidly and at one go "I don't love you I don't love you." Invariably, the person is a poor demented soul seeking a divorce. Many Huhui people lose their minds in the process each year. The so-called "Mandarin Duck Asylum" is an institution especially for housing this sort of demented Huhui. The men and women locked in the Mandarin Duck Asylums do nothing all day long save repeat the words, "I still love you I still love you" or "I don't love you I don't love you" over and over again. For more on the sociology of Huhui marriage, cf. *Sunlon City: Tomb for Romantics* by Professor Tang Huang, published by the Research Institute of Huhui History at the University of Madrid.

Three always had money for the drug, and Ah Wen couldn't do anything with him.

Ah Wen, Ah Two, and Ah Three were all busy in the tavern, and in the kitchen, Ah Four had no time to rest. Frequently he would stick his head out and grumble, "We're all out of snake gallbladder. If a customer orders fried snake gallbladder, we're all out." "There's not much snake soup left. I'll cook another pot; it'll be ready shortly. Who said make just three hundred bowls? That's nowhere near enough." After grumbling, he became his good-natured self again and darted back into the kitchen to make some more snake soup.

Miss Qi was also very busy that night. One minute she was helping Ah Wen serve the customers, another minute she was in the kitchen trying to soothe Ah Four's flaring temper, and another minute she had to do her duty as soul toucher and sing a couple of songs. Fortunately, very few of the customers were paying attention to her singing. Most were focused on discussing the situation in Sunlon City. As busy as she was, she was worried only about the four people in that little room upstairs. When she managed to get the time, she would run upstairs to see if her dada and the Yu brothers had made any progress with the *Five Jade Disks* painting.

In the small room, the three Yu brothers sat with long faces as they stared at the painting on the wall. Old Man Qi sat cross-legged on the bed, wisdom beads in one hand as he flipped without stopping through a copy of the *Art History of Tai Nan* that lay open on the bed.

"Strange," he muttered. "It really is strange. I distinctly remember reading about *Five Jade Disks*, but where? As a man ages, his memory becomes less and less reliable. If only Ah 丑 (chu) were here. The little guy has been gone all day and still hasn't returned. I hope nothing has happened to him."

"I'm sure he is okay," said Yu Jin, looking at Miss Qi, who had just entered the room. "Ah 丑 (chu) is not a child," he continued in an effort to comfort the old man. "He knows where all the Shan checkpoints are located. He wouldn't allow himself to be captured."

The old man manipulated his beads, each of which sparkled beautifully with a rainbow of color. One small bead emitted a chirping sound. The old man placed it in a shallow depression on top of a white globe lamp on the headboard cabinet. The lamp began to glow of its own accord, and words and pictures appeared on the globe. The old man scrutinized it carefully for a while before shaking his head.

"I still can't find it," he said. "I don't understand it. I still can't find it after operating twenty beads synchronously and thoroughly checking all references. Were my wisdom bead calculations incorrect?"

With an air of self-approbation, the old man scattered the beads on the bed. He placed one bead on his left and one on his right Still dissatisfied, he snatched them up and scattered them again. None of the three Yu brothers knew what kind of games the old man was playing. Yu Kui was growing impatient but couldn't very well lose his temper. All he could do was stand before the painting and sigh. Yu Fang wore an anxious expression. He sighed, watching the day slip away as he thought about the Death Commandos dying one by one and the whereabouts of the antidote still unknown. Yu Jin's eyes were fixed on the painting. He had but one question in his mind: What did the painting mean? There were five jade disks, three blue and two green. There were also three people in the painting, each of whom wore an empty, colorless disk on their head.

At his side, Miss Qi tugged on his sleeve, indicating that she wanted him to step outside. Yu Jin left the room with her.

"Yu Jin," said Miss Qi, closing the door behind her, "there's a Gaiwenese downstairs. He looks like the one we saw this morning."

Yu Jin's face went black when he heard what Miss Qi had to say. He was about to go downstairs, but she stopped him.

"Don't be in a rush. There are so many customers it won't be easy to catch him. I'll get him outside where you can deal with him."

"How are you going to get him outside?"

"I have my ways," she said, smiling.

Miss Qi headed downstairs, where she took her seat behind the soul toucher's piano. She began to finger the keys and to sing softly. At first, the sound of her voice was almost inaudible and nearly drowned out by the general clamor of people talking. Suddenly she struck the keys sharply; her voice took on a sad tone that rose, circling ever higher like a coiling green snake. Yu Jin listened as Miss Qi sang.

> *Far away to the north*
> *Stars twinkle in the night sky*
> *I see that girl from Menghan City*
> *Alone and dejected, she*
> *Walks that road of green cobbles*
>
> *O, young lady!*
> *Forget your troubled lot*

Forget your vanished homeland
Let me wrap your dew-soaked clothes
Within these warm affections of mine

Thank you for your good intentions
Kind, kind sir
But the day I was forced to flee from Menghan City
I was doomed my whole life long
To wander without end

O, to wander!
I cannot forget my childhood, free from worry
I cannot forget my beautiful homeland
Nor in the dark of night
Forget my mom and dad

Far away to the north
Stars twinkle in the night sky
I see that girl from Menghan City
Alone and dejected, she
Walks that road of green cobbles.[2]

When Miss Qi finished her song, the tavern was so quiet one could hear a pin drop. After a while, people began to applaud and shout. Yu Jin peeked out from the stairway and saw that the Gaiwenese wept silently, his face covered with tears. As Miss Qi walked by, the Gaiwenese hurriedly stood up. Somewhat embarrassed, he spoke to her.

"Miss Qi, your singing is great. I haven't heard a Gaiwenese folk song in ages. I can't control my tears, please do not think me strange."

"Not at all," said Miss Qi, forcing a smile. "I hope you can visit us often. You look familiar. Have you been here before?"

The Gaiwenese nodded emphatically.

"Of course, Miss Qi. You are my favorite soul toucher. My name is Gai Bo. I've been trading in Sunlon City for more than two years now. I frequent this tavern."

---

[2] The title of this Gaiwenese song is "The Distant North." For more on the genocide of the Gaiwenese, see "Translation of a Poetic Masterpiece" in the *Nebula Suite*.

"So, you're an old customer," replied Miss Qi, smiling. "Are your wife and children here in Sunlon City?"

"I'm not married," said Gai Bo. "Gaiwenese traders make their home wherever they find themselves. It's not easy to find a wife."

Miss Qi knew what he said was true. It was very difficult for the Gaiwenese, accustomed as they were to a life of wandering, to find wives. She thought that perhaps being a spy precluded marriage and kids for him. She looked him up and down carefully. The Gaiwenese all looked pretty much the same, and Gai Bo bore a striking resemblance to the Gaiwenese she had seen on the screen that morning: both had pointed heads and short mustaches. Miss Qi felt bad as she thought about the boy who had sacrificed himself to get a look at the Gaiwenese.

"Mr. Gai Bo," she continued, as if nothing were amiss, "since you've mentioned trading, I've a business matter you might be able to help me with. With the tense situation recently, a friend of mine in the leather business was anxious to leave Sunlon City. He left some leather with me; it's out behind the tavern. Would you be interested? If you are, let me show you."

"I specialize in trading the local products of all planets," replied Gai Bo, overjoyed. "Of course, I'd be interested in leather. If you are not busy, Miss Qi, why don't we go have a look right now?"

The tavern was full of customers. Ah Wen and Ah Two were running around in a sweat through the crowd, and not a trace of Ah Three was to be seen. Miss Qi led Gai Bo out and around to the back of the tavern. She was just about to open the wooden door to the woodshed when a huge hand with nine fingers covered her mouth.

"Don't make a sound, Miss Qi," said the Gaiwenese coldly. "Come along quietly with me."

Then from behind the Gaiwenese someone else spoke in a cold tone of voice: "You got that right, you Gaiwenese pig. Keep your mouth shut and release Miss Qi without making a commotion."

Startled, Gai Bo shoved Miss Qi forcefully in the direction of the voice. Miss Qi screamed, but fortunately Yu Jin was there to catch her in his strong arms. Yu Jin let go of Miss Qi and pointed his snake-shaped blade at Gai Bo. As he did so, the tip of the sword began to glow with a white light. In duels with other warriors, the snake sword could be used as a dagger, and it was also ingeniously designed as a pistol that held ten rounds of traditional bullets and a laser beam as well. Yu Jin took aim at the Gaiwenese's head and shot. Hit, the Gaiwenese fell, but got up again. He had not died, but his face was contorted in pain.

"You Gaiwenese pig," said Yu Jin, spitting. "I'd have to dirty my hands to kill you. Get out of here!"

Gai Bo was in so much pain that he couldn't speak. But he fled, stumbling as he went. After driving away the Gaiwenese, Yu Jin returned his sword to its scabbard, and tenderly took Miss Qi by the hand.

"Are you hurt?"

She shook her head. She leaned close to Yu Jin and said, "Why did you let Gai Bo go? Didn't you want the spy alive?"

"He can't get away. The bullet I just shot into his head contained a miniature skyvision transceiver.[3] Wherever he goes, we'll know. With him showing the way, we might be able to find out what the Shan are planning for us." After thinking for a moment, he continued, "It's strange. He was trying to kidnap you. Perhaps it's another plot. Or have the Shan already discovered that the tavern is a base? It's not safe. I think it best if you and your father go into hiding."

"Where can we hide?" asked Miss Qi, snuggling against Yu Jin's strong chest. "I feel entirely safe here. Dada doesn't get involved in any worldly affairs, and I'm just an ignorant soul toucher. What could they do to us?"

"This won't do." With some alarm, Yu Jin felt the affectionate soul toucher pressing closer. "After the next two critical days have passed," he said sternly, "I'll send someone to escort you out of the city. You can hide on the grassy plains. As far as I can see, there will be a general uprising regardless of whether we are able to save the Death Commandos. The Shan have gone too far! As soon as we get in touch and arrange things, the nine bulu shall rise up together and avenge the dead."

As he spoke, Yu Jin's eyes burned with vengeance. Miss Qi knew that once he got started on the uprising, nothing else mattered. She sighed and gently gathered together her long hair.

"Let's get inside, out of this strong sandy wind," she said.

Yu Jin looked up and saw that the late rain was already falling. The bluish-green flames of the snake lamps at every window flickered. From amid the purple clouds, the bluish shafts of light slowly descended and closed. Yu Jin once again felt that gnawing depression. He knew he would never leave this dangerous city. Years before, he had sworn he would leave Sunlon City and never return. But no matter how far he traveled, no matter how many light years he put between himself and the city, it always called him back. He finally returned, married, and became a father. Every-

---

[3] On the principles of skyvision, see "Romance of a Snipped Dream" in the *Nebula Suite*.

thing seemed settled. But then the fanatical Bronze Statue Cult engulfed the city. He joined the expeditionary force not to spread the faith but rather to satisfy his desire for adventure and hardship. But in the end the followers of the Bronze Statue Cult were defeated, and he lost his wife and child. After so many years, his youthful ideals were the worse for wear and nearly extinct. Only one thought remained: to avenge his wife and daughter. It was the only thing he could do to relieve his guilt.

He hated the city. He hated the starless night, but he had to take responsibility for his life. And he had to save the city.

"Yu Jin, was she beautiful?"

Miss Qi's question interrupted Yu Jin's train of thought. He was somewhat startled.

"Who do you mean?"

"Your wife. Was she beautiful?"

Yu Jin fixed his eyes on the young girl. Her lovely hair was covered with sand. He reached out to brush it away.

"She was not as pretty as you. No, you're both different. She was . . ." Yu Jin muttered hesitantly. "You're different, that's all. Why bring up the past? It's too late. Let's get inside."

They returned to the tavern, which was already half empty of customers. Ah Wen and her butcher husband Ah Two, in complete disregard for the remaining customers, were starting to clean up. Wielding brooms with a vengeance, the two fatties, one man and one woman, swept whatever was left on the tables onto the floor. Miss Qi could vaguely hear Ah Three and Four arguing in the kitchen. She was on the point of asking Ah Wen what was wrong when she spoke first: "Child, don't pay any attention to those two jerks. My fate is a miserable one, so miserable. For a few coppers, my greedy parents married me off to three men without ever considering the possible outcome of a 中 (man) marriage. It's the woman who suffers. My fate is a miserable one."

"Oh, so now you're bad-mouthing me." Ah Two, the butcher, tossed away his broom, nearly striking a customer who was just leaving. "You're miserable. Does that make me lucky? For seven generations, my family have been butchers. Who in the Sunlon market didn't know which girl would be a good 中 (qia)? But no, I had to marry a shrewish (ru-chu)[4] idiot like you. Before 中 (qia) you were 中中 (ru-ru), but afterward you were

---

[4] 中中, pronounced "ru-chu," means "bad-tempered" in Huhui; 中中, pronounced "ru-ru," means "gentle"; 中中, pronounced "chu chu," means "impulsive."

凸凸 (chu-chu). The ancients had it right when they said, 中中 (ru-ru) before 凸 (qia); 凸凸 (chu-chu) after 凸 (qia). Immoral woman, now you're showing your true colors!"

"Sea serpent killer of a butcher! Such affected gentility. I want to puke up the snake soup I ate two nights ago." Ah Wen also threw her broom aside and rushed to hit Ah Two. Yu Jin separated the two of them and said, "No fighting! What sort of impression do you make by fighting in front of the customers? Get to the kitchen, both of you."

Only after they had been scolded by Yu Jin did the two of them pick up their brooms in a huff and head for the kitchen. Once they were inside and all four spouses were together, the fighting got even worse. Miss Qi apologized to all the remaining customers, most of whom simply smiled.

"Well said! Well said!" commented one old man. "'中中 (ru-ru) before 凸 (qia); 凸凸 (chu-chu) after 凸 (qia). Immoral woman, now you're showing your true colors.' All women in a 凸 (man) marriage are spoiled. A long time ago I said we should abolish 凸 (man) marriage."

The old man shook his head, then hooked his arm around that of a young man, and the two of them set off with an air of intimacy.

"凸 (man) marriage is bad enough," said a middle-aged woman, watching the two of them depart, "but this 口 (duan) marriage is even more ridiculous. If everyone were like those two, the Huhui people would have become extinct a long time ago. The golden mean governed by reason and care among people is the only right way."

After she had her say, the middle-aged woman 口口 (lu-mu) a moment, then put her arms tightly around two young men and departed. The two last customers looked at each other and smiled. They took off their caps, revealing full heads of thick hair.

"Hypocrite, hypocrite," said the two of them. "Why must people be such hypocrites? Only the 口 (luan) know true love."

Thus, holding hands, the two young ladies left. As Yu Jin stood there dumbfounded, Yu Kui came hurtling down the stairs. He stumbled and fell and picked himself up immediately.

"He solved it," he said, clapping his hands. "Old Mr. Qi solved the riddle of the five jade disks."

Miss Qi and Yu Jin were overjoyed at the news and together raced up the stairs. The old man was examining the pictures and words that had appeared on the globe lamp.

"Child, my wisdom bead calculations were correct," he said elatedly, seeing his daughter enter with Yu Jin. "I finally found the source of the story."

"Story? What story?"

"Look," continued her father, pointing at the globe lamp. "What do you see?"

Everyone pressed closer for a better look. They saw that the picture on the globe lamp was identical to the painting on the wall.

"It's a story from long, long ago," continued the old man. "Once upon a time, there was a wise and able king who eagerly sought out capable people. He ordered that his minister find the smartest person in the entire realm, so as to appoint him the teacher of the prince. One day he could assist the prince when he ruled.

"The minister himself was extremely intelligent. He scoured the land, leaving no stone unturned, until he found the three smartest people. The minister thought of every way he could to test the three. But unexpectedly, he was unable to determine which one was smartest. The minister was embarrassed because the king had instructed him to find the single smartest person in the realm. He had to do something to find out who it was.

"After giving the matter much thought, he came up with a solution. He assembled the three people and asked them to look at five jade disks on a table. Then he said, 'Three of these jade disks are blue and two are green. I am going to blindfold you, after which I will place one disk on top of your head. Then I will remove the blindfolds. You will be able to see the disks on top of the others' heads but not the one on top of your own. You cannot speak or gesture to one another, and anyone who breaks the rules will be put to death on the spot. The first one to guess the color of the disk on his own head will be deemed the smartest person in the land, and will become the prince's teacher. But if you guess incorrectly, you will be executed at once.'

"So saying, he blindfolded the three smart people and placed one jade disk on top of each one's head. Then he removed the blindfolds. The three people looked at one another for some time, but no one said a word. Finally, one of them got it, guessed the color of the disk on top of his head, and became the prince's teacher. Later he himself became minister and enjoyed wealth and a high position his entire life.

"So what color were the disks on top of the people's heads?"

After he finished telling the story, Mr. Qi's eyes twinkled with satisfaction. The wisdom beads sounded as he rolled them in his hand. The three Yu brothers stared at one another in blank dismay. Yu Kui was the first to say something.

"Mr. Qi, are you just playing with us?" he shouted. "Who knows what color the disks were that the minister put on their heads? Who cares?"

"The painting contains a riddle," said Yu Jin. "No wonder the artist failed to paint in the color of the disks. But even if we solve the riddle, what do we get? We want the antidote for the loyalty pills. And what does that have to do with the riddle?"

"It has a lot to do with the riddle. The solution to the riddle will provide the antidote." Pleased with himself, the old man continued, "A moment ago, I used an apparatus to analyze the chemical composition of the pigments used for the five disks in the painting. I discovered that they contain a mixture of medicines. Clearly, the person who planned this painting really knocked themselves out. All we have to do is guess the color of the disks on top of their heads, mix the medicines proportionately, and it's my guess that we'll have the antidote."

After much thought, the three Yu brothers concluded that what he said was reasonable. Yu Fang immediately bowed three times to the old man and with a great deal of respect said, "Revered Mr. Qi, you are the wisest man in the Sungood bulu. Please announce the solution of the riddle to us. I personally want to thank you on behalf of all the Death Commandos. Thank you for this great favor."

"Hold on!" said the old man sternly. "I have never had any interest in helping the Old Do-Gooder. The Death Commandos are *his* Death Commandos. They're all a bunch of fools, and it would be best if they all died. When you arrived I made up my mind not to help you, but only after my daughter pleaded with me did I promise to help you find the source of *Five Jade Disks*. I have found it. Now you can go ask the Old Do-Gooder to solve the riddle. It's his painting, and the Death Commandos are his men. If he can't solve it, all I can say is that he'll get what he deserves."

"Revered Mr. Qi," Yu Fang began to plead, "I know you have never been pleased with the Old Do-Gooder's ways, but the very survival of the bulu hinges on the fate of the Death Commandos. Can you bear to stand by and not help someone in need?"

As he listened, Mr. Qi remained impassive. Beside him, Yu Kui grew exasperated, and striking his chest said, "Mr. Qi, I have always respected you as the wisest man in the bulu. You and the 丑 (chu) people are the same—you grow complacent in your idleness and have nothing to do. Why does everyone respect you? The elderly are provided for for one thousand days so that they might be of use for one day. The future of our people hangs in the balance. How can you play games with us?"

"Okay, so I'm complacent and have nothing to do," replied the old man, sarcastically. "At least I don't oppress the people of our bulu. What has the head of the bulu you call the Old Do-Gooder done for you? The Death Commandos are almost beyond hope, and has he done so much as lift a finger?"

Yu Kui was about to respond when he was stopped by his brothers. Seeing that the old man was still frowning, Yu Jin offered a few words of thanks in an attempt to smooth things over. He then left with his brothers. Miss Qi followed them downstairs.

"This really is not right," said Yu Jin to Miss Qi. "Your dada already has helped us quite a lot, and all my brother can do is get angry with him. Yu Kui has a bad temper and is only capable of offending people."

"Although Dada seems hard," said Miss Qi, laughing, "he is really a softy inside. How can he not help? He said what he did because he hasn't yet solved the riddle. He is very concerned about saving face but couldn't say so to you. Wait and see—if he solves the riddle he won't be able to keep his mouth shut even if you want him to."

It only took a moment to convince Yu Jin. Yu Kui suddenly felt stupid for what he had said and slapped his own face.

"Miss Qi, I'm hopeless. How could I have had any doubts about a revered man like Mr. Qi? I ought to be whipped."

"It's all right," said Miss Qi. "Since you have angered him so, he'll spend the whole night using his wisdom beads. Knowing Dada's temper, he won't rest until he solves the riddle."

"Great! If he might soon solve the riddle, the Death Commandos will be saved," said Yu Fang happily. "After we save them, we'll settle accounts with the Shan and their accomplices."

"I almost forgot about that Gaiwenese," said Yu Jin to Miss Qi, like one startled from a dream. "We can't let him get away. Do you have skyvision here?"

"It's in the corner."

Yu Jin opened the skyvision control box and inserted the control card. Adjusting the frequency of the crystal of the electromagnetic shaker, he then turned on the skyvision.

Initially the image on the screen was not very clear. There seemed to be a number of what looked like large frogs swimming in the water, one of which climbed out on a rock on the right-hand shore. It opened its mouth and croaked: "Gai, gai."

"He has lost a lot of blood," said Yu Jin, swearing. "His mind is garbled."

"Where is he?" asked Yu Kui. "There are no weird frogs like that within a hundred-mile radius of Sunlon City."

"They're not frogs," replied Yu Jin. "Those are the earliest ancestors of the Gaiwenese. He's half comatose, and so he's recalling the amphibious existence of his forebears. It's a kind of homesickness."

They all stood around the skyvision unit silently watching the half-comatose Gaiwenese retrace his life through memory. On the screen appeared a crowded village, and a small Gaiwenese child at his mother's breast. The child's mother affectionately caressed his face with her huge hand of nine fingers. Then the image on the screen changed again: a huge building in Menghan City appeared. A young Gai Bo, carrying several books, walked beside and chatted with a Gaiwenese girl, who was as delicate and lovely as a flower. Then a scene of utter devastation appeared on the screen as flaming clouds descended from the sky onto the heads of blindly fleeing Gaiwenese, reducing them to cinders. Gai Bo was squeezed amid a throng of people, all of whom were pushing with all their might toward the cabin door of an interstellar ship. Then an ocean appeared on the screen. The earliest Gaiwenese ancestors were swimming and swallowing each other. . . .

"How frightening," said Miss Qi, unable to keep from shuddering. "I hope Sunlon City isn't vaporized like Menghan City. Such an end would be too cruel."

At that moment, the image on the skyvision screen grew clear. The blue flames of the snake lamps appeared in the lower corner of the screen; the top half of the screen was filled with purple clouds.

"He has regained consciousness," whispered Yu Jin. "Let me see. . . . He's already outside Sunlon City on Five Phoenixes Mountain, beyond the eastern gate. That's strange! What's he going there for?"

The image began to sway as the Gaiwenese apparently struggled to stand up and make his way toward the summit. There in the center of the summit stood a shaft of blue light that reached into the sky. The Gaiwenese walked toward the shaft.

"Is he planning to enter the sky shaft?" said Yu Jin, scratching his head. "He doesn't know what he's doing. If he enters the shaft of light, he'll die a horrible death."

The Gaiwenese continued to approach the shaft of blue light until the light nearly filled the skyvision screen. At that moment the blue light gradually turned red, and what appeared to be flames danced all around, filling the shaft. It finally became a transparent golden color; then a blinding flash of white light fell from the sky. Then the shaft suddenly and with great speed began to recede from the ground, vanishing in the blink of an eye.

Those standing around the skyvision screen had never seen anything like that before and were left speechless. Having sharp eyes, Miss Qi noticed something remained where the shaft of light had been. It moved and lifted its head. Startled, Miss Qi shouted: "Ah 凸 (chu)! It's Ah 凸 (chu)."

5

Naturally, Ah 出 (chu), who fell from the sky to the summit of Five Phoenixes Mountain, did not hear Miss Qi scream several kilometers away. This strange guy with eyes on top of his head stood up, aching all over. He felt himself very lucky not to have hit the ground head first. Lowering his head, he looked straight ahead (he had long since lost his 口口 [lu-mu] helmet) and was nearly frightened out of his wits. For there, not more than four meters away, he saw a large, blue-skinned man covered with blood crawling toward him. Blood oozed from the side of his head, and his lifeless green eyes, though looking in his direction, seemed to take in nothing.

"Who are you?" asked Ah 出 (chu), retreating a couple of steps. "What are you doing?" he shouted. "If you don't speak up, I'll let you have it."

The man with blue skin continued toward him. Ah 出 (chu) retreated a few more steps, and after searching his pockets finally pulled out something. With a wave of his hand, he shouted at the advancing Gaiwenese: "You see this stink bomb? If you don't stop, don't blame me for the consequences."

The Gaiwenese paid no heed. Ah 出 (chu) had no choice but to take aim and throw the stink bomb at him. It exploded right in front of his nose, releasing a bluish smoke. The smoke was so vile that Ah 出 (chu) again retreated several steps. But after a whiff of the smoke, the Gaiwenese seemed to perk up and, laughing, said, "It smells so good. I haven't smelled anything that good since I arrived in Sunlon City. Let's be friends, let's be friends."

Who wants to be the friend of a stink lover like you? swore Ah 凵 (chu) to himself. He backed up again and nearly bumped into a tree. He took something else from his pocket and made ready to protect himself. The Gaiwenese pulled himself up and stood towering, then said to Ah 凵 (chu), "Justice cannot be avoided. Where are you going to run, Ah 凵 (chu)?"

Although startled, Ah 凵 (chu) managed to keep his calm and reply, "My knowledge encompasses past and present. Where can't I go? You Gaiwenese are the real fugitives from justice in this universe, detested wherever you go. Why do you want to pursue me? See this scent bomb in my hand? If you don't tell me the truth, don't blame me for the consequences."

The Gaiwenese smiled and said, "Scent is stink; stink is scent. One man's poison is another's pleasure. I alone enjoy them all alike. You have the nerve to call yourself a knowledgeable 凵 (chu) person, but you don't even know that we Gaiwenese have unusual gifts. Stink bombs or scent bombs, throw 'em all this way."

Gai Bo laughed, exposing his mouthful of spiny teeth. Sweat poured down Ah 凵 (chu)'s back.

"Stink is stink; scent is scent," he said, turning his eyes skyward. "The differences are clear. It's because you Gaiwenese cannot distinguish between stink and scent or good and evil that you are a race facing extinction. You mean to say you still don't get it?"

"All you need to do is change the names, and all opposites become one. If I call stink 'scent,' then scent becomes 'stink.' Our forebears understood this, and they united those who eat people and those who are eaten. Those who eat and those who are eaten are all the same. All opposites are made one. This is beyond lowly 凵 (chu) people's wisdom and belief. Who among you understands the lofty philosophy of the Gaiwenese?"

Overjoyed, Gai Bo began to dance with joy. Opening his huge mouth, he began to sing "The Song of the Gaiwenese":

The eater of men opens his mouth and bites
Bites, bites, bites
The cannibalized opens his mouth and screams
Screams, screams, screams
The person standing by and watching opens his mouth and laughs
Ha ha ha
Gai, Oh! Gai, Oh!
Gai, Yo! Gai, Yo!
Whether you bite, scream, or laugh

Bite! Scream! Laugh!
Don't forget to
Gai, Yo! Gai, Yo!

Singing, the blue-skinned Gaiwenese fell head over heels to the ground, completely out of breath.

"Scent is stink, stink is scent; life is death, death is life," said Ah 凸 (chu), heaving a sigh. "Since you Gaiwenese can't tell the difference between scent and stink or good and evil, then life and death must be the same. I see that you live on in death and you die as you live."

"Right!" said the Gaiwenese, opening his eyes. "I think you've got it."

Ah 凸 (chu) thought the Gaiwenese had died, and was so startled that he fell on the ground. Gai Bo actually had lost a lot of blood, and after he had been revived by the stink bomb and his gamboling around, his wound reopened. Although he was still among the living, he was unable to stand up.

"Ah 凸 (chu), the Supreme One figured that you would manage to escape from the shaft of light, so he ordered me here to wait for you," said Gai Bo, his breath as thin as gossamer. "Listen to me: the Supreme One wants you to go of your own accord to report to the South Gate of Heaven, otherwise he will . . ."

Before he could finish speaking, the Gaiwenese dropped his head and apparently breathed his last. Given his previous experience, Ah 凸 (chu) dared not say anything irresponsible or sarcastic. He got to his feet and practically flew down the mountain. He stumbled on across the copper fields and fell clumsily. Fortunately, his sense organs were located on top of his head, and he was unharmed save for a scraped neck. The copper fields were one of the spectacular sights on Five Phoenixes Mountain. Each field was several thousand square meters in size and was filled with copper bamboo shoots, copper melons, and copper beans. Tradition had it that in ancient times, Huhui knights-errant practiced their martial arts on Five Phoenixes Mountain, where they would choose a field and at its edge build a hut. They would practice their kung fu and also observe the copper bamboo shoots, melons, and beans growing. If they practiced sincerely, it was said that the field would produce a copper sword or knife that could be picked and used as a weapon. Therefore, in olden times, the mountain was also referred to as the Mountain of Rising Swords. During the time of the constitutional monarchy, the government prohibited the people from practicing martial arts, and the mountain was given its present name. Strangely, after the name change, the mountain stopped producing copper bamboo shoots, melons, and beans. At the same time, the Bronze Statue in Sunlon City began gradually to increase in size. Many people suspected that this was due to a shift in the position of the veins of copper beneath the ground. But after the Bronze Statue was vaporized, the copper fields on Five Phoenixes Mountain reverted to the way they had been. As a result, the theory of a shift in the copper veins remained unsubstantiated.

But Ah 出 (chu) had tripped over a huge copper bamboo shoot. He was panting like an ox, and took the opportunity to lie in the field and catch his breath. After a brief rest, his breathing returned to normal, but the sound of it remained as loud as before. Ah 出 (chu) thought it strange. He held his breath, but the sound of panting continued unchanged.

The sound seemed to emanate from his chest, but it also seemed to come from beneath the ground. Ah 出 (chu) stroked the smooth surface of the copper field. That shell-like integument felt warm and seemed to rise and fall as if it were breathing. The more he touched it, the stranger it seemed. Rising and falling ever so slightly, the copper field did indeed seem to be alive, and the sound of its breathing grew louder. Ah 出 (chu) could remain idle no longer—turning, he rolled and scrambled away. Just as he did so, the shell-like crust of the copper field was violently rent, and pieces of copper went flying in all directions. Stealing a glance, Ah 出 (chu) saw a long tail and then two claws emerge from the fissure to clench the copper melon vines. Once the claws had a firm hold on the vines, two more claws appeared. After the third set of claws appeared, a shiny, green, triangular head emerged, its three eyes still shut. Then, as if it were just beginning to awake from a dream, it yawned.

"A Serpent baby is born!" shouted Ah 出 (chu) excitedly, almost oblivious to the danger he was in. He had only read about how the oviparous Serpent people laid their eggs in cracks in stone and how the earth would crack open at the hatching of a Serpent baby. But this was the first time that he had actually witnessed the event. Originally, the copper fields had served as nurseries for the infant Serpent people. Ah 出 (chu) could not help but admire their cunning. He stepped closer for a better look at the Serpent baby as it climbed out of the fissure in the copper field. Its long tail coiled, its six limbs all stretched forward, it raised its head and began to cry. Once it finished crying, it opened its three eyes and looked at Ah 出 (chu). Ah 出 (chu) suddenly remembered that according to the books he had read, Serpent babies adopt the first creature they see upon emerging from the ground as their . . .

"Oh no, I'm not your mother. Don't look at me like that." Ah 凸 (chu) turned to flee, but the newly hatched Serpent baby was quicker, and with a flick of its tail, vaulted into the air. With another flick of its tail, it lassoed Ah 凸 (chu) by the fat of his neck, and clutched the panic-stricken 凸 (chu) person tightly in its six limbs. Fortunately, Ah 凸 (chu)'s mouth was located on top of his head, so he was still able to talk after the Serpent baby had a firm hold on his thick and heavy neck.

"Let me go. I'm not your mother."

"Mother . . ." hissed the Serpent baby, mastering the word immediately. "Mother!"

"凸-囗-哷-凷 凸-囗-哷-凷 (chu-lu-ru-mu, chu-lu-ru-mu)," said poor Ah 凸 (chu). "Let me go. If you ☐ (du) your mother to death, you'll end up an orphan. Let go!"

"凸-囗-哷-凷 (chu-lu-ru-mu)," repeated the baby Serpent person. "凸-囗-哷-凷 (chu-lu-ru-mu), Mother."

"You learn to talk more quickly than any adult, you little Serpent orphan," said Ah 凸 (chu), struggling. "Now listen carefully. I am not your mother. I am Ah 凸 (chu)."

"Ah 凸 (chu)," said the baby Serpent, clutching Ah 凸 (chu) by the head and neck. "Ah 凸 (chu), Ah 凸 (chu), Mother," shouted the baby Serpent gleefully.

No matter how hard he struggled, Ah 凸 (chu) could not extricate himself from the baby Serpent's grip. He was afraid that another Serpent baby might come out of the copper field and he wouldn't be able to handle the situation. He ran for the cover of a glen beyond the field. The baby Serpent clung to Ah 凸 (chu) with his six limbs the way a baby clings to its mother.

"Ah 凸 (chu), Mother, Ah 凸 (chu), Mother," it continued crying.

Although Ah 凸 (chu)'s eyes looked toward the sky, his feet never let him down. He ran for all he was worth into the glen, but unexpectedly he ran right into someone. Ah 凸 (chu) fell and hit the ground, the baby Serpent still clinging fast to him, making it impossible for him to get back on his feet. In surprise, the person he'd run into said, "Ah 凸 (chu), what are you doing here? Are you okay?"

But before Ah 凸 (chu) could reply, the baby Serpent spoke for him: "Everything is okay. Mother is okay."

"Ah 凸 (chu), when did you adopt a Serpent baby?" asked the other person, unable to keep from laughing. "We've been looking for you all over Five Phoenixes Mountain. Where have you been taking it easy, enjoying yourself?"

It was Yu Jin who spoke. He took out his snake whistle and blew it several times. In a matter of moments, Yu Fang, Yu Kui, and Miss Qi were there crowding around him. Ah 凸 (chu) had finally managed to struggle to his feet. The Serpent baby still clung to his neck. Wide-eyed and with a good deal of curiosity, it looked everyone over, its long tail standing straight up like a flagpole.

Everyone laughed because the baby Serpent and the 凸 (chu) person seemed to be a pairing made in heaven, but Ah 凸 (chu) did not find it funny.

"Poor me. No sooner am I out of the clutches of that Stranger in Black and able to avoid the pursuit and attack of a Gaiwenese than I run into a Serpent baby emerging from the copper fields. I'm really 口凸口凸 (mu-ru-lu-chu)."[1]

" 口凸口凸 (mu-ru-lu-chu)," said the Serpent baby gleefully. "Mother, 口凸口凸 (mu-ru-lu-chu)."

Everyone laughed.

"Ah 凸 (chu), since the Serpent baby is so good at parroting others, you should adopt him," said Miss Qi. "That way he could provide you with a little diversion when you get bored. What should we name it?"

"What should a Serpent that emerged from the copper fields be called?" Without thinking, Ah 凸 (chu) suggested, "Ah You, let's call him Ah You."

Everyone clapped their hands and shouted in agreement. Ah You seemed pleased and blinked his three triangular eyes; croaking, he said: "Ah You, 凸口凸口 (chu-lu-mu-ru)."

Although the Serpent people were originally oviparous and had three eyes and six limbs, the Huhui mutation was gifted with a talent for language, and able to master any language immediately. Hence the origins of the Huhui saying: "The Serpent people talk the most, the Leopard people are the most deceitful, the Feathered people are the most capable, and the 凸 (chu) people are the wisest." Having been out of the ground for only a brief time, the baby Serpent could speak Huhui. After everyone expressed their admiration, Yu Jin suddenly recalled Gai Bo, and asked Ah 凸 (chu), "Where is that Gaiwenese?"

"He's still on the summit where he passed out." Remembering the Gaiwenese's last warning, Ah 凸 (chu) trembled with fear. No one noticed save Miss Qi. Ah 凸 (chu) at once led everyone to the summit of

---

[1] 口凸口凸 is pronounced "mu-ru-lu-chu" and means "unlucky year" in Huhui, and is the opposite of 凸口凸口 .

Five Phoenixes Mountain, but there was no trace of the Gaiwenese save some blood stains.

"That's strange," said Ah 凸 (chu), surprised. "He was so weak. Where could he have gone?"

Yu Jin and Yu Fang looked at each other. With a dignified air, Yu Fang said in a low voice, "Let's go, otherwise we'll be too late."

With Yu Jin leading the way, they slid down a ravine. Halfway down, Yu Jin signaled that they should all take cover among the trees. Shortly, a group of Shan warriors carrying rifles appeared several dozen meters away. They had fanned out and were slowly making their way up the mountain. Ah 凸 (chu) nervously covered Ah You's mouth; fortunately, the little Serpent person had not made a sound. Once the Shan patrol had passed, Yu Jin quickly led everyone down the mountain under cover of the ravine. Nothing but a poplar forest lay between Five Phoenixes Mountain and Sunlon City. Yu Jin was familiar with the territory. They weaved their way through the wood until they reached a reedy place by the river. From there they followed the soft, loose riverbank for a distance until they reached an opening in the city wall. Yu Jin was the first to top the wall, followed by Yu Fang, who carried Miss Qi; Ah 凸 (chu) and Ah You; and Yu Kui bringing up the rear. Once they had got past the wall, they followed the river to the quay. The river was used by the farmers in the countryside as a waterway to transport grain and produce into the city. Furs and pelts from the grassy plains were brought into Sunlon City by horse caravan, and then were sold throughout the Hu River basin via the river. Since there had been a recent increase in guerrilla activity, the Shan occupation forces had been more thorough in checking arriving and departing boats. Yet in spite of the tight control, three small cargo barges were moored at the quay. Yu Jin signaled to the others and then boarded the first barge to his left.

The small cargo barges on the Hu River all looked like long, rectangular boxes. Water jets were located fore and aft, port and starboard. To propel a cargo barge forward, water was taken in via the forward water jets and ejected through the aft jets. To reverse course, water was taken in through the aft jets and expelled through the forward jets. Although the cargo barges were slow, they performed well and were ideally suited for traveling the narrow tributaries of the Hu River. They were also equipped with rubber tires below, making them amphibious vehicles. For a long time, the cargo barges on the Hu River had been under the control of the Green Snake Brotherhood. But the horse caravans that formed the skeleton of the ground transport system came under the purview of the Leopard Brotherhood. The two chief branches of the Hu River originated on Mount Huihui. The Western Hu River flowed through Sunlon City, around Five Phoenixes Mountain, and then southeast, where it converged with the Eastern Hu River and then flowed into Xinsu Sea. The Green Snake Brotherhood (the Democratic faction) was active throughout the Hu River Basin, from Mount Huihui in the north to the Xinsu Sea in the south and in the vast area east of Sunlon City. But the boundless grassy plains to the north, west, and south of the city were traditionally where the cavalry of the Leopard Brotherhood (the Royalist faction) operated. After the Fourth Interstellar War and the vaporizing of the Bronze Statue, the members of the Bronze Statue Cult fled to both the grassy plains and the river basin, fighting with the other factions for domination. After the Shan occupation forces became masters of Sunlon City, the three factions united to resist Shan rule. For this reason, the power and influence of the factions existed in a jigsaw pattern, making it very difficult to clearly delineate which faction controlled which area. But there was no question that the cargo barges of the Hu River still constituted a basic force of the Green Snake Brotherhood.

Once the three Yu brothers, Miss Qi, Ah 凷 (chu), and the baby Serpent Ah You had boarded the barge, the bargeman glanced at Yu Jin and opened the hold door to let everyone in.

A generator was located in the center of the hold; the rest of the space was piled with sacks of grain. They could barely find enough room to sit. But once they were seated, the generator started and water was heard pumping. Slowly the barge began to move.

"We're in the Sundragon bulu," said Yu Jin. "The head of the bulu has never been very friendly toward us. The barge will take us near Sungood bulu, where we'll jump ship and head back. If we travel in this roundabout way, the Shan will never be able to track us, regardless of how great their abilities."

"They're amazingly fast to act," said Yu Fang, stroking his beard. "We had just arrived at Five Phoenixes Mountain when their patrol showed up. That Gaiwenese had to be an informer of theirs. Strange, but how did they know that Ah 凷 (chu) would be dropped on the summit of Five Phoenixes Mountain from one of the shafts of light?"

As he spoke, Yu Fang glanced unintentionally at Ah 凷 (chu).

"Strange," croaked the Serpent baby, clinging to Ah 凷 (chu)'s neck, "but how did they know that Mother would be dropped on the summit of Five Phoenixes Mountain from one of the shafts of light?"

Ah 出 (chu) wished he could strangle Ah You. The little fellow really was an imp. With a flick of his tail, he landed on top of a pile of grain sacks.

"Last night," said Ah 出 (chu) in a clear voice as he looked at the ceiling, "I went to the Old Do-Gooder's palace to steal the antidote, but was captured by a Stranger in Black. He called himself the Supreme One of the Bronze Statue Cult and, using his ability to manipulate time and space, he took me to the South Gate of Heaven."

"The South Gate of Heaven?" asked Yu Jin, surprised. "Where is that?"

"It seems it was a secret place on Mount Huihui at the beginning of the Anliu Era. If I had some wisdom beads, I could calculate its exact temporal and spatial position."

"Why did the Stranger in Black take you there?"

"I haven't been able to figure that out, because shortly afterward, he left. Perhaps he assumed that I couldn't find my way back, but he underestimated the intelligence of the 出 (chu). I was able to find the shaft of light back without too much effort. But," said Ah 出 (chu), pausing for a moment before continuing, "the moment I returned I ran into that Gaiwenese. He told me that the Supreme One was certain I would flee via the South Gate of Heaven and wanted me to return there on my own. I have no idea how he knew that."

"It sounds like Gai Bo and the Stranger in Black are in the same faction," said Yu Jin, perplexed. "But he is also an informer for the Shan, and the differences between the Shan and the Bronze Statue Cult are irreconcilable. This Gaiwenese is very complicated. Too bad he escaped. It's a good thing I shot him; now he will never be able to elude us."

Miss Qi had remained silent as she sat listening to him, but now she had to have her say. "Ah 出 (chu), when you were captured by the Stranger in Black, did he ask you why you had entered the Old Do-Gooder's quarters?"

"No." Ah 出 (chu) thought for a moment and then began to have some doubts. "That's strange. He only said that he was not interested in helping the Old Do-Gooder. He never asked me what I was doing there. Can it be that . . ."

"Can it be that the Stranger in Black is the Old Do-Gooder?" asked Miss Qi before Ah 出 (chu) could finish speaking. Upon hearing this, the Yu brothers were greatly startled.

"Right," said Ah 出 (chu), nodding his head. "That was precisely my thought at the time, but later I dismissed the idea."

"Why?" asked Miss Qi, still trying to get to the bottom of things.

"Don't forget, though I may not be good at anything else, I do know my Huhui history inside and out," replied Ah厾(chu) after a moment, still looking up. "The Sungood bulu is always termed the most valiant of the nine bulu. Throughout history, the leaders of the Sungood bulu have been brave and good fighters—that is, until the Golden Goose Fort Uprising, when the Royalist faction turned out in full force only to be annihilated by the Democratic faction through trickery. The head of the Sungood bulu and his three sons were all killed in action at that time. Since the uprising, the Wu clan has ruled uninterrupted. The present leader, the Old Do-Gooder, is descended from a collateral branch of the Wu family. He is not known for anything besides bestowing small favors. No one has seen the face of the leader of the Bronze Statue Cult—the Stranger in Black—but he is a strapping, huge fellow. In ten short years he has managed to regroup the members of the Bronze Statue Cult and reassert their prestige. Is that something that the senile Old Do-Gooder could do?"

As Ah(chu) rambled on and on, Yu Kui grew impatient.

"Ah厾(chu), enough of this praise for the ambitions of others while disparaging ours," he complained. "What can the Stranger in Black really do? He just relies on the remaining prestige of the Bronze Statue to spread lies and deceive people! As long as superstitious men and women remain, the cult will always be able to form again. Most people still think that the members of the Bronze Statue Cult are the vanguard in the resistance against the Shan. But think about it, in all the times that resistance has sprung up, when has it ever been initiated by the cult members?"

Before Ah厾(chu) could reply, Miss Qi laughed and said, "Ah厾(chu), you've never had anything good to say about the Bronze Statue Cult. How is it that in one day you have come to admire the Stranger in Black so 厾厾吅吅 (chu-chu-ru-ru)?"[2]

Hearing Miss Qi, Ah厾(chu) blushed. It was a good thing that his face was on top of his head where no one could see it.

"What I mean is that the Stranger in Black's style is entirely different from the Old Do-Gooder's," he hurriedly tried to explain. "I cannot say with complete certainty that the Stranger in Black is not the Old Do-Gooder, nor that they are one and the same. Being historians, the 厾(chu) people value historical fact more than all else. If a historical point of view does not accord with historical fact, it is untenable; and if historical fact does not tally with a historical point of view, it cannot be denied. It still

---

[2] 厾厾吅吅 is pronounced "chu-chu ru-ru" and means "to admire deeply."

remains to be seen if the Stranger in Black is the Old Do-Gooder. This must be proved through textual research."

"Historical fact and historical point of view," said Yu Kui, swearing as he spat, "it's all a load of shit."

Hearing Yu Kui speak, Ah You, the baby Serpent crouching on the sacks of grain, croaked, "Shit fact, shit view, it's all a load of shit!"

Everyone laughed as Ah You croaked. The generator and the sound of water being pumped suddenly ceased. Yu Jin cut their laughter short and said, "Keep quiet, we're coming to shore."

They all became quiet. Silently, the little cargo barge continued forward until it bumped into something. The door to the hold was thrown open, and the bargeman stuck his head in and whispered, "We've arrived."

One by one, they exited the hold. At the end of the waterway was a small dock, and another ten paces beyond was the railing around Sungood bulu. It was late, and the blue shafts from the sky had already receded. All the residents of Sunlon City were asleep. The party hopped the railing and found themselves back in Sungood territory. They made their way through the streets, which were piled with sand. Passing the windows of houses, they occasionally saw the flame of a snake lamp still flickering inside, but most had been extinguished. The darkness was total in the vicinity of the Qi family tavern. Miss Qi opened the back door and let everyone in.

"Keep it down," she whispered. "Don't wake my dada."

"Don't worry." It was the old man's voice coming from the dark stairway. "I'm still up. Has Ah 屮 (chu) returned?"

"Dada," replied Miss Qi, somewhat surprised, "what are you doing up so late?"

"Can I go to bed before I've solved the riddle of *Five Jade Disks*?" said Mr. Qi, stepping out of the shadows. "But I think I've got the solution. Is Ah 屮 (chu) back?"

"I'm right here," said short-necked Ah 屮 (chu) respectfully as he hastened forward. "You've proved yourself a master of the wisdom beads, so the solution to the riddle will not long elude you."

"I'm getting old," Mr. Qi replied, laughing. "I'm not as sharp as I used to be. If I were a young man, I would have had the solution a long time ago. Come along upstairs, all of you, to learn the answer to the riddle."

One by one they went up the stairs to the old man's small room to examine the painting once again. There were five jade disks, three blue and two green. Each one of the three wise men in the painting had a colorless disk on his head. Everyone was still clueless. Old Man Qi laughed and nodded at the painting.

"*Five Jade Disks, Five Jade Disks*, you almost did me in. Ah 㐌 (chu), do you know the tale of the five jade disks?"

"Sir, I have read the Tai Nan histories, and know something of its origin."

"Since you knew that the antidote for the loyalty pills is contained in this painting, you must know its origin. Then," said the old man, stroking his beard, "do you know the answer?"

"I really wouldn't want to hazard a guess." Ah 㐌 (chu) had suddenly grown very modest in the presence of Mr. Qi.

"Mother doesn't want to hazard a guess," said Ah You, the baby Serpent, sitting on Ah 㐌 (chu)'s shoulders. "Mother's getting old; she's not as sharp as she used to be."

They all laughed.

"Nonsense!" said Mr. Qi. "The 㐌 (chu) are all very wise. How could he not know the answer to the riddle? Okay, this is what we'll do—Ah 㐌 (chu), you and I will each write our answer on a piece of paper, and then we'll compare them. It's rare that we get an opportunity to match wits. Don't miss your chance, Ah 㐌 (chu)."

"Sir," replied Ah 㐌 (chu) hastily, "I wouldn't dare to match wits with you. Why not just tell us the answer to the riddle?"

The old man waved his hand in disapproval. He took a notebook from the wooden headboard beneath the white globe lamp and tore out one page for Ah 㐌 (chu) and one for himself.

"There's no need to he polite, Ah 㐌 (chu). Come on, everyone turn around and let Ah 㐌 (chu) write his answer. Have you finished? Fold it up. Okay, it's my turn. Everyone can turn around now. That's it."

Everyone turned around. Ah 㐌 (chu) and Mr. Qi each held a piece of paper in their hands. Then the old man spoke.

"Ah 㐌 (chu), you show yours first."

"No," replied Ah 㐌 (chu) hastily, "you go first."

"No, you go first."

"No, Sir, you first."

As they continued in this fashion, Ah You spoke loudly.

"Mother go first, Mother go first. No need to be polite, Mother. Mother go first."

There was no help for it. Ah 㐌 (chu) unfolded the piece of paper. Everyone pressed in for a closer look. On the sheet of white paper was written "blue." As soon as the old man saw the answer, he laughed and said, "Ah 凸 (chu), can all three of them really be blue?"

Eyes turned upward, Ah 凸 (chu) replied, "That's right. It's the only logical answer. Your answer is the same, right?"

The old man laughed without replying as he unfolded the piece of paper. Everyone looked, but the paper was blank.

"A blank book from heaven," said Yu Kui, jumping. "What does it mean?"

The old man again waved his hand in disapproval and replied, "Don't be so anxious. I have my reasons. Wonderful! Our answers are different! I'm afraid I'll have to ask you to explain why you said all three of the disks are blue."

"You're deliberately pulling my leg," said Ah 凸 (chu), turning his head uncomfortably. "Three blue disks is the only logical answer. How can there be any other? I don't get it. I really don't get it."

"Has there ever been a time when a 凸 (chu) didn't get it?" Mr. Qi was beside himself with joy. Then he turned to his daughter. "You see, my child, your dada has beaten Ah 凸 (chu)."

"Slow down," said Ah 凸 (chu). "I have always respected you, Sir. But just because I don't have the same answer as you doesn't mean I'm wrong. In fact, I am right. It doesn't matter what your answer is, if it's different from mine, it's wrong." As Ah 凸 (chu) spoke, looking at the ceiling, he too began to feel quite satisfied with himself. "Sir, there is a reason for the saying that the 凸 (chu) people are wise. I am a 凸 (chu), and I'm smarter than the average Huhui. Sir, please excuse my lack of manners for saying so, but you are wrong."

"Hold your horses. You still haven't told me why you say that the three disks are blue."

"That's simple. We all know that there are five disks, and three of them are blue and two of them green. If two of the people have green disks on their heads, the third person will immediately know that the one on his head is blue. As the story says, the three of them looked at one another for a long time, and no one said anything. Clearly there couldn't be two green ones and one blue one. But could there be two blue ones and one green one? If there were two blue ones and one green one, then the ones with blue disks on their heads would see one green one and one blue one, but they wouldn't know the color of the one on their own head. They might assume that the one on their own head was green and wait for someone else to speak first. But after they all waited, still no one said anything.

Then it would be obvious that the one on their own head wasn't green, and that two were blue and one was green. Since the three of them were extremely smart, they would know that there were two blue disks and one green one. It wouldn't take long before one of those with a blue disk on his head would say something. But the story says that the three of them looked at one another for a long time. It's clear that it wasn't a matter of one green and two blue disks. Therefore, the only possible answer is that there were three blue disks. Each of them would see two blue disks, but no one would dare say that the disk on their own head was blue. Eventually, someone would figure it out and be the winner."

Ah 㞼 (chu) took a breath only after he finished speaking, leaving Yu Fang and Yu Kui confused. Miss Qi smiled sweetly at Yu Jin. Only Ah You clapped his hands and shouted in approval of his mother. Ah 㞼 (chu), very proud of himself, lowered his head and 鹿母 (lu-mu).

"Ah (chu), your analysis is impeccable," said Mr. Qi, giving a slight nod. "No wonder people say that the 㞼 (chu) are wise."

"Then," said Ah 㞼 (chu), overjoyed, "you concede defeat?"

"No, that's not what I meant."

"If my analysis is impeccable, how is it that you won't admit your error?"

"Ah 㞼 (chu)," replied Mr. Qi, "your analysis was perfect, but you forgot one thing."

"What did I forget?"

"You forgot human weakness. Sometimes, simply by not losing, one wins."

"Sir, the more you speak, the more confused I get," said Ah 㞼 (chu), at a loss. "The riddle of the five jade disks is a question of inference. What does it have to do with human weakness?"

"Well, to put it a little more clearly: sometimes someone else's suffering will make you happier than your own success."

Ah 㞼 (chu) scratched his head, pondering what the old man said. Then it seemed to dawn on him and he broke out in a sweat.

"Do you mean to say . . ." he mumbled.

"Right, now do you understand?"

Their exchange left everyone else in the dark. Yu Kui was the first to lose his patience. "Mr. Qi, what are you and Ah 㞼 (chu) talking about?"

"Mr. Qi," said Yu Fang, "there's not much time, and rescuing the Death Commandos is becoming more urgent. Since you know the answer to the riddle, please tell us. We are not as smart as you or Ah 㞼 (chu). We don't understand the mysteries of the universe."

Mr. Qi was ecstatic and, rubbing his wisdom beads, said, "Okay, I should give you the answer. The color of the disks on the heads of the people in the painting are not necessarily pure, but might be mixed . . ."

At that moment, there was a flash of white light outside the window. Yu Jin's reaction was the swiftest. He immediately extinguished the lamp and drew his sword. He was on the point of opening the door when it opened of its own accord. In shone a bright light, blinding everyone.

"Freeze! Drop your weapons!" someone shouted.

Yu Jin detected the thick accent of a Shan. He swore as he unwillingly dropped his sword. Yu Fang and Yu Kui did likewise. The Shan soldiers outside turned off the searchlight, and gradually Miss Qi was able to see again. The face of the officer in charge looked very familiar. He smiled a big toothy smile at her. Then she remembered where she had seen him before. Their underground headquarters had been taken by the Shan, she thought despondently. She glanced at Yu Jin, who was slowly reaching behind his back.

The idea that he was going to die by his own hand flashed through her mind, but she was too late to stop him.

6

In the final years of the Thousand-Year War, the residents of Sunlon City established a republican government, which was later called the First Republic. The old and new Royalist factions formed a military alliance and besieged the city. Although the Republican army that was defending the city at the time lacked food and ammunition, morale was high. The Royalist faction possessed absolute military superiority and had the support of the Leopard forces, but it was three years before they were able to take the city. The day Sunlon City fell, the senior statesmen of the Republican government gathered together in the Senate, where they immolated themselves, dying as martyrs. The soldiers defending the city fought to the last man—not one surrendered. Luckily, some were able to escape and disappeared among the people; they kept in contact with one another and eventually formed the Green Snake Brotherhood, which became the basic military force of the Democratic faction. It was during this time that Huhui guerrilla warfare started. The Green Snake Brotherhood vowed to restore the Republic and, in fact, the Democratic revolution did succeed and the Second Republic was established. The Royalist faction was scattered over the plains, where they formed the Leopard Brotherhood. In later years, all wars of restoration were related to the activities of this group. During the period of the constitutional monarchy, they were proud of safeguarding the autocratic monarchy, and often found themselves at odds with the Green Snake Brotherhood.

Swordsmen and warriors were all known as "knights" by the Huhui, and they all adhered strictly to the ⊡ □ (du-wu) spirit.[1] To be a ⊡ □ (du-wu) soul according to the ⊡ □ (du-wu) spirit was the Huhui knight's basic principle of self-discipline. But the ⊡ □ (du-wu) spirit was also the highest philosophical plane sought by the Huhui sages. Those who were not Huhui people had a difficult time understanding the true essence of the ⊡ □ (du-wu) spirit. Moreover, various philosophical schools had their own explanations of it. Perhaps the best explanation, and the one most to the point, was the four-line hymn by the immortal ⬚⬚ (man-qia) Sage who practiced the Way on Mount Huihui:

> *Mind is called* ⊡ *(du)*
> *Nonmind is called* □ *(wu)*
> *Transform* ⊡ *(du) into* □ *(wu)*
> *Subdue* □ *(wu) with* ⊡ *(du).*

Later generations explained the immortal ⬚⬚ (man-qia) Sage's hymn in different ways. Some sages emphasized the transformation of ⊡ (du) into □ (wu). They advocated that beginning from the mind, each person, using his or her own powers of cultivation, can arrive at a state of nonmind. This was the Mind Sect. There were other sages who stressed subduing □ (wu) with ⊡ (du). They advocated that a person maintain a natural mind to subdue a cunning heart. This was the Nonmind Sect. The conflict between the two sects represents a significant episode in the history of Huhui philosophy. Yet another school of sages believed that both the transformation of ⊡ (du) into □ (wu)[2] and subduing □ (wu) with ⊡ (du) were biased and that changing □ (wu) into ■ (woo) was more appropriate. This was the Empty Mind Sect, also known as the □ ■ (wu-woo) Sect. Owing to the excessive passivity of its adherents, it was attacked by the other two sects, which found its views heretical, being, they believed, a violation of the ⊡ □ (du-wu) spirit. The sages of the Empty Mind Sect were all vaporized.

---

[1] ⊡ □ is pronounced "du-wu." ⊡ means "shackled" or "fettered"; □ means "liberated," and generally alludes to a physically or spiritually transcendental state. See Heerwen's *A History of Huhui Philosophy*, published by Cambridge University Press.

[2] □ is pronounced "wu" and means "empty." In the language of mathematics, □ is an empty set, whereas ■ is unbracketed, absolute emptiness. Husserel's "bracketing of the world" is a close approximation of the Empty Mind Sect doctrine, and that is why the sect took Husserel as one of its earliest sages.

Naturally, the average Huhui knight could not understand the deeper philosophical implications of the ▣ ☐ (du-wu) spirit. Rather, what the warriors emphasized was the actual practice of the ▣ ☐ (du-wu) spirit. An example is the Sungood bulu Death Commandos who ingested the loyalty pills after seeing the command flag as they prepared to sacrifice themselves for the great uprising. This was the direct result of the influence of the ▣ ☐ (du-wu) spirit. The suicidal mentality of the Green Snake Brotherhood was the final solution of the ▣ ☐ (du-wu) spirit.

The buttons on the green robes of the Green Snake Brotherhood warriors were, in fact, small bombs, which could be pulled off and used as hand grenades. Some extremely skilled warriors could use their inner force to hurl the buttons and kill their enemies. And the golden threads used to sew on the buttons were also fuses, connected to the green snake embroidered on each warrior's back. All one had to do was tug on the snake's tongue, and all the buttons would explode at once. The warriors who wore these robes were in effect living bombs. This was a kind of military suicide. Military suicide was the final option, fully in accord with the ▣ ☐ (du-wu) spirit, used only as a last resort. The most famous story of military suicide in Huhui history was that of Wen Chongwu, the number one ranking warrior of the Sunart people. It was during the Seventh War of Restoration, and he found himself surrounded by 108 famed Sundragon swordsmen. Though severely wounded, he was able to annihilate all 108 of the enemy through his own death. Later generations revered him as the god of military suicide.

If you recall, the Yu brothers, Miss Qi and her father, Ah凸(chu), and the baby Serpent person Ah You were all on the second floor of the Qi family tavern considering the riddle of the five jade disks. Mr. Qi was on the point of revealing the solution to the riddle when the Shan patrol arrived, rounding them all up. Yu Jin was enraged, and was on the point of committing military suicide to annihilate the enemy. Although Miss Qi with her sharp eyes realized his intent, she was not quick enough to stop him. Yu Jin reached behind him, touched the tongue of the snake embroidered on his back, and was about to give it a pull when he felt a sudden heat on his robe. The tall Shan officer had a transmitter in his hand.

"Thinking to commit military suicide?" he said, smiling at Yu Jin. "Go right ahead. I respect nothing more than the ▣ ☐ (du-wu) soul."

Despite his impossible situation, Yu Jin still pulled the fuse, but nothing happened.

"I have burned all the fuses in half with this transmitter," said the Shan officer, laughing. "The small bombs on your robe are all useless. What other tricks do you have? Please give them a try."

Yu Jin was furious at being ridiculed by the Shan officer.

"Don't let temporarily getting the upper hand go to your head," said Yu Jin, remaining outwardly calm. "There will come a day when you Shan bastards will fall into our hands, and then you'll get yours."

"I have already had a taste of your ⊡ (du) cage. I would like to invite you to sample the grand banquet we have prepared for all of you."

He signaled to his subordinates with a glance. The entire group was escorted downstairs. Outside, two patrol cars were waiting, and their searchlights made the area around the Qi family tavern as bright as day. Towering between the two cars was a tall, blue-skinned man, his head bandaged. His huge mouth opened a crack as he looked at them.

"It's Gai Bo," exclaimed Miss Qi.

"That's right," replied Gai Bo. "That's me, my friends. I am indebted to you for not forsaking me. After you implanted that skyvision transmitter in my head, I spent half the day as a broadcasting station and nearly died from loss of blood. Fortunately, I was not meant to die and was saved by Captain Mai's men. I was indeed lucky, or as you say in Huhui, I was ⏊⊣▯⊤▯⊢ (chu-lu-ru-mu). In spite of my better judgment, I should return this skyvision transmitter to you."

Gai Bo took out a pistol and aimed it at Yu Jin's head, but Yu Jin didn't even flinch. Gai Bo laughed coldly, turned, and aimed at Miss Qi. Yu Jin began to shout and Miss Qi closed her eyes, waiting to die. Suddenly, someone rushed forward and knocked the gun out of Gai Bo's hand.

"Quit horsing around. Who told you to threaten the prisoners with a pistol?"

Miss Qi opened her eyes and saw that the person who had saved her was none other than the tall Shan officer.

"Captain Mai," said Gai Bo, all smiles, "I was just fooling around with them, having a bit of fun. We're all friends here."

"We don't joke around in the military. It is not permitted to threaten a prisoner with a pistol, especially a defenseless prisoner." Without expression, he continued, "You Gaiwenese are primitive cannibals, and the Huhui are a backward people; otherwise you wouldn't behave in such an uncivilized way toward a defenseless enemy. But we Shan are different. We could never be so uncivilized. Bear in mind, Gai Bo, that though you are a spy, you must respect our laws and control your barbarous nature."

Assenting several times, Gai Bo bent down to retrieve his pistol, then departed. Smiling, Captain Mai turned to Miss Qi.

"Sorry about that. These Gaiwenese are savages. On behalf of the Shan occupation forces, I offer you our apologies ㄔㄖㄔㄖ (chu-ru-chu-ru)."[3]

"On behalf of the uncivilized Huhui, I offer our thanks to the civilized Shan occupation forces," said Miss Qi in a sarcastic tone of voice. "You Shan are so advanced, using the most civilized means to vaporize us. Are not the targets of your interstellar warship also defenseless enemies? Why do you consider yourselves civilized, and everyone else barbaric?"

Captain Mai was left speechless, momentarily stunned.

"What a ㄖㄔ (ru-chu) nasty, cunning young lady," he replied angrily. "You don't even know who your friends are. I save your life and you laugh at me and call me a savage. Take them away!"

Once they were all locked inside the patrol car, they set off. They all swayed in the dark with the movement of the car. Fortunately, Ah You's eyes gave off a greenish light in the dark. Taking advantage of that light, old Mr. Qi stood up and thrust a wisdom bead into the palm of each one of them.

"Here's a wisdom bead for each of you. Hang on to it. Pay attention now. When we get out of the car and I yell 'now,' throw your beads and run for all you're worth. Anyone who escapes must make their way back to the tavern and prepare the antidote for the Death Commandos."

"The antidote?" asked Yu Fang. "What is the antidote?"

"It's quite simple. Scrape both the blue and green pigments off the painting and mix them together. Then go to any pharmacy and tell them to make up an identical prescription, and you'll have the antidote."

"You get the antidote by mixing the colors together?" asked Yu Jin. "That's all there is to it? What, then, is the answer to the riddle?"

"I don't have time to explain," replied old Mr. Qi impatiently. "Ah ㄔ (chu), do you agree with me?"

"Mr. Qi is so brilliant, while all I can do is lament my own shortcomings," said Ah ㄔ (chu) reverently. "If your understanding of human nature is correct, then your explanation is also correct."

"Well put, well put," replied Mr. Qi, laughing loudly. "I can't compare with you when it comes to analytical reasoning, but when it comes to an understanding of human nature, you can't compare with me by a long

---

[3] ㄔㄖㄔㄖ is pronounced "chu-ru chu-ru" and means "a breach of etiquette."

shot. But if we disregard the human factor in the riddle of the *Five Jade Disks* painting, then it's not worth talking about."

He stopped laughing and turned to his companions. "Press the wisdom beads into the palms of your hands and rub them there."

Everyone did as instructed. The wisdom beads gradually grew warm and seemed to quiver.

"Keep rubbing them and make sure you keep them moving," continued Mr. Qi. "Concentrate and exercise your ▣ □ (du-wu) spirit and let the beads clearly understand your intentions."

Although they didn't fully understand what the old man was talking about, none of them disobeyed. They all concentrated as they rubbed the beads. The patrol car finally came to a halt, and the Shan soldiers opened the doors. Yu Jin could see that they were near the Golden Palace and knew that they were at the headquarters of the Shan occupation force located in the city center. At that moment Mr. Qi shouted: "Now!" Yu Jin quickly threw his bead out the door and was followed by the others.

The beads exploded before they hit the ground. Almost immediately, the three Yu brothers, Mr. Qi and his daughter, and Ah 凸 (chu) were standing outside the patrol car. Each of them ran off in a different direction. The Shan soldiers let out a cry and some of them pulled out their guns, firing at the smoking decoys of the exploding wisdom beads.

"Now it's our turn, gentlemen," shouted Mr. Qi. "凸-刂⊓⼞- (chu-lu-ru-mu)!"

After she had gone some distance, it dawned on Miss Qi that she was running the wrong way. She had run toward the restricted area where the Shan warship was moored. By the time she was aware of her mistake, it was too late: several Shan soldiers, their guns raised, surrounded her. She had no choice but to give up without a fight.

After a while, the shooting on the square died away. The smoke screen raised by the wisdom beads also gradually dissipated and finally disappeared. Miss Qi looked around her. Her father, unable to run, had remained standing where he was, laughing beside the patrol car. Yu Kui was captured and escorted back by two Shan soldiers. Ah 凸 (chu) had tripped and fallen and Ah You was by his side, anxiously trying to help him up. But Yu Fang and Yu Jin had disappeared. Miss Qi was pleased. Since the two of them had escaped, the Death Commandos would be saved. After a spell of confusion, Captain Mai was able to bring his men to order. He knew he had been fooled.

"Lock them inside the warship, all of them!" he barked furiously after some of them had been recaptured. "Let's see how far they can get. Lock them all up."

Miss Qi and her father, Yu Kui, Ah 凸 (chu), and Ah You were surrounded by Captain Mai, Gai Bo, and several Shan soldiers and escorted into the restricted area around the warship. It was the first time that Miss Qi had had the chance to examine the huge ship at such close quarters. Its bluish gray hull seemed to stretch off in all directions and countless gun turrets protruded from the hull at every angle. A small circle of lamps illuminated the strange steel hulk. As Miss Qi looked up, she couldn't help but admire the impressive technological achievements of the Shan engineers. She also recalled her dada once telling her that the Bronze Statue of Sunlon City was even larger than the Shan warship. She found it mindboggling trying to imagine how magnificent the incomparable statue must have been. No wonder the believers were so fanatical in their worship of it. Wouldn't even the wisest person not tremble with fear upon seeing its huge form with their own eyes?

The Shan soldiers escorted them into a freight elevator directly beneath the center of the warship. They slowly began their ascent into the heart of the ship. From the elevator, the inside looked like a steel honeycomb and the crew members like minute ants moving over the hive. Miss Qi was stunned.

"Miss, please observe the greatness of Shan civilization," said Captain Mai with an air of pride. "No planet could produce such a ship save the Golden Planet, the center of interstellar culture."

"Oh, really?" said Miss Qi, not to be outdone. "During the Fourth Interstellar War, the Expeditionary Fleet of the Huhui Empire had many ships like this."

"If you'd had ships like this, you wouldn't have been conquered by us," said Captain Mai with a wave of his hand. "All the warriors of the Huhui world put together could not stand up to the firepower of this warship. Yet you're still trying to rebel. And how? With just your ▣ ☐ (du-wu) spirit?"

Ridiculed this way by Captain Mai, Miss Qi was just about to reply when Ah 凸 (chu) bowed deeply to the Shan officer.

"Captain Mai, what you say is not entirely true. Everyone knows that the G Supergalaxy has repeatedly experienced civil unrest. Although you Shan people have the ability to build armored warships with quick cannons and conquer other worlds, you lack the ability to rule them. I think the ancient Huhui Sage 凸·☐ said it best: 'If the sight (du-wu) of something makes you want to fight (du-wu), this is not singular awareness (du-wu) but a poison (du-wu).' The ⊡ □ (du-wu) spirit of the Huhui is the spirit of wisdom. ⊡ (du) is feeling; □ (wu) is reason. It is through singular awareness that we attain ⊡ □ (du-wu). But because you see something you don't like you foolishly want to fight, eventually becoming a poison and hated by one and all. One is wisdom (du-wu) and one is poison (du-wu). The difference between good and bad is readily apparent. In the end ⊡ □ (du-wu) will conquer poison!"

Captain Mai couldn't keep from laughing. "What you say is gibberish and all sounds the same.[4] What is it you are getting at?"

Ah 凸 (chu) shook his head and with his eyes turned upward replied, "You are unwise and fight; we possess singular awareness (du-wu) of ⊡ □ (du-wu). That is the basic difference between the Shan and Huhui cultures. Poison (du-wu) will never conquer singular awareness (du-wu)."

"But," protested Captain Mai, "poison (du-wu) and singular awareness (du-wu) sound the same. How do you know if it's poison that won't conquer singular awareness or if it's singular awareness that won't conquer poison? Or are you saying that singular awareness won't triumph over singular awareness?"

"You've got a point," said Ah 凸 (chu) by way of praise. "Captain Mai, you are beginning to understand a little of the Huhui ⊡ □ (du-wu) spirit. Naturally, poison can't conquer poison; nor can singular awareness conquer singular awareness. Both are logically impossible. That leaves only two possibilities. Can poison conquer singular awareness? Of course not. Why? Although the two sound similar, singular awareness is superior to poison. The reason is clear. Thus the only possibility is that singular awareness must conquer poison!"

"I still don't get it," said Captain Mai.

"I don't either," said Gai Bo, opening his huge mouth. "Gaiwenese philosophy holds that all opposites can achieve synthesis. Scent is stink, and stink is scent. Life is death, and death is life. Thus, singular awareness

---

[4] Captain Mai's comment is justified. As the reader can see, untranslatable puns on the words "du-wu" abound. The Huhui language is the same as ancient Chinese. Thus the sound of individual characters can lead to confusion. Zhao Yuanren's tongue twister 施氏食獅史 (all characters are pronounced "shi," and the sentence means "a history of the lion-eating Mr. Shi") is one example. Another example, involving binomial compounds, is Yi Cigong's tongue-twister, composed of a series of compounds all pronounced "jinshi"; it means roughly, "modern scholars are completely nearsighted."

is poison, and poison is singular awareness. The Huhui must be friends with the Shan. Everyone be friends."

"What a shallow philosophy," said Ah 出 (chu) disdainfully. "No wonder you Gaiwenese are the wanderers of the universe. According to Huhui philosophy, all that is united can be broken down into opposites. There is no way for singular awareness to be poison, but what's more, singular awareness is of necessity superior to poison. This is the ⊡ □ (du-wu) spirit."

"Forget it," said Captain Mai, yawning. "What's all this ⊡ □ (du-wu) poison? We Shan people have only one philosophy: 'Power comes from the barrel of a gun.' We can conquer you, therefore we are civilized and you are barbarians."

At that moment, their ascent at an end, the freight elevator came to a halt at the top deck. Captain Mai escorted them down two corridors to the ship's brig. He locked Mr. Qi, Ah 出 (chu), Ah You, and Yu Kui in one cell, and Miss Qi in another. Having been placed in solitary confinement, Miss Qi couldn't help but feel alarmed, wondering what Captain Mai's intentions might be. The big, tall Shan officer with his ruddy complexion seemed to have a favorable impression of Miss Qi. Hadn't he prevented Gai Bo from threatening her with a gun? Although she had made fun of him several times, he was never really angered. Thinking of his bright, piercing eyes, she had no peace of mind. She wished Yu Jin were there, but she was glad he had managed to escape. He certainly must have returned to the tavern and perhaps had mixed the antidote and, taking advantage of the dark, had administered it to the Death Commandos. They had been successful—that is, as long as her dada was right. She still couldn't figure out how he had arrived at his solution to the riddle, but that was unimportant. She had faith in her dada.

As she sat thinking, Miss Qi drifted off to sleep. Perhaps she had just dozed off for a moment, but when she opened her eyes, she discovered that someone was standing in front of her. Startled, she jumped off the bed.

"It's all right," said the person at once, "it's all right."

When Miss Qi saw who it was, she covered her chest with one hand.

"Captain Mai, What are you doing here?

"N-n-nothing," said Captain Mai, suddenly stuttering. It was only then that she noticed he had changed clothes. He was now wearing the blue uniform of the Shan Imperial Fleet.

"Did . . . you sleep well?"

"All right," she said, brushing her hair back with her other hand. "How long was I asleep?"

"Seven hours. It's already daylight," he said, smiling. "Unfortunately, the purple sun of your Huhui planet cannot be seen from here."

"Seven hours!" And she thought she had only dozed off. Suddenly she was vexed with herself. "Captain Mai, what is it you are really after?"

"Nothing. I just wanted to ask you some . . . questions," he said, somewhat embarrassed. "You know that we must ask questions of all Huhui people we invite here. It's just routine, nothing important."

"Ask whatever you like—after all, I am your prisoner," she replied ingenuously. "Why are you here to interrogate me? You are a captain in the Shan occupation force, a pretty high rank. Aren't you wasting your time by questioning a Huhui prisoner?"

"You have a sharp tongue, Miss Qi," he said, so embarrassed that his ears turned red. "Are you hungry? Would you like me to have someone bring you some breakfast?"

Her initial reaction was to say no, but after thinking about it, she changed her mind, perhaps because she felt sorry for him. "Okay."

He seemed to relax a bit, and left her cell immediately. He returned momentarily, followed by a Shan soldier carrying a tray of food for her. Breakfast consisted of fried fish fritters. He watched as she wolfed them down.

"Miss Qi, what do you say if we talk while you eat?" he said, perfectly calm and collected.

"As you wish, Captain Mai."

"How long has your father—your dada—run that tavern?"

"I don't know. I remember it from when I was a child. We live above the tavern."

"And Ah 凸 (chu) and Ah Wen? Did they work in the tavern at that time?"

"Ah 凸 (chu) is my kindermann. He has looked after me since I was small. Ah Wen has also been with us for a long time. But when I was little, she hadn't yet married. It was only later that she 凹 (qia) Ah Two, and later Ah Three and Four. It was only after they arrived that business improved at Dada's tavern."

"Why does Ah Wen sometimes call you 'fourth child'?"

"Don't you know Huhui? Then how could you not understand?"

"Of course I understand, but it means that you are the fourth child. Then you have three older brothers or sisters?"

"Right."

"Where are they?"

"The same as my mother. They were all killed by you."

"I'm sorry." After a moment of silence, he continued softly. "I have to ask. War is hell, I hate it."

"That's all right. You did say that you conquered us, which makes you civilized and us barbarians."

"Did I say that?" His ears turned red once again. "I'm very sorry. Sometimes I don't think before I speak. That's how I was trained in the military academy. Over and over again; you hear it so much that if you're not careful, you'll find yourself talking the same way. Actually, I don't believe all that crap."

"That's okay. Are you training the next generation in the same way?"

"It's only like that in the military academies." He paused for a moment before continuing. "I'm an orphan. My mother and father both died in a terrible war you've never heard of. Anyway, there will always be war in this galaxy of ours, and orphans. Fortunately, orphans like me always supply new blood for the military academies. They always send people like me to defend the farthest outposts. They know that if we never return, at least no one will miss us."

A slight note of anger could be detected in Captain Mai's voice. Miss Qi knew a little about the strict class system of the Shan. She wanted to ask him what class he belonged to, but thought better of it.

"Occupation soldiers—like myself—are divided into two groups," he continued. "Regular troops are sent home once a newly occupied planet is pacified; but the other type are stationed there and are doomed to remain behind forever. I am of the latter type. When I was assigned to the Huhui planet nine years ago, I knew I was fated to defend the Shan empire and die in battle far from home. They didn't treat me unkindly. Before I left they cast a bronze grave marker for me that reads: 'Here lies Captain Natang Mai / He gave his blood and life / Defending the honor of the empire.' No place or date was included, because they have no meaning in the vast time and space of an interstellar empire. What matters is that they have already decided that I should give my life for the empire. As to where and when I die, they will leave that up to fortune."

Captain Mai paused before continuing. "Every night now for nine years, I have led patrols into Sunlon City to capture Huhui revolutionaries. I don't know how many I have captured, but I quickly realized that the numbers weren't important. What really mattered was how to stay alive. At first, when I would hit the sack each night, I would think about that bronze tablet. I told myself that it was all a lie. I was determined to show it for what it was and never submit to them. I was going to survive and perhaps become one of the first generation of Shan colonists on the Huhui planet.

"Each night when I lead a patrol into Sunlon City, I try to apprehend the revolutionaries as quickly as possible. The work has meaning, because only by eliminating the revolutionaries will the Shan colonists be able to survive in the city. Perhaps this is what they hope I will do. Perhaps it's only a small part of a comprehensive policy of colonization. But I don't care. What matters to me is proving that bronze tablet false."

Although Miss Qi knew that she was looking at a Shan officer who had executed countless numbers of her compatriots, she couldn't bring herself to hate him. He seemed to be telling someone else's story.

"I've learned to speak Huhui. Since I'm determined to be a first-generation Shan colonist here, I've had no choice. One night I went on patrol in the Sundragon bulu in civilian dress, and no one recognized me as a Shan. Perhaps I had made progress in learning Huhui. I sat under a tree in the center of town. A small boy attracted my attention. He was pestering his mother to buy him an action figure—a Shan soldier. I wondered why he would choose such a toy. He sat down on the ground beside me, and taking out a small knife, proceeded to slowly and carefully cut it to pieces.

"It was only at that moment that I really understood the hatred among peoples. From that night on, I never again believed that the words on the bronze tablet were false. I knew I'd die here, giving my blood and my life, defending the honor of the empire."

At that point, Captain Mai stood up.

"Sorry I've talked so much. We'll never conquer you, but the struggle will go on because I have no choice."

"Nor do we," replied Miss Qi. "We have never been ruled by another people for very long. You won't succeed."

"Sometimes," said Captain Mai shrugging his shoulders, "I think that it might not be so bad to die in Sunlon City. You may not believe me, but I really like this place. I'm really taken with your language and culture."

"Wonderful!" said Miss Qi. "You're a colonist who has a way with words. All colonists say that they are taken with the culture of the colonized and that they love the land they colonize. But no matter how nicely they put it, they all have one goal: to rule forever and exterminate the culture and the will of the colonized to rebel."

Captain Mai was on the point of replying when someone outside the cell laughed.

"Wrong! No matter how nicely colonialism sounds, the goal is to make friends with the colonized. You make friends with me; I make friends with you. We're all friends; everyone is friends."

"Gai Bo," said Captain Mai, frowning, "I'm interrogating Miss Qi. Why are you eavesdropping?"

"I'm not up to anything," replied the blue-skinned fellow hastily. "I wouldn't dare. The commander has ordered that all prisoners be brought to the bridge so that the he can interrogate them himself."

Captain Mai seem startled. Miss Qi noticed a look of surprise and bewilderment cross his face, and realized that the situation was unusual. Miss Qi's curiosity was piqued. After all, although the Shan were the mortal enemies of the Huhui, the Huhui still had a great deal of respect for the little commander of the occupation forces. If it hadn't been for his flexible political stratagems and ingenious military strategy, the Shan would have been annihilated by the Huhui long ago. Without him, they wouldn't have ruled as long as they had, even with their warship.

Most Huhui had never seen the Shan commander. Those who did manage to see him went in 凸 (chu) but came out 凸 (ru).[5] Did it mean they were going to be executed now that the commander himself wished to interrogate them?

Miss Qi looked for an answer in Captain Mai's face. Sure enough, he did look uneasy. But to obey is a soldier's sole duty. He ordered his subordinates to bring Miss Qi and the others. They were all escorted back to the freight elevator, but they were not put into it. Instead he opened a steel door beside the elevator. It led to a stairway up to the bridge. They all climbed the steps to the highest level, where the bridge was located. As they peered upward, a look of surprise passed over their faces.

The bridge was actually a glass structure shaped like a mushroom. The huge purple sun, as it shone through the bridge, looked larger than ever. Ah 凸 lowered his head to avoid the bright light. As Miss Qi gazed out through the glass, she noticed that the hull on top of the ship appeared to be paved with black flagstones.[6] She couldn't figure out the reason for the stones. Then she turned to look around the interior of the bridge. She saw a group of Shan officers in neat blue uniforms clustered around a short

---

[5] 凸, pronounced "chu"; 凸, pronounced "ru." The phrase means "to enter alive and leave dead."

[6] The black flagstones Miss Qi observes are produced on Blackstone planet and are the most effective for absorbing light. The power and firepower of the interstellar warship are derived from the light absorbed by these stones. See "Shangrila" in the *Stardust Suite no. 2*.

figure with glasses. He was not in uniform, but rather dressed in a black ceremonial robe that seemed much too large for him. He was bald and had a big nose. Miss Qi couldn't believe that that little guy was the commander of the Shan occupation force, but Captain Mai, who was standing beside her, clicked his heels and saluted him sharply.

"I report that all prisoners are present."

The bald man pulled a handkerchief from his pocket and blew his nose loudly; he replaced his handkerchief, his nose twitching. Only then did he speak in a loud voice.

"The morning is like a window, the day like a wall, the night like a mirror. A window is a mirror, a mirror is a window."

When the bald man finished speaking, Mr. Qi, Ah 凸 (chu), and Gai Bo nodded. Ah 凸 (chu) bowed to the little man and in a sharp voice recited:

> *Mind is called* ▣ *(du),*
> *Nonmind is called* □ *(wu),*
> *Transform* ▣ *(du) into* □ *(wu),*
> *Subdue* □ *(wu) with* ▣ *(du),*
> ▣ □ *(du-wu) singular awareness!*

When Ah 凸 (chu) had finished speaking, Ah You wagged his tail and croaked.

"▣ □ (du-wu) singular awareness, unpleasant sight makes one want to fight, poison, poison, singular awareness, wisdom, ▣ □ ▣ □ (du-wu, du-wu)!"

When Ah You had finished croaking, Gai Bo suddenly stepped forward and in praise said, "Life is death, and death is life; scent is stink, and stink is scent. Let's be friends, let's be friends!"

As the three of them carried on unconcernedly, Yu Kui was fuming. "What's this?" he roared. "Unfortunately, I've been arrested, otherwise I'd kill you and cut you all to pieces. I wouldn't leave so much as an eyebrow intact. Such politeness, I can't stand it. Take me out and finish me off."

"What a boor," said the bald commander, blowing his nose. "He doesn't even know a poem for setting the stage for himself. You're a disgrace to the Huhui. Brother Wu, please explain things to him."

As the Shan commander finished speaking, the officers in blue made way for three people standing behind them. When they saw the old man who seemed to be the leader, they were dumbfounded. Yu Kui was the first to lose his calm and shout: "Old Do-Gooder, you traitor!"

7

The old man was none other than the Old Do-Gooder, the spiritual leader of the 170,000 people of the Sungood bulu, one of the nine bulu of Sunlon City, capital of the Huhui planet. Behind him stood the ■ (woo) Bearer of the Gilded Mace and the □ (wu) Bearer of the Gilded Mace,[1] two huge Sungood bodyguards. Seeing the old man smile as he stepped forward so angered Yu Kui that his face went black with rage and he daringly leaped forward and grabbed the old man's neck in his viselike grip.

"Traitor! So you were behind the plot to induce the Death Commandos to take the loyalty pills. You'll die with me!"

Of course the two bodyguards to either side of the Old Do-Gooder could not let Yu Kui have his way. They each grabbed an arm and lifted

---

[1] Both the ■ Bearer of the Gilded Mace and the □ Bearer of the Gilded Mace originated from the Chamberlain of the Imperial Insignia of ancient China. Before Han Guang Wu ascended the throne, he uttered the brave words, "To marry a wife I want Yin Lihua; to be an official I want to be commander-in-chief." Later, on the Huhui planet the position became two. Accordingly, Huhui officialdom was divided into two main systems. The □ officials were also referred to as "earth" officials and were required to pass seven exams. Their salaries rose with seniority. The ■ officials were also referred to as "heaven officials." They all had special abilities and were selected and promoted without order. Therefore, the common saying, "The two ways of ■ □ are of one heart and mind, and take turns assisting the ruler in governing, 凸-口呻卜." The □ officials were popularly referred to as "white officials," while the ■ officials were popularly known as "black officials." On the Huhui official system, see *The Huhui Exam System and Official System* by Kaoski, published by the Moscow Institute for the Study of Official Systems.

him up. Both were fully 270 centimeters in height. Suspended in the air, Yu Kui shouted in fury but was powerless to do anything. The Old Do-Gooder coughed drily a couple of times.

"Well, well!" he said, rubbing his neck. "You have quite a grip. If I didn't have such a strong neck, that might have been the end of me. Yu Kui, what should be your punishment for raising a hand against your superior?"

Yu Kui wanted to hit the old man in the mouth. The old man motioned with his eyes, and the two bodyguards squeezed Yu Kui until he could scarcely speak. The Old Do-Gooder turned away, his square face all smiles, and spoke to the Shan commander.

"Brother Yifu, these youngsters are all in need of a little discipline. If they give you any trouble, just 凸凹凸凹 (chu-ru-chu-ru)."²

The Shan commander took out his handkerchief and blew his nose forcefully until it was red and swollen. Only then did he put his handkerchief away.

"Brother Wu, with all respect, your people horse around too much, flout the law, lack discipline, and are just plain stupid. We've been aware of their every move. Are we simply to let these rebels go unchecked?"

"Well, well," said the old man, smiling, "hand them over to me. I guarantee that they won't be any more trouble."

"Bulu Chief Wu," said the short, bald Shan commander as he rubbed his nose, "I must be able to count on your word."

"Brother Yifu," said the Old Do-Gooder, making a □ (wu) gesture, "when have I ever gone back on my word or broken faith with you? We Sungood people are not your enemies."

"You're right," said the bald commander as he looked over the prisoners. Then he continued slowly, "Nor are we your enemy. In fact, we have never wished to be the enemy of a single Huhui person. I was a student of philosophy, and I always admired the ⊡□ (du-wu) philosophical system more than any other. How could a people who developed such a philosophy be our enemy? We Shan people are prone to resort to force; we should, in the future, he open-minded and study ⊡□ (du-wu) philosophy. Both peoples should keep the peace."

"Right, right," Gai Bo quickly echoed. "Let there be peace forever among peoples. Everyone should be friends!"

As Gai Bo spoke, the Huhui people present all stood silently with their

---

²凸凹 凸凹 means "a breach of etiquette."

heads lowered. Miss Qi recalled what Captain Mai had said and thought that it was much in the same vein as what the Shan commander had said. She couldn't help but feel irritated. She ignored Captain Mai's anxious looks and boldly spoke her mind. "What you Shan people say sounds nice, but if you really love peace, why did you invade our planet? Why don't you withdraw and let us live our own lives in freedom?"

"Let you live your own lives in freedom?" said the bald-headed commander in surprise. "What does 'freedom' mean? Who is really free? Look at the Gaiwenese. In the past, they ate one another, but they were also friends with one another. That's pretty free. But if you happened to be one of those who was eaten, you wouldn't be too happy, would you? Do you want the freedom to be eaten? Or would you rather lose the freedom to eat others and thereby gain freedom from being eaten?

"And look at you Huhui people. You were much freer in the past, especially with your Thousand-Year War, the Snake and Leopard War, and all the countless dead. Then came the rise of the Bronze Statue Cult, which forced its beliefs on all the Huhui people and even on the people of neighboring planets. That is why the Golden Planet Alliance was forced to intervene. Our Golden Planet is the most advanced and the most civilized. If we weren't doing this for your own good, why would we dispatch occupation forces to civilize you?"

"So your occupation forces were sent to civilize us?" said Miss Qi. "Didn't you just say you admired our ⊡ ☐ (du-wu) philosophy? Isn't that a contradiction?"

"This young lady has a way with words!" exclaimed the bald-headed commander, laughing. "Too bad you don't understand ⊡ ☐ (du-wu) philosophy. What is ⊡ ☐ (du-wu)? ⊡ (du) is to be imprisoned; ☐ (wu) is to be liberated. It's human nature to he enmeshed in one's own web—that's ⊡ (du). The ability to break that web and attain liberation is ☐ (wu). Therefore, our rule over you is, on the surface, ⊡ (du). Actually, our civilizing mission is to help enlighten you, to help you attain ☐ (wu)!"

"Right," countered Miss Qi, "our being under your rule is ⊡ (du), and for that reason we rebel. If our revolution is successful, then we'll be ☐ (wu)." Miss Qi and the bald commander were diametrically opposed in their battle of words. Those listening all broke into a cold sweat for different reasons, and no one dared say anything. But then the Old Do-Gooder laughed for a while before speaking in a resonant voice.

"Brother Yifu, you are worthy of being called a philosopher. So vast is your learning that it even encompasses our shallow ⊡ ☐ (du-wu) philosophy. Well, well. I'm ashamed to be the head of a bulu and not be able to control my people, and also to know nothing about ⊡ □ (du-wu) philosophy. Miss Qi is young and hotheaded, but still the extent of her knowledge is nothing to be sneezed at even when compared with that of Commander Yifu. Brother Yifu is right in saying that the Shan and the Sungood peoples are not enemies. We are friends, and what is more, our friendship will be long-lasting and close."

The Old Do-Gooder's words appeared to smooth things over. "We're all one big family," said the commander, taking advantage of the situation. "Without discord there can be no concord. Today we have had the rare opportunity to exchange views frankly and honestly. I believe you'll now be able to control your people. Captain Mai, you will escort Bulu Lord Wu and the others back to the Sungood bulu. Be very careful because I will hold you personally responsible. You may go."

No one expected that the bald commander would just up and let them go. Captain Mai was especially happy and immediately led them from the bridge. As they were leaving, Miss Qi saw the commander take out a large hankie and blow his nose. Ah 凸 (chu) noticed her.

"Baldy is still harboring a lot of evil designs," he whispered to her. "He's got too many philosophical notions. See how brilliant he is at breaking things down. But he is allergic to the bugs of the Huhui world. He spends all day wiping his nose, and that's enough to keep him occupied."

"You 凸 (chu) people are also philosophers and historians. Thats why you're always harboring evil designs," Miss Qi said, snickering.

"We're different," replied Ah 凸 (chu) derisively. "We have a ⊡ □ (du-wu) soul, and our loyalty and devotion can overcome everything. What do the Shan have? Their power comes from the barrel of a gun. That's the way things are; everything else is false."

After they had exited the interstellar warship, Captain Mai returned them all to the Sungood bulu in a patrol car. The car stopped in front of the Sungood bulu lord's palace. Captain Mai assisted each one out. When it came to Miss Qi, he gazed at her with a great deal of affection, but she pretended not to notice. He couldn't help but sigh. Then he got back in the car by himself and drove away. Yu Kui shouted: "Get out of here, you bastard. The hour of reckoning has arrived. Wu, you're the head of the bulu, but you have dealings with the foreigners and harm your loyal followers. You are shameless. Why shouldn't I kill you right now? Prepare to forfeit your life."

Yu Kui snatched up a large rock and charged forward to strike the Old Do-Gooder, but was prevented from doing so by his bodyguards. Grunting with contempt, Yu Kui said, "I didn't want to make a scene in front of the Shan. But if you don't step aside this minute, don't blame me for what happens."

The two bodyguards made no reply. The ■ (woo) Bearer of the Gilded Mace took out a ■ (woo) staff; the □ (wu) Bearer of the Gilded Mace took out a □ (wu) staff. They stood opposite each other forming the character ⼞ (qia). Yu Kui watched but was unaware what kind of formation it was. Just as he was about to make his move, old Mr. Qi hurriedly shouted from behind, "Don't be hasty. That's a formless ■□ (woo-wu) formation, and can't be overcome."

"What do you mean a formless ■□ (woo-wu) formation? I'm not afraid of any real formation, much less a formless formation. There's nothing to fear. Just watch."

Summoning all of his strength, he hurled the rock at the two guards. With a wave of their staffs, the rock disappeared. Stunned, Yu Kui couldn't believe it. Again he snatched up a rock and hurled it at the guards. And again, with a fanning of their staffs, it disappeared. Yu Kui stopped because his arm was sore. The Old Do-Gooder stood laughing with his hands behind his back. "Did you think a boor like you could break a formless ■□ (woo-wu) formation? The formless will always triumph. Well, well. Just forget it, Yu Kui."

"Not so fast," said Mr. Qi in a heavy tone of voice. "Brother Wu, I haven't seen you in years, but you're still the same old hypocrite. You think that no one is capable of overcoming your formless formation?"

"More or less," said the Old Do-Gooder. "Brother Qi, you've lost all your wisdom beads, and without them you're helpless. What do you have to overcome my formless formation?"

"Spears!"

Upon hearing this, the Old Do-Gooder's expression changed immediately. After being silent for a while, he replied sadly, "It's you who are unbeatable, Mr. Qi. I admit I've met my match. For years I have been hoping that you'd join me, but you have always refused. If we could have joined forces, Sungood bulu, no, Sunlon City, would never have fallen to its present state. From the days of old, it has always been difficult to use men of genius. I confess I don't have your wisdom. But what has your steadfastly and haughtily refusing to take up a post done for the Huhui people? Haven't you let down Sunlon City?"

"Such is the will of heaven; there is nothing I can do."

"What will of heaven? You just have to do everything you can."

Mr. Qi and the Old Do-Gooder stood staring at each other for a long time without saying a thing. Yu Kui could no longer restrain himself. "I'll go get a spear to break his formless formation. Mr. Qi, you don't have to keep speaking in riddles to this shameless old dog."

"Enough of your nonsense," said Mr. Qi. "He might not necessarily be all bad."

"He is dealing secretly with foreigners; he's trying to harm the Death Commandos. Why do you say he's not necessarily all bad?" asked Yu Kui. "Don't be deceived by the old dog."

"I've known him all these years, how can he deceive me?" Then Mr. Qi spoke to the Old Do-Gooder: "Brother Wu, tell the truth now, was it you who tried to do in the Death Commandos?"

"I don't have to explain myself to anyone," he replied haughtily. "But it wasn't I who harmed them."

"Given the fact that you saved my daughter today, I believe you. Even if you are a hypocrite, I'm still grateful."

"Well, well. Genuine or hypocrite, time will tell."

Having had his say, the Old Do-Gooder turned and strode into the palace. The two bodyguards broke their formless formation and carefully backed away, covering the old man. Yu Kui stamped his foot and said, "He's fooled you, Mr. Qi. How can you believe him?"

Sighing, Mr. Qi replied, "It's like he said, only time will tell if he is genuine or a hypocrite. I know him only too well and that's why I won't work for him. But there are times when I have my doubts. Even if he is a hypocrite, he still might do some good. Who knows? Perhaps he's right. Maybe that's the only way to do anything for Sunlon City. I don't know."

Miss Qi had stood by watching coolly, but she could no longer control herself. "But the Old Do-Gooder is in cahoots with the Shan, and that's treason. How can you say he's right?"

Looking at his daughter, Mr. Qi replied warmly, "He saved your life today, and ours too. How can I destroy him?"

"I . . . I guess I'd rather have died in prison."

"Nonsense." Mr. Qi turned and asked Ah 出 (chu), who had all along been silent, "Ah 出 (chu), what do you think?"

"I don't want to be rash," said Ah 出 (chu), bowing deeply. "I don't have your understanding of human nature, and I can't say if the old man is genuine or false."

"Mama doesn't dare say," said Ah You, leaping about. "Mama doesn't dare say. Mama wants to 口 (qia)."

"Mr. Qi," said Yu Kui, filled with admiration, "the formless formation is so strong. How did you know how to overcome it?"

"Actually, it's just another method of transforming time and space. Most such methods only can be implemented at night with the appearance of the heavenly shafts. The Old Do-Gooder's formless formation makes use of the ■ (woo) shaft to cover heaven, and the □ (wu) shaft to cover earth. They only need be disposed correctly where the heavenly shafts appear, and whatever enters the formation will be transferred to another time and place. The rocks you hurled a moment ago perhaps ended up at the South Gate of Heaven at the beginning of the Anliu Era. It's not hard to overcome—just throw spears quickly, one after another, with a frequency surpassing the transformational speed of time and space.[3] The guards won't have enough time to resist. In this way, they will be forced to change their ⊡ (qia) character positioning and the formless formation will collapse of itself."

At the mention of the South Gate of Heaven, Ah 凸 (chu) couldn't help but think of another old devil. "Surprisingly, the Old Do-Gooder knows how to transform time and space, and also knows how to use the formless formation in broad daylight. That makes him more powerful than the Stranger in Black."

"The Stranger in Black," mumbled Mr. Qi. "Right, the formless formation was once only practiced by the followers of the Bronze Statue Cult. How did he learn it? Ah 凸 (chu), we'll have to get to the bottom of this. . . ."

At that moment, the purple sun seemed to swell, emitting a dazzling light, a burning light. It was noon. The Huhui planet was seared like sausage in a skillet, and the surface of the ground creaked. Everyone hurried for the shade beneath the eaves. Sweltering, Miss Qi was dripping wet. As she wiped the sweat away, she thought about how upon a word from the Old Do-Gooder, the bald Shan commander had released them. Clearly he had saved them, but was he still secretly plotting against them? Did he know that Yu Jin and Yu Fang had escaped to prepare the antidote? When he let them have the painting of the five jade disks, did he already know the answer to the riddle? Had he been collaborating with the Shan to hammer out interlocking stratagems to ensnare and harm the Green Snake Brotherhood?

---

[3] According to Nexson, if the basic rate of change in time and space can be doubled, then time and space can be reduplicated elsewhere.

"Dada," said Miss Qi, returning to that old question after much thought, "what is the solution to the riddle of the five jade disks? You still haven't told us."

"That's right." Mr. Qi laughed, stroking his beard. "I ought to tell you the answer. The key to the riddle is bound up with the thoughts of the three wise people. If they all harbor □ (wu) thoughts and cleave to the right way, then Ah 凸 (chu) is right—the three disks are blue. But if the three harbor ⊡ (du) thoughts and are bent on harming others, then the issue becomes much more complicated."

"I still don't understand," said Miss Qi. "If they answer correctly, then they'll become minister. Isn't that good? Why harm anyone?"

"Don't forget that the three intelligent people heard the prime minister say that those answering incorrectly would lose their head!"

At that moment the purple sun flared twice, and then darkened. Mr. Qi continued, "If you wanted someone to lose their head, what would you do? If you knew one of the others wanted you to lose your head, what would you do? As the old saying goes: 'You can't have a mind bent on harming others, but you must have a heart set on protecting yourself. Or the saying, 'A person might not want to harm a tiger, but a tiger has its mind set on harming a person.' Though you may not wish to harm someone else, can you prevent them from harming you?"

As Mr. Qi was happily expounding his point, someone began to laugh coldly.

"So it's a sage. Although a tiger has a ⊡ (du) heart, it is not as ⊡ (du) as the hearts of men. Everyone thinks about doing someone else harm; everyone has to protect themselves from others. No wonder everyone walks the path of the ⊡ □ (du-wu) spirit."

All present were startled and looked in the direction of the voice. Out walked a tall, masked man dressed in black. Ah 凸 (chu) immediately felt his legs give way, and blurted out: "It's the Supreme One."

"At your service," said the man in black. "The twenty-seventh Supreme One, Paramita Hare Krishna Holy Holy Holy Law of Moses, Below the Honored Bronze Statue Never Sinking Dharmapala Mountain God 7113218. I salute you revolutionaries, one and all. ⊡□ ⊡□, 凸-◻⊡◻- (du-wu du-wu, chu-lu-ru-mu)."

"凸-◻⊡◻- (chu-lu-ru-mu)," replied Mr. Qi in a deep voice. "Followers of the Bronze Statue Cult rarely appear in Sunlon City in broad daylight. You call yourself the Supreme One and show yourself in the Sungood bulu during the day. What is it you want?"

The Stranger in Black laughed heartily as if wailing. Ah You was so frightened that he leaped on Ah 凸 (chu), who, regardless of how he tried, couldn't free himself from the baby Serpent person's long tail. Miss Qi took a careful look at the stranger. He was wearing a bronze mask that was absolutely ferocious and horrible, the way legend described the Statue just prior to being destroyed. A small bronze statue hung at his chest. In his hands he carried a pair of strange bronze weapons shaped like the Bronze Statue. This cult member was covered with bronze statues. The Stranger in Black stepped forward and, ignoring Mr. Qi, spoke to Ah 凸 (chu).

"I presume you have been well since we parted. I ordered that you be told to return to the South Gate of Heaven. What are you doing here?"

Ah 凸 (chu) was so frightened that he hugged Ah You and was unable to respond. The Stranger in Black continued, "You are well. But you still haven't been eaten by that big worm. Don't you know that the little Serpent person you are holding might take a couple bites out of you when you least expect it?"

Ah 凸 (chu) was scared out of his wits and fell to his knees.

"Supreme One, I wouldn't dare. If you want me to return to the South Gate of Heaven, I'll do so at once."

The Stranger in Black laughed coldly. "That won't be necessary now. This is the place to be. Even I thought I'd come and join. Not just me, but another ten thousand followers of the Bronze Statue Cult."

"Ten thousand Bronze Statue Cult members!" said Mr. Qi, Miss Qi, Yu Kui, and Ah 凸 (chu) in unison, all somewhat startled.

"Not only that, but General Shi and seven thousand swordsmen from the Leopard Brotherhood as well."

"General Shi and seven thousand swordsmen from the Leopard Brotherhood!" said Mr. Qi, Miss Qi, Yu Kui, and Ah 凸 (chu) in unison, all somewhat startled.

"Not only that, but also the Sungood Death Commandos and nine thousand Green Snake Brotherhood warriors!"

"The Sungood Death Commandos! Nine thousand Green Snake Brotherhood warriors!" said Mr. Qi, Miss Qi, Yu Kui, and Ah 凸 (chu) gleefully in unison.

"The great uprising! The great uprising!" shouted Yu Kui, beside himself. "It has finally arrived!" Ah 凸 (chu) and Ah You hugged each other and capered around. Mr. Qi and his daughter laughed so much that tears flowed from their eyes, because they knew that Yu Jin and Yu Fang had succeeded in saving the Death Commandos. They all joined together in an uproar of laughter.

The Stranger in Black raised his pair of strange bronze statue weapons above his head and said in all seriousness, "Enough of this uproar. I didn't come here to listen to this; this is not the time to celebrate. The Shan have not yet been destroyed, and the situation in Sunlon City is more dangerous than ever. If you cause a ruckus again, I'll have you all sent back to the South Gate of Heaven."

They all became quiet. "Then you mean that the organization of an anti-Shan united front of the Bronze Statue Cult, Leopard Brotherhood, and Green Snake Brotherhood has finally been successful?" asked Mr. Qi.

"Right," said the Stranger in Black angrily. "This is the first time in history that our three great factions have united. Only in this way do we have the strength to undertake a decisive battle against the Shan. I have been put forward as the Supreme Commander of the United Revolutionary Army; it was decided at this morning's joint military affairs meeting. The Shan are still unaware of this. But the bald commander, who has eyes and ears everywhere, will find out about it sooner or later. Once he learns that we are working together, he will adopt the severest measures to suppress us. He might even vaporize Sunlon City. That's why we have to act at once. The great uprising is set for tomorrow morning, the moment the purple sun rises."

"Long live the great uprising," shouted Yu Kui, leaping to his feet. "The united front is great; things are getting better, they can't get any better!"

"Keep it down!" said the Stranger in Black angrily. "There's not much time; listen and I'll give you your assignments. Yu Kui, your brothers in the Green Snake Brotherhood are waiting for you. Hurry back to HQ. With the three great Yu brothers together, the Death Commandos and the Green Snake Brotherhood can start the uprising. Mr. Qi, the sages of Sunlon City are gathered in the Sunwork bulu. They are manipulating their wisdom beads to formulate the best plan for tomorrow's uprising. You are one of the senior sages, so please report to the Sunwork bulu at once to advise at the Revolutionary Army's headquarters. Miss Qi, you and Ah 凸 (chu)—and the little Serpent person—head west out of the city to the grassy plains."

Miss Qi was momentarily stunned, then she protested. "Why are Ah 凸 (chu) and I being sent out of the city? I want to be with Dada. Or I can go to Green Snake Brotherhood headquarters and join the three Yu brothers in the uprising."

"Military orders are orders; there's no room for you to act independently," said the Stranger in Black impatiently. "You and Ah 凸 (chu) have assignments of your own."

"How can you have no use for us? You want to protect us by tricking us into leaving the city so that we can't join the uprising. Sorry, but I don't need your kindness."

"Child!" said Mr. Qi, hurriedly trying to hush his daughter. "The Supreme One is the supreme commander of the United Revolutionary Army. You can't disobey."

"So what if he is the supreme commander?" said Miss Qi, pouting. "Who isn't thinking of ways to trick me into leaving?"

The Stranger in Black laughed heartily. "Such a filial daughter! But I'm not the least interested in saving anyone's life. All our strength must be hurled into this final decisive fight. If you want to come back tomorrow, I won't stop you. But before tomorrow morning, everyone must obey my orders. General Shi's cavalry is at this very moment gathering on the grassy plains to the west of the city. They will be the main force in tomorrow's attack. And although he agreed to take part in the united front at today's meeting, he sent only one representative; he himself failed to appear. I know that he has never trusted me, but that doesn't matter as long as everything comes off the way it should. Miss Qi, I'm entrusting you with this key to our secret code to give to the general. Detailed and encoded battle plans will be sent by the headquarters of the general staff to the general's command post via skyvision."

Hearing this, Miss Qi bit her lip and hesitated before speaking. "So that's my job. What happens if I'm intercepted by the Shan and am unable to deliver the key to the code?"

"That's why I'm also sending Ah 凸 (chu) by a different route. If you are unable to deliver the key, Ah 凸 (chu) ought to be able to get through. Although he doesn't have the key, 凸 (chu) people are very smart and he should be able to break the code."

"What happens if he can't break it?"

"Then General Shi will have no way of knowing the details of our battle plan," said the Stranger, laughing coldly. "He is a little on the eccentric side, and there is no guarantee that he will follow the plan even if he knows the details."

"That being the case, then you really don't care if he has the full details of the plan," said Miss Qi. "But there is another problem: if I am captured and the Shan obtain the code key, won't that jeopardize our plan?"

"Good question." The Stranger in Black laughed, tilting his head back. "First of all, I can't believe that a clever girl like you would be captured by the Shan. Second, if you were captured, I'm sure you would find a way to destroy the key. Third, if you were captured and could not destroy the key, and the Shan obtained the details of our plan, it wouldn't mean that it is our real plan."

"Good god," interjected Ah 占 (chu), unable to restrain himself, "you mean you believe General Shi will not follow the plan? But you're not necessarily giving him the real one. No wonder he doesn't trust you."

"But I don't necessarily trust him either," said the Stranger in Black.

"That's a really strange united front—no one trusts anyone else," said Ah 占 (chu), shaking his head. "What's the point of having a plan then?"

"Any plan is better than no plan, right?" said the Stranger in Black triumphantly. "Besides, those who make plans are different from those who carry them out. By making plans, someone will be occupied and they will have a sense of being useful. Is there anyone foolish enough to carry out someone else's plan? Certainly no one on the Huhui planet. Not playing by the rules will allow one to be victorious in a hundred battles. That's the ⊡ □ (du-wu) spirit. ⊡ □ (du-wu) means singular awareness. If two people cooperate, then it's not singular awareness!"

Ah 占 (chu), as usual, bowed deeply. "Supreme One. It's not that I like arguing, but perhaps you have misunderstood the meaning of the ⊡ □ (du-wu) spirit. The 中口 (man-qia) Sage said it best:

> *Mind is ⊡ (du),*
> *Nonmind is □ (wu),*
> *Transform ⊡ (du) into □ (wu)*
> *Subdue □ (wu) with ⊡ (du).*

That's the true essence of the ⊡ □ (du-wu) spirit."

"The (man-qia) Sage was not a follower of the Bronze Statue," said the Stranger in Black scornfully. "The 97th Supreme One of the Bronze Statue Cult, the 口中 (qia-man) Sage, also has a four-line hymn to explain the ⊡ □ (du-wu) spirit:

> *That which has form is ⊡ (du),*
> *That which has no form is □ (wu).*
> *Transform ⊡ (du) into □ (wu)*
> *Subdue □ (wu) with ⊡ (du).*

This is to say that the Bronze Statue of Sunlon City with form is ▣ (du); the formless Bronze Statue of Sunlon City is ☐ (wu). We want to transform our worship by prostrating ourselves before the Bronze Statue into faith in the formless Bronze Statue in our hearts. Once we possess this firm inner faith, external forms become unimportant. This is really the true essence of the ▣ ☐ (du-wu) spirit."

"Sorry," said Mr. Qi, butting in, "war is coming, so this is hardly the time to talk philosophy. Supreme One, initially I was not opposed to you sending my daughter to the grassy plains to deliver the code key to General Shi, but she has spent all her days in Sunlon City and is completely unfamiliar with the plains. And you want Ah ㅂ (chu) to take a different route. I'm worried that my daughter will lose her way."

"Don't worry," replied the Stranger. "I've thought of everything. Miss Qi need not take any risk on her own—she will be escorted."

As he finished speaking, he banged the two strange bronze statue weapons together, giving off a metallic clang. A person stepped out from behind the Stranger in Black.

8

"It's you again!' said Miss Qi in a huff. "Gai Bo, you're involved in everything. Have you no shame?"

Gai Bo opened his dark, cavernous mouth in a stupid grin but made no reply.

"Supreme One," said Yu Kui angrily, "this bastard is a Shan spy. Don't trust him."

"He's a Shan spy sent to keep an eye on us," the Stranger in Black said. "He's also a double agent whom we have sent to keep an eye on the Shan."

"And how do you know," asked Ah 凸, "that he's not a double-double agent working for the Shan?"

"How do you know," retorted the Stranger in Black, "that he's not a double-double-double agent working for us?"

"But he might be a double-double-double-double agent," said Miss Qi.

"He might be a double-double-double-double-double agent," said the Stranger in Black.

"I hear that some people specialize in the shady business of being double-double-double-double-double-double agents," added Mr. Qi.

"You know," replied the Stranger in Black, "that some people are even engaged in the trade of being double-double-double-double-double-double-double agents."

"Let's not argue; let's be friends," said Gai Bo, raising his arms. "Being a double agent is the most thankless task; it's like Piggy in the novel *Jour-*

ney to the West, who looks at himself in the mirror—what he sees is not real. You have doubts about me, and you have reasons for your doubts. But I have gone through the severest training to become a professional double agent. If you don't believe me, just look at my diploma from counterespionage school."

Gai Bo took out a small black book with gilt lettering. Everyone gathered around; on the title page was written "IT IS RIGHT TO REBEL" in gold lettering.

"It is right to rebel?" asked Ah 出 (chu), somewhat confused. "Is that the school motto?"

"Correct," said Gai Bo proudly. "A double agent can make himself into a double-double agent at any time, but a double agent who has received strict training must respect certain principles regardless of how many doubles he adds. Hence the words, 'it is right to rebel.'"

Miss Qi couldn't help laughing. "So that's what it means. So why do you rebel?"

Gai Bo immediately flipped to the last page in the book and pointed to something for all to see. It read: "Diploma, 1–2–3 Period, Academy of Counterespionage, Highest Honors, National Advanced Examination for Counterespionage, Master Spy Gai Bo, 2n+1 Double Agent #700."

"See, I'm a 2n+1 first-equation spy. I can be a double agent, a double-double-double agent, and so on . . . but I could never be a double-double or a double-double-double-double agent. On account of this, you can fully trust me."

"That's reasonable," said Ah 出 (chu), filled with admiration. "You actually have a master's degree in espionage; that's impressive."

"Of course. 'Master spy' sounds better than 'spy' or 'intelligence operative.' These days, you need a title; otherwise, how can you make a living?"

When Gai Bo mentioned his title, his own success seemed to go to his head. Then he began to sing:

> *Everyone needs a title,*
> *Otherwise, how can a living be scraped out?*
> *What with so many scholars*
> *Seeking the truth from the facts*
> *B.A., M.A., Ph.D.*
> *There's philosophers and post-docs.*
> *A taxi driver is a meter man,*
> *The outspoken is a reclusive scholar (chu shi).*

"Right on," said Ah 出 (chu). "That makes me a 出 (chu) man (*chu shi*)."

> *Everyone needs a title,*
> *Otherwise it's hard to scrape out a living*
> *There being so many scholars*
> *Leads to lots of problems.*
> *People who like money are breadwinners,*
> *Brigands are strongmen (qiangshi).*

"That's reasonable," said Yu Kui. "Someone who forces (*qiangshi*) you to leave is a strongman."

> *One who steals information is a spy,*
> *A dishwasher is also a dish master*
> *Everyone needs a title*
> *Only with a title can a living be scraped out.*

Gai Bo was just getting started, but fortunately the Stranger in Black couldn't bear his singing. "Gai Bo," he said, sneering, "haven't we had enough? Time is running short; everyone knows what they have to do; let's get to it."

The Stranger in Black looked up and gave a long whistle. Then he clanged the two strange weapons shaped like bronze statues together above his head, and recited the following lines:

> *Though fruit and flowers must fall, scattered by the wind,*
> *Sunlon City will be reborn!*

"Bear in mind, one and all, the city's fate hangs on this battle!"

As he finished speaking, he stretched out his arms. His black robe swelled, and suddenly he vanished. Everyone stood around stupefied, their eyes as wide as saucers. "He can transform time and space in broad daylight and in full view," said Mr. Qi. "He's a notch above the Old Do-Gooder."

"Dada," said Miss Qi, "did you ever think that the Stranger in Black might actually be the Old Do-Gooder?"

"It's possible." Mr. Qi sighed. "If he is the Old Do-Gooder, then I'll have to be a little more respectful. Time really is short. Let's go."

They all went their separate ways. Yu Kui returned alone to the Green Snake Brotherhood's underground headquarters; Ah 出 (chu), along with the little Serpent baby Ah You, took off down an alley; as Mr. Qi was about to depart, he took Miss Qi aside and whispered, "Daughter, watch your step with Gai Bo; he's very complicated. He says he is the #700 double agent working for us, but he could just as easily be the #700 agent for the enemy."

"I'll be very careful. Dada, you be careful yourself."

Father and daughter parted in tears. After Mr. Qi left, Gai Bo carefully put his black-and-gold diploma away. "Let's go, Miss Qi. The quickest route is through the center of the city to the Sunbright bulu, then out of the city to Cavalry Camp. But it would be better not to go looking for trouble, so I suggest we take a roundabout route through the Sunevil bulu to Sunnew bulu and then along the Jinsuo rail line to the plains. There will be less chance of encountering Shan patrols. What do you think?"

"Whatever you say." Miss Qi didn't really trust him, but she didn't want to go back to the city center. "Anyway, you know the way."

"I'm not from around here, so how can you say that I know the way better than you do? But I use this route all the time. There's a Gaiwenese Drifters' Club in the Sunevil bulu that I frequent, so I guess that qualifies me to be a guide."

Of Sunlon City's nine great bulu, Sunevil bulu was the smallest; it was also the poorest and most populous, with 250,000 people crammed into the small, narrow trapezoidal area. The bulu was number one for criminal activities such as drug dealing, prostitution, and robbery.[1] It was no surprise that a Gaiwenese Drifters' Club should be located in such a bad neighborhood. In spite of a large population, political consciousness was low, and neither the Republicans nor the Royalists were active there. Whenever the three Yu brothers, Mr. Qi, or Ah 出 (chu) brought up the bulu, they did so with a note of disdain. The only thing Sunevil bulu could be proud of was the fact that they had the best ball team in the city; they had won the Huhui Cup five years running. Armed fights would break out at the end of the matches in which many Sunevil people would be killed or injured. Fortunately, the large population made such losses insignificant.

Miss Qi braced herself as she and Gai Bo entered a narrow alley. The people of the Sunevil bulu were standing in twos and threes in the doorways. Some were strenuously soliciting clients on the streets or selling

---

[1] The drug sold by the Sunevil people is called ▣ ☐ pills, and is much more potent than morphine. Most Huhui people bitterly hate Sunevil drug dealing. They don't call the drug "du-wu pills," referring to it euphemistically as "elation pills."

drugs, while others were eyeing passersby to see if they were worth robbing. Fortunately, Gai Bo was big and tall, so no one gave him a second look. They stepped out of the alley into a small square that was filled with people, pushing and shoving, fighting over a small wooden block the size of an orange. When one team got the block, they'd rush for the square-shaped goal at the square's center, where the other team would pile up to block the goal.[2] When the other team got the block, they would all push toward the goal from the opposite direction, and the other team would push forward to cover the goal. They were playing ▣ ☐ (du-wu) ball. Amid the frenzy of the game, Gai Bo stopped in the crowd to watch. Miss Qi had always detested the sport and she called Gai Bo several times, but he ignored her. All she could do was stroll around the square and look at the shops.

The square was one of five in the Sunevil bulu. At its center was the ▣ ☐ (du-wu) ball court; at the end of the square was a fountain. The statue in the fountain—a writhing mass of men and snakes—was covered in a green patina. Shops were located all around the square, all selling pretty much the same thing: dried sea serpent meat, candied snake liver, and toys. There were also two theaters; one was showing *The Story of Wen Chongwu*, which was about the life of the Spirit of Military Suicide. The program of the other theater was *I Love You 100,000 Times*. A row of hawkers at the theater entrance were handing out playbills to the passersby. Miss Qi look one. It read:

Real people and real events come to the silver screen. An epic tale of love. The male lead is a victim of the ☐ (man) marriage; the hero is ☐ (qia) to a wicked woman who deserts him. See how he stands outside her window mumbling 99,999 times how much he still loves her. In the end, heaven is moved and he wins back the beauty's heart. When the picture was shot, the male lead repeated the words "I still love you" so many times that he fainted. The whole film is in fifty parts and lasts twenty hours. *I Love You 100,000 Times* must be seen.

---

[2] The "du-wu" ball court is square with a single square goal at the center. The two teams attack the goal from opposite sides. For this reason the opposing goalies stand back to back. There is no limit to the size of a team except that dictated by the size of the court. Players are allowed to hit, kick, and strangle one another, but they are not permitted to carry weapons on the court. Players who are killed during play may be replaced. Players can beat the referees (normally there are 49 of them) but may not kill them. For a detailed description of the rules of du-wu ball, see *The Spirit of Du-wu Ball and Its Players* by Rui Er, published by the Athletic Association of the Universe.

Miss Qi found the playbill interesting and considered taking it back to show Ah Wen when suddenly a huge hand with nine fingers reached from behind her to cover her eyes. Miss Qi knew that this did not bode well. As she struggled, she shouted, "Gai Bo, I knew you were a traitor. Let me go!"

But the person who had hold of her didn't respond. One hand covered her eyes; the other grasped her about the waist and dragged her backward. Although she shouted for help, the lively and merry sounds of the match drowned out her voice. And kidnappings were such a common sight to the people of Sunevil bulu that she knew no one would help her. She was dragged into an alley, and then through a narrow doorway into a room. Then she heard a voice.

"Okay, let her go."

The hand was removed from her eyes; Miss Qi pushed away the long arm that was around her waist. Two large, blue-skinned men, both strangers, stood before her. Startled, she whirled around. The Gaiwenese who had grabbed her stood there smiling at her.

"Who are you? Where am I?"

"There's no need to be alarmed, miss," said the Gaiwenese. "This is the Gaiwenese Drifters' Club. My name is Gai Bao; I'm one of Gai Bo's sworn *bazi*."

Miss Qi was fluent in Gaiwenese and knew that a *bazi* was a sworn brother.

"Why did you bring me here? Where's Gai Bo?"

"He's already gone," said Gai Bao. "He ordered me to take you to the cavalry camp on the plains. That's why I sent our seventh brother to bring you here. I'm afraid you are making much ado about nothing. I must ask you to forgive me my little ruse. Let's be friends. Let's be friends."

Miss Qi gnashed her teeth as she listened. She wondered what Gai Bo was up to, and regretted her own lack of caution. Now she found herself in the clutches of three Gaiwenese. Weighing the situation, she saw that it would be difficult to make a break for it. She turned back to him and smiled.

"So, Gai Bo has already left and didn't say a word to me. I don't want to trouble you to take me. I'm quite familiar with the streets of Sunlon City. I can get there on my own."

"How can I let you do that?" asked Gai Bao. "If I didn't take you and Gai Bo were to find out, he would rebuke me for my lack of courtesy. Isn't that right, Seven and Eight?"

"Right," they replied in unison. "We'd rather die than show a lack of courtesy. Let's be friends."

When Miss Qi heard them reply in one voice, she knew she wouldn't be able to get rid of them.

"Well, then I'll have to trouble you just this once. How are we going to get there? Time is short; I must get to the cavalry camp before nightfall today."

"Just leave it to me," said Gai Bao. "Please wait a moment while Seven, Eight, and I get ready."

At once, they busied themselves with a strange machine that looked like neither plane nor car. They filled it with gas, recharged the battery, and filled it with air. As Miss Qi boarded the craft, she examined the Gaiwenese Drifters' Club. They called it a club, but it was nothing more than a big, empty room. There were long, bright lights in the corners, and there were about one hundred Gaiwenese lying around on the floor. At first she thought they were drunk or had just taken some elation pills. She never expected that at the ring of a bell they would all get up excitedly and fix their eyes on the wall, where a ticker display of stock prices from the Sun-lon City market was located. As they watched, they grew more excited and started trading. When the exchange closed, they would lie down and go back to sleep. When the bell rang they would all jump up again. Miss Qi understood then that the Gaiwenese Drifters' Club was actually their stock exchange. She found it amusing that the Gaiwenese, who were accustomed to careful calculations and strict budgeting, never stopped doing business. Gai Bao and the others had readied the contraption. Gai Bao nodded to Miss Qi.

"Everything is ready. Please step aboard."

"Where am I supposed to sit? It looks like a frog!" asked Miss Qi, a bit perplexed. The body of the craft was short and bulky; two steel struts with wheels attached jutted out from the front. At the back of the craft were affixed two grasshopperlike legs; two more wheels brought up the rear. There were two lights forward, below which was located the grillwork of a vent. At first glance it might have been confused for a frog.

"Right you are," said Gai Bao, with a commendatory tone. "You are very smart. This is the famous Gaiwenese Froghopper, a mode of transportation we invented."

As he spoke, he opened two doors revealing two seats—one behind the other. "Miss Qi, please have a seat in the back; the front seat is for the pilot. I'll sit in front since I'm piloting the Froghopper."

After they had taken their seats, Gai Bao started the engine; the Froghopper shook and made a lot of noise. The roof of the Gaiwenese club slowly opened, revealing a patch of purple sky. As if entirely unaware, the one hundred or so Gaiwenese remained asleep on the floor. Out of curiosity, Miss Qi asked, "Can this Froghopper really jump? How far?"

Before she could finish, the craft gave a violent shake as the hind legs kicked, shooting it out through the roof. It soared more than 100 meters into the air before rapidly descending again in a parabolic arc. Flames shot from the rocket exhaust pipes located at the bottom of the craft, softening its landing. Miss Qi breathed a sigh of relief, clapped her hands, and laughed. "This is fun. It actually leaped over several streets; it really does work."

"Of course it does," said Gai Bao, quite satisified. "Our planet is covered with swamps; if not for Froghoppers, how would we ever get around? To pilot the Froghopper, one needs good eyes and a quick hand. Once airborne, you have to find the next landing spot. You see these two accelerator pedals? They control the spring in the legs; and the pilot's wheel is used to adjust the trajectory. In the past, we used to have an annual piloting competition on our planet; inexperienced pilots often landed in the water. Terrible!"

"You must be a first-rate Froghopper pilot."

With Gai Bao at the controls, the Froghopper jumped higher and higher. Miss Qi felt as if she were on an amusement park ride. Several times, the Froghopper nearly landed on a rooftop or on top of some pedestrians, so scaring Miss Qi that she closed her eyes.

"Why don't you go a little slower? What happens if the landing spot isn't so good?"

"That'll never happen. I forgot to tell you that I am the champion Froghopper pilot. This kind of long-range obstacle course will never trip me up."

Proud of himself, Gai Bao began to sing in a high-pitched voice:

> One Froghopper and one mouth
> Two eyes and four legs
> Boing! And in the water it lands
> Two Froghoppers and two mouths
> Four eyes and eight legs
> Boing! And in the water they land . . .

Miss Qi sighed to herself. She well knew how the Gaiwenese loved to sing. But Gai Bao was indeed a first-rate pilot. In a matter of a few hops, they had gone from Sunevil bulu to Sunnew bulu. Most of the buildings in Sunnew bulu were new, gray skyscrapers. Hopping among them seemed alarmingly dangerous. But they effortlessly cleared the last building and the city wall to land outside. The plains seemed to stretch as far as the eye could see, and Gai Bao grew even more daring, sending the Froghopper on a huge leap.

Sitting in the Froghopper, Miss Qi had the opportunity to examine the plains, something she had never before had the chance to do. The plain near the city was a patch of fresh green dotted with Huhui farming villages. Farther away, the green fields gave way to the yellowish plain; there were no villages, and occasionally herds of cattle or sheep could be seen.

Shortly, the Froghopper crossed some railroad tracks.

"That's the Jinsuo Line," remarked Gai Bao, pointing to the tracks. "The trains used to go directly to the Golden Goose Fort. Recently, General Shi's cavalry has been active, often blowing up the tracks, and so the train no longer goes through."

"Gai Bao, have you ever met General Shi?" Miss Qi recalled having seen a slogan on the wall at the mouth of an alley in Sungood bulu that read:

> *A great wind rises*
> *Fierce warriors gather*
> *The general gives his orders*
> *Orders solely to be obeyed.*

She grew very excited as she realized she would soon be meeting the general in person. "What is he like?"

"I don't know; I've never seen him. My business clients all reside within the city walls; I'm not like Gai Bo, who frequently journeys to the plains outside," said Gai Bao, yawning. "Piloting the Froghopper on the plains is not very interesting. Fortunately, we'll be there soon."

"We'll be there soon?" Miss Qi gazed into the distance as the Froghopper ascended. "I don't see Cavalry Camp where they are supposed to be encamped."

"That's just a name, Miss. Perhaps a cavalry was stationed there in ancient times. General Shi wouldn't put his troops around here, not out in the open."

"Then how are we going to find his headquarters?"

Gai Bao shrugged his shoulders and said nothing. The Froghopper hopped three more times before it landed next to a huge black boulder. Gai Bao turned off the engine. "We've arrived."

Gai Bao got out first. Miss Qi jumped out without waiting for him to help her. Upon closer inspection, the rock was huge and looked perfectly square, as if carved by human hands. Miss Qi gasped with surprise as a big person with blue skin appeared from behind it.

"Hello, Miss Qi, I've been waiting for some time."

"Gai Bo! How did you get here before me?"

Gai Bo and Gai Bao looked at each other and then grinned foolishly. Gai Bao said good-bye to Gai Bo and Miss Qi. He climbed back into the Froghopper, started the engine, and hopped away. Gai Bo waited till the Froghopper was some distance away before addressing Miss Qi.

"I arranged for Gai Bao to bring you; I felt it would be safer if we arrived separately. I hope you don't mind."

"How could I? You've done a wonderful job," Miss Qi said somewhat insincerely. "Is this Cavalry Camp?"

"It's another five miles from here. Gai Bao and I decided to meet here because the landmark is easy to spot. We'll have to walk the rest of the way."

Gai Bo didn't wait for Miss Qi to reply before he strode off across the plains. Miss Qi had no other choice but to follow. After a short distance, she regretted that Gai Bao's Froghopper was not there. From the air, the plains looked smooth, but walking on them was another matter. She gritted her teeth as she trudged through the waist-high, yellow grass. Twice she stepped in a hole and nearly twisted her ankle. Gai Bo, who was walking ahead of her, didn't even look back; he was just a blue silhouette far, far ahead. Miss Qi had to do her best to catch up, but she wasn't careful and fell. She felt like crying but didn't shed a tear; she sat in the grass and rubbed her ankle. She looked up and saw Gai Bo standing in front of her, grinning foolishly. She didn't know when he had come back for her.

"What are you smiling about? Someone gets hurt and all you can do is smile. What an idiot."

"We're almost there," said Gai Bo, trying to comfort her. "The way is hard. Come on, get up; we'll have a rest down by the water."

"What water?" asked Miss Qi, feeling very thirsty. "Is there a lake on the plains?"

"No, but there is a stream. Let's go."

Once again Gai Bo strode off. Miss Qi had no choice but to stand up and hobble after him. After a hundred steps or so, Miss Qi did in fact see a small stream shining in the purple afterglow of the sun. She gave a cheer.

"What a lovely little stream! Too bad it doesn't have a name; it'll just stay buried here on this vast plain."

"It has a name. It's called 'Sword-Cut Water.' "

" 'Sword-Cut Water'?" said Miss Qi suspiciously. "Gai Bo, you're talking nonsense again."

"No I'm not. Just watch this." Gai Bo unsheathed the sword at his waist and walked over to the stream, and with a light swipe of his blade, cut the water in half. "When you cut the water with a sword, it stops flowing; that's why it's called 'Sword-Cut Water.' "

"How is that possible?" asked Miss Qi as she undid the snake blade from her waist. She walked over to the little stream, which was no wider than two arms' length. She sliced slowly, cutting the stream. She couldn't believe her eyes. She got down on her knees for a closer look. Reaching out, she lifted a piece of bright stream water up with two hands. The small yellow flowers covering the stream bank caught her eye; then it dawned on her.

"That's it. When the fruit of the small yellow flowers fall into the stream, the water freezes. It ought to taste good."

She took a bite of the piece of water in her hands. It was cool, thirst-quenching, and fragrant. Being very thirsty, Miss Qi soon gobbled down the water. Gai Bo watched as she polished it off.

"Good?"

"Yeah! Why don't you try it?"

"Haven't you ever heard that when the Sword-cut Water ceases to flow, drink a cup to relieve sorrow and the sorrow is gone. The sorrow is gone means . . ." Gai Bo began to look blurred to Miss Qi. "It means . . . Actually, actually . . ." Miss Qi felt like speaking, but her tongue was numb and she couldn't say a thing. She staggered and fell to the ground.

After Gai Bo ascertained that she was unconscious, he took something from her and hurried off. Miss Qi lay amid the tiny yellow flowers beside the stream. As the purple sun weakly sank away, the sky gradually grew darker and a fierce wind sprang up. The wind carried a fine sand that quickly covered the plains like a yellow carpet. It passed over the plains and enveloped Sunlon City, and gusts of sand fell over the gray skyscrapers of Sunnew bulu; over the broken statue in the fountain in the small square of Sunevil bulu; over the greenish snake lamps in the doorways of Sungood bulu; and over the bluish gray interstellar Shan warship next to the Golden Palace. On the bridge of the warship, a young, dark-skinned officer was gazing at the yellow sand roiling beneath the purple clouds. He thought for a moment about that stubborn young lady. On the wooden staircase of a tavern in Sungood bulu, a short warrior dressed in green was staring silently at the sand falling outside the window and thinking about that passionate young soul toucher. The young woman they were thinking about was at that very moment lying amid the small yellow flowers along the banks of the Sword-cut Water, her body covered by a layer of yellow sand. She was sleeping like a baby.

After a while, the wind died away. The blue heavenly shafts reappeared, and the heavenly colonnade gradually closed. The girl was still sleeping beside the stream when a new movement appeared on the plains. The sound of horses's hooves approached. Troop after cavalry troop appeared out of nowhere, moving as quickly as ghosts and goblins. When the troops came together, a shout was heard.

"Gen-er-al . . ."

The call was repeated across the plains. The galloping drew closer, and the shouts grew nearer. The girl sleeping by the stream awakened and brushed the fine sand from her hair and clothes. The shouts were coming from all around her. She picked up her snake blade, not knowing which way she should run. One troop came galloping along the stream. Just as the lead soldier was about to run into the girl, he pulled the reins and veered away to one side.

"Who are you?" he growled angrily.

"I've come to see the general," said Miss Qi indifferently. "I'm a messenger from Sungood bulu to see the general."

"What makes you think you can see the general?" asked the horse soldier. "Get along with you. No one is permitted to see the army assemble."

"I must see the general," said Miss Qi firmly. "I have important intelligence information that I must give him in person. It has to do with the success or failure of tomorrow's great uprising and the very survival of Sunlon City. I have to see him at once!"

As soon as some of the horse soldiers heard her mention the "great uprising," they exchanged looks of surprise. The lead horse soldier bent forward and lifted Miss Qi to his horse's back.

"Okay. I'll take you to see the general, miss."

Sitting behind the soldier on the horse, Miss Qi could see more clearly. She saw countless horsemen surging all around her and she heard their shouts for the general rising to the sky. Above a group of soldiers, surrounded by countless cavalrymen, an awe-inspiring general in golden armor sat motionless astride a white horse and looked in the direction of Sunlon City.

"Gen-er-al!"

"Gen-er-al!"

Miss Qi felt her heart skip a beat. It was him, the famous General Shi!

The cavalryman urged his horse forward. He dismounted beside the soldiers and helped Miss Qi down from the horse. He took the opportunity to whisper a command to her.

"Once you've given the intelligence information, you should leave without delay."

"I understand."

Miss Qi followed him past the soldiers. He knelt before the general in gold. "General, this girl says she is a messenger from Sungood bulu," shouted the cavalryman. "She says she has important intelligence information for the general."

The general in gold slowly turned his eyes from Sunlon City. Miss Qi looked up at the warrior in gold who, though white-haired, she still found awe inspiring.

"Hurry up!" urged the horse soldier beside her. Miss Qi reached into the leather bag at her waist and her heart sank at once.

The key to the secret code was gone!

"Oh, no, it's gone!" said Miss Qi, blushing. She knew that Gai Bo was responsible. The horse soldier who had brought her continued to urge her to speak.

"Hurry up! The army has assembled and is awaiting orders and can't wait for you. Do you have intelligence for the general or not?"

"It's gone," replied Miss Qi angrily. "This is Gai Bo's doing."

She raised her voice and was overheard by the general.

"What's gone?" asked the general. "Take your time, Miss; it's okay."

His manner of speaking was affable, which encouraged her. She looked at the general's face. Under the purple clouds of the Huhui planet, she saw that he was old and tired. Just a moment before, as he gazed at Sunlon City, he had appeared so self-assured. But now, from her present vantage point, the golden-armored general, who had a moment ago been cheered by the troops, was, in fact, a tired old man. Yet when he spoke, the fatigue seemed to vanish from his face and his wrinkles seemed less pronounced.

"Did you just arrive from the Sungood bulu in Sunlon City, young lady? What is it like there?"

"The Death Commandos had been saved, and the Sungood warriors, under the command of the three Yu brothers, are gathering for the great uprising."

"Excellent, excellent," said the general, with a smile that vanished as quickly as it had appeared. "What about the head of the Bronze Statue Cult?"

"He entrusted me with delivering the key to the secret code, and said that he would transmit detailed battle plans to you via skyvision. But, unfortunately, I was robbed of the key on my way here," said Miss Qi, her voice faltering.

"That's all right; all I need to know is whether the head of the Bronze Statue Cult is planning to take part in the uprising. I agree that he should be made commander; that way he'll be sure to send troops. His actual plans are unimportant," said the general warmly. "You're a very brave young lady, an asset to the Sungood people."

"I'm ashamed that I wasn't able to complete my mission. The key . . ."

"It's not important. You've already delivered the most important piece of information." The general then addressed his bodyguards.

"Did you hear that? The Green Snake Brotherhood and the Bronze Statue Cult are all going to join the rebellion. We have help inside the city, and can therefore throw everything into the fight. Children, make ready."

"Make ready!" A flurry of shouts came from both sides. Then the standard bearers lifted the large, square banner of the Leopard Brotherhood with the general's name emblazoned on it. When the Leopard Brotherhood warriors saw the banner, they roared with joy and began to chant rhythmically:

"Gen—er—al!"

"Gen—er—al!"

"Gen—er—al!"

By this time, the drummers were beating their great war drums in time with the chanting. As the drums sounded, the cavalry began to move. Each company was composed of four groups of ten horsemen; four companies formed one battalion; four battalions formed one regiment; and four regiments formed one brigade. Soldiers were dispatched to inform the general as the troops were marshaled.

"The ninth regiment of the Valiant Cavalry is assembled."

"The first brigade of the Dragon Cavalry is assembled."

"The fifteenth battalion of the Routing Cavalry is assembled."

The general stood firm and erect as he received the soldiers; his face seemed expressionless. The guerrilla tactics of the Green Snake Brotherhood, by comparison, now seemed like child's play. As she was absorbed in the spectacle, someone tapped Miss Qi lightly on the shoulder.

"Miss," said the soldier who had brought her, "the general is going to set off. He will be issuing orders in a moment, and you shouldn't stay. I'll take you to the general's camp."

"Can't I stay here and watch?" Miss Qi pleaded. "I won't get in the way."

"Military matters are classified; it would be disastrous if they were revealed. You'd best come along with me."

Miss Qi had no alternative but to accompany the soldier. He helped her up and then mounted the horse himself. All around them the troops had already formed battalions. The Brave Cavalry armed with curved scimitars, the Dragon Cavalry armed with lances, and the Routing Cavalry armed with pistols had all formed rows. Miss Qi could imagine what a sight it would be to watch them attack. No wonder the general was known for his military prowess and struck terror in the Shan.

"With such crack troops," said Miss Qi in all sincerity, "tomorrow's uprising will surely be a success. The Shan will be scared out of their wits when they see the general's banner."

"Is that so?" said the soldier behind her. "The Shan will think otherwise; ten armored vehicles will be sufficient to stop our attack, not to mention the firepower of their warship. Unless the surprise attack proves effective, we won't be able to beat the Shan."

Miss Qi was surprised by the soldier's depressing assessment.

"Whose side are you on? Don't you think the general can beat the Shan bastards?"

"Of course, of course; we all must believe. In any case, a person only lives once, and tomorrow we should carry on the ▣ □ (du-wu) spirit." The soldier sighed. "The general firmly believes that his cavalry can break through the Shan line of defense. Unfortunately, he was born two thousand years too late; he could have been a hero of the Thousand-Year War. You see how he marshals his troops in accordance with the ancient system. He can't forget the glorious past of the plains. But he has forgotten it was precisely because the cavalry was no match for the infantry of the Republic that the Royalist party suffered such a miserable defeat at Golden Goose Fort."

"Why are you here if you don't believe in the general? Why join the cavalry?"

"It's not that I don't believe in the general. He's the greatest hero of the Royalist party and a warrior of a sort rarely encountered," whispered the soldier. "For generations, we members of the Ma family have been Royalists. If I don't follow the general, who should I follow? We'll follow him to the end, even if he leads us to our deaths. Anyway, you only live once. Besides, the ancient books contain a prophecy: Though fruit and flowers fall, scattered by the wind, Sunlon City will be reborn! Perhaps we will sacrifice ourselves tomorrow for this prophecy."

They cut through the orderly ranks of the Dragon Cavalry and shortly returned to the stream.

"Is this stream really called 'Sword-Cut Water'?" asked Miss Qi out of curiosity.

"Yes, it is. Unfortunately, the water cannot be drunk; if a person does drink of it, they will drift off into a deep sleep," said the soldier. "Miss, you said that the intelligence information was missing and that Gai Bo was behind it. Who is this Gai Bo?"

"A Gaiwenese spy," replied Miss Qi angrily. "He tricked me into drinking from the stream so as to steal the key."

"A Gaiwenese? That's strange. You don't suppose that it's that munitions merchant?"

"What munitions merchant?" Miss Qi asked hastily. "Have you seen him? What does he look like?"

"He's tall and blue-skinned," replied the soldier. "The Gaiwenese all look pretty much the same. Without some special characteristic, I can't describe him."

"He has a head injury and his head is wrapped in a white bandage."

"I don't know if he has a head injury; he was wearing a hat." The soldier suddenly spurred his horse, and as they galloped off, he said, "There are always a lot of munitions merchants from other planets around the general, and that has always made me nervous. Since you can recognize the Gaiwenese spy, let's hurry back; he might still be there."

The general's camp was at the head of the stream. The source of the stream was Clear Lake, at the center of which water welled up. The lake was ringed with the tiny yellow flowers. The lake water formed blocks before flowing into the stream. Spurring his horse, the soldier and Miss Qi bolted into the camp, which was in an uproar.

"Catch the spy! Catch the spy!" someone yelled.

"There really is a spy," said the soldier, leaping from his horse. Holding the reins, he helped Miss Qi down. A group of people had surrounded someone in the empty space between the tents. The soldier and Miss Qi pushed into the crowd. The spy, who was covering his head, was curled up on the ground and was being kicked back and forth like a leather ball. When Miss Qi saw the spy, she couldn't help shouting.

"Ah 出 (chu)!"

Hearing his name, Ah 出 (chu) looked up, but unfortunately was kicked in the belly. He doubled up in pain and passed out.

"Don't kick him; he's not a spy!"

The soldier helped Miss Qi restrain the men.

"We caught more than one; there's one more."

"A little Serpent person?" asked Miss Qi. "He's not a spy."

The other spy that had been captured was indeed Ah You. He had been hung by his tail and was croaking strangely. The minute he saw Ah 凸 (chu) on the ground, tears welled from two of his three eyes and he cried out, "Mama, don't die."

When Serpent people cry, their middle eye is unaffected. This is a natural means of defense. As the saying puts it: "the heart of a woman, the tears of a Serpent person"; in other words, fickle and unpredictable.

Ah You cried until Ah 凸 (chu) slowly came around. When he saw Miss Qi, he said, "Miss, have you been well since we parted, 凸-乜凸乜 (chu-lu-ru-mu)?"

"Ah 凸 (chu)," said Miss Qi, laughing, "how could you be mistaken for a spy and be beaten like this?"

"When I encountered the soldiers, I was unable to reason with them." Ah 凸 (chu) forced himself to sit up. "It's because Ah You kept calling me his mother; the soldiers assumed I was a female spy wearing a mask. I couldn't explain, no matter how I tried. They insisted upon peeling off my mask. Fortunately I have a strong neck; otherwise they would have twisted off my head." As he spoke, he was once again filled with fear. "The uprising isn't until tomorrow, and I don't feel like exercising the ⊡ ☐ (du-wu) spirit today. Miss, how did you get here?"

Miss Qi gave him an account of her journey, and how Gai Bo took advantage of her falling asleep after drinking the water from the stream to steal the key to the secret code.

After hearing her account, Ah 凸 (chu) looked up and said, "I knew Gai Bo was no good. In addition to being a Shan spy, he also is a secret agent for the Bronze Statue Cult, and heaven knows what else. It's a good thing I'm here; I can break any code. Stealing the key won't do him any good."

Miss Qi was accustomed to hearing him boast and didn't think anything about it, but the soldier's expression changed; skeptically, he asked, "Aren't you being a little overconfident, Mr. Ah 凸 (chu)? Is the code that easy to break?"

Still looking skyward, Ah 凸 (chu) snorted contemptuously. "If I say I can break it, I can break it. And who might you be, sir?"

"My name is Ma You. An old *zhihuang* who will never pass the national exams now.[1] I serve the great general and am responsible for intelligence and security."

"Oh, so that's the case, 凸卟凸卟 (chu-ru-chu-ru)," Ah 凸 (chu) lowered his head, and his expression changed to one of respect. "Since you are in charge of intelligence and security, you must be familiar with all sorts of secret codes."

"I wouldn't say that," said Zhihuang Ma. "I know a little about one or two. I have often heard of how smart the 凸 (chu) people are, and you yourself claim that you can break any code. We'll have to rely on your brains tonight."

Ah 凸 (chu) regretted his boast, and Miss Qi had to laugh to herself. Zhihuang Ma was about forty years old; his skin was the color of purple beech leaves, and he had a short mustache. He was strong and very capable looking. He led Miss Qi, Ah 凸 (chu), and Ah You into a tent that was filled with all sorts of electrical equipment for counterintelligence and monitoring. When Ah You saw the shiny gauges, he shouted with glee.

"Look at all the video games! Ma, I want to play."

"These are not video games," said Zhihuang Ma. "These things are really useful. See, this one shows the present location of the Shan warship."

On the screen, they could see a map of the Huhui planet. A flashing marker was moving ever so slightly at the center of the square that was Sunlon City.

"The warship is lifting off!" gasped Miss Qi.

"Yes," replied Zhihuang Ma, frowning. "It's quite unusual for the warship to take to the air at night. I fear that the Shan might already know about the great uprising planned for tomorrow morning. If they get the detailed battle plans, the army will be put at a disadvantage."

"Fortunately, no one knows the army's plans," said Miss Qi, as she re-

---

[1] Young Huhui intellectuals who wish to attain official rank must take a series of seven exams. Those who have not sat for a single exam are called *zhiqing* (short for "intellectual youth"). Once they pass one level, they are called *zhiqing* (short for "young and wise"). Those who pass the second level earn the title *zhishi* (short for "wise person"), while the third level receives the moniker *zhilao* (short for "wise senior"). Young Huhui intellectuals who have no desire for an official position are generally satisfied with achieving the third level. Those wishing to continue on to an official position must enter the □ official system and must pass four more specialized exams that test their abilities in policy making, organization, responsiveness, and diplomacy. By special appointment, the *zhiqing*, *zhiqing*, *zhishi*, and *zhilao* can enter the ■ official system. There are some older *zhiqing*s who spend their whole lives without ever passing an exam. They are called *zhihuang*. The expression "everything increases in value save always turning out exams" is indicative of the dejected lot of a *zhihuang*.

membered the Stranger in Black's words. "If we don't even know, how much less likely it is that the enemy does. Although the leader of the Bronze Statue Cult promised to send the plans via skyvision, they weren't necessarily going to be the real plans. The general wasn't going to follow them anyway."

"That might be, but we want the Shan to believe that the plans will be followed. They have the key that Gai Bo provided, so they must know the plans. We must know the plans too, in order to counter the Shan deployment. Besides," Ma chuckled, "with Ah 凸 (chu) on it, it'll be easy to break the code and turn the tables. Perhaps Ah 凸 (chu) would care to demonstrate."

Ah 凸 (chu) knew that Ma had no ill intentions, but he had boasted and now had to make good on his boast. He still had one hope in a thousand.

"We don't know if the leader of the Bronze Statue Cult has sent the plans or not."

"Rest assured," said Ma, pointing to a machine, "we have a complete record of all skyvision transmissions from Sunlon City tonight. Ah 凸 (chu), perhaps you'd care to get to work right now. You are wise and smart, not like us *zhihuang* who lack knowledge and ability. With you here, we ought to be able to break the code at once."

Fool, cursed Ah 凸 (chu) to himself. He had no choice but to take his place in front of the machine. With the push of a button, the skyvision broadcasts began to replay on the screen. "You can control the speed of the broadcast," said Ma. "The machine has the usual mathematical keys for decipherment. But you are a 凸 (chu), so I don't need to tell you anything. One look and you ought to be able to use it. It's up to you now, Mr. Ah 凸 (chu)."

After finishing what he had to say, Zhihuang Ma led Miss Qi out of the tent, leaving Ah 凸 (chu) and Ah You behind to stare blankly at the screen. At first, Ah 凸 (chu) was a bit agitated, but after observing the broadcasts for a while, he became intrigued. After a while, Miss Qi and Zhihuang Ma returned. Ah 凸 (chu) and Ah You were enjoying a program titled *Purple Sun, Golden City*. Miss Qi didn't know if she should laugh or be angry.

"Ah 凸 (chu), you were asked to break the code, and here you are watching a show. Do you think that's right?"

"Stop complaining," said Ah 凸 (chu) with a wave of his hand. "I've nearly got it; the Bronze Statue Cult leader's battle plans are in this program."

Zhihuang Ma was startled when he heard that Ah 凸 (chu) was on the verge of breaking the code. He hurriedly looked at the screen and saw three sweet and charming soul touchers singing together. He listened for a while, then he spoke without hesitation.

"Mr. Ah 凸 (chu), though I have little talent and less learning, I can't make out what they are singing. What could it have to do with the cult leader's plans?"

"There are many things you don't know," replied Ah 凸 (chu) with an air of superiority. "The more sophisticated the code, the greater the philosophical content. This should be obvious, given how smart the leader of the Bronze Statue Cult is, shouldn't it? The philosophy behind the secret code is to find war in peace! See how these three young ladies are singing softly and dancing slowly? Actually, they're signaling the battle plans. Look at how the girl on the left holds her arms out with her fingers spread—this indicates the second regiment of the tenth brigade. The right arm of the one on the right is at eight o'clock; this means that they should enter the city and attack the Shan from the southwest. The one in the middle is singing 'Love you, love you, love you.' Those three 'love yous' mean 'hate you,' and this means that the third battalion should lead the attack and the first battalion should he held in reserve."

When Zhihuang Ma heard Ah 凸 (chu)'s explanation, he broke out in a sweat and fell to the ground in front of him.

"So the song and dance of three young ladies on the skyvision has such a serious significance! You've explained it so well, you have my admiration."

"You're too kind, you're too kind," said Ah 凸 (chu). "Finding war in peace and using song and dance to tell one's ambitions is the ultimate expression of the ⊡ □ (du-wu) spirit. Brother Ma, please get up. Henceforth you should spend a little more time studying the philosophy of ⊡ □ (du-wu)."

Ah 凸 (chu) talked excitedly, his saliva flying. Outside, hoofbeats were heard rapidly approaching.

"The general has returned," said Zhihuang Ma.

They rushed out of the tent. The general was galloping back to the camp, followed by ten of his most trusted men. Zhihuang Ma hurried forward to respectfully make his report.

"General, we have obtained the battle plans of the leader of the Bronze Statue Cult using the secret code!"

"I know," said the general with an impatient wave of his hand, without dismounting. "Break camp at once. We are marching on Sunlon City and must reach our objective before sunrise."

But Zhihuang Ma would not drop the matter. He stepped forward again to respectfully make a report.

"General, would you like to hear the plans of the leader of the Bronze Statue Cult, just for reference? The Shan might prepare their defenses in accordance with the plans."

"I know," replied the general. "The head of the Sungood bulu sent his chamberlain Lai Fu to deliver the plans of the leader of the Bronze Statue Cult. The leader is really stubborn. But I've already made up my mind. The cavalry will attack as planned when the sun comes up. Hurry and break camp."

The general cracked his whip; his trusted followers fell in around him, and they all galloped east. Zhihuang Ma stood there, stunned. Unable to bear it, Miss Qi tried to console him.

"You needn't waste your breath since the general wants to attack as planned. You did all you could; don't be upset."

"I'm not upset. I know the general all too well. He wouldn't lightly change his plans. But I do find it strange that someone else delivered the plans."

Miss Qi also thought something was fishy.

"The leader of the Bronze Statue Cult sent Ah 凸 (chu) and me. And now the Old Do-Gooder has sent his chamberlain Lai Fu with the plans. Did he know that Gai Bo would steal the key? Unless . . . unless the Old Do-Gooder himself is the leader of the Bronze Statue Cult."

As she was pondering the possibility, a loud explosion was heard from the west. Having sharp eyes, Miss Qi saw a golden beam of light recede into the purple clouds and vanish in an instant.

"Ah 凸 (chu), quick, look, someone is using the heavenly shafts to transform time and space!" In a flash, Miss Qi had an inkling of who it might be. "Someone has returned to the South Gate of Heaven to report to the leader of the Bronze Statue Cult. Who is it? Lai Fu? Or Gai Bo? Let's go have a look, Ah 凸 (chu)."

"Go where to have a look?" asked Ah 凸 (chu), pale with fear. "Miss, let's not go looking for trouble."

"We have to go to the South Gate of Heaven. I won't be able to rest until I figure out this mystery. Maybe we have all been tricked by the Old Do-Gooder, or should I say the leader of the Bronze Statue Cult."

"Miss Qi," said Zhihuang Ma, "I think you should just forget about it; you can't deal with the cult leader. With the uprising so close, it's more important that we get to Sunlon City."

Miss Qi wouldn't listen. She turned and walked away. Ah 凸 (chu) could do nothing but grab Ah You, heave a sigh, and fall in behind her. Zhihuang Ma thought for a moment, shook his head, and gave the order to break camp. He then led his troops to catch up with the general's vanguard.

It was already the middle of the night, and the blue shafts of light were moving quickly over the grassy plain. It was as if someone were operating the heavenly colonnade, broken into several smaller groups, each of which was revolving around a single stationary shaft. But at night the grassy plain was actually full of life. Prairie squirrels, hundred-pacer snakes, drought frogs, and stealthy cats were all on the prowl for food. There was also a pale red to light purple-colored flower that blossomed only at night. When the sky grew light it would shrink back into the soil. It was popularly known as "mistress flower" or "too-shy-to-be-seen." At night the ground was covered with the flowers, which looked extremely attractive against the yellow sand.

Miss Qi, Ah 凸 (chu), and Ah You crossed an area covered with the flowers and made their way to the nearest stationary shaft of light. Ah 凸 (chu)'s fear increased with each step closer to the shaft. He kept repeating himself as he spoke to her.

"Miss, forget it. I don't know where the South Gate of Heaven is, and even if we find it, the leader of the Bronze Statue Cult won't necessarily be there. If by chance he is there, it will just mean more trouble. What would your dada think? Your dada . . ."

Miss Qi paid him no heed and, without consulting anyone, leaped into the shaft of blue light. Her white clothes immediately shone with a purple glow. Ah 凸 (chu) gritted his teeth and put Ah You down.

"This shaft can only support two people," he said to Ah You. "So I can't take you with me. If you are smart you'll find your way back to the Sungood bulu."

"Ma!" Ah You called with fear. "I'm afraid. I don't want to leave you."

Ah 凸 (chu) leaped through the air into the shaft of light. It slowly began to change color, and what looked like flames seemed to spring up around Miss Qi and Ah 凸 (chu). Ah 凸 (chu) appeared to mutter incantations and began to recite the "Song of the 凸 (chu)":

> 凸呫 *(chu-ru)*
> 凸呫 *(chu-ru)*
> 口匚-口匚 *(lu-mu-lu-mu)*

‑◫‑ ‑◫‑ *(lu-mu-lu-mu)*
▣ ☐ *(du-wu)*
▣ ☐ *(du-wu)*
┰┥ *(chu-ru)*
┰┥ *(chu-ru)*[2]

Just as Ah ┰ (chu) began, the shaft of light changed from blue to purple to red, and the flames seemed to dance up and down, filling the shaft. It finally turned a clear gold, and the two people shrouded within emitted a blinding white light. Then a loud tearing sound was heard as the shaft left the ground and quickly receded into the sky; the two people inside also rose and disappeared into the purple clouds. Seeing the two of them vanish that way, Ah You departed, filled with fear.

Miss Qi felt as if she were in a pitch-black corridor. There seemed to be some light in the distance toward which she struggled to make her way. The point of light grew in size, and the loud tearing noise sounded again. Miss Qi was ejected in mid-air; she turned a few somersaults before landing on the ground.

Miss Qi got up. She found herself in a green grassy area in a valley. It was the most bountiful stretch of the Hu River Basin, and everything was a fresh green color. The countryside was divided into regular small squares, within which were located the hamlets of the Huhui farmers. The mountains were massed on the other side of the valley. Miss Qi was moved.

"So this is the South Gate of Heaven? It's beautiful, Ah ┰ (chu). Ah ┰ (chu)!"

She searched for a while before finding Ah ┰ (chu) lying across a large rock. She shook him for a long time before he finally came to. He rubbed a big bump on his neck and sighed.

"This really is ◫┥┰ (mu-ru-lu-chu).[3] I'm going to lose my life one of these days if I keep this up."

"Ah ┰ (chu), is this the South Gate of Heaven?"

He looked around and shook his head.

"No. This is the southernmost valley of Mount Huihui. It's called Green Valley. The South Gate of Heaven is on a mountain not too far

---

[2] This portion of the "Song of the ┰" can be roughly translated as: "salute / salute / look left, look right / look right, look left / awaken the du-wu soul / exercise the du-wu spirit / salute / salute."

[3] ◫┥◫┰ means "unlucky year."

from here. I must have left out a line when I was reciting, so we ended up being thrown so viciously to the wrong place. But that's okay; we won't attract any attention if we climb to the South Gate of Heaven from the valley floor."

From the bottom of the valley they began their ascent. Miss Qi was startled to notice that the purple sun seemed to have shrunk substantially. Then she recalled that they were in a different age and that what she was seeing was the purple sun of the past.

"Ah 出 (chu), are we really at the beginning of the Anliu Era?"

"Yes. As chance would have it, 2,201 years separates us from our age!" said Ah 出 (chu). "I don't know why the leader of the Bronze Statue Cult would choose this place at this time for his headquarters. He must have a reason."

"Listen, Ah 出 (chu)."

Ah 出 (chu) listened carefully. The sound of wood cutting was coming from the forest on the slopes. After a while a person was heard singing.

> Mountain trees ought not to grow alone
> I clasp my knees and sing a mountain song
> Ah! Sing a mountain song
> Everyone says I'm a playboy
> There must be beauty in this rotten life
> Ah! There must be. . . .

Finished singing, the woodcutter went back to chopping wood, the sound of his axe echoing long and steady through the valley. Ah 出 (chu) laughed.

"In this age, the Huhui farmers really loved to sing mountain songs, but they are not so popular in our day."

"It's great to be able to sing." Then Miss Qi thought once more about Gai Bo. "You just don't want to be like Gai Bo, opening his big mouth to sing at any time and at any place, annoying one and all."

Ah 出 (chu) laughed.

"That's just the nature of the wandering Gaiwenese. What kind of wanderers would they be if they couldn't drink and sing?"

Miss Qi grew worried thinking of Gai Bo and his followers Gai Bao and Gai Seven and Eight. "Gai Bo is an evil influence, not just for ma-nipulating the Gaiwenese club but also for joining up with the Shan, the

Bronze Statue Cult, and the Old Do-Gooder. I wonder what his intentions are."

"Don't worry about it; we'll go to the South Gate of Heaven and see."

Ascending the slope, they saw the ancient Sunlon City as if carved out of gold on the plains beyond the mountains. Miss Qi stood silently for a while before saying anything.

"Ancient Sunlon City really was beautiful! I wouldn't have believed it unless I saw it with my own eyes."

"The ancient city is both our glory and our nightmare. Do you see the statue? That's the Bronze Statue of Sunlon City."

Miss Qi looked in the direction that Ah 凵 (chu) was pointing. There in the center of the city stood the shining statue. Being so far away, she couldn't make out the expression on its face. But without question, the statue lent a dignified if not sacred air to the city. "The Bronze Statue of Sunlon City. It gave meaning to our Huhui world, but it also nearly destroyed us," said Ah 凵 (chu) solemnly. "Miss, do you remember the ancient poems I had you memorize as a child? Those poems of praise and blame were for this very statue. It is our original sin and our atonement."

"I remember," said Miss Qi softly. She wished that Yu Jin were also here to savor this moment with her. Suddenly she understood why the Huhui people lived, struggled, and died. The beautiful valley, the woodcutter's mountain song, the golden city, the shining statue; all of these things belonged to the Huhui world she so loved. Perhaps the Stranger in Black had chosen this time and place for his camp for that very reason.

"Let's go."

Ah 凵 (chu) led the way. Nearing the top of the slope, they came to a pine forest. Outside the forest, Miss Qi noticed two stone pillars of unequal height about twenty paces apart. The pillars were covered with markings that formed no recognizable words.

"Miss," whispered Ah 凵 (chu), "this is the South Gate of Heaven. Heaven's southern gate."

10

Curious, Miss Qi examined the two mottled and uneven stone pillars. Was this the South Gate of Heaven? She ⊣⊟⊢ (lu-mu) for a while. There was nothing there other than the two stone pillars and the pine forest.

"This is the South Gate of Heaven? Where is the camp of the leader of the Bronze Statue Cult?"

"Don't underestimate the pillars," whispered Ah ⣥ (chu). "A pivot in the flow of time is located between them."

"If we enter the gate, can we travel to any other time?"

"Almost any, but not all. Each pivot in the flow of time is compatible only with those on the same basic frequency—about half of them. The other half can be reached through the North Gate of Heaven."

"Where is the North Gate of Heaven?"

"Hey, listen!"

Miss Qi listened carefully.

"It's the wind in the pines. Don't be so jumpy, Ah ⣥ (chu)."

"It's not just the wind in the pines," said Ah ⣥ (chu) nervously. "I hear some other sound in the woods."

Miss Qi didn't believe him. She pulled out her snake blade, walked around the pillars, and stepped into the forest. Ah ⣥ (chu) followed. They crossed a stretch of ground, soft with pine needles. The light of the purple sun poured through a break in the woods onto the green moss, where it shone back softly. Miss Qi looked around for a while and was on the point of abandoning the search when she too heard the sound.

"There's someone in the forest," whispered Ah 凸 (chu). "Miss, be careful."

They followed the sound deep into the forest until they came upon a spring. A man dressed in black sat cross-legged on top of a boulder beside the spring, playing chess. At his side stood a small, blond girl. Each time he moved a chess piece, a "ping" was heard.

"So it's the leader of the Bronze Statue Cult," said Miss Qi. "Who is the girl next to him?"

Ah 凸 (chu) shook his head. The Stranger in Black had been concentrating on the chessboard atop the boulder. Suddenly, he raised his head in the direction where they were hidden and spoke.

"It is boring to play ⊡ □ (du-wu) chess alone. Why don't the two of you come and play?"

They knew it was pointless to hide, so they stepped out from behind the pine tree. The Stranger in Black gave an odd laugh.

"Well, Miss Mei, what do you say? I guessed correctly. Those who ought to come will, and those who shouldn't—well, you won't be able to get rid of them. I knew I'd have visitors before the start of the final battle with the Shan. Miss Qi, Ah 凸 (chu), I haven't seen you in ages."

When Ah 凸 (chu) heard the Stranger in Black's shrill laugh, his heart pounded and his knees shook.

"Supreme One," he stammered, "we would never think of disturbing you. Actually, we made a special trip to warn you that first Gai Bo, the counteragent, stole the secret code, and then the Old Do-Gooder sent his chamberlain Lai Fu to deliver the battle plans in person. We were worried that you had been tricked and that the battle plans might he compromised."

"What a joke," said the Stranger in Black, unamused. "What kind of person am I to be tricked by the likes of them?"

"But with my own eyes I saw someone ride a heavenly shaft here," said Miss Qi. "If it wasn't Gai Bo, then it was Lai Fu. If you say that they haven't tricked you, then you are tricking us."

When Ah 凸 (chu) heard Miss Qi, he broke out in a sweat and nearly fainted from fright. Hastily, he smiled apologetically.

"Supreme One, Miss Qi is young and hot-tempered. She might have spoken a little rashly. Please forgive her."

But the Stranger in Black was not angered.

"Gai Bo and Lai Fu are both my faithful servants," he said, smiling. "They have always recited the Bronze Statue Cult scriptures; they have always listened to the cult; and they have always done things in accordance with the directives of the cult. To make certain that General Shi saw the plans and that we could fight in unison, I sent Gai Bo to assist Miss Qi in delivering the key to the code; I also sent Lai Fu to deliver the battle plans."

"But," said Miss Qi, protesting, "you know that General Shi will not follow the plans. So why all the trouble?"

"I am successful if he receives the plans," said the Stranger in Black. "General Shi is no fool—he will adopt the appropriate measures once he sees them. To put it another way: if the general sees my plans and we are successful tomorrow, history will say that it was due to my careful planning; if by chance we lose, General Shi will be blamed for not listening to orders and trying too hard to make himself the hero. No matter what, history will recognize my contributions; I can't lose."

"So that's it," said Miss Qi. "But you forget, Ah 凸 (chu) was once an official historian, and most of his 凸 (chu) friends work in the National Office of History. If what you just said ever becomes known, how will history judge you? Aren't you afraid of being called unscrupulous, a person who succeeded by scheming?"

The Stranger in Black laughed coldly.

"Miss Qi, there's nothing wrong with that. A true hero is not afraid of being criticized. Womanish benevolence will never lead to success, and frequently leads to disaster. How my merits are judged in the future is predetermined. Miss Mei," he said, pointing to the blond-haired girl beside him, "is a historian from the future. That I am the most unscrupulous schemer of the age is a judgment that can be passed only when the coffin is nailed shut."

"So that's the way it is," said Miss Qi as she gave Miss Mei a careful once-over. They were about the same age, but Miss Mei was a little taller. She never stopped smiling and she seemed interested in everything that was going on around her. "Miss Mei, is he really an unscrupulous schemer?"

"My name is Mei Xin," said the blond girl, smiling. "I am here from Earth to study the entire history of the Huhui planet. As historical researchers, our first commandment is that we cannot break up the completeness of Huhui history. Thus, we cannot interfere in the unfolding of the Huhui past, and we cannot reveal the tendencies in the future of Huhui history."

"Then," interjected Ah 凸 (chu), "she can't tell us if tomorrow's uprising will be a success or a failure."

"Sorry," Miss Mei apologized. "I can't reveal that."

"But you have told the leader of the Bronze Statue Cult that he is an unscrupulous schemer," said Miss Qi, dissatisfied. "Isn't that a little unfair? According to you, if he wasn't that way initially, then he'd have to become that way."

"Right," said the Stranger in Black, and laughed. "Unscrupulous schemers lack ⊡ (du), and a man should improve himself. But Miss Mei never clearly told me that I was an unscrupulous schemer. However, when we met she slipped and said, 'You're that bad egg of a leader of the Bronze Statue Cult, aren't you?' From what she said, I realized what my historical status was. Miss Mei, you are inexperienced."

"A bad egg isn't necessarily an unscrupulous schemer," said the blond-haired girl, blushing. "A bad egg is just . . . a bad egg."

"What's a bad egg?" asked a voice in the forest. "A bad egg is a rotten egg; a rotten egg is a bad egg. You don't have to eat a bad egg to know that it's bad; one whiff and you'll know."

"Gai Bo!" said Miss Qi, who knew who it was without looking. "You have the nerve to show up here?"

A blue-skinned man walked out of the woods.

"Scent is stink; stink is scent," he said, opening his big black mouth. "Let's be friends, let's be friends."

Everyone noticed that Gai Bo was wearing a seven-pointed hat, with three orange tassels dangling from each point. He wore a dark yellow raincoat with the collar hanging open. But he couldn't hide the two gill slits on his pointed head. Seeing Gai Bo in such a strange getup, Ah 出 (chu) bowed deeply.

"You are no doubt wearing a master spy's robes."

"Correct. At least I've met someone who knows what's what," said Gai Bo happily. "Each time I pull off a beautiful bit of espionage, I put on my robes and celebrate. At least you'll know that my title of master spy wasn't something conjured out of thin air."

"Leader of the Bronze Statue Cult," said Miss Qi, "Gai Bo stole the key to the secret code and surely gave it to his Shan masters. Did you encourage him to do this? Or weren't you aware that he was a traitor?"

The Stranger in Black snorted.

"Gai Bo, you tell them."

Gai Bo raised himself slightly before speaking.

"Everything was done with the Supreme One's knowledge. The Shan had someone follow the Froghopper that Gai Bao and Miss Qi took to the plains. After lifting the key, I was stopped by a Shan military patrol. The key was sent to the bald commander, who no doubt knows all the army's battle plans."

The Stranger in Blacked nodded his head.

"Well done. Everything went smoothly. What is there to worry about?"

"The Supreme One can anticipate things with miraculous skill. You have my admiration," said Gai Bo, taking the opportunity to continue. "If there is anything you want me to do, please don't hesitate to ask."

"There's nothing else. We ought to be getting back to Sunlon City to take part in the great uprising." Quite satisfied, he addressed Miss Qi and Ah 出 (chu). "You heard that Gai Bo followed my orders to the letter. That's the function of a counteragent. He can leak the intelligence we want our enemies to have and make them believe that it's genuine."

"But the intelligence a counteragent leaks is always false; your counter-agent here, on the other hand, leaked the real article," said Miss Qi. "What good will it do us to let the Shan know all our battle plans?"

"As head of this cult, I have my reasons," replied the Stranger in Black, looking up at the purple sun. "It's late, we should be getting back to Sun-lon City. Miss Mei, will you accompany us?"

"I have to get back to the Research Institute because I have a mid-term paper that I must turn in," said Miss Mei sweetly. "I'll return to Sunlon City to investigate after your uprising and collect materials for my final paper."

"That's too bad; by then we might all be with the ancients," said the Stranger in Black proudly. "That's all right. Fruit and flowers must fall, scattered by the wind, but Sunlon City will be reborn."

"Good-bye, everybody." Miss Mei waved. The air around her began to move rapidly, as if she were wrapped in a transparent cocoon. Then the blond-haired girl vanished. Ah 出 (chu)'s curiosity was piqued.

"That's the first time I've ever seen that way of altering space and time."

"It's not a way of altering space and time," said the Stranger in Black. "The people of the future have constructed corridors through time to every other age. Unfortunately I haven't been able to locate the entrance. Let's go."

The Stranger in Black retrieved his two weapons shaped like bronze statues from the boulder and strode off through the forest. Gai Bo, Ah 出 (chu), and Miss Qi followed him back to the South Gate of Heaven. The Stranger in Black stood before the two pillars, then turned to address Miss Qi and Ah 出 (chu).

"Take another good look at this land of enchanting beauty. You might never make it back here, but always keep in mind that this is the way the Huhui planet should be."

He turned away and boldly strode through the South Gate of Heaven. Suddenly, there was a flash of light between the pillars, and he turned into a whirl of purple light and disappeared. Ah 屮 (chu) waited till he had vanished entirely before speaking.

"The leader of the Bronze Statue Cult is an amazing individual. Without him, I'm afraid we Huhui would never be able to unite in a great uprising."

"But he's no good," said Miss Qi. "Even Miss Mei Xin said he was no good."

"What's wrong with even the worst?" Gai Bo laughed. "The bad are good and the good, bad. Frankly, if I didn't admire the head of the Bronze Statue Cult, I wouldn't be helping the Huhui people. You ought to be aware that in the business of counterespionage, the least slip-up can cost one his life."

Miss Qi didn't know whether to believe this cunning Gaiwenese or to laugh at him. As she paused, blue-skinned Gai Bo stepped through the South Gate of Heaven to become a whirl of purple light. Only Miss Qi and Ah 屮 (chu) remained there at the edge of the forest. Ah 屮 (chu) slowly looked around and sighed.

"Miss, it doesn't matter if the head of the Bronze Statue Cult is good or bad. What he said was right: the Huhui planet ought to be like this. Unfortunately, those to come are not worthy and can't defend the golden city of the purple sun. Now I understand that the head of the cult had his reasons for bringing me to the South Gate of Heaven the night before last. If I hadn't fled, I might have had the honor of being his counterespionage agent instead of Gai Bo. I'm ashamed of my own uselessness; the 屮 (chu) are a useless lot, and that's the truth."

Miss Qi had rarely seen Ah 屮 (chu) so emotional. She remembered how in his company she had learned to read, wield a sword, and sing. He could do anything, but she had never seen him take anything seriously. Even when he learned to manipulate the wisdom beads with her dada, he just looked at the sky and didn't put much thought into it. He wasn't like her dada, who would go without food or sleep when he manipulated the beads. She heard her father say that Ah 屮 (chu) had once been a famous Huhui historian, but Ah 屮 (chu) never brought up the past. She was surprised that Ah 屮 (chu), who normally seemed to have no cares, was now so emotional. She tried to console him.

"We still don't know if Gai Bo is good or bad. Nor do we know what the Bronze Statue Cult leader's intentions really are. We can't even determine for sure if he is the Old Do-Gooder. So why blame yourself?"

"Not being able to die protecting Sunlon City is something I'll regret for the rest of my life. Fortunately, I'll soon be able to atone for that crime," said Ah 凸 (chu). "Miss, take a careful look at the landscape and see how charming it once was. What will it become in the future?"

The purple sun was half hidden by the horizon, and vast was the land. Far away, the Bronze Statue in Sunlon City glowed in the fading light. Its head suddenly sparkled strangely like a giant diamond, and like a giant flaming torch that burned the entire city. The long Hu River also seemed to be set aflame, and shone like a long, gorgeous serpent. The square fields in the verdant valley at the foot of the mountain were various shades of green and resembled belts of jade. A song was heard rising from the valley floor.

> *The purple sun sinks in the west*
> *Once again*
> *Evening has come*
> *A sudden look back*
> *Only to see that*
> *Solitary city*

Ah 凸 (chu) watched in awe as the purple sun slowly sank and disappeared. He sighed and stepped into the South Gate of Heaven. Miss Qi lingered until the light vanished from the statue's head before she reluctantly stepped between the pillars.

In what seemed like the blink of an eye, she found herself in front of the gate to the Sungood bulu. The sky was just beginning to get light and the gate was still shut. Squatting in front of the gate were a number of people in black, whom Miss Qi recognized as members of the Bronze Statue Cult. But the Stranger in Black, Gai Bo, and Ah 凸 (chu) were nowhere to be seen. She was just about to ask the people in black when someone called her from behind.

"Miss Qi."

"Brother Yu Jin."

Yu Jin was carrying a heavy cloth sack on his back. He was followed by the Death Commandos of the Green Snake Brotherhood, all of whom carried identical cloth bags. Members of the Leopard Brotherhood, who were holding scimitars, stood next to their mounts. Miss Qi saw that they

belonged to the vanguard of the cavalry. The members of the Bronze Statue Cult, the Green Snake Brotherhood, and the men and horses of the
Leopard Brotherhood had all arrived, and the uprising appeared to be on
the point of beginning. Miss Qi could feel that everyone's nerves were
stretched taut and ready to snap.

"Yu Jin, are you going out through the gate?"

"Very soon," replied the short warrior. "What took you so long to get
here? Your dada's about to keel over with worry."

"Has Ah 出 (chu) returned?"

"A long time ago. You better hurry back to the tavern and let your dada
know that you are okay."

"I thought he was still at the Sunwork bulu."

"The leader of the Bronze Statue Cult sent him back to the Sungood
bulu to coordinate the military action. Hurry back."

Yu Jin repeatedly urged her to go. At first Miss Qi had a lot to say, but
now out of anger she held her tongue. She turned to leave, but Yu Jin
called for her to stop.

"Miss Qi."

Miss Qi stopped in her tracks, and Yu Jin thought for a while before
speaking.

"Take care."

Miss Qi, on the verge of tears, nodded. She knew he would say no
more. Perhaps it would be their final farewell, but what else could she expect? As if relieved of a heavy burden, Yu Jin hastened to the gate, where
he had the door bar removed. The thick, heavy wooden doors were slowly pushed open.

She knew that time was short, so she started back to the tavern at a run.
Fully armed warriors lined both sides of the narrow alley, silently awaiting the order to attack. Every able-bodied man of the Sungood bulu had
mobilized; even the young men, who were armed with swords and half
pikes, waited in ambush behind the windows. Sungood bulu was unusually quiet; only her footsteps were heard in the alley, breaking the silence
before the storm.

Miss Qi rushed into the tavern. Ah Wen, the fat servant woman, was
wiping her nose and tearful eyes as she packed for her butcher husband Ah
Two, her taxi driver husband Ah Three, and her cook husband Ah Four.
She griped the whole time.

"Go! Go! Don't bother about anything in the house. The worst that
can happen is that you'll all die and I'll play the widow."

"Who wants you to be a widow?" said Ah Two the butcher. "It is commonly said that 'a woman should remarry, and a husband should not practice two arts.' If you don't get rid of an old husband, you can't expect to get a new one. Cheer up, Ah Wen."

"You would have to be that way at a time like this!" cried Ah Wen, her tears moistening Ah Four's cuff. Ah Four frowned. "Ah Two, Three, and Four, listen carefully to what I say. As soldiers you must be extra careful; look after and care for one another."

Ah Two looked at Ah Three and Ah Three looked Ah Four and Ah Four looked at Ah Two. They all nodded.

"Ah Wen, where is my dada?" asked Miss Qi.

Without saying a word, Ah Wen pointed upstairs. Ah Two, Three, and Four fell in line and marched outside. Ah Wen fell to the floor, weeping. Miss Qi tried to console her with a few words before heading upstairs. There, in the small room, Mr. Qi and Ah 出 (chu) sat facing each other on the wooden bed, absorbed in studying the multicolored wisdom beads.

"I'm back."

Mr. Qi tossed aside the beads, smiled, and stroked Miss Qi's face.

"Child, we've succeeded. All the troops have arrived at the meeting place. The Shan will never suspect the Huhui of being capable of launching such a large-scale uprising."

"What about their interstellar warship?"

"It has landed again; it's in the city center," said Mr. Qi, his white beard shaking. "This is the best time for the uprising. We must break through the Shan line of defense, and our shock troops must try to take the ship by sacrificing everything. Once we capture their warship, that'll be the end of the Shan."

"But what if we don't take the warship?" asked Miss Qi, growing increasingly nervous with each word. She suddenly wondered what was in the bag Yu Jin carried. "If by chance the shock troops should fail, the warship will take off and vaporize Sunlon City."

"That's right,' said Ah 出 (chu), putting in his two cents. "That's why they must succeed; they can't fail. This is a time when we must exercise our ⊡ ☐ (du-wu) spirit."

Miss Qi was silent. There was no way of knowing if Yu Jin and the shock troops had already slipped into the city center. The enemy he encountered might just be Captain Mai's patrol. She recalled Captain Mai's words: "I'll die in battle here; I'll sacrifice my blood and my life for the glory of the Shan empire." She knew he meant what he said. Then she thought of Yu Jin and how the fire of revenge forced him to look at death unflinchingly. There was no escaping it: the Huhui had to rebel, Sunlon City had to be reborn, and the Shan had to fight to the end. She wondered how Miss Mei Xin, the history student, would write about this moment. Would she sympathize with the Huhui or the Shan? Or would it just be an unavoidable tragedy?

Once again Mr. Qi and Ah 凵 (chu) manipulated the wisdom beads. Mr. Qi was satisfied. "All the data is right: our chance of success is great. We've done all that we can. Now we just have to wait for the final attack."

They went downstairs and Ah 凵 (chu) turned on the skyvision. All the rebels from Sunlon City's nine bulu ought to have put on their skyvision transceivers, with which they would stay in contact. Miss Qi saw the cult members in black, the Green Snake Brotherhood members in green, and the Leopard Brotherhood swordsmen in yellow lying in wait in every corner of the city. The Stranger in Black, the three Yu brothers, the Old Do-Gooder, the Death Commandos, Gai Bo, Gai Bao, General Shi, Zhi-huang Ma, all of them certainly were waiting for that decisive moment.

"Dada, you never told me the answer to the riddle of the five jade disks. How did you find the antidote for the loyalty pills?"

"It actually was very simple," said Mr. Qi slowly, glancing at Ah 凵 (chu). "If the three intelligent people in the painting harbored no evil designs, then Ah 凵 (chu)'s answer was correct: they were all blue.

"But what if they did harbor evil designs and wanted to get someone? For instance, if there were two green disks and one blue one, then the one with the blue disk on his head would know how to respond. But if he didn't let on and let the others guess, perhaps incorrectly, then they would lose their heads. Perhaps they all harbored ⊡ (du) thoughts. Even if they didn't want to harm someone, they'd have to prevent others from harming them. If there were two blue disks and one green disk, the two people with blue disks on their heads wouldn't dare make a move and chance guessing incorrectly, only to lose their lives for nothing because the other might have intentionally not let on."

"I know," continued Miss Qi. "Even if all three of them had blue disks on their heads, they still wouldn't dare do anything rash, because the disk on their own head might be green. As a result, no one would say anything."

"That's right," said Mr. Qi, nodding. "If the prime minister possessed □ (wu) thoughts, then he would put a blue disk on each one's head. But if he harbored ⊡ (du) thoughts, he might give them two green disks and one blue one, or two blue ones and one green one. And then there's the chance that he could be in cahoots with one of them! Therefore, there is no one correct answer to the riddle in the painting. Only then did I realize that the pigment of all the plates should be scraped off and mixed together for the antidote."

"You're the wise one," said Ah 出 (chu) by way of praise. "That's the only solution for the enlightened of the Huhui world."

The three of them looked up at the painting hanging on the wall. The three intelligent people in the painting were looking at one another. Only then did Miss Qi notice that they all had the same look of utter helplessness. She couldn't help but think of the Stranger in Black, General Shi, and the three Yu brothers. Could the cult followers and different brotherhood members all fight together as one? Were the Stranger in Black and the Old Do-Gooder one and the same? Had the Old Do-Gooder intentionally tried to harm the Death Commandos? Would Gai Bo, the self-styled counterespionage agent, sell out the revolution? Why did the Stranger in Black want to leak the battle plans to the Shan? Would General Shi act in accordance with the Stranger in Black's plans? Doubts and suspicions for which no answers existed filled Miss Qi's mind.

"It has started!" Mr. Qi suddenly shouted with excitement.

Sure enough, one short and three long whistles were heard from a snake whistle—the signal for the uprising. Shortly, snake whistles were heard all over. Mr. Qi stood up and ran outside, with Miss Qi and Ah 出 (chu) right behind him. The Green Snake Brotherhood members who had lined both sides of the narrow alley had unsheathed their snake blades and were rushing toward the bulu gate. They ran as fast as they could on the tail of the lead warriors. The three gates of the Sungood bulu were open, and the warriors surged through like a tide toward the city center. Gunfire could be heard in the vicinity of the Golden Palace.

Mr. Qi was out of breath by the time he reached the gate. Miss Qi and Ah 出 (chu) helped him up to the lookout tower beside the gate. Miss Qi could clearly watch the uprising from there. She couldn't help gasping at such a magnificent spectacle.

Wave after wave of green-clad warriors, mostly from the direction of the Sungood bulu, drove north toward the Shan battle position. Two Shan patrol cars had been hit and were aflame, sending up clouds of thick smoke. Looking much like ants, the black-clad cult followers attacked the Shan from Sunart and Sundragon bulu in the east, from Sundark bulu in the north, from Sunnew bulu in the west. No sooner did one person fall than another took his place; the fighting was hand-to-hand as they at-

tacked the enemy positions, and as a result casualties were heavy. Wave after wave of all sorts of warriors from Sunbright, Sunevil, and Sunold bulu
made suicidal attacks on the Shan. But the most heart-stopping attack
came from the Sunwork bulu.

General Shi's small vanguard cavalry force had been dispersed among
the nine bulu to coordinate the action. The main force of three brigades
was concentrated in the Sunwork bulu to the northwest. Sunwork bulu
traditionally had been the center of Royalist influence, and because the
Leopard Brotherhood had ambushed several Shan patrols there, Shan suppression had been severe. But in one night, General Shi miraculously had
been able to slip his principal force into Sunwork bulu from the plains.
The general's cavalry had slowly deployed for battle outside the earthen
wall of the bulu. The second brigade of the Valiant Cavalry was on the
left; the third brigade of the Routing Cavalry was on the right; and the
crack first brigade of the Dragon Cavalry was in the center. The ordered
rows of horsemen formed three square arrays.

At the very center of the troops, under a yellow banner carrying the
general's insignia, was the general in gold armor. He raised his whip, and
the great leopard-skin drums resounded. The three brigades of seven
thousand warriors urged their horses forward. The Valiant Cavalry horsemen on the left unsheathed their scimitars; the Routing horsemen were
armed with pistols; and the Dragon horsemen in the center held lances.
The seven thousand fine horses began at a trot, but nearing the Shan positions, they picked up speed and charged at a full gallop. The cavalrymen were dressed in yellow. The three charging brigades raised immense
clouds of yellow dust and struck the Shan positions like three huge yellow waves.[1]

The Shan occupation forces consequently found themselves engaged in
an arduous struggle on all fronts: to the south, the Green Snake Brotherhood; to the north, east, and west, the Bronze Statue Cult members; to
the northwest, General Shi's cavalry. Smoke and powder rose on all sides
of the Shan position. The shock troops that were the first to slip into the
city center had undertaken their mission of detonating bombs. After a series of huge explosions, a thick smoke began to rise.

---

[1] This is the famous Cavalry Charge at Sunlon City. According to military historians, there are
only three such charges in human history worth recalling: the charge of the English Light
Brigade during the Crimean War; the charge of the French army during the Battle of Water-
loo; and the Cavalry Charge at Sunlon City.

At that moment, the gigantic purple sun of the Huhui planet once again began its slow rise to stand imposingly over Sunlon City. Under the glow of the purple sun, the Shan occupation forces, the Bronze Statue Cult, the Green Snake Brotherhood, and the Leopard Brotherhood fought in their final struggle without regard for life or death. The combatants slaughtered one another; they exchanged blows over the fallen bodies of friend and foe. Those who lost their weapons fought with tooth and nail against their enemy. The purple light of the sun also changed the color of the flowing blood. But everyone continued fighting to their last drop of blood for the glory of the Shan empire or for the rebirth of Sunlon City.

Shortly after the purple sun rose, the huge bluish gray interstellar warship rose into the sky from what once was the site of the Bronze Statue at the city center. On the battlefield, the soldiers, exhausted from killing, perhaps took no notice; but the three people on the watchtower next to the gate of Sungood bulu clearly observed the ill-omened object.

"Dada, look," said Miss Qi softly.

"I see it," said Mr. Qi calmly. "Ah 凸 (chu), what do you say?"

"Sir, there is only one thing left to do," replied the strangely shaped 凸 (chu) person. "Let's get out of here."

The three descended the tower and headed toward the smoking battlefield at the center of the city. The giant sun continued to rise, coloring the façade of every building in the city as well as the blood-spattered bodies of the soldiers who continued to fight. When the sun reached its zenith, it emitted a bright light for just a moment. But an ashen pall gradually covered the Golden Palace of the capital.

As the light of the giant sun dimmed even more, the battling soldiers gasped and raised their heads. Everyone saw the ill-omened object in the sky.

It was almost all over.

Or was it just beginning?

The shadow of death hung in the sky; the cry of death spread over the land. Death shone in the old sun, shone in the people's eyes. Everyone trembled, waiting. At that moment, time stopped.

TWO

DEFENDERS OF THE DRAGON CITY

1

Dawn in Sunlon City.

Through the smoke and ash, the giant purple sun took on a rust color. The center of the city still smoldered, and thick smoke continued to rise. On the scorched black square on the former site of the Bronze Statue next to the Golden Palace, the dead were heaped high. The Shan had made their last stand and been annihilated. Half the nearby buildings had been toppled by shell fire; the walls still standing were heavily pocked. The devastated city was burning. But the Huhui revolutionaries were victorious.

The victors stood amid the rubble, surrounded by corpses of friend and foe alike. The victors watched as the giant purple sun set. The price of victory was death. So Sunlon City was victorious.

Shortly after the last Shan stronghold was overcome by the revolutionaries, the Huhui people who had been in hiding began to come out. Wild with joy, they rushed toward the Golden Palace. The grateful populace surrounded the army; the young women kissed the soldiers and the aged embraced them. Merchants offered wine; the children gave them flowers. The people danced and shouted with joy in the square. Sunlon City was finally victorious!

"Long live the Huhui empire!"

"Long live the ▣ ☐ (du-wu) spirit!"

"Long live the true spirit of the Bronze Statue!"

Millions rejoiced at the happy news. Everyone discussed how the Shan had been defeated this time. In the morning, the army launched a full-scale attack, and before the day was out, the Shan forces had collapsed. Speaking then with the wisdom of hindsight, many said that the Huhui should have launched an uprising to throw off the yoke of Shan tyranny years earlier. Others had their doubts and wondered why the Shan hadn't used the firepower of their warship to vaporize the city. Some said that at noon, when the fighting was fiercest, the Shan warship actually did take to the air, but crashed and was destroyed. Those from the Sunwork bulu in the east confirmed that around noon they had seen a huge ball of fire fall in the direction of Five Phoenixes Mountain. But others swore by heaven and the sun that the warship never crashed, that instead it cruised once around the city and then headed swiftly away to the north. Rumor followed rumor, but it was undeniable that the Shan occupation force in the city was finished. The people and the soldiers embraced and shouted.

"Long live the Huhui empire!" shouted the Royalists.

"Long live the ▣ ☐ (du-wu) spirit!" shouted the Republicans, not to be outdone.

"Long live the true spirit of the Bronze Statue!" yelled the Bronze Statue Cult members, shouting themselves hoarse.

But the atmosphere in the Audience Hall of the Golden Palace was completely different from that outside. Despite the shouts of joy coming from the square, the leaders of the army in the hall all looked solemn and sad. Yu Fang and Yu Kui of the Green Snake Brotherhood stood with sad expressions. Deep in thought, General Shi of the Leopard Brotherhood sat in one corner, stroking his beard. His staff officer Zhihuang Ma stood beside him. The black-clad leader of the Bronze Statue Cult stood in the center of the hall, but no one could see his face for his mask. Yu Kui was the first to erupt in anger.

"Leader of the Bronze Statue Cult, what was your reason for leaking the battle plans to the Shan bastards? Lucky though we were to succeed, we did so only by sustaining enormous losses. We began with nine thousand warriors, of which only three thousand remain. Not one of the Death Commandos who was sent out to blow up the Shan warship has returned alive. Our brother himself died for our righteous cause. As you have harmed so many, what should we call your crime?"

Hearing these words, the Stranger in Black snorted contemptuously.

"Yu Kui, do you think only your Green Snake Brotherhood suffered heavy losses? Of the 20,000 cult followers who looked at death unflinchingly and who were the first to break through the Shan line of defense, only five or six thousand remain. Have we suffered any less than the Green Snake Brotherhood?"

"You Bronze Statue Cult members have always acted with an utter disregard for life," replied blond-haired Yu Fang angrily. "There is nothing strange about your losses. But we, the members of the Green Snake Brotherhood, love one another like brothers. This disastrous victory is the first of its kind in the history of our brotherhood. My brother is right. Why did you harm so many people?"

"It wasn't me who chose this strange strategy," answered the Stranger in Black sarcastically. "If Gai Bo hadn't utilized the ruse of inflicting an injury to gain the confidence of the enemy by leaking the plans to the Shan commander, do you think he could have won the trust of the Shan and wormed his way into their warship? Without Gai Bo working with us from inside the warship, do you think your brotherhood's bomb squad would have succeeded? If the warship hadn't been destroyed, we would have been vaporized, along with the entire city, a long time ago. Why are we arguing?"

Yu Kui and Yu Fang were furious and were about to unsheathe their swords and spring forward, but they were stopped by Zhihuang Ma.

"Stop! Control your anger and listen to me. Although the leader's plan was harsh, it was unspeakably difficult for him. The revolution has just succeeded, and many things remain to be done. If we become embroiled in internal conflicts, the Huhui people will be disappointed and we'll become the laughingstocks of the universe! And although the Green Snake Brotherhood and the Bronze Statue Cult have suffered great losses, the same can be said of the Leopard Brotherhood. Even if the two of you are displeased with the leader, why don't you first listen to what General Shi has to say?"

Yu Kui and Yu Fang both found his suggestion reasonable. But the General remained silent, stroking his beard, deep in thought. Yu Kui grew impatient.

"General Shi," he asked, "what sort of losses did you sustain?"

The general still was silent. Zhihuang Ma stood up and spoke.

"I will answer for the general. The charge began with 7,680 horsemen; when it ended, only 800 remained. The general is a kind and generous man, and this immense suffering has silenced him."

Everyone was moved.

"To face the guns of the Shan armored vehicles with scimitars and pistols was indeed exceedingly brave, but also exceedingly stupid," said the

Stranger in Black, and sighed. "When I made this plan, I knew we would lose many men and horses, but I never dreamed that you would dash ahead with no regard for your own safety. I can't be held responsible."

Yu Fang's temper had gradually cooled, but when he heard the cult leader speak, he was enraged.

"Cult leader," he said, "to accommodate you we accepted the fact that the plans had been leaked, but because we tried our best to stick to the letter of the plans, we suffered enormous losses. But now you shirk all responsibility and try to shift the blame to others. One can't help thinking that you must have ulterior motives. Because of the vastly superior number of your followers, you make us fight a war of attrition so that now the war is over, the Bronze Statue Cult remains the only viable power able to dominate Sunlon City. Cult leader, don't you think you are too cold-hearted?"

Hand on his sword, Yu Fang spoke, and his eyes flashed. Yu Kui was eager to have a go at it. After a moment of general terror, the Stranger in Black raised his head and laughed insanely.

"The power of the Bronze Statue Cult has always been the greatest. Even if the Green Snake and Leopard brotherhoods had joined forces, you never would have been able to overcome us. Why would I have to make use of such a lowly strategy? Okay, so you still doubt me. To prove that the cult is open and aboveboard, I order that the cult withdraw from Sunlon City!"

The Yu brothers were stunned; they never expected the Stranger in Black to be so generous. The Stranger in Black continued: "Since the Bronze Statue Cult is withdrawing to outside the city, the Green Snake and Leopard brotherhoods ought to do the same, in all fairness."

Before the Yu brothers could reply, General Shi, who had been silent until then, suddenly heaved a long sigh and spoke.

"I wholeheartedly admire you for being willing to withdraw your troops. My cavalry will return to the plains this very day, and never enter the city again."

The two Yu brothers looked at each other.

"Since the two of you have decided to withdraw," said Yu Fang, "the Green Snake Brotherhood will not delay. We will move to Hehe Village in the Hu River Basin."

The tense atmosphere in the Audience Hall suddenly relaxed. Zhihuang Ma tapped his forehead.

"That the heroes can give way to each other for the good of the country bodes well for the rebirth of the city. If everyone agrees, I would ask the leader of the Bronze Statue Cult, in his capacity as supreme commander, to issue a statement saying that the combined army is withdrawing to outside the city in order to calm the citizenry. And also that henceforth the city is an open city to be ruled jointly by the heads of the nine bulu, so that the nation might rest and rebuild."

There was no dissension from those present to Zhihuang Ma's fair and reasonable statement.

"It's getting late." The Stranger in Black gestured impatiently. "Let Staff Officer Ma handle it. I'll take my leave first."

As he finished speaking, his black robe billowed and in an instant, he disappeared. After the Stranger in Black's departure, General Shi slowly rose to his feet and gestured courteously to the Yu brothers.

"The Shan are finished. I ought to lead my forces out of the city. Staff Officer Ma, stay behind and look after things and assist the heads of the nine bulu in rebuilding the city. After the general populace has regained a sense of normalcy, you can return to Golden Goose Fort and see me."

General Shi staggered out. He seemed to have aged considerably. Head hanging, he slowly exited the Audience Hall. The shouts of joy on the square beside the Golden Palace grew louder than ever. The Huhui people had no idea of how the leaders had just jockeyed for power in the Audience Hall. All they understood was how to sing victory songs. As before, the various political factions shouted slogans.

"Long live the Huhui empire!"

"Long live the ⊡ ☐ (du-wu) spirit!"

"Long live the true spirit of the Bronze Statue!"

The sun had nearly set beyond the horizon and the purple clouds in the sky joined to form an immense purple carpet. The glowing blue shafts of light reached from the empyrean to the earth like a colonnade to protect the wounded capital. The shouts of the people in the square grew fainter until all that remained was the weeping of those who searched the rubble for lost family members. Among them was a young lady who was followed by a fat 凸 (chu) person. Dejected, they combed the battlefield. The girl cried anxiously: "Dada, Dada! Where are you?"

"Miss, perhaps your father was wounded and saved by someone in the rear. We'll search again tomorrow."

Miss Qi was naturally unwilling to listen to Ah 凸 (chu)'s advice. Her eyes brimming with tears, she continued her search, removing debris from the dead bodies with her bloody hands. By her side, Ah 凸 (chu) helped her pull one corpse after another from the rubble. He knew the odds didn't look good for her father. At the time of the last concerted attack, they had been separated by the charging crowd. Ah 㢅 (chu) stuck close to Miss Qi because he remembered Mr. Qi's orders that his first and foremost duty was to protect her regardless of what happened. Most likely, Mr. Qi was dead, but he had died a worthy death. Though he was saddened, still a fierce sense of pride welled up in Ah 㢅 (chu)'s breast. He was lucky enough to have taken part in the most important battle in Huhui history. How should he, as a historian, record the event? He knew that the victory gave value to all the sacrifices—Yu Jin and Gai Bo destroying the Shan warship; the Royalist cavalry bravely throwing themselves into the Shan line of fire; and the cult members always stepping forward to take the place of their fallen comrades. But how should he narrate the events?

He felt the weight of his responsibility and nearly forgot where he was. He didn't recover his wits until he heard Miss Qi's grief-stricken cry, and then he rushed to her side, stumbling and picking himself up as he went. Miss Qi was squatting beside her father. He lay with his eyes closed, his body covered with blood. Ah 㢅 (chu) merely glanced at Mr. Qi and knew that he would never wake. Miss Qi stroked her father's face and smiled.

"Dada, Dada, I've finally found you. Let's go home."

"Miss, Miss . . ." Ah 㢅 (chu) wanted to stop her, but she was completely unaware of his presence and continued to speak softly to her father.

"Dada, Dada, the war is over. We can go home."

"Miss . . ." Ah 㢅 (chu) wanted to persuade her to stop, but suddenly he found himself in tears. He remembered how, shortly after he had graduated from the Academy of History, he had decided to walk the length and breadth of the Huhui planet, visiting its famous mountains and rivers. He lost his way on Mount Huihui and mistakenly wandered into the restricted area of the Feathered people, where he had been captured by them and was in peril of losing his life. Fortunately, Mr. Qi, who had come to the mountain in search of herbs, rescued him—three bottles of ▣ ▢ (du-wu) pills for his life. They had become friends for life. After the Shan took over Sunlon City, Ah 㢅 (chu) quit his job as historian and became the Qi family kindermann. Every day he and Mr. Qi drank and played chess. Such a good friend and master had left him silently without so much as a final farewell. Grief-stricken, he cried and collapsed beside Miss Qi. It was Miss Qi who consoled him.

"Ah 㢅 (chu), don't cry. Let's take Dada home."

"Yes, Miss, let's go home."

Mistress and servant bore Mr. Qi away. The Huhui planet's heavenly shafts of blue light glowed. The flames from the burning buildings shone on the people moving like ghosts slowly about the square. The wind howled, and the Huhui planet slowly sank into the depths of the sorrowful night.

2

Dusk in Sunlon City.

That incomparably large purple sun hung over the battlements, as if hesitating to set. The fierce wind, carrying sand, blew over the city wall, whipping the people in the streets. The gale-force wind of the Huhui planet howled through the streets and avenues of the city. Even the gray stone skyscrapers of the Sunnew bulu seemed to shudder in the wind; but that was simply the mistaken impression of the pedestrians, because those living in the skyscrapers had no fear of the wind. If they looked out of their windows, they would see the yellow dust rolling through the city in giant yellow waves. Normally they might complain that there was too much wind-driven dust, but the waves of yellow dust that night were associated with happy thoughts. Hadn't the huge waves of cavalry under the command of General Shi fearlessly charged the Shan positions much the same way on the very same day the year before?

This was the first anniversary of the Huhui planet's successful uprising against the Shan. Inside, all families were celebrating despite the wind. The wealthy held banquets and the poor steamed a dish of sea serpent in honor of those who had given their lives. Of course, each household honored someone different: a follower of the Bronze Statue Cult, a warrior of the Green Snake Brotherhood, or a swordsman of the Leopard Brotherhood.

But Sungood bulu was by far the noisiest. Groups of young people in green uniforms carried snake swords and roamed the narrow, windy streets. The old people lit the snake lamps, which flickered with a blue flame, in their windows in memory of those who had given their lives in battle. The small food stands and the taverns were crammed to overflowing. The people loudly discussed the uprising of the previous year and the annihilation of the Shan occupation forces. Although only a year had passed since the uprising, it had already become the stuff of legend on the Huhui planet. Those who had survived the battle by luck were now treated as local heroes. Those who could tell a story sat in the taverns and never lacked an audience. Nor did they ever have to pay for food or drink. Later, the most eloquent of them became storytellers. It is said that the Huhui folk tradition of ■□ (woo-wu) speak[1] got its start with these veterans at the end of the Anliu Era.

In one tavern on this particular night, the storyteller told one tale after another, his spit flying as he jabbered away. The more he spoke, the more magical and far-fetched his stories became. The fat butcher Ah Two told how he charged the Shan with his cleaver and how he dispatched thirty-six Shan soldiers. He kept hacking away, drubbing the Shan bastards who lay groaning on the ground, but without inflicting any cuts. He thought it strange and when he looked, he saw that his cleaver was bent. He simply threw it aside and began choking the enemy soldiers to death with his bare hands, and in this way he killed another eighteen Shan bastards. But Ah Three, the taxi driver who was sitting beside him, dampened his spirits.

"No more ■□ (woo-wu) speak, Ah Two. If you . . . you were any braver, your two fat, we-weak hands would not be enough to . . . s-s-strangle anyone. A-a-actually, I was the o-o-one that dealt the fatal blows to the Shan bastards."

The taxi driver Ah Three then slickly told how he had stealthily climbed aboard a Shan military vehicle, killed the driver, and got away with the vehicle. At that moment, General Shi's cavalry was making its final charge, meeting the Shan head-on, only to fall and die in droves. When Ah Three saw what was happening, he attacked the Shan military vehicles from the rear, destroying seven at one go. His actions allowed the cavalry to punch through the Shan lines and overrun their position. Ah Three stuttered, and when someone else wanted to say something, he raised his voice, drowning them out. He grew more excited with each word and soon jumped up on the table and, gesturing wildly, demon-

---

[1] ■□ speak. ■□ is pronounced "woo-wu." Woo-wu speak is comparable to ancient Chinese storytelling, and a *woo-wu speaker* is a storyteller. Later generations apparently forgot this and erroneously understood the term *woo-wu speaker* to mean a university professor.

strated how "pow" he destroyed one vehicle to the left, and "pow," he destroyed another to the right. Pow, pow, pow, he killed with relish, until, unexpectedly, chubby Ah Wen grabbed him by the ear and forced him down from the table.

"Ah Three, I keep calling you and you pay no attention. It's just "pow, pow, pow." Didn't you hear me tell you to serve the snake soup?"

Ah Two and the guests laughed. "What an artilleryman. He can't even defend his own ears. How could he fight the Shan bastards?"

"So you think it's funny!" said Ah Wen, turning to Ah Two after collecting Ah Three. "If you're so good with a cleaver, why don't you get your ass in the kitchen and chop that umpteenth sea serpent into little pieces?"

The customers all laughed. "What a blade! He's skilled enough to make mincemeat out of the Shan, so he can go dice sea serpent meat."

The atmosphere in the tavern was a jovial one. Ah Wen was happy to have put two of her husbands in their places. Of her three husbands, two were heroes of the war against the Shan. Only Ah Four, her husband the cook, was satisfied with his lot. But no hero was a match for Ah Wen, which meant that she was better than any Shan warrior. She was feeling pleased with herself when someone spoke. "Ah Wen, what about the soul toucher of the house? Having no soul toucher at such a happy time is no fun. Ah Wen, ask Miss Qi to come."

The other customers applauded the request. Ah Wen looked uneasy. All the taverns but theirs had a soul toucher. But she knew that Miss Qi was in no mood to sing that night. All she could do was talk to the customers and have Ah Two and Ah Three pour more wine and tell more stories. Given free rein by Ah Wen, Ah Two and Ah Three began to brag about their exploits in the war.

Ah Wen went inside, where she found Miss Qi in full white mourning on her knees before Mr. Qi's spirit tablet. Ah 出 (chu) knelt beside her. The snake lamp flickered, and tears came to Ah Wen's eyes as she thought of her old master.

"Miss Qi, it's so late. Get up and have a bite to eat."

Miss Qi shook her head. Beside her, Ah 出 (chu) mumbled scripture with his head bowed.

"Ah Wen," said Ah 出 (chu), turning to speak, "Who's outside the door?"

"No one." Still, Ah Wen was startled. She pulled back the curtain; there wasn't a sign of anyone out in the hallway. She figured that Ah 出 (chu) was just being oversensitive again. Ever since the old master had died, Ah 出 (chu) had had no peace of mind. He would get out his ▪ □

(du-wu) chess manual and then make a big to-do that someone had been messing with his chessboard. Ah 㠪 (chu) seemed to know what was on Ah Wen's mind.

"Ah Wen, my 㠪 (chu) senses are never wrong. Go downstairs and see who it is."

Ah Wen was somewhat reluctant to leave the room, because the people in the upstairs hall were all very spirited. Someone led them in the "Song of Sunlon." Ah Three and a Serpent person jumped up on a table and, hand in hand, sang:

> *Sun, Sun, Sun, Sunlon!*
> *Soul of the Huhui planet.*
> *Sun, Sun, Sun, Sunlon!*
> *Master of the Huhui planet.*
> *Sun, Sun, Sun, Sunlon!*
> *The purple sun shines on the Golden Palace.*
> *Sun, Sun, Sun, Sunlon!*

The Serpent person's right and left eyes were closed, and the one in the middle was half open. He flicked his forked tongue as he repeated "Sun, Sun, Sun" over and over again as if intoxicated. Ah Wen gave the Serpent person a nasty look, because she couldn't stand it when Serpent people sang. She felt they always managed to ruin a song with all their obligatory hissed "Ssssuns." It was so boring. But it was a day of celebration, better let the Serpent people sing.

A group of Huhui people were gathered in the stairwell, keeping time. Ah Wen recognized them all as butchers from the Sungood market. Ah Two was among them, but seeing Ah Wen, he shrank away. Ah Wen pretended not to notice him and squeezed her way downstairs. The seats there were all taken, mostly by the tavern's usual customers. Ah Wen figured it had to be Ah 㠪 (chu)'s oversensitive nerves. She checked outside; the wind was still blowing. As she was about to go back inside, she heard a voice behind her.

"Ah Wen, I haven't seen you in a long time. How are you?"

The fat servant woman's mouth dropped open with fear. Ah 㠪 (chu) was really something! The person who spoke was dressed in black and wore a mask; he resembled a follower of the Bronze Statue Cult. But Ah Wen thought it strange. After the uprising succeeded, the Bronze Statue Cult and the Green Snake and Leopard brotherhoods had withdrawn, declaring that unless it were an absolute necessity, no one from any of the three factions would enter the city. What was a cult follower doing in the city?

"Ah Wen, is Ah 凸 (chu) in?"

"Who . . . who are you?"

"Don't worry about who I am," said the man in black impatiently. "Take me to see Ah 凸 (chu), it's urgent."

The fat servant woman had always been afraid of the Bronze Statue Cult followers. They had no fear of death and didn't seem to have the slightest idea of what it was. Many cult members had died during the uprising; they had all passed with a smile on their face. For a cult member, death possessed the ultimate glory of reuniting one with the Bronze Statue. Ah Wen was secretly happy that Ah Two, Three, and Four had not been corrupted by the cult; otherwise, how could she control her three husbands?

Again, the man in black spoke as if giving an order: "Ah Wen, hurry up and take me to see Ah 凸 (chu)."

Ah Wen dared not ask any more questions. She led the man in black upstairs. When the people in the tavern saw him, they suddenly stopped singing, their mouths hanging open. A cult member in the city! The customers shot inquiring glances at one another. Did this mean that the Bronze Statue Cult was breaking its promise? Ever since the three factions had withdrawn and Sunlon City had become an open city, stability and prosperity had returned. Everyone valued the peace. Why was the Bronze Statue Cult so flagrantly going against the wishes of the Huhui people?

Ah Wen led the man in black inside. Miss Qi remained kneeling before her father's spirit tablet; Ah 凸 (chu) stood by her side, his eyes looking skyward as he calmly spoke.

"凸-口品口 (chu-lu-ru-mu). Who are you? What do you have to say?"

The man dressed in black slowly removed his mask. The fat servant woman and the kindermann were both startled. Ah 凸 (chu) spoke with surprise: "So it's you!"

"It's Yu Fang," cried Ah Wen.

Yes, it was the eldest of the three great Yu brothers, Yu Fang with the blond beard. Hearing the news, Miss Qi stood up and, holding back her tears, said, "Elder brother Yu."

Yu Fang stepped forward and tightly clasped the hands of the pale and wan Miss Qi. He wished to comfort her, but after thinking for a while could only say, "Miss Qi, don't be sad."

Fighting back her tears, Miss Qi nodded. The short, fat 凸 (chu) person snorted through his nose.

"Yu Fang, have you come all the way from the village just to tell Miss Qi not to be sad? I am moved by such a great kindness. Too bad you've come a year late."

"Sorry," said Yu Fang, paying no heed to Ah 凸 (chu)'s sarcastic tone. In all sincerity, he addressed Miss Qi: "I wanted to come and pay my respects to your dada a long time ago, but the leader of the Bronze Statue Cult, General Shi, and I had prior commitments, and no one could enter the city without prior authorization. But tonight I have been able to fulfill my wish."

So saying, he bowed three times to Mr. Qi's spirit tablet.

"Mr. Qi, do you remember me? It's Yu Fang. You solved the riddle of the five jade disks and saved the Sungood Death Commandos, which allowed the uprising to succeed. Your favor has permitted the Huhui people to enjoy freedom. Now the Shan are staging a comeback, and we must renew our efforts. I hope that your spirit in heaven will preserve the success of our revolution. Please accept my respects."

"The Shan are returning to the Huhui world!" Ah 凸 (chu) leaped up in fright, the five organs on top of his head shrinking together. He reached up and scratched his nose. "Yu Fang, is what you say true, that the Shan are returning?"

"I'm not kidding you," said Yu Fang, standing up. "Ah Wen, go out and take care of the customers. Don't breathe a word of what you just heard."

Poor Ah Wen. The fright affected the way she looked. She was nearly frozen with fear and she trembled. Making an effort to keep calm, Miss Qi tried to elicit more information.

"Yu Fang, if the Shan are returning, why hasn't the city been informed? Is the city government hiding it to keep the people from panicking?"

"No one in the city knows about this," said Yu Fang, shaking his head. "That's why I hurried in. People as close as Five Phoenixes Mountain have seen Shan patrols. As far as we can judge, they are the advance party of a Shan counterattack. They are as yet unwilling to make their presence known near the city, probably because they are waiting to hook up with the main force, after which they will attack Sunlon City and reassert their rule over the Huhui planet."

The atmosphere in the room suddenly became solemn. Ah 凸 (chu) rubbed the nose on top of his head until it became red, something he did whenever he was nervous. He rubbed his nose and shook his head.

"It can't be; it's impossible. In the last year, all I have accomplished is to repair the spy satellite. Each bulu has one listening station manned by a 凸 (chu) person. We are telepathic, and if a warship even approached the Huhui planet, we would certainly know about it. The internal strife in the G Supergalaxy has already lasted fifty years, so there is no way the Shan could dispatch another warship to attack us. To put it bluntly, our little planet isn't all that important to them."

"They are not reinforcements from beyond the planet," said Yu Fang, "and we know there has been no increase in the number of Shan warships in the galaxy. But small Shan patrols have been sighted at Five Phoenixes Mountain, and that is a fact. Where are these troops from? There is only one possibility. . . ."

Before he could finish speaking, Miss Qi excitedly continued for him. "Are you saying that the Shan warship was not destroyed in last year's uprising? Then the rumors floating among the people are true."

Miss Qi's mind was filled with so many thoughts. If the warship had not been destroyed, then Yu Jin could still be among the living, not to mention Captain Mai and Gai Bo. Perhaps they hadn't died. Her heart jumped. She couldn't say if she was happy or sad. Her pale white face once again showed a little color. Seeing this, Ah 凸 (chu) was secretly glad.

"You have surmised correctly," said Yu Fang. "We thought about it for a long time, and that is the only possible explanation. Perhaps after the ship was damaged by the explosion it lay concealed in the mountains, where it was repaired over the last year and now is again ready for action. If we fail to locate its whereabouts and destroy it, disaster could be in the offing. That's why I sneaked into the city. I wanted to pay my respects to Mr. Qi and also to ask for Ah 凸 (chu)'s help."

"Ask for my help?" said Ah 凸 (chu), at first startled and then pleased. He was not willing to let anyone see the pleased expression that faced the ceiling. "I'm just a deformed 凸 (chu) person. How can I be of help?"

"The 凸 (chu) are wise. If we don't ask for your help with this, whom are we to ask? Of the nine 凸 (chu) people of the Huhui planet you are esteemed as the smartest. We need your help to locate that warship in the mountains. Besides, you are the most familiar with the terrain of Five Phoenixes Mountain."

Ah 凸 (chu) recalled with no little shame the time he had been caught on the mountain by the leader of the Bronze Statue Cult.

"You flatter me," he replied with hesitation. "Actually, the most complex feature is the underground veins of copper and the copper fields.

Where those veins extend, even the 凸 (chu) don't have a clue. Besides, the warship might have been destroyed a long time ago, and the Shan troops that have been sighted are nothing more than remnants of the occupation force."

"That's true," said Yu Fang. "But still we must eliminate these remnants, for if the G Supergalaxy sends reinforcements, they could act in coordination, making for a difficult situation."

Head raised, Ah 凸 (chu) was still thinking hard. Yu Fang, who was very direct, was losing patience and tried to coerce him along.

"Ah 凸 (chu), we musn't lose a minute. Let's go. You can consider any plan you might have when we're on the road."

"Hang on!" suddenly said Miss Qi, who had been listening to everything. "I want to go too."

"Miss Qi, it's not that I'm unwilling to take you, but locating the warship could be very dangerous," answered Yu Fang. "You are your dada's only child, and whatever you say, I cannot allow you to risk it."

Miss Qi pouted and said angrily, but in a still charming way, "Didn't I go anywhere I wanted even when Dada was alive? If you don't let me go, I won't permit Ah 凸 (chu) to go."

Yu Fang was helpless; he looked at Ah 凸 (chu). Ah 凸 (chu) knew that what she said was true. When Mr. Qi was alive he could do nothing with her. Now, Ah 凸 (chu) would do anything she said. The 凸 (chu) were a people that could not reproduce. His love for Miss Qi was no different from Mr. Qi's. The five sense organs of the 凸 (chu) were located on top of their heads, and everyone knew that they were arrogant and egotistical, but no one knew that they were far more sensitive than most people. Ah 凸 (chu) was little concerned about his deformity; he figured it was the price for his wisdom. After enthusiastically reading the histories of the Huhui planet in their entirety, he knew that the Huhui people were destined for all sorts of suffering, and that ultimately Huhui civilization would decline. But what sort of sufferings? Each time Ah 凸 (chu) thought about this, he would feel oppressed with gloom. Mr. Qi's death in battle had been a great blow to him. Having experienced the great uprising, he knew that history showed no mercy. The Green Snake Brotherhood, the Leopard Brotherhood, the Bronze Statue Cult, the Shan, the good and the bad alike could not escape death. But then who really was good, and who bad? Would all they did, all the sufferings and sacrifices, actually change the course of history? The more Ah 凸 (chu) considered the matter, the more perplexed he became. Fortunately, on Miss Qi's account he was forced to bestir himself and go on living. In order to care for the beloved daughter left behind by his master, Ah 础 (chu) could not afford to give himself up to despair.

"Ah 础 (chu), Yu Fang won't let me go. What do you have to say?"

Ah 础 (chu) lowered his head and smiled. "Of course you can go, Miss. But I must make a few simple rules beforehand. After we set off, you must listen to Yu Fang, and not run off on your own. If you promise, Yu Fang will surely let you go."

"Of course I promise," said Miss Qi, hastily. "Yu Fang, I'll obey your every order. If I don't, you can treat me according to military law."

Yu Fang laughed. As he was about to reply, Ah Wen ran in in a panic.

"Oh no! The police are here to arrest Yu Fang."

The three of them were startled. Yu Fang quickly put on his mask. Ah 础 (chu) indicated that he should hide in the closet, then he and Miss Qi left the room. Several policemen were arguing with Ah Two and Ah Three, who were blocking the stairway to prevent them from going upstairs. Angrily, one policeman pulled out his pistol.

"No guns!" someone suddenly shouted from behind. "He must be taken alive!"

Ah 础 (chu) found the voice familiar. The policemen grabbed Ah Two and Ah Three, and the officer in charge strode up the stairs. Seeing the officer, Ah 础 (chu) had to laugh.

"So, it's you."

3

The person who arrived was perhaps forty; he had purplish skin and a short mustache, and was slightly plump. He wore an orange robe. When the customers upstairs saw him, they all spoke: "Mayor Ma, ㄓㄌㄖㄇ (chu-lu-ru-mu)."

Mayor Ma greeted them.

"Residents, ㄓㄌㄖㄇ (chu-lu-ru-mu). It's dark and the tavern ought to close. Everyone please leave peacefully. ㄓㄌㄖㄇ (chu-lu-ru-mu)."

No one dared to stay; they all left in a matter of seconds. Only then did the mayor address Miss Qi and Ah ㄓ (chu). "I haven't seen the two of you in a while."

Mayor Ma was none other than Zhihuang Ma, General Shi's staff officer in charge of intelligence. When the three factions had agreed to withdraw from Sunlon City after the uprising, Zhihuang Ma had been ordered by General Shi to remain behind and assist the heads of the nine bulu in the rebuilding process. Shortly thereafter, he had undergone a metamorphosis: he had become Mayor Ma. It is said that he was chosen by the bulu heads, which made him a ■ (woo) official. Although there was no justification for his position, still he had the bulu heads behind him, and no one could do anything against him. None of the nine bulu heads was willing to see one of their number become the leader, so they promoted Zhihuang Ma to take the reins of power. He had gone from being an unknown and lowly *zhihuang* to an upstart with immense powers. His high spirits are easy to imagine. Miss Qi remembered how on the plains he had taken her to see the general.

"Mayor Ma, how is the general?"

At the mention of the general, Ma's expression changed, and he waved his hand.

"Miss Qi, I have had nothing to do with the general for quite some time. He is who he is, and I am who I am; we don't have anything to do with each other. Henceforth, do not mention his name in my presence."

Ah 出 (chu) laughed.

"You are now the number one ▣ (du) man in Sunlon City; of course you can't favor any one of the three factions. What brings you to Sungood bulu, territory of the Green Snake Brotherhood?"

Zhihuang Ma 吅卟 (lu-mu). Suddenly his eyes shone brightly. He hesitated before speaking.

"I hear that a member of the Bronze Statue Cult came to this tavern. Is that correct?"

"Mayor Ma, are you speaking ■□ (woo-wu)?" asked Ah 出 (chu). "Would a cult follower be allowed to flagrantly enter the territory of the Green Snake Brotherhood? Besides, the three factions have all agreed not to interfere in the city. The mayor knows that, otherwise he wouldn't keep repeating that he has nothing to with the general. Wouldn't it mean breaking the peace agreement for a cult member to enter the city?"

"That is precisely what I am concerned about," said Zhihuang Ma, scratching his face as he paced back and forth in the hall. Although he was the mayor of Sunlon City, he had worked in intelligence. So when he heard that a cult member had slipped into the city, he hurried over with a few trusted subordinates. On the one hand it was his duty, but on the other, he was itching to show his mettle. He looked at Ah 出 (chu) and Miss Qi and then at the policemen. "Search the place," he shouted.

Several policemen scurried around inside and out. After a while, they reported that there were no suspicious characters. Miss Qi knew that Yu Fang already had escaped, and that was a burden off her mind. Zhihuang Ma was greatly disappointed and spoke in a vicious tone to Miss Qi and Ah 出 (chu): "Do you have any idea how serious it is for a cult member to enter the city? If the other two factions were to find out, they might lead an army in, plunging the people into an abyss of misery. You understand that as residents of Sunlon City you are breaking the law if you know anything and don't report it?"

The 凸 (chu) person turned his meatball-like head, trying to think of how best to respond. He knit his brows and came up with a scheme.

"Mayor Ma, it is indeed a serious matter if a cult member enters the city without authorization. If the army were to re-enter the city, it would not only be bad luck for the residents but would also make your position as mayor quite tenuous. You have my concern."

"I don't need your concern," replied Zhihuang Ma angrily. "I have my own ways of handling this."

Zhihuang Ma talked tough, but Ah 凸 (chu) didn't realize that it was all just a façade. He smiled.

"Mayor Ma, there were a lot of customers here a little while ago. Perhaps there was a cult member among them, we really couldn't say. Do you think there could be any connection between our two factions given, our vast differences?"

Zhihuang Ma realized the truth of the statement and grew quiet, and Ah 凸 (chu) continued heatedly.

"Mayor Ma, in my humble opinion, while the nine bulu will never unite, they are all, without exception, opposed to conflicts among the three factions. It would be better to get the heads of the nine bulu together and have a joint meeting to deal with the situation. If cult members really are active in Sunlon City, then everyone can be apprised of the truth. Although the leader of the cult might be ambitious, he certainly is not willing to risk universal condemnation and will take steps to mitigate the situation."

Zhihuang Ma rolled his eyes.

"Ah 凸 (chu), what you say is true, and I am much obliged. Miss Qi, I forgot myself a moment ago. I respect your father and, regardless of the circumstances, I could never suspect his descendants. But," said Zhihuang Ma, pointing at Ah Two and Ah Three, "these two had the audacity to resist an officer and his men, for which there is no excuse. I will have to take a statement. If nothing else turns up, they will be released and allowed to return."

Miss Qi didn't really expect Zhihuang Ma to take them into custody. Ah Wen cried loudly.

"Mayor Ma," said Ah Two and Ah Three, "we are heroes in the fight against the Shan. We ask that for the services we rendered in the fight that you pardon us. When you speak on the skyvision, don't you always say that the Huhui people ought to implement democracy? Then why arrest us?"

"Democracy, democracy." Zhihuang Ma sighed. "How many crimes have been committed in the name of democracy? You have no conception of the true essence of democracy. You are the people and I am the master. Someone come and take them away."

The policemen immediately bound the two men. Miss Qi was about to protest when she was stopped by Ah 出 (chu). After Zhihuang Ma had departed, she complained to Ah 出 (chu).

"Poor Ah Two and Ah Three, to be taken away like that. Why don't you think of some way to save them?"

"Zhihuang Ma needed a way out," said Ah 出 (chu), laughing. "He won't do anything to them. We have some serious business to take care of."

"What serious business?" grumbled Ah Wen, wiping her tears away. "Lousy Ah 出 (chu), you don't know the pain because it's not your own flesh and blood. My poor Ah Two and Ah Three are going to suffer. You and your big mouth. If anything happens to them, I'll never forgive you."

Ah Wen cried, sorely grieved. Ah Four the cook heard this and in a fury picked up his cleaver and came out of the kitchen. Normally, he didn't get along with Ah Two and Ah Three, but suddenly he felt sorry for them and wanted to give Ah 出 (chu) a whack with his cleaver. Having no desire to stand around and wait, Ah 出 (chu) took off. Amid the general uproar, a man suddenly leaped in through the window.

"That's enough," said Yu Fang, who had returned. "It's late; let's go."

The fighting came to a halt and no one dared continue. Ah Wen wiped her tears away and packed a bag for Miss Qi, clucking over her like a mother hen, telling her to be careful. Miss Qi thought of how Ah Two and Three had been arrested and now she and Ah 出 (chu) were going to Five Phoenixes Mountain with no idea when they'd be back; the family was falling apart, and she couldn't help feeling sad. Only after Yu Fang urged her to hurry up several times was she finally ready. Dressed in a tight-fitting purple outfit with a snake sword at her waist, Miss Qi appeared a wonderful woman warrior of the night. Ah 出 (chu) was wearing his 卢目 (lu-mu) helmet equipped with a periscope, and a string of forty-nine shining wisdom beads left to him by Mr. Qi around his neck. Although he was short and fat, he still looked quite spirited.

"Let's get a move on," shouted Yu Fang. Then he opened the window and jumped out, followed by Miss Qi and Ah 出 (chu).

Sunlon City's huge shafts of blue light were beginning to shift. Miss Qi and Ah 出 (chu) were right on Yu Fang's heels as they made their way quickly between the shafts of light. After running for a while, Ah 凸 (chu) was panting and said something was wrong. He caught up with Yu Fang.

"Haven't we gone the wrong way?" asked Ah 凸 (chu). "The road out of the city is to the east."

"We don't want to leave the city just yet," said Yu Fang without stopping.

"We don't? Then where are we going?"

"We're going to see the Old Master."

"We're going to see the Old Do-Gooder?" Ah 凸 (chu) nearly fainted. "You're delirious. Have you taken too many ⊡□ (du-wu) pills? Since when do we want to see the Old Master?"

Yu Fang paid no attention to Ah 凸 (chu)'s protests and shot ahead. Ah 凸 (chu) knew that Yu Fang, the leader of the Green Snake Brotherhood, was a most upright man, and that he was loyal to Wu Zhongyan, the head of the Sungood bulu. He sighed over his bad luck. Miss Qi caught up, and Ah 凸 (chu) told her that Yu Fang was going to see the Old Do-Gooder. Miss Qi angrily stamped her foot.

"Yu Fang is a fool. After what the Old Do-Gooder did to us, he still hasn't figured it out."

Despite their complaints, they continued after Yu Fang. When they got to the palace, the two of them refused to go inside. Yu Fang knew that they didn't want to see the Old Do-Gooder, so he alone jumped over the palace wall. As soon as he landed on his feet, he found himself surrounded by palace guards. The palace was brightly lit. In the hall, an old man with white hair and a large mouth sat, surrounded by servants listening to a song. The guards brought Yu Fang in. When Yu Fang saw the old man, he spoke respectfully: "Yu Fang to see the Old Master. 凸-叮-叮- (chu-lu-ru-mu) to our leader."

"Well, well, enough of the ceremony," said the old man, turning his shining dark eyes toward him. "Yu Fang, you know that the city is not defended and that the members of the three factions are not allowed in. Why have you come?"

"The Old Master is very observant." He then told him about the recent sightings of the Shan patrols on Five Phoenixes Mountain. "If the Shan warship was not destroyed, they'll be back to attack Sunlon City. As leader of the Green Snake Brotherhood, I can't shirk my responsibility and must fight them to the end. I think that eventually the city will have to prepare."

"Oh! It is no small matter if the Shan warship survived." The old man stroked his white beard and thought for a while. "Well, well, we'll just have to muddle along. After all, it's just your hunch; you don't know how many Shan soldiers there are roaming around. It would be hard to bear a year hiding in the mountains with no food; they will have to come out and steal something to eat. Yes, they will have to."

"Master, the old saying puts it best: 'Don't be afraid of what is known; fear the unexpected'," admonished Yu Fang. "Take advantage of the present unprecedented unity of the nine bulu and sound the call to action; you would be sure to get results."

The Old Do-Gooder laughed, and his mouth seemingly cut his face in two. "Unprecedented unity? Are you dreaming? When have the Huhui people ever been united? Unprecedented unity? Well, well, well. If the nine bulu are so unified, I swear on the purple sun above that I'd willingly yield my seat to you."

The Old Do-Gooder laughed without stopping. His servants all laughed with him. He clapped his hands and spoke to his chamberlain Lai Fu: "Yu Fang is urging the Huhui people to unite. Invaluable advice. Let's all sing the 'Song of Unity' together."

Lai Fu led, and all the servants began to sing:

> *Unite, unite*
> *Huhui children*
> *Build a new Sunlon City*
> *With our flesh and blood.*
> *Unite, unite*
> *Huhui children*
> *Leave your cunning*
> *Or I must fight.*
> *Unite, unite*
> *Huhui children*
> *Sing the song of unity*
> *The world is one big happy family.*[1]

When they finished singing, they all burst into laughter. Yu Fang was speechless with anger but felt it improper to lose his temper before the Old Master, so he hastily bowed and left the palace. Just as he was about to vault the palace wall, Lai Fu the chamberlain came after him.

---

[1] The "Song of Unity" is a Huhui children's song that everyone can sing. See *Five Thousand Huhui Folk Songs*, compiled by the Huhui Ancient Culture Society. Unfortunately, the more the Huhui sing the song, the less the unity.

"Yu Fang, you came to deliver some secret information. Your devotion and friendship are praiseworthy. The leader told me to see you out of the city, to avoid any unwanted situations along the way."

"There's no need," said Yu Fang, enraged and shaking his head. "I can take care of myself."

"Yu Fang," whispered Lai Fu 口口 (lu-mu), "my lord suffers unspeakably. You don't understand the open and veiled struggles among the bulu lords. Even if my lord stepped bravely forward today, the other eight lords probably wouldn't be convinced, and might ruin things."

Yu Fang was very straightforward, and when he heard Lai Fu's explanation, his anger gradually subsided.

"Don't be deceived into thinking that my lord only wants to indulge in sensual pleasures," continued Lai Fu. "He's doing this for others to see. If the Shan really are staging a comeback, the Sungood bulu will be the first to offer resistance. You don't know that my lord is secretly training troops."

"So I have misunderstood my lord's suffering," said Yu Fang, genuinely moved. "Now that you've told me this, I can rest assured. So long."

Yu Fang insisted that Lai Fu need not accompany him. Lai Fu didn't force the issue and ordered the guards to open the gate. Miss Qi and Ah 凸 (chu) were waiting anxiously. When they saw him come out in a happy mood, they breathed a sigh of relief. Miss Qi was the first to speak.

"Did you see him?"

Yu Fang nodded. He told them everything about his meeting with the Sungood bulu lord as well as what Lai Fu had told him. Ah 凸 (chu) listened but didn't openly express his suspicions. He knew how stubborn Yu Fang was, and it was pointless to argue with him.

"Yu Fang, you saw who you came to see. Shouldn't we be going?"

Yu Fang laughed heartily and took off. When he was happy, he ran faster than usual, making things harder for Miss Qi and Ah 凸 (chu). The three soon passed the Sungood bulu fence and shortly came to the little Sundragon bulu wharf on the West Hu tributary. Yu Fang took out his snake whistle and blew three times. Soon a long, armored boat sailed out of the darkness shrouding the river. The three of them boarded the barge.

"Leader of the Brotherhood," whispered the boatman, "something happened on Five Phoenixes Mountain today."

"What happened?" asked Yu Fang, startled, as he leaped into the cabin. The boatman waited until Ah 凸 (chu) and Miss Qi had stepped into the cabin and then closed the door. The engine made a pumping noise and the barge got under way.

After the three of them had boarded, a member of the Green Snake Brotherhood who had been hiding hastily stood up, saluted Yu Fang, and spoke, his voice filled with emotion: "Leader, it's not good. It looks like the Shan are going to be foolhardy to the end."

"Slow down," said Yu Fang. "What happened?"

"It's the Wufeng copper fields," he replied. "The enemy has occupied them."

"And Yu Kui?" asked Yu Fang angrily. "Did he lead troops and horses to Five Phoenixes Mountain?"

The messenger proceeded to give a detailed account of the fierce fighting for the Wufeng copper fields.

4

———

The Wufeng copper fields were among the most spectacular sights on Five Phoenixes Mountain. There were about ten fields along the foot of the mountain. Each was several thousand square meters in area; they were barren of grass but covered with copper bamboo, melons, and beans. The newly sprouted copper bamboo was purple in color, but as it grew it gradually took on a patina. Some fields were better for bamboo than others and were covered with groves. The bamboo grew no taller than 180 centimeters in height; from a distance it looked square, but when viewed up close, it was actually round. The Huhui warriors of ancient times harvested the bamboo to make swords, which were called copper bamboo swords.

From ancient times, the Serpent people frequented the Wufeng copper fields. With three eyes and six limbs, the oviparous Serpent people were, according to legend, the offspring of gods and men. They were also one of the three native peoples of the Huhui planet. They were cave dwellers and had great facility for imitating other languages. The Feathered people and the Leopard people were solitary and kept their distance from men, but Serpent people would occasionally form long-standing friendships with them. For once the bonds of friendship were established, a Serpent person was a friend for life. They were known even to sacrifice themselves for a friend. But they would show their meanness and cruelty to those who were not their friends. This unusual quality forced anthropologists to admit that although the Serpent people were oviparous, they actually possessed a number of the basic primate characteristics.

Serpent people had always been active on both sides of the West Hu River. They were known to sometimes join together and attack merchant caravans, but most of them acquired some skill necessary to the Huhui people with which to earn a living. Some performed in variety shows; some traded pelts; some became skilled copper artisans; and some were fishermen. Traditionally, the territory under Green Snake Brotherhood control included the area where the Serpent people were active. Over a long period of time, the two groups maintained friendly relations. Occasionally, the Serpent people would attack a Huhui village or the Huhui would get together and kill Serpent people. When such incidents occurred, the head of the Green Snake Brotherhood and the leader of the Serpent people would mediate. Normally, the two groups lived in peace with each other.

After the success of the uprising, the main force of the Green Snake Brotherhood moved to Hehe Village. Yu Fang knew that the chaos in the G Supergalaxy would one day end, and at that time the Shan would try to stage a comeback. As in the past, he continued to train troops and expand his power over the Hu River Basin. All the land between Red Iron Village in the north to River Mouth City in the south was controlled by the Green Snake Brotherhood. With one command, legions would rise; the brotherhood was at the height of its power. Nothing that occurred in the river basin escaped their notice.

It took no time at all for the informers of the Green Snake Brotherhood to become aware of the reappearance of a small Shan force on Five Phoenixes Mountain. As soon as Yu Fang was informed, he dispatched Yu Kui and one thousand brotherhood members to garrison the mountain, and he himself hastened to the city to get Ah 出(chu)'s help and to notify the Sungood bulu lord. No one expected that Yu Kui and his force would encounter formidable resistance soon after reaching the mountain.

Although the brotherhood's numbers were great, they had grown too rapidly in the past year, which was both good and bad. The only troops who were really experienced fighters were those who had taken part in the uprising against the Shan. Green Snake Brotherhood losses had been great and of that fighting force, only a little more than three thousand survived; they all had moved to Hehe Village with the Yu brothers. The force of more than one thousand warriors that Yu Kui had led to Five Phoenixes Mountain was composed of these experienced fighters, who knew they were up against the powerful Shan and therefore were cautious. Despite being somewhat coarse, Yu Kui was a diamond in the rough as a military commander. He divided his force into three columns that advanced on the mountain.

Yu Kui's middle column was deployed slightly ahead of the other two, and thus was the first to arrive at the copper fields. It was high noon; the sun had reached its zenith and had changed from purple to gold. That huge, feeble sun suddenly emitted a flash of light, as if it had recovered its former majestic appearance of a million years earlier. Yu Kui knew that it would be hard to fight in the bright light and heat, so he motioned for the column to halt its advance to allow the soldiers to rest for a while in the cool shade.

The soldiers were nearly overcome by the heat and lay down in the shade of the trees. The sun was at its intensest at noon, and if they didn't get out of the heat, they might have been toasted. From their position among the trees they could see the copper fields apparently boiling and throwing up a green smoke at the foot of the mountain. The copper bamboo grove trembled, and the bamboo and beans emitted a screeching sound. The copper beans seemed to jump of their own accord. Yu Kui found it curious.

"You see the copper fields?" he said to those on either side of him. "It looks like the god of heaven is cooking. Isn't that funny?"

"That's called 'copper bamboo fried with beans'; it's one of the marvels of Five Phoenixes Mountain," replied one of his more worldly subordinates. "Wufeng is famous for a dish called 'bamboo fried with beans,' which was supposedly invented by a warrior-cook after he saw this noontime marvel of the copper fields. It must be prepared with a lot of oil at a high temperature, and must be cooked quickly so that it is both crisp and tasty."

As everyone sighed with admiration, the purple sun had dimmed somewhat, and the screeching sound from the copper fields gradually subsided. The copper beans came to rest on the ground; the bamboo stopped trembling; but the air actually seemed to grow hotter and drier. Yu Kui was just about to blow his snake whistle to have the troops reassemble when he heard someone shouting:

"Jade spring water, cool and thirst-quenching. Just one ▣ (du) a cup."

The brotherhood members saw that it was a big, tall Serpent person. Carrying the jade spring water, he called out as he approached slowly from the foot of the mountain. Being thirsty, everyone took out their money. Yu Kui suddenly found it odd.

"No one is to buy any water," he shouted. "You □ (wu)[1] Serpent person, come over here."

The Serpent peddler heard and came over. He was really big and tall and was covered with shiny greenish-yellow scales. The three eyes on his triangular head glared angrily. Yu Kui didn't like what he saw. He unsheathed his sword and pointed it at the Serpent person.

"You □ (wu) Serpent person," he said, "what kind of drugged water are you selling? Are you trying to ⊡ (du) us?"

The Serpent person put down his burden and curled his tail. "In this time of peace," he said, "what's wrong with doing a little business? My jade spring water is made by steeping plums and lingzhi fungus in well water from the Jade Fountain Temple on Five Phoenixes Mountain. In addition to being cool and thirst-quenching, it's also good for the liver and brain. If you don't want to buy any, fine! Why bullshit around? Don't think you can mess with me because you have so many people backing you; if you've got the ⊡ (du), fight me man-to-man!"

Infuriated, Yu Kui stuck his sword in the ground and tried to grab the Serpent person by the tail. Yu Kui was proud of his own strength and would never give in. Several jibes from the Serpent person were enough to set him off and make him fight bare-handed. Yu Kui swung, but the Serpent person jumped back, and all he hit was air. The Serpent person stuck out his tongue and smiled mischievously. He supported himself with his hind limbs and long tail; his four front limbs were readied in the shape of a 廾 (man) character, waiting for Yu Kui's attack. Weighing the situation, Yu Kui slowly advanced on his foe. The Serpent person suddenly turned and thrust his tail vigorously below Yu Kui's waist. Yu Kui leaped into the air, then hit the ground and rolled to avoid the thrust. Missing with his tail, the Serpent person tried to grab Yu Kui with his four front limbs. Yu Kui waited, rubbed his hands, and then with four consecutive blows warded off the Serpent person's claws. Yu Kui was using the ■□ (woo-wu) singular awareness fist, a special skill at which the Green Snake Brotherhood members were especially adept. Yu Kui gave a good account of himself, and the soldiers cheered. Seeing that he had missed with tail and claws, the Serpent person emitted several strange cries. The Serpent person's usual moves consisted of a thrust and a grab; having used both tricks, he seem to grow discouraged and lose heart. He roared and swept his tail, but Yu Kui was ready. As quick as lightning, Yu Kui grabbed the Serpent person

---

[1] When □ is used as an auxiliary, it has no meaning.

by the tip of his tail and, giving a vigorous shake, threw him off balance and down he went. Yu Kui pinned the Serpent person's tail to the ground with his foot and then, taking up the sword that he had thrust in the ground, he hacked off his opponent's tail, sending green blood spurting everywhere. The Serpent person gave a bloodcurdling scream, then passed out from the pain. Yu Kui laughed.

"How disgusting! How dare you treat me, a real ▣ (du) man, with such disrespect," said Yu Kui. "Now that I've chopped off your tail, we'll see how tough you are."

The soldiers all cheered. As Yu Kui savored his victory, several hundred Serpent people unexpectedly emerged from the cracks in the copper fields round about. They attacked the Green Snake Brotherhood from all sides with half pikes. Taken by surprise, several dozen warriors were killed by the Serpent people in a matter of moments. Yu Kui knew they had fallen into a trap; he hastily blew his snake whistle and motioned for the warriors to form a tight circle to ward off the attack. Within a range of two hundred feet, the Serpent people were deadly accurate with their half pikes. The middle column of the Green Snake Brotherhood found itself surrounded. The Serpent people hurled their pikes, killing many more warriors. When the situation was at its most desperate, the other two columns rushed to the rescue just in time. The Serpent people found themselves attacked from both sides and couldn't hold out, so they fled screeching toward the foot of the mountain. Pulling victory out of defeat, Yu Kui blew his snake whistle to order pursuit of the enemy. Unexpectedly, the Serpent people ran to the copper fields, where they disappeared into a hole in the ground. By the time the Green Snake Brotherhood arrived, there wasn't one Serpent person to be seen. Yu Kui took count of his troops and found that he had lost more than seventy warriors; and more than one hundred Serpent people had been killed. Although the small victory had gone to the Green Snake Brotherhood, Yu Kui was very upset to lose so many of his brothers-in-arms. Liu Qi, the experienced commander of the right column, said: "Brotherhood Leader Number 3, Serpent people rarely act in groups, but now hundreds of them have attacked us for no reason. It's strange. Given the unusual situation, I think it would be best if we temporarily withdrew from Five Phoenixes Mountain."

When he heard this, Yu Kui flew into a rage.

"Withdraw? The Green Snake Brotherhood doesn't know the word! This is an opportune moment for us to exercise our ▣ ▢ (du-wu) spirit. How can you speak lightly about withdrawing? Don't talk ■□ (woo-wu)."

Liu Qi dared not say more. Wang Liu, the experienced commander of the left column, offered his advice: "Brotherhood Leader Number 3, Liu Qi is right. The Serpent people have never openly provoked us. Isn't it safe to assume that the Shan are behind this? Caution should be our first priority."

Yu Kui stamped his foot with fury.

"You read books on singular awareness; you cultivate a spirit of singular awareness, but what have you learned? If everyone were as 卟卟 (ru-ru)[2] as you, could the Green Snake Brotherhood show its face in the world of warriors and martial artists? No, we will not withdraw. Fall in, form one long snake formation, and advance!"

Normally, Yu Kui was fairly prudent, but now he was beside himself with anger. The more he was provoked, the more hot-tempered he became. Liu Qi and Wang Liu were aware of his temperament, but they had to keep admonishing him when it was a matter of success or failure. Yu Kui's mind was already ▣ (du); he strode to the fore, and the warriors had to array in a snake formation and advance behind him to the peak of Five Phoenixes Mountain.

"Brothers, sound off!" shouted Yu Kui.

The warriors shouted in unison:

"One, two, three, four,

卟卟卟卟 (chu-lu-ru-mu)

One, two, three, four!

卟卟卟卟 (chu-lu-ru-mu)

One, two, three, four!

卟卟卟卟 (chu-lu-ru-mu)."

"Liu Qi, you lead," shouted Yu Kui, in high spirits. "Everyone sing the ▣ □ (du-wu) military song. One, two, three, sing!"

The warriors had no other choice, and like crows they began to sing:

> *Army of singular awareness! Army of singular awareness! Army of singular awareness!*
> *We are the army of singular awareness of the Huhui planet*
> *Singularly aware and ambitious are we*

---

[2] 卟卟 is pronounced "ru-ru" and means gentle and modest in demeanor.

Army of singular awareness! Army of singular awareness! Army of singular awareness!
The 凸-𠃌𠮟𠃊 *(chu-lu-ru-mu) army of singular awareness. . . . .*

Before they had finished singing, the troops at the rear of the column started to shout. Yu Kui turned to see that several Serpent people had come out of the copper fields in a sneak attack on the Green Snake Brotherhood troops. Already, one warrior had fallen, hit by a pike. Enraged, Yu Kui turned back, leading his troops to the rescue. The Serpent people disappeared at once into a hole in the copper fields. Courageous as the warriors were, in the copper fields they were no match for the Serpent people. On one side, the Serpent people vanished into a hole in the ground; elsewhere, they came out of a copper bamboo grove. Attending to one group, the warriors would lose sight of the other; the snake formation was soon twisted into a knot. The troops were led in circles around the copper fields by an angry Yu Kui without capturing a single Serpent person. Half a day had been wasted, dusk was falling, and all the Green Snake Brotherhood had accomplished was to lose another ten warriors or so. Seeing how the situation stood, Liu Qi and Wang Liu once again admonished Yu Kui: "Brotherhood Leader Number 3, we can't keep this up. Sound the withdrawal."

Although he was unwilling to retreat, after weighing the situation he knew they couldn't continue in this fashion. Liu Qi and Wang Liu took out their snake whistles and blew. Everyone ran for their lives down the mountain. Fortunately, the Serpent people were all underground at the time and didn't pursue. The army retreated to the foot of the mountain, where they regrouped. After a head count, they found that they had lost 20 percent of their force.

"Since the great uprising," said Yu Kui, his face covered with tears, "the army has won every battle; it has been all-conquering. But today we have been defeated at the hands of the Serpent people. How can I return to face my brother?"

Yu Kui wanted to take his own life, but Liu Qi hastily intervened.

"Number 3, you can't! As the saying goes: 'Where there is life, there is hope.' Even though the Serpent people are ferocious, we killed plenty. Have no fear, tomorrow we'll lure the bandits out of their hole and exterminate them."

Yu Kui refused to listen. Just as he and Liu Qi were arguing, Wang Liu suddenly shouted: "Shan bastards! So it was the Shan bastards!"

The two of them looked in the direction Wang Liu pointed. Three Shan warriors with scarlet capes had appeared in the middle of the copper fields. Although far away, they could be seen clearly, and their clothing was beyond a doubt Shan. Yu Kui ground his teeth and wanted to charge them with his sword, but Liu Qi and Wang Liu did everything they could to hold him back. The three Shan warriors walked around in the copper fields a while, then disappeared into the copper bamboo grove.

"The Shan hate living in caves," said Yu Kui. "Isn't it strange that they are living with the Serpent people?"

Wang Liu, though a boor, was fairly resourceful. People called him "Brains Wang." He addressed Yu Kui: "Leader Number 3, it's true they don't relish living in caves. A moment ago, in the heat of battle with the Serpent people, they didn't lend a hand. Why would they appear at this moment? There has to be a reason. Serpent people have poor eyes. In the light of day they are okay, but at nightfall they might as well be blind. Does that mean that the Shan are now taking their turn on duty to defend the copper fields?"

Yu Kui suddenly understood.

"The Serpent people hit us with everything they had, which is unusual considering the fact that they normally won't engage in a pitched battle. And now the Shan have appeared. There's something peculiar going on in the copper fields. Liu Qi, choose forty daredevil warriors to check out the copper fields under cover of darkness."

Liu Qi was overjoyed with his orders. He was 270 centimeters in height, and his face was as black as a skillet. He was good with twin daggers and was known as "Sharp Knives Liu." He was a famous Green Snake Brotherhood warrior. He liked fighting at night, and during the uprising he had knifed thirty-eight Shan warriors. When he heard they were going to fight that night, he was excited and immediately chose forty warriors from his own column.

The purple sun was sinking in the west, and the sky was growing dark. Five Phoenixes Mountain cast its huge shadow over the copper fields at its foot, throwing them into darkness. But in the dark, a hissing sound was heard as if thousands of poisonous snakes were shaking their tails. Hearing the sound, the Huhui warriors were absolutely terrified. Yu Kui knew that it was the Serpent people in their hole, doing their best to frighten the Huhui people as well as exchange information. He laughed loudly and ordered all the soldiers to blow their snake whistles. For a while all that could be heard below the mountain was the sound of snake whistles. So one side played the part of the snakes, and the other side played the snake charmers; they seemed pretty well matched. Originally, the Green Snake Brotherhood had been organized by snake catchers, who gradually became warriors and later developed a political consciousness, only to form the basis of the military power of the Republican faction. Normally the Serpent people feared the Green Snake Brotherhood, but today they had dared to wage war against them. It was very odd, indeed.

Both sides tried to create as much noise as possible, but the Serpent people gradually gave up their hissing because they were drowned out by the snake whistles. Wang Liu had the eyes of a hawk; he saw something wriggling in the dark.

"Leader Number 3," he said lowering his voice, "they've released snakes."

Yu Kui couldn't help but laugh.

"Releasing snakes in front of the Green Snake Brotherhood! They must really overestimate themselves. Wang Liu, you take your men and go catch the snakes. Liu Qi, take your men and detour around to the copper fields. The Serpent people will think we are completely occupied with catching the snakes and will never expect us to launch a surprise attack. Let's catch them with their pants down."

The two set off after receiving their orders. The snakes slithered toward the Green Snake Brotherhood position. Suddenly the sky lit up as Wang Liu's men shot several flares. The snakes had no place to hide. They were everywhere: rat snakes, vipers, giant pythons, green snakes, cobras, and rattlesnakes. Each one of Wang's men had a sack, and when Wang blew his snake whistle, they all began catching snakes. Yu Kui watched with interest.

"Releasing snakes to attack the Green Snake Brotherhood is like herding lambs into the wolf's mouth." He laughed. "All right kids, catch the snakes and tomorrow we'll have a feast."

While feeling amused, he heard the sound of gunshots from the rear. In the light of the flares, a Shan officer in a scarlet cape could be seen leading Serpent people, each of whom clutched four half pikes, one in each forelimb, in an attack on his rear. The warriors were caught off guard and suffered heavy casualties. Yu Kui realized that he had again fallen into a Shan trap. They had tricked the Green Snake Brotherhood into setting off flares to give away their position and then hit them as they were busy capturing the snakes. The Serpent people took advantage of the light to hurl their pikes. The brotherhood members fell one after another. Yu Kui was both angry and anxious and ordered his remaining troops to counterattack, but they were pinned down by two Shan laser machine guns. The brotherhood couldn't hold out.

"Spirit of singular awareness," shouted Yu Kui, "⊡□! ⊡□! (du-wu)! (du-wu)!"

The Green Snake Brotherhood knew the order as the last resort and were filled with grief and indignation, and were prepared to fight the Shan and the Serpent people to the bitter end. At that moment, the sound of a whistle was heard far away. Soon the sound of many whistles was heard all around.

"Reinforcements have arrived!" Their spirits rose, and they continued the fight with renewed vigor. Steeling himself, Yu Kui charged a Shan officer close by. The officer raised his gun but was cut down by Yu Kui. Two Serpent people beside him, who had already hurled all their pikes, leaped to grab him. Yu Kui killed the first one with a thrust of his sword, but was grabbed by the second. Struggling, the two of them rolled around on the ground. The Serpent person grabbed Yu Kui's throat in his mouth. Yu Kui thought it was the end; he closed his eyes and reached for the embroidered green snake on his back, and was about to pull the lead wire to detonate the bomb. At that moment, the Serpent person shook in a sudden spasm, and his four limbs loosened. Yu Kui saw that the Serpent person was dead in his arms. The blond-bearded man who had killed the Serpent person bent down to examine him. Yu Kui was overjoyed. They both spoke at the same time.

"Yu Fang!"

"Yu Kui!"

5

The moment Yu Kui saw his brother, he felt ashamed. He pushed away the dead Serpent person and got up hastily.

"Yu Fang," said Yu Kui, "I'm sorry."

"Let's finish off the enemy first," said Yu Fang. Motioning to the members of the brotherhood around him, he said, "Brothers, it's time to repay a blood debt!"

They all shouted and began slaughtering the enemy, quickly killing every Serpent person and Shan involved in the surprise attack to the last man. By the time Ah 出 (chu) and Miss Qi arrived with the rear guard, the Green Snake Brotherhood was already clearing the battlefield. Miss Qi felt sick when she saw the huge pile of dead green Serpent people.

"So many Serpent people! I've never seen so many dead ones."

"Ah 出 (chu)," said Yu Fang, "the Serpent people have never organized, never had any discipline. But they launched a huge surprise attack against us, something I never would have expected. I hate to think what would have happened if we had got here a little later. Yu Kui said that they were led by Shan officers. If the Shan have been able to train the Serpent people, we're facing a serious problem. It is imperative that we find their secret camp as soon as possible and destroy them."

Ah 出 (chu) remembered his Huhui history and lowered his head in silence. But perhaps history could be changed. Had it possibly been recorded incorrectly? In any event, they had to try. Ah 出 (chu) sighed without saying a word.

"The Serpent people fought with everything they had and died defending the copper fields," said Yu Kui. "There must be a reason. Before their attack, we sent Liu Qi to reconnoiter. I don't know if he's back yet or not."

"He's back!" someone shouted. Sharp Knives Liu, with two shining daggers in his belt, had returned. He was covered with blood and was leading a string of prisoners by a rope—one Shan officer and two Serpent people.

"Liu Qi," said Yu Kui gleefully, "you're the greatest."

Proudly, Sharp Knives Liu pointed to his prisoners and said, "These guys were hiding in a big hole under the copper fields. We groped our way into the fields and killed the sentries at the entrance to the hole. The enemy soldiers who found it too late to flee were either taken captive or killed. I brought the prisoners back."

"Did you find the Shan warship?" asked Yu Fang anxiously. Liu Qi shook his head. "The hole wasn't big enough to hold the warship. But there were underground passageways everywhere. Where they lead, I have no idea. We didn't have time to check."

"The prisoners will know." Yu Fang walked over to the Shan officer and struck him squarely in the face. Sternly he asked, "Who are you?"

"I'm an advisor to the Serpent People's Revolutionary Army," he replied. "When their revolution succeeds, you Huhui will be finished."

"Serpent People's Revolutionary Army?" asked Yu Kui in surprise. "I've never heard of it."

"True," replied the Shan prisoner. "You Huhui people were too busy thinking about rebelling against the Shan to notice. Now the Serpent People's Revolutionary Army is rebelling against the Huhui. It's your turn to see what it's like."

"Nonsense!" Yu Fang struck him another blow to the face. "The Serpent people have never understood the concept of rebellion. We have treated the Feathered people, the Serpent people, and the Leopard people like brothers. Although they were the original inhabitants, we have always considered them to be compatriots related by blood. That being the case, why would they rebel?"

"The Shan also treated the Huhui as brothers. Why did you rebel?"

Yu Fang was furious.

"The Shan are foreigners. They are not part of us, and their hearts are □ (wu). How could the Huhui be ruled by foreigners?"

"The Serpent people see you as foreigners. Why should they be ruled by you?"

Yu Fang was so angry that he couldn't speak.

"Yu Fang," said Yu Kui, "why argue with such an obnoxious character? Have him executed."

"You can't kill me," replied the Shan prisoner. "I am an unarmed advisor. Interstellar law stipulates that you cannot kill unarmed advisors as you please. In retribution, the entire Huhui planet can be vaporized."

"I don't care!" said Yu Kui, pulling out his snake sword, but Ah 亍 (chu) interceded.

"Leader Number 3," said Ah 亍 (chu), "what he says is true. If he really is an advisor, we can't kill him. Otherwise, if the Golden Planet were to find out, the Huhui planet really would be vaporized!"

"Why are you singing the same tune as the Shan bastard?" asked Yu Kui angrily. "You'll have to make a strong case for your position."

"No problem!" Ah 亍 (chu) bowed deeply and took out a small red book. "This is the Interstellar Public Code. Look, Article 16,056 stipulates that unarmed advisors are to be treated as noncombatants and not as war criminals. Article 24,523 stipulates that when two planets go to war, noncombatant prisoners should be treated well and that when the fighting is over the Interstellar Peace Tribunal will oversee prisoner exchange."

The Shan prisoner listened with satisfaction. Yu Kui was fit to be tied, and wanted to beat the daylights out of Ah 亍 (chu). Ah 亍 (chu) put away his book and addressed the Shan prisoner: "Since you are an advisor, do you recall the three major laws and eight regulations governing advisors?"

There was a slight change in the prisoner's expression, and he forced a reply: "Of course I remember them."

"Since you remember them, please recite them for us."

The Shan prisoner thought for a while, then beads of perspiration appeared on his forehead.

"The three major laws are . . . ," stammered the prisoner. "I forgot."

"You forgot the three major laws? What about the eight regulations?"

"The eight regulations are . . ." The Shan prisoner could not recall them no matter how hard he tried. He hastily protested: "What difference does it make if I can't remember? I memorized them a long time ago and now I've forgotten them."

"You just said you remembered them. How is it now that you have forgotten them?" Ah 亍 (chu) once again took out the law book and read: "Interstellar Public Law, Article 1700 stipulates that if an unarmed advisor is unable to recite the three major laws and eight regulations, he is to be punished as if he were a spy. How could you forget something so important?"

As if refusing to admit his mistake, the Shan prisoner replied, "You made it all up. How come I've never heard of either the three major laws or the eight regulations?"

"You've never heard of them? Well, let me recite them for you." Ah 厶 (chu) leisurely recited:

"The Three Major Laws for an advisor are:

Number One: After going to the bathroom an advisor must wash his hands before eating.

Number Two: No eating or buying snacks between meals.

Number Three: If he can get away without advising, he should do so."

"Those are the three major laws governing advisors?" asked Yu Kui, surprised. "If being an advisor is so easy, then I want the job."

Ah 厶 (chu) paid no attention to Yu Kui's interruption. He continued to leisurely recite the eight regulations.

"The eight regulations are:

Pay attention to results, not causes;

Ask about causes, not results.

Pay attention to life, not death;

Ask about death, not life.

Advise the good, not the bad;

Ask about the bad, not the good.

Pay attention to the small, not the big;

Ask about the big, not the small."

"That's much more profound," said Yu Kui, scratching his head. "Ah 厶 (chu), what do they mean?"

"I don't know," said Ah 厶 (chu), closing the little red book. "They must be right because they are in the little red book. Since this guy couldn't recite them, he is without a doubt a spy. Someone take him out and dismember him!"

The Shan prisoner went pale when he heard this. He fell to his knees and kowtowed as if he were crushing garlic. "Great Mr. 厶 (chu), I'm not a spy, so don't have me dismembered. If you want to kill me, have me vaporized."

"If you're not a spy, then what are you?" shouted Yu Fang. "Hurry up, out with the truth!"

"My name is Archimedes. I'm just an army cook; I'm not a combat soldier. Please spare me!"

"The Shan never ask for quarter," said Ah 厶 (chu), laughing. "You can't be a Shan if you are so afraid of death."

"What you say is true," said Archimedes. "I'm a Wula, and was taken prisoner and forced to work for the Shan and brought here against my will. I was happy when the Shan were defeated. Please free me and let me go home."

The Golden Planet of the Shan was the most powerful planet in the G Supergalaxy. The people on the Purple and Blue planets were dominated by the Shan. The Blue Planet of the Wula people was a third-rate planet in the G Supergalaxy. The Wula people love to eat and are all good cooks. As a result, they were employed as chefs by the people of other planets. Ah 凸 (chu) held conference with the two Yu brothers.

"What he's saying is true. He's no military advisor; most of them are cooking consultants. But chefs usually have the best information. We can probably obtain excellent intelligence information from him."

"Great!" said Yu Fang. "Hold him. We won't waste our time interrogating the two Serpent prisoners then. Liu Qi, you take care of them."

Sharp Knives Liu assented gladly. He took out his two daggers. The two Serpent people knew they were done for, and tears began to flow without stopping from their outer two eyes. The middle eye still glared with hatred at everyone. Ah 凸 (chu) noticed that the smaller of the two kept staring at him. Suddenly, something came to his mind; he approached the smaller Serpent person for a closer look.

"Ah 凸 (chu)," said Sharp Knives Liu impatiently, "it's late. If you don't mind, I'll take them out and dispose of them."

"Wait a minute," said Ah 凸 (chu), stopping Sharp Knives Liu. He took another look at the Serpent person and recognized him. "Ah You, is that you, Ah You?"

The Serpent person cried and shouted: "Mama!"

"Ah You, Ah You," replied Ah 凸 (chu).

That year, just before the uprising, when Ah 凸 (chu) had accompanied Miss Qi to the plains to deliver the battle plans to General Shi, they had leaped into the heavenly shaft to go to the South Gate of Heaven to ascertain the whereabouts of the leader of the Bronze Statue Cult. Knowing that the heavenly shaft could only carry two people, Ah 凸 (chu) had told Ah You, who had accompanied him, to return to Sunlon City by himself. Since then, he had lost track of the baby Serpent person. Ah 凸 (chu) assumed that he had been eaten by some beast in the desert; he never expected to run into him on the field of battle. Miss Qi had stepped to one side when the prisoners were being interrogated. When she heard Ah 凸 (chu) shout Ah You's name, she came running. Her heart was good, and she was all tears. She stooped and untied Ah You.

"Ah You, what are you doing here?"

"Miss," cried Ah You, the little Serpent person, "save me, Miss. Save me, Mama."

"Don't worry, they won't hurt you." Miss Qi then addressed those assembled: "He's still a child. Do you want to kill him as well?"

Ah 出 (chu) looked at Sharp Knives Liu; Sharp Knives Liu looked at Yu Kui; Yu Kui looked at Yu Fang. Yu Fang thought for a while.

"Since he's Ah 出 (chu)'s 囗 (du) child, he should be spared. But he joined the Serpent People's Revolutionary Army and has been influenced by them, so how can we trust him?"

"I haven't joined the SPRA," argued Ah You. "Me and Archimedes are in the same boat—we didn't join voluntarily."

Archimedes, the Wula person, spoke on Ah You's behalf.

"Everything the little Serpent says is the truth. The SPRA is an organization that was created by the Shan. Not all Serpent people are willing to cooperate with the Shan; those who don't cooperate are labeled counterrevolutionaries. They only are allowed to work as coolies in the copper fields. If you don't believe me, go down in the hole and see for yourselves."

Yu Fang remained silent for a while.

"What you say is reasonable. I suggest we rest right now, and when the sun comes up we'll return to the copper fields to see if we can discover what secret is held underground. Ah 出 (chu), we'll turn Ah You over to you. Since you are his mom, we'll look for you if anything goes wrong."

Ah 出 (chu) immediately bowed to Yu Fang. Miss Qi took Ah You by the hand, and she and Ah 出 (chu) took him the tent that had been set up for her in the camp of the Green Snake Brotherhood. The three of them sat down for a heart-to-heart talk, when suddenly they heard a scream outside. Ah You blanched and dived under the carpet. Miss Qi knew that Sharp Knives Liu had just executed the other Serpent person. She was saddened, for she had seen and heard many dreadful things since the uprising. She wondered if the Huhui had always been so cruel, or if they had become cruel in the course of their resistance to the Shan. Everyone she knew had changed; even Ah 出 (chu) was no longer the gentle, affable person he had been. The short, fat 出 (chu) person lowered his head so that his five sense organs were visible like anyone else's. He looked so mournful.

"Ah 出 (chu)," said Miss Qi, "how many people must die before we have peace?"

Smiling bitterly, Ah 屮 (chu) shook his head.

"I don't know. Even if I knew, I couldn't bring myself to tell you. Don't be sad for that Serpent person. He himself knew he couldn't escape death. If any Huhui were taken prisoner by the Serpent people, they would be dealt with in the same fashion. Who told the Serpent people to help the Shan fight us?"

"But perhaps the Serpent people didn't do it willingly," said Miss Qi, brushing her hair back. "Ah 屮 (chu), I remember when I was little my dada would take me to the western part of the city and show me the boundless plains. He told me that my mother and three brothers lay buried somewhere under the yellow sand. When they were fleeing as refugees, they were killed by the Shan. At that time I hated the Shan. I asked my dada if he hated them. He said he didn't. I thought he was lying to me. And now he too has been done in by the Shan. Sometimes I think I should hate them, but I don't. It's not hate, but . . ."

Miss Qi stopped talking.

"What is it, Miss?"

"It's a kind of indescribable sadness. Certainly I hope that we can defeat them, and I'm willing to sacrifice myself doing so, but it's not for revenge. Do you understand?"

The short, fat 屮 (chu) person looked at Miss Qi without responding. He turned and slapped the little Serpent person under the carpet.

"Ah You, come out!"

He crawled out from under the carpet. Ah 屮 (chu) saw that he had more than doubled in size over the last year. He was a young Serpent person. Serpent people grew very quickly, reaching maturity in two or three years. They might live eighty or ninety years. Because of their short youth, they never seemed to mature. Ah You was still a child: he smiled at Ah 屮 (chu), having entirely forgotten the danger of a moment ago.

"Ma, 屮-口口- (chu-lu-ru-mu)."

"屮-口口- (chu-lu-ru-mu)," said Ah 屮 (chu). "Where have you been in the last year? Tell us, okay?"

"I've been lots of places," said Ah You, becoming excited; his six limbs and tail were all moving at the same time. "Didn't you tell me to return to Sunlon City on my own? I didn't know where it was, so I just started walking. I came to a river where I ran into Uncle Zhi-Hu."

"Who is Uncle Zhi-Hu?" asked Miss Qi, interrupting, but guessing the answer at once. "Was he another Serpent person?"

Ah You nodded and continued his story.

"Uncle Zhi-Hu was very good to me. He knew I was lost and asked me where I wanted to go. I told him I wanted to go to Sunlon City to find my mama. He took me, even though he wasn't really willing. We walked and walked until we suddenly saw a patch of light in front of us. Uncle Zhi-Hu said that we couldn't go to Sunlon City because of the fighting, so we ran back to the river. We saw a huge fireball appear in the sky and watched it go thundering by. Uncle Zhi-Hu said it was bad, that the sky was falling. We ran for our lives all the way to the mountains. When we got to the copper fields, I recognized the place—it was the place where I was born! Not long after that, lots of other Serpent uncles and aunts came back. After discussing the situation, everyone decided to hide out in the copper fields for a while, until the war was over, and then go back."

The little Serpent person stopped speaking, but Miss Qi had to ask: "And after the war you stayed here?"

Ah You looked around furtively and refused to speak.

"Ah You, tell your mom what happened then," said Ah 凸 (chu).

"I can't tell you." Ah You began crying. He looked here and there as the tears flowed from his eyes. "If I tell you, they will kill me. Not only kill me but make snake soup out of me. Ma, I don't dare say."

"Don't be afraid, Ah You. They can't hurt you," said Ah 凸 (chu), trying to comfort him. "Who are *they*? The Shan, right? The Serpent people are under their control; they've become Shan slaves, right?"

Ah You remained silent and trembled. Ah 凸 (chu) wanted to ask more, but Miss Qi spoke: "Ah 凸 (chu), don't ask any more questions. Can't you see how frightened he is? Poor thing. If he doesn't speak the Green Snake Brotherhood will kill him; if he speaks, the Shan will kill him. What's he supposed to do?"

Ah You began blubbering and curled up in a ball on the floor. Ah 凸 (chu) and Miss Qi tried to coax him with some kind words, but he just cried all the more loudly. As he was crying, someone poked their head in the door of the tent.

"Who's making all the racket?" asked Yu Kui, his eyes as big as brass bells. Ah You became silent at once. "My brother spared you after seeing the look on Miss Qi's and Ah 凸 (chu)'s faces, little guy. If you make another peep, I'll send Liu Qi for you!"

"But . . ." Ah You was about to argue when a black face appeared below Yu Kui's in the tent door.

"Are you looking for me? Who's keeping us up with all the noise?" Liu Qi's eyes fell on Ah You. "Leader Number 3, this little Serpent person's ■ (woo) mouth and □ (wu) tongue are intolerable. Let me get rid of him."

Ah You was under the carpet in a flash. Yu Kui and Liu Qi roared with laughter.

"Do you really want to kill him?" asked Miss Qi, unable to restrain herself. "I guarantee he won't cry and keep you up anymore."

"Who wants to kill him?" said Yu Kui. "This is not the time to sleep. Yu Fang has ordered that the entire army be ready to march once they have eaten."

"Where?" asked Ah 凸 (chu). "To the copper fields?"

"Yes, we're going to explore that hole."

6

Before the purple sun rose, the crack troops of the Green Snake Brotherhood had surrounded the Wufeng copper fields. Everything was quiet on Five Phoenixes Mountain; the birds, beasts, and insects were all still asleep. Yu Fang, Yu Kui, Sharp Knives Liu, Brains Wang, Miss Qi, Ah 凸 (chu), Ah You, and the Wula prisoner Archimedes stood outside the bronze bamboo grove. In the dense grove, they saw the black hole.

"That's the entrance to the underground cave," said Liu Qi, pointing at the hole. "This is where we entered last night."

"This is the lair of the Serpent people," said Yu Kui, grinding his teeth. "Yesterday we lost a lot of men; today we're going to smash their lair. Let's go, Yu Fang."

"Don't be in such a hurry!" said Ah 凸 (chu) rapidly, waving his hand. "Don't be in such a hurry. Let me get everything clear, and then we can discuss it."

Yu Fang, who had always respected Ah 凸 (chu), was quick to ask: "What are you thinking, Ah 凸 (chu)? Might there be an ambush awaiting us underground?"

Ah 凸 (chu) kept waving his hand, and lifted his head skyward and began pacing. Everyone knew he was considering some thorny problem and held their breath in anticipation. After some time had passed, he was still pacing back and forth, deep in thought. Yu Fang lost his patience.

"Ah 凸 (chu), the purple sun will rise any moment now. What are you thinking about?"

"Keep quiet," said Ah 凸 (chu). "Can't you see that I'm busy thinking?"

Yu Fang had no choice but to wait. Ah 凸 (chu) continued his pacing.

"Ah 凸 (chu), we have to get started," said Yu Fang, no longer able to restrain himself. "Would you tell us what you're thinking about?"

"Okay," said Ah 凸 (chu), heaving a long sigh. "I was wondering why you have to attack the hole so early and why no one can have a decent night's sleep."

"Why . . ." said Yu Fang. "That's the way of the *Art of War* by the 凸口 (man-qia) Sage. Haven't you read him?"

"Of course I have," replied Ah 凸 (chu) proudly. "What book haven't we 凸 (chu) people read?"

"The 凸口 (man-qia) Sage says that the early bird catches the worm. Do you understand?"

"True," said Ah 凸 (chu). "Rising early is good for birds. But what about the worm? Won't the early worm be eaten by the bird? When I read the *Art of War* by the 凸口 (man-qia) Sage, I was outraged by the injustice suffered by the worm."

"Good lord, and I thought you were thinking about something of importance," said Yu Fang angrily. Then he turned to the Green Snake Brotherhood soldiers and said, "Let's not lose any more time; down in the hole we go."

"Hang on," said Ah 凸 (chu). "I know you're planning to play the early bird. Let me ask you: What should the worm do?"

"Ma is right," said Ah You, parroting Ah 凸 (chu). "What should the worm do?"

"What should the worm do?" asked Yu Fang angrily. "The worm should accept its fate and let the bird eat it."

"Or perhaps not get up early," said worldly Brains Wang. "Anyway, the lazy worm won't be eaten by the bird."

"Or perhaps it should get up even earlier," said Ah 凸 (chu), "and not wait to be eaten by the bird. It should take off."

Yu Fang thought and thought and then understood what Ah 凸 (chu) was getting at.

"What you mean is that the Shan are expecting us to attack, and they have already decamped? Then why are you taking so much time and preventing us from entering the hole?"

"Because I figure that when the Shan commander ordered the Serpent people to retreat, they positioned a suicide squad to defend their rear. That squad, I'm sure, is composed of Serpent people. There are so few

Shan that they wouldn't sacrifice even one of their own. Although the Serpent people are selfish by nature, they would give their lives to cover the retreat of their fellows. Once the old and the weak and the women and children have been evacuated, the suicide squad will then also run away. If we put off entering the cave a little longer, we won't run into any crack suicide squad or sacrifice anyone on our side."

In spite of what Ah 㢊 (chu) said, the Green Snake Brotherhood warriors were not willing to wait any longer. With an angry shout and brandishing his sword, Yu Kui led the charge on the hole. Sharp Knives Liu and Brains Wang, who were to lead the troops in a surprise attack, followed on his heels. Yu Fang shook his head and brought up the rear with Ah 㢊 (chu), Ah You, Miss Qi, and Archimedes. The tunnel was narrow and winding, so everyone had to crawl on their hands and knees. After some distance, the cave opened out and they could walk upright. After walking farther, they entered a huge cave under the copper fields, the lair of the Serpent people, one of the three original peoples of the Huhui world.

Miss Qi's eyes roamed as she breathed the cool air. It was the first time she had seen such a big cave. From ancient times, the veins of copper had existed beneath the copper fields. Some people suspected that they ran all the way to the center of Sunlon City, where they had inflated the Bronze Statue, gradually making it the huge object it became. But that was just a surmise; no one really knew for certain where the copper veins ran. Only after she saw the huge cave did Miss Qi draw the connection between the copper fields and the growth of the statue.

In the light of the warriors' flashlights, countless small black holes were visible in the walls of the cave. Pointing at the small holes, Ah 㢊 (chu) addressed Yu Fang and Miss Qi: "Those are the dens of the Serpent people. They spend their days wandering, but when they reach the time of mating and giving birth, they always return to the copper fields. As long as an old Serpent person can still walk, he'll return here to die. Those holes were all bored by the Serpent people: those are their homes, and their graves."

Miss Qi carefully examined the holes, where she did see the dried, black corpses of Serpent people. She shuddered and dared not look again.

"Serpent people are cruel and belligerent," continued Ah 㢊 (chu). "No one would dare enter their lair. In the past, when the Shan tried to buy over the Serpent people, they were never successful. It's strange that they are now able to control them."

Yu Fang grumbled.

"If it weren't for you, we would have captured the Shan bastards. What should we do now?"

"We wouldn't have entered here with such ease if the Serpent people were here to fight," said short, fat Ah 出(chu), bowing. "We should at least determine if the warship wasn't destroyed and was concealed here. Perhaps we should ask him where the Shan have fled."

Ah 出(chu) was pointing at Archimedes, who was so frightened that his knees were knocking together. He thumped to his knees and said, "Warrior Yu Fang and Mr. 出(chu), I'm just a cook. I've never been to this place before, much less know where everyone has gone."

"Nonsense," said Yu Fang. "You were working for the Shan. Why wouldn't you know? Listen carefully: tell us where the warship is and you'll be spared; otherwise, don't expect ever to leave this cave!"

Archimedes was in tears. He pleaded, "Warrior Yu, do you think a small potato like me would be allowed on the warship? I'm just a cook for the 71st Company of the Border Defense Corps of the Shan Occupation Army. My company was stationed at Red Iron Village. After the Huhui uprising, we fled with the company commander to Mount Huihui. Last month, the company commander received word that we should proceed at once to Five Phoenixes Mountain. The commander told us that the Serpent People had organized a revolutionary army and that we were going to join forces with them and retake Sunlon City. We've been fighting a guerrilla war this month, and our company is nearly decimated. I honestly don't know where the warship is."

"Oh," said Yu Fang suspiciously. "Your company commander never told you the whereabouts of the warship? Where is the Shan headquarters?"

Archimedes shook his head.

"He might be speaking the truth," said Ah 出(chu) to Yu Fang. "I think the Shan commander's plan is pretty obvious. He is inciting the Serpent people to rebellion; he's probably doing the same with the Feathered people and the Leopard people. He knows the Serpent people lack discipline, so he sends the remnants of the Shan forces here to act in concert with them. Once the three original Huhui peoples have rebelled and the Huhui forces are tied down, Sunlon City will be isolated and defenseless. Then he'll muster the Shan forces and attack Sunlon City. His plan is nothing less than pure treachery."

"If that's the case," said Yu Fang, "then the main Shan force is not on Five Phoenixes Mountain at all. Where is it, then?"

Yu Fang paced about in an agitated state of mind; the Green Snake

Brotherhood warriors who had gone out to search had all returned to report that there wasn't a trace of a Serpent person or the Shan. Yu Fang knew that it was pointless to keep searching. He ordered them to eat their field rations. He called a meeting of the Green Snake Brotherhood cadres. They sat down in a circle to discuss their next step.

Yu Fang then related to everyone what Ah 丑 (chu) had just said. Yu Kui leaped up and said, "What are we doing here if the Shan do have such an evil plan? Let's get back to Sunlon City. If we lose the city, the Huhui will be finished."

"Don't get so excited," said Yu Fang. "Sunlon City is an open city, and we can't enter it on a whim. We must first have the agreement of General Shi and the leader of the Bronze Statue Cult. The three parties must be of one mind in the defense of the city."

"You're wrong," said Yu Kui. "Why should we cooperate with a deceitful person like the cult leader? There's not much left of General Shi's crack cavalry, so there is no need to work with him. I think that when it comes to the fate of the city we can rely on no one but ourselves, the Green Snake Brotherhood!"

Everyone applauded and said this was well spoken. Sharp Knives Liu stood up and said, "Yu Kui said what we are all thinking. We all want to return to Sunlon City. Who doesn't want to go home when our families are all there? With the Shan staging a comeback, it is only natural that we should return and protect the city. General Shi and the leader of the Bronze Statue Cult might be displeased, but they have no reason to oppose us. I am in favor of withdrawing and returning immediately to Sunlon City!"

Everyone clapped and said this was well spoken. Yu Fang cut off their applause so that Ah 丑 (chu) could stand and speak. Ah 丑 (chu) bowed to the company.

"Green Snake Brotherhood officers and honorable revolutionaries, the Shan have stirred up rebellion among the Serpent people, to the anger of gods and men alike. At present, Sunlon City is not in danger. If the Green Snake Brotherhood enters the city, we will provoke an attack by the Leopard Brotherhood and the Bronze Statue Cult, which will only lead to infighting among the three factions. Even if the Green Snake Brotherhood triumphs, its strength will be diminished, giving the Shan the chance they are looking for. Having studied Huhui history, I have come to the conclusion that defending the city to the death will destroy the nation. I won't speak of distant things; the Shan are a good recent example—they sought to hold the city to the last and were defeated by our combined army. The Shan retreated to the mountains to wage a guerrilla war and to stir up the original peoples; this can be characterized as a □ (wu) formation. If we return to Sunlon City and defend it to the end, that will create what could be described as a ⊡ (du) position. The ancient ⊟⊡ (man-qia) Sage said it wisely: 'transform ⊡ (du) into □ (wu); subdue ⊡ (du) with □ (wu).' The Shan strategy coincides with this truth. Their retreat from Sunlon City is to transform ⊡ (du) into □ (wu); to surround ⊡ (du) with a □ (wu) position is to subdue ⊡ (du) with □ (wu). Shan headquarters appears to have competent men who should be taken seriously."

Nobody said a word. Yu Kui was the first to object.

"There's no reason to strengthen their ambitions while destroying our own power and prestige. What's the big deal about the Shan collaborating with a few Serpent people? We destroyed their warship, so why be scared of a few surviving troops?"

"Don't be so hasty," said Yu Fang. "Ah 凵 (chu), in your view, what should we do?"

"In my humble opinion," he said, without missing a beat, "the worst thing we could do would be to return to Sunlon City and wait for a fight; to fight with the Serpent people of Five Phoenixes Mountain is only slightly better; to launch a direct attack on the Shan command should be our first priority. Even if we fail to locate the warship, we can keep up our attack on the Shan, forcing them off balance and preventing them from forming a □ (wu) formation. In this way they will never be presented with an opportunity to attack Sunlon City. The ⊟⊡ (man-qia) Sage said . . ."

As Ah 凵 (chu) spoke, proud of his own eloquence, no one noticed a person moving toward the edge of the cave save for Miss Qi, who had sharp eyes.

"Someone is getting away!"

The warriors were eating their rations of salty rice balls and sea serpent when they heard Miss Qi shout. They stood up, but too late—the person ducked into a hole. Several warriors ran to the cave, where they pointed their flashlights.

"Who was it? Who was it?" asked Yu Fang.

Everyone present looked at everyone else. Miss Qi looked around and then said, "It was Archimedes, the Wula prisoner, and . . ."

Before she finished speaking, Yu Kui shouted furiously: "That little Serpent person Ah You also ran away. Brothers, catch them, quick!"

The warriors were on the point of dividing up when someone shouted,

"Over there!" They looked to the opposite end of the cave, where they could see a rapidly moving shape struggling up the slope. They took out their laser guns and shot. Miss Qi was scared for Ah You, but he was gone in a flash. Yu Kui grabbed Ah 凸 (chu) by the neck and picked him up.

"You useless 凸 (chu) person. First you wouldn't let me go down in the cave, allowing all the Shan bastards to escape; then you opposed returning to Sunlon City so as to pursue the Shan bastards instead. And now your little adopted son has run off. All your ideas are lousy. 凸 people are wise. . . . I think you're as a dumb as a sea serpent."

Yu Kui had hold of him as if he were a chicken and shook him in the air. Fortunately he was unharmed because the 凸 (chu) have thick necks. Yu Fang ordered Yu Kui to stop several times before he reluctantly put Ah 凸 (chu) down. As soon as Ah 凸 (chu)'s feet touched the ground, he bowed deeply to Yu Fang.

"Yu Fang, 凸-凸哻凸 (chu-lu-ru-mu), felicitations are in order. Archimedes and Ah You have fled, providing the Green Snake Brotherhood with a course to follow. I suggest that the troops divide up and pursue them to the end and see where they go."

Yu Kui was so angry he nearly collapsed.

"You see how deceitful the 凸 (chu) are," said Yu Kui to himself. "His adopted son runs away and not only is he not ashamed, but he even congratulates Yu Fang! Now he wants us to give it our all to pursue them deeper underground. I can't believe that there is such a scoundrel under the purple sun. But the scoundrel has pulled the wool over my brother's eyes; my poor brother still believes he has wise counsel to offer. Okay! When my brother isn't looking, I'll fix him!"

His mind made up, Yu Kui spoke to Yu Fang: "Brother, Ah 凸 (chu) is right. As the saying goes: 'You can't catch a snake unless you enter his lair.' We should do as he says and divide into two groups to pursue them."

"That's what I was thinking," said Yu Fang, nodding. "There must be tricks to these underground passageways. We'll each take ten suicide soldiers and go in pursuit. The rest of the men should return topside to the copper fields and await further news."

Yu Kui shook his head.

"You are the head of the brotherhood, and cannot ignore your responsibility as leader. If we both go down in the cave, who will be left in command? It would be better to let Liu Qi and Wang Liu lead one group while Ah 凸 (chu) and I lead the other. If we don't come out within five days, don't wait for us. Protecting Sunlon City is more important."

Yu Fang listened without offering any opposition. He just ordered them all to be extra cautious. Ah 出 (chu) moaned and groaned but couldn't say he didn't want to go. He hastily said good-bye to Miss Qi. Miss Qi was sad because she knew that this time, things would most likely be difficult for the 出 (chu) person. Before Miss Qi could say anything, Yu Kui, laughing malignantly, had already picked him up with one hand.

"Ah 出 (chu), let's explore farther underground. We'll have to rely on you to guide us through the labyrinth. But if you come up with any more lousy ideas, it won't be me who is in trouble. Let's go find your adopted son!"

Ah 出 (chu) was half pulled and half pushed into the hole in which Ah You had disappeared. Ah 出 (chu) struggled and said, "Yu Kui, I don't know where this passageway leads. We must be careful to avoid any danger."

"Ha ha." Yu Kui laughed in the dark. "You were the one who said we have to give it our all. And now it's you who is saying we have to avoid danger. You can trick my brother with that act of yours, but not me. You wise 出 (chu) people just rely on your mouths. Come along, you lead the way since you're so capable."

Yu Kui really did put Ah 出 (chu) down. Nothing scared the short, fat 出 (chu) person more than the dark. With fear and trepidation, he felt his way forward. When he slowed down, Yu Kui prodded him along with his sword. Ah 出 (chu) cried out for help but to no avail; he just had to steel himself and continue forward. Covering one stretch, he noticed he was moving faster and faster, and Yu Kui no longer prodded him. Ah 出 (chu) was secretly happy, and with Yu Kui no longer right on his tail, he sat down to rest. He reached out to one side and touched a bunch of icy scales. Startled, he tried to sound out who was there.

"Is that you, Ah You? Here you are, and you've made your poor ma look all over for you. Let's go back together."

He continued touching the scales as he spoke. The Serpent person sitting there didn't move in the slightest. The more Ah 出 (chu) touched, the more frightened he became. As he was about to pull his hand back, a huge hand grasped him tightly. Poor Ah 出 (chu) screamed and nearly had a heart attack. Behind him, Yu Kui laughed.

"What are you screaming about? Why scream when you've found your son?"

Yu Kui turned on his flashlight and was nearly frightened out of his wits. It wasn't Ah You sitting beside Ah 出 (chu), but rather the biggest Serpent person he had ever seen. It was entirely covered with green scales and twice as big as any Serpent person he had fought the previous day. Its three eyes shone with a greenish glow. It held Ah 凸 (chu) with one hand and blocked the way with the other five. Its huge tail was coiled behind it. Yu Kui had never seen such a nasty-looking Serpent person and couldn't help being afraid. Ah 凸 (chu) struggled desperately and shouted. His tears also began to flow. Impatiently, the Serpent person used another hand to cover his mouth. When Yu Kui looked back and saw the ten suicide soldiers had come up behind him, he felt a little calmer and stepped forward bravely.

"You □ (wu) Serpent person! Why are you blocking the way? You should know that a good dog doesn't block the road, and a good snake doesn't block the hole. Put him down and get out of the way this minute! Otherwise you risk losing your head."

As he listened to this, the gigantic Serpent person's three eyes blinked and he swung his tail and smiled.

"Oh my! Methinks to have my head sundered from my body is not a thing so fine. A stranger to shame I am not, for I have failed to cultivate virtue. Will he who first stops the cave not be followed? No, no. I like not to empeach the way, but I am obliged."

When Yu Kui heard the Serpent person's odd, old-fashioned speech, he was so startled that he nearly dropped his snake blade. He asked, "You □ (wu) Serpent person, who are you?"

The gigantic Serpent person raised his two forelimbs and pumped them up and down as a greeting.

"I am hight Zhi-Hu Zhe by name. Zhi-Hu is my double surname; Zhe, my given name. For generations I have guarded 凸 凸 (chu-ru) Pass. Maistre Zhi-Hu am I ycleped by all."

Yu Kui listened without saying a word. Ah 凸 (chu) freed his mouth with ease from the Serpent person's grasp.

"So this is 凸凸 (chu-ru) Pass," said Ah 凸 (chu), panting. "There is a saying that goes: 'Those who enter and exit are all heroes, and he who quails is not a man.' Who would have thought that we would stumble on the Huhui planet's Number One Underground Pass?"

Hearing this, the gigantic Serpent person was mighty pleased. He immediately put Ah 凸 (chu) down.

"Sorrowe subdews mee to see the world so declined. There are no more men of wisdom. Knowing of the Number One Underground Pass, certes you must a 凸 (chu) person be, no?"

Ah 凸 (chu) bowed to the gigantic Serpent person.

"I am pleased to meet you, Mr. Zhi-Hu. You are a Serpent person, and Zhi-Hu is the grandest of Serpent surnames. Are you not then the senior member of the Serpent People Clan?"

Zhi-Hu Zhe was overjoyed.

"I am none other. Might you be Ah 凸 (chu), the Huhui sage? No wonder so clearly wise you seeme."

"You flatter me," said Ah 凸 (chu), bowing. "Mr. Zhi-Hu, it has been ordained that we should meet. I am pleased to meet your awe-inspiring personage, but never thought to make your acquaintance underground. Your reputation is well deserved."

Zhi-Hu was so flattered by Ah 凸 (chu)'s remarks that he scarcely knew where to put his tail. Watching the two of them boast and fawn, expressing regrets that they had not met earlier, Yu Kui was furious. He ordered the soldiers to raise their laser guns and aim and fire at the gigantic Serpent person. Ah 凸 (chu) was startled at the turn of events.

"We're all friends here; we can talk things through. We're all good friends—tell the soldiers to lower their laser guns."

"No," said Yu Kui, angrily. "I've never heard of a 凸口 (chu-ru) Pass underground, and that it's called the Huhui planet's Number One Underground Pass. If he is the hero who guards this pass, I want to see what he's made of."

"Don't cause trouble. Number One Pass separates the world into ■ (woo) and □ (wu). If we discuss it with Mr. Zhi-Hu, I don't think there will be any problem for him to let us go to the ■ (woo) world. . . ."

Before Ah 凸 (chu) had finished speaking, Yu Kui gave the order to fire. Zhi-Hu was big and fast. He didn't wait for anyone to open fire, but with a forceful spring of his tail he bounded deeper into the cave. The laser beams hit the stone wall. Zhi-Hu Zhe laughed crazily in the darkness. Yu Kui ordered the soldiers to push forward. As they hesitated, two copper doors slowly closed, sealing off the passageway. Everyone was startled.

"This is bad," said Ah 凸 (chu). "Run for your lives!"

Before he finished speaking, two more copper doors closed behind them, sealing off the return route. The warriors panicked and shot at the doors, but they were thick and impervious. Ah 凸 (chu) blamed Yu Kui.

"It's all your fault. You pissed him off, and we're all done for."

Although he had regrets, Yu Kui refused to admit his mistake. He faced the copper doors and shouted: "Zhi-Hu Zhe, no real man would take a path of action like yours. If you've got any ⊡ (du) at all, you'll come out and fight like a man."

He shouted several times before a small window in the copper doors opened. Zhi-Hu poked his head in and said, "⊥ ⊤ (chu-ru) Pass is the first underground pass. True knights be those who enter and exit again; he who quailes is of manhood fraile. I bolt the pass and I unbolt the pass. If thou but hazard thy life, passage wilt be rendered facil for thee. If thou wilt but assay to fight with mee in single lists and succeed in ouerthroing mee, I shall passage open for thee."

Everyone just stared blankly. Ah ⊥ (chu) bowed to Yu Kui.

"Mr. Zhi-Hu has challenged you. Let us see your glory."

Yu Kui gasped, then steeled himself and approached the door. The copper doors opened halfway, allowing Yu Kui to enter, after which they closed once again. Everyone listened carefully. The sound of fighting could be heard on the other side, then suddenly all was quiet. After a while, the window opened again and Zhi-Hu poked his head out and said, "Next!"

Everyone paled with fear. Ah ⊥ (chu) addressed the soldiers: "Never could today's turn of events have been imagined. Since you are all suicide soldiers, you must prepare to exercise your ⊡ □ (du-wu) spirit."

Hearing this, the soldiers all went pale. Again Zhi-Hu called for one of them. One quaking soldier approached the door. Shortly after he entered, the window opened again. Zhi-Hu once more shouted: "Next!"

One by one, the ten soldiers all entered through the door until only Ah ⊥ (chu) was left. Again, the Serpent person opened the door and shouted: "Next!"

Ah ⊥ (chu) -▯▯- (lu-mu). He really was the only one left. In a quaking voice he said, "Mr. Zhi-Hu, I am a sage and have never studied the art of insult. Your victory will be won without a fight. Wouldn't it be better just to spare me?"

"That I cannot do. One and all ⊡ □ (du-wu) must assay. You mean you are incapable of singular awareness?"

Frightened, Ah ⊥ (chu)'s legs nearly gave out; he couldn't budge. The gigantic Serpent person waited impatiently before opening the door and coming out. Ah ⊥ (chu) knew there was no escape, so summoning what courage remained, he sadly shouted: "Long live the spirit of singular awareness!" Then he charged.

7

On Five Phoenixes Mountain, Miss Qi and Yu Fang waited a long time at the copper fields for the return of the suicide soldiers who had gone underground. Before they knew it, five days had passed. On the morning of the fifth day, Liu Qi and Wang Liu came out of the cave, their faces as pale as ghosts. Of the ten soldiers who had accompanied them, only five remained. They told Yu Fang that the underground passageways were as close-knit as spiderwebs. Shortly after entering, they had lost their way and wandered around for three days before they were luckily able to find their way out. Miss Qi knew that the other group must have been less fortunate and she couldn't help but shed a tear. At nightfall, there was still no news of Yu Kui and Ah 出 (chu). Yu Fang gave orders to break camp. Miss Qi asked to stay behind and wait for Ah 出 (chu), but Yu Fang would not hear of it. He reminded her that because the Serpent guerrillas were still active on the mountain and the soldiers' chances were slim, there was no reason to risk waiting.

That night, the principal Green Snake Brotherhood force withdrew from the copper fields, crossed the West Hu River, and assembled on the eastern outskirts of Sunlon City. Yu Fang knew that the Shan-controlled Serpent people who had escaped the copper fields would attack again. His order that the barges should undertake armed patrols to defend the city from attacks by the Serpent people spread down the Hu River Basin like wildfire. He also ordered that the Green Snake Brotherhood forces be stationed in a defensive line from Red Iron Village to Hehe Village to River

Mouth City to be especially alert and prepared at any time for the enemy to cross the Hu River for a large-scale battle.

The news of the fierce fighting between the Green Snake Brotherhood and the Serpent people at the Wufeng copper fields spread rapidly through Sunlon City. The inhabitants of the city were jittery, and it was widely rumored that Shan reinforcements had landed at Five Phoenixes Mountain and that a fleet of dragon-class dreadnoughts had entered and were cruising in the Huhui galaxy. Bombings occurred continuously all over the city, and Serpent People's Revolutionary Army slogans appeared everywhere. With these frights, some people began preparing to flee. Although the nine bulu lords jointly tried to calm the public—Mayor Ma was constantly on the skyvision calling for calm—still panic buying occurred as the people swarmed to the market to buy food and canned goods. There was price inflation in the city, and needless to say, profiteers were active. The city government arrested a bunch of Huhui profiteers and vaporized several Gaiwenese speculators but could not control the violent inflation. The more pessimistic residents fled the city with their valuables. But most of the Huhui people adopted a wait-and-see attitude. Sunlon City was facing misfortune, something that had happened all too frequently in the past. Thus, most of the fatalistic Huhui people, who had often lived as refugees, waited until the last minute before leaving the city. The poor feared that leaving meant death; the rich wanted to keep up their lives of comfort and ease. Whatever the reason, they would always be too late for regrets.

The Green Snake Brotherhood forces, which had assembled on the eastern outskirts, saw the trickle of refugees coming out of the city, and morale began to sink. Most of the warriors were from Sungood bulu; it had been more than a year since they left the city after the uprising, and they couldn't help but feel homesick. Rumors pervaded the city and spread among the Green Snake troops outside the walls. It was rumored that the city government had surrendered unconditionally to the Shan. It was also rumored that the Sungood bulu lord unfortunately had been killed in interbulu quarrels. Rumor also had it that the Bronze Statue Cult was already in complete control of the city. As the rumors increased, the troops grew more restless. Older warriors such as Liu Qi and Wang Liu hurried to see Yu Fang, the brotherhood leader.

"Sir, the men are restless. If we don't enter the city quickly, we might not be able to maintain discipline."

"Previously we agreed with the Bronze Statue Cult and the Leopard Brotherhood that none of us would enter the city alone," said Yu Fang, stroking his beard. "If we go back on our word now, who will trust us in the future?"

"Sir," remonstrated Liu Qi, "inside and outside the city, everyone is panicky. By entering, we will not be going back on our word but rather proving to the thousands of Sunlon City residents that it is the Republicans who care most about the people."

Shaking his head, Yu Fang would not consent.

"Already I have sent letters asking General Shi and the leader of the Bronze Statue Cult to send troops. I figure that the Leopard Brotherhood cavalry will be here in a matter of days. The cult leader will get wind of it soon enough, as he has spies everywhere. When they arrive, we will join forces and enter the city."

Wang Liu and Liu Qi knew that Yu Fang's mind was made up, so they said no more. The Green Snake Brotherhood soldiers who assembled to the east outside the city began making an uproar. The green-clad soldiers held demonstrations beneath the city wall and shouted a slogan: "Give us back Sunlon!" Some ran to the city's eastern gate and cursed the policemen on guard there for not allowing them in. But in fact, how could the twenty or so city policemen watching the gate keep the thousands of Green Snake Brotherhood warriors out? Due to the severity of the Green Snake Brotherhood rules and the fact that they had not obtained their leader's permission, the warriors dared not rashly enter the city. All they could do was shout. But the noise they made soon attracted a crowd of residents. The skyvision reporters got wind of what was happening and also showed up at the eastern gate. They reported on the experiences of the warriors during the uprising, how they defeated the Serpent People's Revolutionary Army at Five Phoenixes Mountain, and how they had rushed back to protect the city but were denied entry. The soldiers who appeared on the skyvision screens spoke with their faces covered with tears. The Huhui people who saw them were moved and sent messages of protest with their brainwaves to the government via skyvision. Soon Zhihuang Ma, the mayor, showed up in person to entertain the troops. They were given wine, fresh fruit, snake soup, and Sungood bulu specialties such as sea serpent jerky and blue wine. The warriors were overjoyed and cheered. Mayor Ma shook hands with the troops and wished them ㄔㄌㄖㄇ (chu-lu-ru-mu). These precious images naturally appeared simultaneously on the skyvision screens. The people were satisfied with what they saw. The residents were comforted to know that the troops were right outside the city. Feeling much easier, a number of those who had made up their minds to flee now decided to wait.

Puffed up and satisfied with the way he handled the troops, Mayor Ma went to see Yu Fang in his tent. Miss Qi, who was there as an onlooker, discovered that Mayor Ma, that frustrated zhihuang who had once been one of General Shi's staff officers, was attired much differently from the last time she had seen him at the Qi family tavern. At that time, he was dressed in the orange robes of a civil official, but now he was wearing a sharp khaki military uniform with a belt across his shoulder. A laser gun was stuck in the belt at his waist; he wore black riding boots, had three rows of medals on his chest, and had a slight paunch. When Zhihuang Ma met Yu Fang, he clicked his heels together and made a singular awareness salute.[1]

"Brotherhood leader, ㄎ-ঢ়ᆍ-, ⦿□ ⦿□ (chu-lu-ru-mu, du-wu du-wu)!"

"Mayor Ma, ㄎ-ঢ়ᆍ- (chu-lu-ru-mu)." replied Yu Fang. "Not only are the troops grateful that you personally have come to entertain them, but also you have my admiration. You are an official who truly loves the people as if they were his own children."

"You are far too polite; it is my duty as mayor," said Zhihuang Ma, his expression unchanged. "Your loyalty shines. You led your troops to defeat the Serpent people on Five Phoenixes Mountain and then rushed here to protect the city. I am moved. But after the uprising, the three factions agreed that Sunlon City would be inviolably an open city where troops would never be stationed again. You yourself signed the agreement. So why have you violated the treaty and brought an army here?"

"I am aware of all that," said Yu Fang. "That's why I have given the order that no one is to set foot inside the city. The Green Snake Brotherhood will not enter without the agreement of the other two factions."

"You really can be counted on," said Zhihuang Ma. "But soldiers, like snakes, are easily released but difficult to recall. The Green Snake troops are stationed outside the city now, but that might change at the slightest sign of trouble, and then you won't be able to control the situation. Therefore, I think it best that you return to Hehe Village. If the city finds itself in danger, then you can come to our rescue."

Hearing this, Miss Qi couldn't help asking, "Mayor Ma, Sunlon City is already facing great danger. If the Shan can incite the Serpent people to

---

[1] The du-wu salute consists of a mouth and hand gesture. First a person opens their mouth and sticks out their tongue, as represented by the character ⦿ . Then the person forms a circle using the thumb and index finger of the right hand, as represented by the character □. The right hand is raised in a salute of polite respect. This is the unique Huhui du-wu salute.

rebellion, they can do the same with the Leopard people and the Feathered people. Won't it be too late if the city goes undefended at this critical juncture? Must you wait until the city is attacked?"

Zhihuang Ma laughed.

"Don't worry, Miss Qi. I have made thorough preparations. My plan is top secret, otherwise I would tell you about it. Anyway, you need not worry about a thing." He then turned and spoke to Yu Fang in an earnest tone. "Not that I'm boasting, but with me here, Sunlon City doesn't have to worry. Please believe me when I say that the Green Snake Brotherhood can fall back to Hehe Village with no worries."

While Yu Fang didn't entirely trust Zhihuang Ma, he did believe that he was fairly sincere about protecting Sunlon City.

"To tell the truth, I already have sent letters to General Shi and the cult leader requesting that they send troops. When they arrive, we will join forces and enter the city together."

Zhihuang Ma's expression changed when he heard this. "Sir," he said angrily, "what you are doing is wrong. If the city really were in a desperate situation, then naturally, the nine bulu lords would authorize me to invite the three factions in. We have not yet reached that moment. Because you've taken it upon yourself to ask for reinforcements, some might suspect that you have an ulterior motive."

"You cannot say that," replied Yu Fang angrily. "When the fate of the Huhui hangs in the balance, every ⊡ (du) man has a responsibility. From inside the city you cannot see the seriousness of the situation outside, and if you don't organize a united army, things might get out of hand. Do you yourself have an ulterior motive for wanting me to pull my army back to Hehe Village?"

The two of them continued with their heated exchange. The more they spoke, the worse the situation became. At that moment, Liu Qi rushed into the tent.

"Sir, Mayor, the reporters are here."

A group of reporters appeared immediately behind Liu Qi. Zhihuang Ma shot forward, all smiles, to address the reporters.

"Gentlemen, this is my close comrade in arms, Yu Fang, the leader of the Green Snake Brotherhood. Out of loyalty, he has brought his troops to save Sunlon City. We are moved with admiration. On behalf of the Sunlon City government and the thousands of residents, I thank you, Yu Fang."

The reporters pressed forward, some snapping photos, others filming for skyvision. Zhihuang Ma clasped Yu Fang's hand and did not let go of it. He smiled, showing a mouthful of yellow teeth as the cameras snapped. Yu Fang was actually very bashful and didn't say a word. Watching from the sidelines, Miss Qi found the spectacle fascinating and couldn't help smiling. After the reporters left, Miss Qi laughed.

"Since you two are such close comrades in arms," said Miss Qi, "from this moment on, you can't argue anymore."

Zhihuang Ma laughed, but almost immediately once again assumed his serious demeanor.

"Yu Fang is of course my closest friend. Although we must keep private and public business separate, that doesn't mean I agree with what he does. You just saw that there are lots of reporters in Sunlon City and they have complete freedom in reporting the news, which is what's good about an open city. If the united army were to enter and heroes like General Shi and the cult leader were to return, would the people continue to enjoy their freedom?"

"But," said Miss Qi, rolling her eyes, "I clearly remember you saying that the essence of democracy is that we are the people and you are the master."

"Right," said Zhihuang Ma without batting an eye. "The essence of democracy is that on occasion, you are the people and I am the master; at other times those roles are reversed. Democracy is the concept of reciprocity. You can't quote me out of context, right?"

Tongue-tied, Miss Qi said nothing, but thought to herself, "Is he just quibbling or did I misunderstand him?" But before she could say anything, Zhihuang Ma turned to speak to Yu Fang.

"Yu Fang, please consider carefully and don't make any rash decisions. The nine bulu lords would never agree to allowing a united army into the city. Sure, there is danger, but there is also security. We haven't reached the critical juncture." After having his say, Zhihuang Ma hastened back to the city. Miss Qi had wanted to ask him about Ah Two and Ah Three, but didn't. The reporters departed like a cloud of locusts in the wake of Zhihuang Ma. Cooking after having received the food and drink, the troops were less restless for the time being. Dusk had come, and the huge purple sun sank in the west. Someone in the camp sang:

> *The purple sun sinks in the west*
> *Once again*
> *Evening has come*
> *A quick look back*

Only to see that
Solitary city

Standing outside the tent and listening to the sad song, Miss Qi could-n't help thinking about the past. Mr. Qi, Yu Jin, Captain Mai, the Shan officer, Ah You, and Ah 占 (chu) had all left her. Some had died, the where-abouts of others were unknown, and she now found herself all alone with loyal warriors filled with ardor to protect their city, who in fact weren't re-ally welcome there. As she thought, she shed tears for her lot and for the situation in which the Green Snake Brotherhood found itself.

In her sadness, Miss Qi saw a flash. Some thirty feet away in an open space between two tents, a man dressed entirely in black and wearing a mask with a bronze statue pendant at his chest suddenly appeared.

"The leader of the Bronze Statue Cult. Supreme One!"

"Right you are," said the Stranger in Black. "The unfortunate death of your father affected me deeply. But he sought and he found ⊡ ☐ (du-wu); he had no regrets. I hope you can put aside your grief and accept what has happened, and that you have the strength to continue on."

"Thank you for your concern," said Miss Qi, wiping her tears away. "What brings you to the camp of the Green Snake Brotherhood? Are you looking for Yu Fang?"

Then a voice was heard behind her. "Of course he is looking for me. How have you been, cult leader?"

The Stranger in Black strode forward.

"Yu Fang," he said, "I received your letter. According to my intelli-gence, the Leopard people have already formed an alliance with the Shan. The Leopard force is training near Silverfield Village; they are prepared to head south at any moment. It looks as if the Shan are planning to mount a large-scale attack on Sunlon City."

"So things are happening exactly the way Ah 占 (chu) expected." Yu Fang sighed. "Unfortunately, Zhihuang Ma refuses to listen to reason. You were the one who suggested that all three factions withdraw from the city. The situation is different now, and the united army ought to return to the city."

"Hold on," said the Stranger in Black. "The men and horses of the Green Snake Brotherhood already are gathered outside of town. The Bronze Statue Cult is everywhere; we can return to the city at any time. But the Royalist cavalry has not arrived. According to our agreement, if one party is absent, no action can be taken."

Yu Fang nodded and said, "I already have sent someone to inform General Shi. He is utterly devoted to the country. If he knows that Sunlon City is in danger, he will certainly lead the cavalry here on the double."

"I'm afraid that might not be the case," said the Cult Leader, laughing coldly. "The Royalist cavalry suffered immense losses during the uprising and they still have not fully recovered. Even if General Shi chooses to take action and the Shan are aware of it, the forces of the Leopard people will attack them en route. I don't think that General Shi will be here anytime soon."

Yu Fang never expected to hear the leader of the Bronze Statue Cult speak this way and was momentarily stunned. After a while he said, "Even if he doesn't arrive, we can still take action. Frankly, only the Republicans and the Bronze Statue Cult are capable of mobilizing the people for a showdown with the Shan."

"True," said the Stranger in Black with an even colder laugh. "The power of your brotherhood has grown rapidly in the last year, so much so that it appears that the entire Hu River Basin is in your hands. But bear in mind that the power of the Bronze Statue Cult spreads far and wide and that it might far surpass that of your brotherhood."

Yu Fang restrained himself after these provocative words.

"Sunlon City is in danger, and I suggest that we enter at once. When the Leopard Brotherhood cavalry arrives, we'll welcome them with open arms into the united army. Believe me, General Shi will not take it amiss."

"No," said the Stranger in Black. "If any one of the three factions is absent, we can't just discard the agreement. To you, as leader of the Green Snake Brotherhood, such ▣ ▢ (du-wu) morality and justice can't be any clearer. Besides, if we want to act unilaterally and break our promise, the nine bulu lords who sympathize with the Royalists will never consent to our two factions entering the city. The situation is chaotic enough as it is, and if we start another internal squabble, I dread to think what might happen."

The Stranger in Black spoke with the force of conviction. And Yu Fang, who had never had much of a way with words, suddenly found himself without a reply. Miss Qi felt anxious for him. The man in black raised both arms and said, "I have something important to do and must leave. When General Shi and his cavalry arrive, we'll discuss whether or not the united army should enter the city."

"Cult leader!" replied Yu Fang anxiously, "this is no time to be impulsive. Sunlon City is depending on us. . . ."

"Don't worry," said the man in black, the lower half of his body already having disappeared. Before he vanished completely, he said,

"Though fruit and flowers must fall, scattered by the wind, Sunlon City will be reborn!"

After the Stranger in Black disappeared, Yu Fang lowered his head submissively. Miss Qi knew that Yu Fang, who feared nothing, thought only of Sunlon City and the Green Snake Brotherhood. He was entirely different from Yu Jin. Yu Jin thought only of revenge, but really didn't care much about, and maybe even despised, the city. Perhaps it was Yu Jin's disregard and constant thought of leaving the Huhui planet that most attracted Miss Qi. Yu Jin had fulfilled his desire for revenge; now it was her turn. But she didn't really hate the Shan. She didn't hate anyone; she was just profoundly sad. She finally had come to realize why Yu Jin wanted to leave the planet. Oh, Yu Jin. Where was he at that moment? Would she ever see him again?

"Miss Qi," Yu Fang suddenly called out, "you should return to Sunlon City tonight."

"Why?" she asked in surprise. "Is the Green Snake Brotherhood going to enter the city? Or are you preparing to withdraw to Hehe Village?"

"We have no alternative." Yu Fang sighed. "Zhihuang Ma does not welcome our presence in the city; the cult leader is also opposed to it; General Shi hasn't arrived yet; we are powerless to dispatch troops. But if we don't enter the city and remain outside, the army will fall apart. We can only return to Hehe Village and wait for a more opportune moment. Perhaps Ah 凸 (chu) was right—defending the city to the end is the worst strategy. If we can locate the Shan command and destroy their warship, there will be no need to enter."

"Too bad Ah 凸 (chu) isn't here," Miss Qi said, laughing. "I think you need a military advisor. I'll be your temporary advisor and help you make decisions. Okay?"

"You be my military advisor?" Yu Fang laughed. "I watched you grow up and I know all your wily tricks and games. But these are affairs involving national defense, not drinking games."

"Don't be in such a rush to get rid of me," said Miss Qi. "If Sunlon City is threatened, then aren't you sending me to my death by having me return?"

Yu Fang saw that there was some truth to what she said.

"Zhihuang Ma and the cult leader all have selfish motives," continued Miss Qi. "Zhihuang Ma is afraid that if he lets the united army into the city he'll lose his job as mayor; the cult leader doesn't want to relinquish any of his power in the city to the Green Snake Brotherhood. They will be elated if we withdraw. We should send someone to General Shi at once and ask him to come. Once the general is here, Zhihuang Ma, being his old subordinate, won't have anything to say. And the cult leader won't have any excuses. The people will be put at ease when the united army enters the city. At that time, troops can be sent out to locate the Shan command, thereby putting the enemy on the defensive with no opportunity to attack."

Miss Qi spoke with confidence and composure, and Yu Fang just had to nod his head.

"You're right, we can't withdraw," said Yu Fang. "You've really thought of everything. But if General Shi fails to send troops, we'll be in deep trouble."

"Why don't I go and see the general?" asked Miss Qi. "I'll deliver the message. Perhaps I can convince him to send troops."

"No, it's too dangerous," replied Yu Fang, shaking his head. "If anything were to go wrong, how could I face Mr. Qi? If Ah 出 (chu) found out, he would curse me up and down."

"It's not that dangerous," said Miss Qi, refusing to give in. "I'm not a child. I can take care of myself."

Yu Fang continued to shake his head. Miss Qi knew that once he had said no, there was no changing his mind. She rolled her eyes and said, "Since you don't want me to go, there is no point staying here either. I'm going back to Sunlon City."

"Okay, okay, that's more like it. Although the city is threatened, it is still safer there than here."

"But it is too dangerous for me to return alone. Can you have someone see me back?"

Seeing the reasonableness of her request, he called Liu Qi and ordered him to escort her back. By that time, the purple sun already had fallen below the horizon, and the wind had whipped up the sand. Liu Qi chose four warriors and escorted her to the East Gate. Miss Qi turned and spoke to Liu Qi.

"By agreement, the Green Snake Brotherhood cannot enter the city. Go on back. Tell Yu Fang that tomorrow morning I'll take the train to Golden Goose Fort to see General Shi. I'll bring good news within the week."

Sharp Knives Liu was surprised by what she said.

"Does Yu Fang know that you are going to see General Shi?"

"It's none of his business," retorted Miss Qi. "Besides, there's nothing dangerous about taking the train."

"Miss Qi. . . ."

Miss Qi didn't give him a chance to protest as she headed directly through the city gate. The gate was locked, but there was a small side door guarded by two policemen. Seeing her pass through the door, the skinny policeman yelled, "You □ (wu) girl. Where are you going at this time of night?"

"I live in Sungood bulu," said Miss Qi. "During the day, I went to see a sick relative. I didn't watch the time, and that's why I'm coming back so late."

"You're too late," said the skinny guard. "Didn't you see that the gate is already closed? Come back tomorrow."

"But the side door is open. Why can't you let me in?"

"This door is for the use of public servants," said the thin policeman. "It's not to be used by the residents. Are you a ■ (woo) official or a □ (wu) official? Do you have a privilege card? If you don't, forget about coming in."

"What do you mean, a privilege card?" asked Miss Qi angrily. "My family has lived in Sunlon City for generations. I've never heard anything about having a privilege card. I'll show you my ID card."

"I don't want to see your ID card," replied the policeman, laughing. "What good is that? I want to see your privilege card."

The other policeman, who was fat, spoke to the skinny cop: "She has a privilege card. I know her family. I'll go with her to get her card and show you."

"Oh? So you know her. Why didn't you speak up sooner? Go on. But," he said to Miss Qi, "next time you go out, don't forget to take your privilege card. If you have one, you had better use it. Understand?"

The fat policeman repeatedly offered his thanks and then dragged Miss Qi away. After entering the city, Miss Qi turned and spoke to the fat policeman: "Fortunately it was you I ran into, Ah Two. How did you get to be a policeman standing guard at the East Gate? What about Ah Three? When did Zhihuang Ma let you out?"

The policeman was, in fact, Ah Two the butcher. As Miss Qi asked one question after another, he raised a finger to his lips and whispered, "Shhhh, this is no place to talk. I can't begin to tell you all I've seen in the last few days. I'll take you home. We'll talk as we walk."

"Don't you have to go back and stand guard?"

"It doesn't matter," said Ah Two, taking something from his pocket, "I have a privilege card."

8

———

Although Miss Qi had been away from Sunlon City for only two weeks, she felt for some reason that the place had changed a lot. With Ah Two the butcher, she made her way back to Sungood bulu along the main thoroughfare of Sundragon bulu. It was near closing time and the fine sand was raining down. Fewer and fewer people were seen on the streets; yawning, the shopkeepers were closing up. Most of the buildings in Sundragon bulu had two stories and were painted with lime. Shops were located on the ground floors while people lived above. Iron bars covered the wooden-shuttered windows facing the streets. Murals of historical personages or scenery were sketched above the windows. The two sides of the black-tiled roofs came down in vivid dragon-shaped flying eaves that made the buildings appear especially large.

Miss Qi recalled her childhood, when her dada took her through the alleys of Sundragon bulu examining the murals ornamenting the windows that had been painstakingly sketched by artisans down through the ages. Some of the murals were almost a thousand years old; some had nearly disappeared due to the action of the sand, leaving the scenes and portraits vaguely discernible. Her dada had told her that this was true Huhui folk art, and he told her some of the stories associated with the historical figures. The ▣ □ (du-wu) Sage who achieved enlightenment on Mount Huhui in the early days of the Anliu Era and Wen Chongwu, the chief warrior of the Sunart people during the Seventh War of Restoration, were most frequently depicted in the murals. Through military suicide, Wen

Chongwu had killed 108 Sundragon swordsmen. But ironically, it was the Sundragon people who later most revered his actions. Mr. Qi always said that in the past, the Huhui people were of decent character and never held a grudge, but in more recent times they had become increasingly intolerant. He told her countless tales, few of which she now remembered. What she did remember was the warmth and affection between father and daughter experienced during those visits.

As she and Ah Two walked down the streets of Sundragon bulu, she couldn't fail to notice that on the sand-covered streets under the streetlights the murals seemed somehow different than in the past. Looking closer, she made out the image of the Stranger in Black, and . . . Zhihuang Ma! Softly, she couldn't help asking Ah Two, "Were the murals changed recently?"

"You've got sharp eyes!" replied the fat butcher. "The city government just recently established a historic preservation corps. The city's key cultural relics and historical sites are being repaired and renovated. Ah Three was assigned to be a driver for the Department of Historic Preservation."

Hearing Ah Two mention Ah Three, Miss Qi was quick to ask, "When did Mayor Ma let you two go?"

"Who said he let us go?" Ah Two replied angrily. "The night we were arrested we were both beaten severely. The next day, the mayor judged us guilty of resisting arrest. We were not allowed to defend ourselves. He gave us the choice of going to jail or volunteering to serve the people of Sunlon City. So I volunteered to be a policeman, and Ah Three volunteered to be a driver. The residents are apprehensive, and many public servants have left their jobs and fled. Zhihuang Ma is using this means to force the residents to continue the work of his city government."

"So," Miss Qi said, "that's why you have a privilege card. It sounds like you're doing okay."

Hearing this, Ah Two laughed.

"What kind of person am I? I'm a seventh-generation butcher, and who doesn't know me in the Sungood market? I repeat, who doesn't know me? If they want fresh sea serpent meat, they have to kiss up to me, right? A privilege card, or PC, is nothing. Tonight I decided I didn't want to stand guard. Who is going to say no? Ah Three is also getting along pretty well at the Department of Historic Preservation; he's been able to rip off a lot of antiques and sell them. But it has been hard on Ah Four. Since we were taken away, he's been busy as hell every day, and Ah Wen just orders him around. It's a real case of being 口 (qia) to a bad wife."

"What is a PC?"

"It's a new invention of Zhihuang Ma's." Ah Two took out his privilege card and gave it to Miss Qi to examine. It was a gold-plated bronze card, on the front of which were engraved the characters ⊡ □ (du-wu) and several rows of numbers. On the back was Mayor Ma's portrait. "Not long ago, our great mayor spoke on the skyvision and said that given the difficulties facing the nation, special privileges had to be eliminated. He said special privileges were to be feared because they lacked form and shape, but were pervasive. He said if special privileges could be quantified so that everyone knew what they were, then everyone would possess some and they wouldn't be so disgusting. Now there are ads for PCs in the papers and on the skyvision every day. I traded 100 kilos of sea serpent meat for a second-class card."

"What is it good for?" asked Miss Qi in a skeptical tone.

"That depends on the class of the card. Fourth- and fifth-class cards aren't good for anything; you can't even cut in line with them. They're good only for tricking children. Third-class cards are the most basic. Second-class ones can actually be used to get things done when dealing with the city government. First-class and super-class PCs are even more magical. But still, the most effective, as in the past, are the special privileges that lack shape and form and are pervasive. I suspect that Zhihuang Ma is pushing the cards just to make some extra money." Ah Two, the fat policeman, laughed. "Miss Qi, I'll sing the advertising jingle for the special privileges cards."

He then sang aloud the following song:

> *Privileges, O privileges*
> *Without shape or form*
> *All-pervasive*
> *I really hate you*

> *Privileges, O privileges*
> *No one else should have you*
> *I can't be without you*
> *I love you deeply*

> *Privileges, O privileges*
> *Invented by Mayor Ma*
> *There are six classes*
> *Everyone loves to use you.*

"The song even mentions Zhihuang Ma?" Miss Qi laughed. "The whole thing is dull and makes no sense."

"Sales haven't been bad," said Ah Two. "Zhihuang Ma will go down in Huhui history solely for having invented privilege cards."

Chatting, the two of them entered Sungood bulu without noticing. Although closing time was approaching, the narrow lanes of the bulu were still crowded. The buildings were different from the antique two-story brick structures of the Sundragon bulu. Most were single-story wooden buildings; two-story buildings were seen only in the commercial district. The second floor was usually quite low, so they still looked like single-story structures. The Sungood people usually went to bed late; long after the Sundragon people had retired, the Sungood night market was still busy. It was especially true in these unsettled times. People stayed at home during the day and came out at night for the latest news. Black-market peddlers also took advantage of the night to come out and sell their wares. As Miss Qi and Ah Two crossed a small square, a number of Huhui people were shouting and beating a peddler who happened to be a Serpent person. The leader of the group pointed at the six-limbed Serpent person, who seemed to be breathing his last, and said that he was a spy for the Serpent People's Revolutionary Army. The people there beat him and looted his wares. Seeing what was happening, Miss Qi couldn't help but say, "Ah Two, you're a policeman, do something!"

"You've got to be kidding," said Ah Two nervously. "In their resistance to the Shan, the people get very excited and indignant, especially when it comes to the Serpent people. If I interfere, they will think I'm a spy for the foreigners, and if I'm not beaten, I'll surely be cursed."

"If the Serpent people are aware of the danger, why do they still come to Sunlon City?"

"Perhaps he really is a spy, or maybe he's just a descendent of the □ (wu) Serpent Faction."

During the Thousand-Year War, the Serpent people sympathized with the Huhui Republicans and fought shoulder to shoulder with the Green Snake Brotherhood. But there was a small faction of them that sympathized with the Royalist Party, and they were called the □ (wu) Serpent Faction. They were banished by the Serpent majority. Historians refer to the Serpents who sympathized with the Republicans as the ■ (woo) Serpent Faction and those who sympathized with the Royalists as the □ (wu) Serpent Faction. The descendants of the □ (wu) faction could not return home, so they began a life of wandering. All the beggars and smugglers on the Huhui planet were either descendants of the □ (wu) Serpent Faction or Gaiwenese. At the thought of the Gaiwenese, Miss Qi couldn't help but recall Gai Bo and Yu Jin, both of whom had disappeared.

"I didn't see any Gaiwenese as we were walking. They like to speculate, so why aren't they around?"

"It's strange. Ten days ago, the city government caught five Gaiwenese speculators and vaporized them. It was all broadcast on skyvision; after that, all the Gaiwenese vanished without a trace from Sunlon City. Perhaps they all left because they were afraid of being vaporized."

How was it possible? wondered Miss Qi. The Gaiwenese were the wanderers of the universe and had never feared being arrested by the government. As long as there was business to do, the Gaiwenese would be there. They knew very well that business opportunities were scarce, so there wasn't a trace of them anywhere. The Serpent peddlers knew that it was dangerous, but still they were active in the city. Zhihuang Ma clearly knew that the Shan and the three original peoples of the Huhui planet were going to attack the city, but he remained calm and composed and was vigorously engaged in historic preservation and the selling of privilege cards. The portraits of Zhihuang Ma and the Stranger in Black appeared in the city like exotic flowers and strange plants in the desert after rain. Sunlon City really had changed, thought Miss Qi uneasily—it was like the desert just before a storm, when some animals fled and others took the opportunity to become more active.

They reached the Qi family tavern. The place had just closed and Ah Wen, along with Ah Three and Ah Four, was cleaning up. They were overjoyed at the appearance of Miss Qi and Ah Two. They surrounded Miss Qi and all questioned her at once. Ah Wen wiped her tears away, then wiped her runny nose; then she hugged Miss Qi and cried aloud.

"You've returned safe and sound. The purple sun has eyes. What about Ah 凸 (chu)? Why hasn't Ah 凸 (chu) come back?"

Miss Qi gave them an account of what she had done over the last two weeks and how Ah 凸 (chu) had pursued Ah You into a cave beneath the copper fields and unfortunately had never returned. Everyone sobbed as they listened. Miss Qi also informed them that she was planning to go to Central Station and take a train to Golden Goose Fort to look for General Shi, leader of the Leopard Brotherhood. When Ah Wen heard this, her tears flowed like a cataract.

"I don't mean to scold you, but for a person to leave just after returning home! If your dada were here, he wouldn't let you traipse around like this.

Nor would Ah 忄 (chu), if he were here. Don't go; Ah Two can go in your place. Ah Two is from Jinjiakou, and he knows the way across the plains."

With Ah 忄 (chu) gone, Ah Wen naturally considered herself the head of the Qi household, and she began to order people about. Miss Qi laughed to herself, but she also felt the sweetness of being home, the joy of having someone look after her. But she steeled herself and replied somewhat coldly, "I have to go. The Green Snake Brotherhood won't be able to enter the city unless General Shi sends troops. The city is in danger. We can't just think of ourselves at such a desperate time. Besides, there's no danger."

Ah Wen knew that she couldn't prevent Miss Qi from going.

"Then let Ah Two go with you," said Ah Wen. "Ah Two, did you hear me? Hurry up and get ready."

"No," said Miss Qi. "Ah Two is a policeman and has work to do, as do Ah Three and Ah Four. It will be simpler if I go alone."

"Can I let you do that?" asked the three men in unison. "I'll accompany you."

"I have a privilege card, which will make things very convenient," said Ah Two.

"I c-c-can take you in the Department of Historic Preservation c-c-car," stuttered Ah Three.

"I may not have a privilege card or a car, but I'm a mean cook, and I'm popular everywhere," said Ah Four.

After discussing the matter, everyone decided that Ah Two the butcher would accompany Miss Qi to the Golden Goose Fort; Ah Three would drive them to the train station; and Ah Four would prepare the food for their trip. Ah Four went to the kitchen and fixed four roast chickens, ten kilos of salted sea serpent meat, and a big bag of steamed bread. Ah Two packed the food in a backpack, and complained that it wasn't enough. Ah Wen wanted Miss Qi to go upstairs and get some rest, but Miss Qi found it impossible to sleep. She knelt in front of her dada's spirit tablet, and thinking of how he and Ah 忄 (chu) taught her to manipulate the wisdom beads, wept with sorrow. She seemed to have dozed off for a moment, when Ah Wen shook her.

"Miss, Miss, it'll be light soon. You should get going."

Miss Qi rubbed her sleepy eyes and followed Ah Wen downstairs. Ah Three was waiting outside with the big gray car from the Department of Historic Preservation. Ah Two had shouldered the big pack and stood waiting beside the car. Ah Wen's and Ah Four's eyes were red from crying, especially Ah Wen's. She clung to Miss Qi as if unwilling to let her go. Ah Wen held her so tightly that Miss Qi could hardly breathe.

"If you can't find General Shi," said Ah Wen, "come home directly. There are lots of poisonous snakes and wild animals on the plains. You must be careful."

"I know."

Miss Qi and Ah Two got in the car, and Ah Three started the motor. The wind had already stopped, the sky was still dark, and several blue shafts of light still lingered over the city. It was a little chilly in the car; Miss Qi buttoned her coat. As he drove, Ah Three spoke to Miss Qi.

"Actually, I c-c-can take you all the way to Golden Goose Fort. It will be more c-comfortable than the train. Everyone is r-r-running away and the trains are c-c-rowded."

"This car belongs to the Department of Historic Preservation. How can you just leave the city?"

Ah Three shrugged his shoulders and replied, "It d-d-doesn't matter. They are f-friendly at the department. No one will say anything. In addition to all the living people, Sunlon City is filled with historical landmarks. The th-th-things that the department should preserve are too numerous to be c-c-concerned about."

"Whose idea was it to put the cult leader and the mayor in the murals in Sunlong bulu?"

"I-i-it wasn't me," said Ah Three, speeding along. "Nor was it anyone in the d-d-department. But it's said that lots of high-ranking city government officials are c-c-cult members. The department just follows orders."

Miss Qi thought that perhaps when the cult leader said that the power of the cult pervaded the city, it was no idle boast. Perhaps Zhihuang Ma and the cult leader were in cahoots and using each other. If the nine bulu lords were the cult leader's puppets, then the situation of the Green Snake Brotherhood was perilous. As she considered the situation, the car pulled up to the station.

Although it was still dark, the square in front of the station was already crowded with Huhui people fleeing the city. Ah Three parked beside the square. To protect Miss Qi, the two men took up position on either side of her as they pushed toward the station. Some people glared at them. Ah Two took out his privilege card and barked, "Move aside. Move aside. We have privileges, move aside."

As expected, the people parted to let them squeeze through. But nearing the steps to the station, they found their way blocked. Ah Two once again took out his privilege card and shouted, "Move aside. We have privileges. Everyone move aside."

"Quit shouting," said a large, middle-aged man, glaring at Ah Two with loathing. "Who doesn't have privilege cards here? Why shout? Just get in line and wait your turn."

But Ah Two wouldn't give up. He took out his card and asked, "□ (wu) you Mister, what class PC do you have?"

The man whipped out his own card and asked, "What class do you have?"

"Second class!" said Ah Two. Everyone doubled over in laughter. The middle-aged man laughed coldly.

"A little second-classer actually has the gall to try to pull rank around here. Let me tell you, everyone here has first-class cards. We'll bow to the inevitable if you have super-class privileges. But a second-class card just won't get you anywhere."

Ah Two regretted having been so quick to show his card. The middle-aged man shoved him with his elbow and said, "Get lost. Second-class PC holders should stand to one side. Look, here comes another group of first-classers. Move aside."

There indeed was another group of people, all of whom were smiling, holding their cards. They pushed Ah Two, Ah Three, and Miss Qi behind them. The three of them waited in line for a long time, and got farther and farther behind. Ah Two began getting anxious.

"If I'd known this would happen, I would have got a first-class PC. No, I'd have got a super-class one, which would make everything more convenient. This way we'll never get to the head of the line."

Miss Qi laughed. "You still don't get it? You have a second-class card; other people have first-class ones. If you get a super-class one, other people can too. If things go on this way, it will never end. It would be best if everyone just took their turn in line."

"St-st-standing in line like this won't work. I'll drive you to the West Station in Sunbright bulu. If you can't get a train there, I'll t-t-take you to the next st-t-tation to the west until you get one."

Miss Qi and Ah Two agreed that it was the only way. They had a difficult time getting out of Central Station, and when they looked back, they saw that the place was busier and more chaotic than ever. The Huhui people, all of whom had privilege cards, were stepping on each other's toes and swearing at each other. People were climbing over one another until there was a mountain of them in the station doorway. And each person had a card. Ah Two couldn't help sighing.

"Zhihuang Ma was up to no good when he pitched the cards. Privileges can't be obvious. If everyone has them, then they no longer exist."

Seeing all the cards, a thought suddenly flashed through Miss Qi's mind.

"It's not Zhihuang Ma's scheme, but rather the cult leader's," said Miss Qi. "He is planning to rule the city through the use of those bronze cards."

"What?" said Ah Two, looking at the card in his hand. "Is that possible? But it's Zhihuang Ma's picture on the cards, not the cult leader's. Zhihuang Ma is selling them to make money; it has nothing to do with the cult leader."

"But why, then, are they made out of bronze?" Seeing that mountain of people in front of the station, Miss Qi had a feeling she was back at the South Gate of Heaven at the beginning of the Anliu Era, looking at the Bronze Statue in Sunlon City. "It's got to be a huge plot."

"Th-th-the train is going to leave soon," said Ah Three, urging Miss Qi on. "If w-we don't leave soon, we won't be in t-t-time for the train at West Station in Sunbright bulu."

Miss Qi and Ah Two got into the big gray car. When Ah Three drove away from Central Station, Miss Qi looked out the rear window. That mountain of people with bronze cards was slowly breaking up like a clay sculpture being dissolved and swept away in all directions in the rain.

Miss Qi trembled; she suddenly had a bad premonition.

9

West Station in Sunbright bulu was even busier than Central Station. It seemed as if all the residents of Sunbright bulu had decided to flee; they stood on the hills on either side of the station, craning their necks. There was no way Ah Three could get through. Ah Two climbed on top of the car for a look; after a while he jumped down.

"We can't get through," he said to Miss Qi. "Let's go on to the next station."

It doesn't m-matter," said Ah Three optimistically. "I might as well t-t-take you all the w-w-way to Golden Goose Fort. It could be fun."

"What's the next station?" asked Miss Qi. "Is it Jinjiakou?"

"Jinjiakou is another 480 kilometers," said Ah Two, wiping the sweat from his face. "There are three or four small stations before you get to Jinjiakou. And it's another 800 kilometers from Jinjiakou to Golden Goose Fort. That's 1,280 kilometers. You can get there by car in three days at the earliest. It takes two whole days by train."

Miss Qi calculated that even if she had no trouble locating General Shi after arriving in Golden Goose Fort and he agreed to send troops at once, it would still be ten days before the Leopard Brotherhood cavalry could get to Sunlon City. Could the Green Snake Brotherhood troops encamped outside the city hold out that long? Would the Shan and the Serpent army cross the Hu River and attack before then? And what if General Shi was unwilling to send troops?

Ah Three guessed what was going through Miss Qi's mind and tried to console her. "I . . . I . . . I guarantee that I'll get you to Golden Goose Fort within th-th-three days. I used to drive this road all the time; I could drive it with my eyes s-s-shut."

Hearing Ah Three brag, Ah Two commented, "I'm from Jinjiakou and know the road across the plains. If Ah Three gets lost, I can still get us there."

"I-I won't get lost. Don't talk n-nonsense," said Ah Three, blushing. "When we leave the city, just watch me g-g-go."

Ah Three was right: he sped up after exiting the city from the West Gate in Sunbright bulu and shot across the plains. Between the mountains to the north and the vast ocean to the south lay desert and plains. The plains were sparsely populated, and one could drive a long way before encountering a village. These so-called villages weren't much more than about ten families, or four or five stone houses along the road. The houses were made of piled stone; they had doors but no windows in order to keep the sand out. Occasionally a few shepherd girls were seen herding their flocks, walking slowly along the road. Miss Qi noticed that they all wore small bronze statues. It certainly looked as if the power of the cult had penetrated into the plains.

Ah Three drove like crazy until they reached a relatively large village. It was the first train stop on the plains. A number of tents, which served as temporary quarters for the refugees from Sunlon City, had been pitched next to the station. When Miss Qi, Ah Two, and Ah Three managed to squeeze into the station, they at once were surrounded by a bunch of real estate brokers.

"Do you want to buy a piece of land? The land is fertile, there are springs, and Sunlon City is not too far away. You can buy a piece of land on which to settle your family. Tomorrow, after the war is over, you still can use it for a country house," said one broker.

"A good location, a good location. Garden. Villa. Pasturage. We'll throw in a milk cow and ten sheep. Specially priced, don't miss your chance," said another broker.

"Buying land and an estate is the best investment," said a third broker. "How good are our ranch houses? Words cannot describe them; please come and see for yourselves. You will be well taken care of at the ranch, entertained by the Shasha song and dance troupe. Come and see this free ranch show."

Ah Two and Ah Three escorted Miss Qi out of the clutches of the land brokers. Ah Two pushed his way to the ticket window, took out his privilege card, and immediately purchased two tickets. He was quite proud of himself.

"In Sunlon City," said Ah Two, "there's nothing special about second-class cards, but in a place like this, they work great."

As he was boasting, a skinny little black-skinned guy snatched his card, shouting, "Down with privileges; long live equality," and ran out of the station. Ah Two and Ah Three were in hot pursuit when he slipped into the refugee camp and disappeared. Annoyed, Ah Two shouted: "□ (wu) you, you no-good bastard. Stealing my card! I'm telling you, if I meet up with you in Sunlon City, I'll make mincemeat out of you and feed you to the sea serpents, or I'm not a real man."

Pretty soon the refugees came out of their tents to see what all the shouting was about. Somewhat embarrassed, Miss Qi pulled at Ah Two's sleeve and said, "Forget it. Those privilege cards aren't anything to be proud of. If it's gone, it's gone."

But Ah Two wasn't willing to give up. By then the camp was astir, and the refugees all stood there talking and pointing at the horizon. Miss Qi, Ah Two, and Ah Three looked in the direction they were pointing and saw a small black speck falling rapidly to the ground to the south. But the speck shortly reappeared, ascending, before falling again. The speck drew closer and closer, and the refugees grew louder and louder. The speck seemed familiar to Miss Qi; then she realized what it was.

"It's a Froghopper. It's a Gaiwenese Froghopper!"

A few more jumps, and the Froghopper landed in front of the station. By then, everyone could see the strange object that was neither car nor airplane. The fuselage was like a car, but there were two small steel struts up front that ended in two tires. In the rear there was a pair of grasshopperlike legs. There were two more small tires where the rear touched the ground. At the front there were two riding lights, beneath which was grillwork that covered an air intake. Miss Qi informed Ah Two and Ah Three that it was a Froghopper, a mode of transportation invented by the Gaiwenese. The hood opened and out stepped a blue-skinned Gaiwenese. He walked toward Miss Qi, but she didn't recognize him. But the Gaiwenese smiled his toothy smile at her.

"It has been a while, Miss Qi. Let's be friends. Let's be friends, everyone."

"Wh-wh-who are you?" stuttered Ah Three. "Miss Qi doesn't know y-you."

"Miss Qi really doesn't recognize me? Well, I can't say that I'm surprised, because we Gaiwenese all look the same to you Huhui people. I'm Gai Bao, the bazi of Gai Bo. Just before the uprising, under orders from Gai Bo, I took Miss Qi to the plains in a Gaiwenese Froghopper. Do you recognize me now?"

Miss Qi smiled, and Gai Bao made a singular awareness gesture.

"Let's be friends. Let's be friends, everyone. I never expected to meet you here after leaving you on the plains. What a coincidence. Let's go someplace and have a nice friendly chat."

Gai Bao then broke into song without regard for all the people watching:

Pretty flowers don't last long
Pretty scenery isn't around forever
Good friends don't meet often.
The bright moon wavers
After parting tonight
When will we meet again?

All the refugees clapped and cheered when Gai Bao finished his song. He then bowed elegantly. Miss Qi had a thought and blurted out: "Meeting again in this place is too much of a coincidence, isn't it?"

"It sure is," replied Gai Bo immediately. "To tell the truth, someone sent me here to get you."

"Who?" asked Miss Qi with curiosity. "Who?"

"I can't tell you just now," replied Gai Bao in all seriousness. "Having been entrusted with this mission, I must faithfully carry it out. I would rather die than break faith with an old friend. Come with me. You needn't ask any more questions."

"You've got to be joking," responded Ah Two angrily. "You Gaiwenese can't be trusted. How can she go with you? Who knows what's in that Froghopper of yours?"

"I have some urgent business," said Miss Qi. "I have to get to Golden Goose Fort. Unless you tell me who wants to see me, I can't go with you."

"It's . . ." Gai Bao hesitated, "I can't tell you."

"Is it Gai Bo?"

At the mention of Gai Bo's name, Gai Bao began to weep, and his skin turned an ashen gray. When happy or sad, the skin color of the Gaiwenese would change to match their mood. Thus, the actors in a Gaiwenese opera would change color as they sang, to make the show more thrilling.

"Don't mention his name," said Gai Bao through his tears, "he's already become a gaixian.[1] I'll never see him again."

"Well, if it's not Gai Bo, then who is it?"

"I can't say, and that's all there is to it," said Gai Bao, his sadness turning to anger. "Are you coming or not? I'm busy and don't have time to discuss it with you."

"She's not going with you," said Ah Two, answering for Miss Qi. "No more tricks; we don't trust you."

Without so much as a word, Gai Bao got in his Froghopper and closed the hood. The thing started with a horrendous racket. As the hind legs sprang, the rockets fired and it leaped into the sky, accompanied by the cheers and applause of those present. Watching the Froghopper depart, Miss Qi felt a tinge of regret.

"I should have convinced Gai Bao to take me to Golden Goose Fort. I'd be there today if I took that Froghopper. How long must I wait here until the next train?"

"D-d-don't worry; it's coming," said Ah Three, pointing eastward. Soon the train was heard tooting, and it wasn't long before it pulled into the station. Many of the refugees from Sunlon City got off the train. This being the closest station to the city, many decided to watch from there to see if the situation improved. If so, they could return. Getting off the train, the refugees were immediately surrounded by a swarm of brokers. A truck to take people to see the ranch show drove up to the station. Miss Qi and Ah Two shouldered their packs and boarded the train with relative ease. After seeing them onto the train, Ah Three shouted from outside, "Take care!" Then, crying, he drove back to Sunlon City in the big gray car from the Department of Historic Preservation.

The train slowly got under way. Miss Qi sat by the window and watched the rows of tents slip by and disappear. New tents were being set up at the edge of the village. Little shepherd boys were herding their flocks away from the village in search of water and pasturage. The men and women from Sunlon City sat outside their tents, unable to adjust at once to their new surroundings. But perhaps the camp would soon become a small Sunlon City. Miss Qi sighed to herself. The city had such charisma.

The train gradually picked up speed. Miss Qi noticed groups of men and women standing beside the tracks. At first she thought that they were

[1] The Gaiwenese refer to the living as *gaiwen* and the dead as *gaixian*, or Gaiwenese immortal. A *bazi* is a sworn brother.

waiting for the ranch show. Then she noticed that they were all expressionless. They were wearing small bronze statues, or they were holding bronze cards. Immediately she called to Ah Two.

"What are those people doing?"

Ah Two looked, then grew so excited that he nearly fell out of the train.

"□ (wu) that no good bastard! He stole my card. Don't run away!"

"Miss Qi quickly pulled Ah Two back into the train. Amid the crowds was a small, skinny, black-skinned guy. His face was without expression, and he held the card he had stolen high above his head. Miss Qi understood at once what was going on.,

"It's a good thing he stole your card, otherwise you'd be standing there instead of him! The cult leader apparently has some secret way of controlling those people. I wonder what evil business he is planning?"

The train continued to pick up speed, leaving the cult members far behind. Miss Qi couldn't help but recall how that mountain of people with bronze cards had broken up like a clay sculpture dissolved by rain. That bad premonition struck her again. She was sure that Sunlon City was facing a disaster of gigantic proportions. Zhihuang Ma was just a puppet, and it was the omnipresent cult leader who was pulling the strings from behind the curtain. The cult leader knew that the Shan were staging a comeback and inciting the three original peoples of the Huhui planet. And he continued to deny the Green Snake Brotherhood entry into the city. Did he think that the cult followers could ward off a Shan counterattack? Or did he have another plan? The Serpent people would soon cross the river and attack the city. Would Yu Fang be able to control the Green Snake Brotherhood and thwart them? Had Ah 凸 (chu) become a prisoner of the Serpent people? Gai Bao said someone wanted to meet her. Who was it? Was it Gai Bo? Was it Yu Jin, whom she thought about constantly? Perhaps the Gaiwenese were controlled by the Shan. Then was it Captain Mai who wanted to see her?

Her mind filled with such thoughts, Miss Qi soon dozed off. When she woke, the purple sun was falling in the west and the wind had risen, obscuring the plains. There was only yellow sand to be seen. Ah Two had already prepared a supper of steamed buns, roast chicken, and sea serpent meat. Miss Qi was not hungry, so Ah Two voraciously gobbled down the food alone. Smelling the roast meat, the other passengers took out their food and ate. Some people had brought the blue wine Sunlon City was famous for and passed it around for everyone to take a swig. The tipsy passengers then started to sing the "Song of Sunlon City":

Sun, sun, sun, Sunlon City!
Soul of the Huhui planet
Sun, sun, sun, Sunlon City!
Master of the Huhui planet
Sun, sun, sun, Sunlon City!
The purple sun shines on the city of gold
Sun, sun, sun, Sunlon City!

Miss Qi had never liked the song, but hearing it sung by the refugees on a speeding train at sunset made her feel sad. The passengers sang it again and again. She watched from the window as the purple sun gradually sank from view and the plains were shrouded in darkness. In the distance a single blue heavenly shaft appeared. Light flashed in the clouds near the shaft, like a lightning storm. After a night of rain, the plains would be reborn at dawn, covered in countless beautiful, colorful flowers. . . .

Sun, sun, sun, Sunlon City!
Soul of the Huhui planet
Sun, sun, sun, Sunlon City!

Miss Qi gazed at the blue shaft of light far away. The flashing lightning lit up the plains thereabouts. In a moment the dry grass was afire, the plains a patch of flaming red. Fanned by the wind, the patch seemed to roll into a ball of fire. The darkness outside the window was suddenly filled with flying fireballs.

Sun, sun, sun, Sunlon City!
The purple sun shines on the city of gold
Sun, sun, sun, Sunlon City!

Miss Qi once again turned her attention to the amazing scene outside the window. The fireballs had arrayed themselves in neat rows and moved rapidly. Miss Qi wondered how the fireballs could arrange themselves in such an orderly fashion. Suddenly she realized that the fireballs were actually torches held in the mouths of huge leopards the size of small horses. They were in fleet pursuit of the train. As they turned their heads, Miss Qi could clearly see that the leopards had human faces. She shouted with fear, "Leopard people!"

"Right," said Ah Two, "they are Leopard people. When they feel like it, they can run faster than a train at 110 kilometers per hour. Ten, twenty, thirty . . . goodness! I've never seen so many Leopard people!"

The passengers abruptly stopped singing. They all peered anxiously out the windows at the Leopard people running alongside with torches. Suddenly a group of them sped up and headed toward the engine. Shortly, the train gradually began to slow down and finally came to a complete halt. The lights in the carriage flickered. The female passengers began to cry, the men to swear. A Huhui policeman suddenly appeared in the doorway and addressed the passengers: "The train has been hijacked by the Leopard people. Compatriots, exercise your spirit of singular awareness and vow to fight the enemy to the end."

Ah Two immediately stood up and whipped out a dagger. The braver male passengers all took out knives and guns, getting ready to fight the Leopard people to the bitter end.

From the train window, Miss Qi saw that all the Leopard people were standing at attention. When they stood upright, they looked more like human beings; they resembled huge men dressed in animal skins. The leader of the Leopard people, who was the biggest of them all, actually stood taller than the train. The others were all at least 360 centimeters in height. Holding torches in their mouths made it look like they were smoking. Awe-inspiring, they stood, awaiting orders from their leader. The tallest Leopard person fumbled around at his waist and finally removed from a leather bag a red silk ribbon, which he placed across his chest. By the light of the torches, Miss Qi could see crookedly written words on the ribbon: BATTLEFRONT COMMANDER, LPRA (LEOPARD PEOPLE'S REVOLUTIONARY ARMY).

The other Leopard people also took out red ribbons on which were written the letters LPRA and put them on. The commander then shouted at the train: "Huhui comrades! This is the first brigade of the Leopard People's Revolutionary Army. You are surrounded. Surrender immediately and you will be spared. Otherwise, you will all perish!"

The commander shouted several times, but no one dared leave the train. Angered, the commander bared two rows of sharp teeth and howled. He was soon joined by the other soldiers. Ah Two whispered to Miss Qi, "Remember, when the Leopard people come into the carriage, dive under a seat and play dead. They are bloodthirsty killers. We're finished!"

At that moment, the carriage started to rock violently. Miss Qi tightly grasped the seat to steady herself; then she saw them lift the carriage.

"They're going to roll it," shouted Miss Qi.

The words were scarcely out of her mouth when a screeching sound was heard as the Leopard people tipped over the carriage.

The Leopard, Snake, and Feathered peoples were considered the three indigenous peoples of the Huhui planet. And together with the 亼 (chu) mutations, they were called the "four strange peoples." Legend had it that they all had a single origin: they were said to be descended from the early human explorers of the Huhui planet. Save for their strange appearance and exceptional intelligence, the 亼 (chu) were the most like ordinary people of the four. Not only did the Feathered, Snake, and Leopard peoples look odd, their customs were also vastly different from those of human beings. This was especially true of the Leopard people; only their faces appeared human, and they were cruel and cunning by nature, a hundred times worse than the Serpent people. Influenced by a thousand years of Huhui civilization, the Serpent people at least had accepted the philosophy of singular awareness and got along peaceably with the Huhui people. But the Leopard People resisted being assimilated by the Huhui.

During the Snake and Leopard War, the Royalist generals rose in revolt several times, using the Leopard people as their vanguard. The Leopard people cooperated on the condition that the Huhui recognize their independence and autonomy. To obtain their support, the Royalist party not only gave the northern plains to them but also adopted the leopard as their symbol. During the constitutional monarchy, the Huhui government dispatched troops several times to subdue the Leopard people. Although they suffered huge casualties, they would not submit and fled to the northern plains, Silverfield Village, and the mountainous region to the west, from where they continued a guerrilla war. The Huhui government was unable to exterminate the Leopard people and had to tacitly acknowledge the existence of a Leopard kingdom.

At the beginning of their rule over the Huhui planet after the Fourth Interstellar War, the Shan also considered exterminating the three indigenous peoples but soon abandoned the plan, adopting a conciliatory policy instead. The Leopard people not only rejected the Shan policy as false but also murdered the science and technology transfer team sent by the Shan. The Shan commanding officer was infuriated and sent an interstellar warship to suppress them. But even after he had vaporized several mountains, the Leopard people couldn't be forced to surrender, and eventually the Shan troops withdrew. The fiercely independent character of the Leopard people was world famous.

After the successful uprising against the Shan, the Leopard people, who were fond of their independence, declared their freedom. Once the united army concluded their agreement to withdraw from Sunlon City, making it an open city, the chances of interfering in the self-determination of the Leopard people grew even remoter. The Leopard people, who functioned as an independent kingdom, suddenly had moved south to attack the Jinsuo rail line. Not only were the Huhui passengers sore afraid, but the Leopard people themselves knew little about the reasons behind their leader's actions.

We said that Miss Qi and Ah Two were on the train to Golden Goose Fort that was hijacked by the Leopard people. They were endowed with enormous strength, and they overturned the train of eight cars. The train was immediately filled with cries of misery. Miss Qi fell on top of Ah Two, and fortunately was uninjured. Ah Two had fallen hard and was moaning. Miss Qi quickly helped him up, and saw he had a huge welt on his head and one black eye. Eighty percent of the passengers were injured, and their will to fight was gone. They helped one another out of the train. By torchlight, the Leopard people rounded up the Huhui and made them sit on the ground with their hands on their heads. Commander Hua, the huge, stalwart leader, removed a piece of paper from the pouch at his waist and read aloud:

From the General Headquarters of the Leopard People's Revolutionary Army.
The plains area from Silverfield Village to Jinjiakou has belonged to the Leopard People from ancient times. It is off limits to all other peoples. In

these extraordinary times, anyone who willfully intrudes into the area will be dealt with in accordance with the LPRA articles of martial law.

After reading the military order, Commander Hua laughed and addressed his Huhui prisoners: "Huhui compatriots! You have entered a restricted area without authorization. The punishment for this crime is death. But given the common origin of the five peoples[1] and the virtue of our purple sun, we shall spare you. Instead we will send you to the Silverfield Village Labor Camp, where you will do hard labor."

When Commander Hua finished speaking, a general hubbub arose, but no one dared to argue. They merely gestured to one another. Miss Qi stood up and said, "Previously, you made no such announcement. How were we supposed to know we were entering a restricted area? Therefore, how can you say we are guilty?"

Commander Hua replied impatiently, "The restricted area is the same as our range of activity. Wherever we go, the area is restricted."

"That doesn't make sense," said Miss Qi. "If that's the case, then are you saying that the entire plain is restricted?"

"That's the way it is," said Commander Hua, laughing. "If we want to place it off limits, who is to say we can't?"

When he laughed, Commander Hua's fat face looked very funny. Miss Qi felt like laughing but dared not. Commander Hua guessed what she was thinking, so he put on a grave expression and said, "No more arguing; otherwise you'll be executed!"

The Leopard people then proceeded to tie the Huhui prisoners into strings of ten, each led by one Leopard soldier. Ah Two and Miss Qi found themselves in the same string, which was led by Commander Hua. At first the Leopard people walked slowly, but soon they picked up speed. The Leopard people were accustomed to running on the plains, and the poor Huhui people had to force themselves to run in order to keep up. The Huhui refugees—businessmen and women who normally lived an easy life—couldn't take it. After running a short distance, they would fall to the ground. If one person fell, the whole string went down. Those who fell didn't catch up again. The Huhui prisoners knew this didn't bode well, so, fearful for their lives, they forced themselves to run. But the Leopard people seemed to be punishing them. They ran faster and faster and, once again assuming their true animal nature, ran on all fours. One string of

---

[1] The five peoples are the Huhui, 凸 (chu), Serpent, Leopard, and Feathered peoples.

prisoners after another was lost in the dark. Soon only the string that included Miss Qi and Ah Two remained. Miss Qi ran until she was exhausted, then she felt a pull from behind. She knew that the three people behind her had fallen, and there was no way she could drag them. Then she fell too. Soon the entire string lay gasping on the ground. Commander Hua turned around and, laughing malignantly, opened his mouth.

"Can't go any farther, eh? You're useless. I can make a snack out of you."

The Huhui people lying on the ground shouted with fear. He gulped down the woman at the head of the string in two or three bites. The others watched her being eaten but couldn't believe their eyes. After eating her, Commander Hua burped and said, "I'm full. That's all for right now. Take a break. When you've recovered your strength, we'll hit the road again. I'm a nice guy, and I'm no glutton. If you work with me on this, maybe only a few of you will be eaten on our way to Silverfield Village."

Then everyone understood that the strings of prisoners were the rations allocated to each soldier. Some people wept, others prayed. The commander tied the rope to his leg and fell asleep. Of course, none of the Huhui prisoners could sleep; they lay there trying to think of some solution to their predicament. Some advocated fighting the Leopard person to the death as a group, especially those at the head of the string, who were particularly agitated. Those at the rear were against acting rashly. They talked and talked, and argued. The more they argued, the louder they got until they woke Commander Hua. He said, "You no-good Huhui people. I say I'm not going to eat you and you cause a ruckus. So be it; I'll have another!"

He leaped up and ate the Huhui businessman at the end of the string. After eating, Commander Hua wiped his mouth and said, "You see how fair I am. I eat one from the front and then one from the rear. Everyone has an equal opportunity. No one can complain about anyone else."

After eating the businessman, Commander Hua once again fell asleep. The remaining eight prisoners broke into two factions: those at either end of the string favored forceful action, while those in the middle didn't want to rush things. Once again they started arguing. Miss Qi had to speak: "We'll all soon be eaten by him, so why is everyone arguing? If we don't think of a plan now, we'll all be done for when he wakes up."

Ah Two, the butcher, asked Miss Qi if she had some brilliant scheme in mind. Miss Qi whispered her plan to them. They listened, and soon they stopped arguing and all settled down and rested.

After he had been asleep for a while, the commander felt a gentle tugging at the rope. Leopard people have keen senses, and he smiled inwardly but pretended to be asleep. After a short time, he got up. The rope had been cut, and the eight prisoners were gone! Commander Hua laughed and said, "Fools. Playing games with me. When I catch you, you'll wish you had been eaten."

The crafty Leopard people were accustomed to toying with their captives, then finding some excuse to eat them. So when Commander Hua saw that his prisoners had escaped, instead of being angry, he was pleased. He stood erect and sniffed the air. In a moment he scented the direction they had gone. He let out a howl and set off in pursuit on all fours. After a while he saw the string of Huhui prisoners running in front of him. Commander Hua laughed coldly and said, "Stupid people don't know enough to run in different directions and hide in a dark place to make it harder for me to find them. In the light of that heavenly shaft I can see them as plain as day. Where can they go?"

The commander shot forward and blocked their way. Frightened, the Huhui people dropped to their knees and pointed at Miss Qi, saying, "Commander Hua, it was all her doing. Eat her first."

"Don't be anxious," replied Commander Hua scornfully. "You'll all get your turn. I'll eat the tender one first."

He approached with the intention of eating Miss Qi. But unexpectedly they were upon him and pinned him down. Caught off guard, he found himself shafted, thrust into the blue light of the heavenly shaft. He knew this was bad and began to shout: "Save me. I'm being imprisoned in a shaft of heavenly of light! Save me!"

Seeing Commander Hua trapped in the shaft of light, the Huhui prisoners clapped and laughed. At first the Leopard person struggled. The shaft of light changed from blue to red, then a golden red. Commander Hua turn into a white silhouette, and there was a huge rending sound, after which the shaft of light rose off the ground and quickly receded into the sky. Commander Hua rose with the light and disappeared into the purple clouds. A wave of fear swept over Ah Two's face.

"That was too close for comfort. We nearly ended up as wandering ghosts on the plains."

The Huhui people all thanked Miss Qi. She smiled and said, "Driving away leopards and protecting the people is the lot of my generation. The commander will end up in some other little corner of Huhui history. He'll get his."

They were lucky to be alive, but they were also afraid of being attacked by other Leopard people. After discussing the matter, they all decided to head off on their own. Only after the other six prisoners had set off did Miss Qi and Ah Two start off slowly southward. By that time, the sky was growing light, and the shafts of blue light had vanished. The huge purple sun rose slowly over the boundless plains. After walking a while, Miss Qi couldn't help sighing.

"What are we going to do?" she asked Ah Two. "We don't even know where we are, much less where Golden Goose Fort is."

"Don't worry," replied Ah Two with confidence. "Jinjiakou is only forty kilometers from here. If we head south, we'll run into the railroad tracks, and then we just have to follow them west. At Jinjiakou your worries will be eased, because I know lots of people there and we'll be able to get a car to take us to Golden Goose Fort."

"If I'd known things would turn out this way, I would have let Ah Three drive us," said Miss Qi. "If I could have convinced Gai Bao to take me, I'd be there by now."

"There's no need for regrets," said Ah Two, striding ahead. "As long as you're alive, there is no need for regrets. You won't accomplish anything by thinking about the past."

Seeing Ah Two's strong back, Miss Qi silently caught up with him. She wondered if Yu Jin had any regrets. As she walked along, she thought about Yu Jin and tugged on the dry grass beside her. She recalled Yu Jin as he was about to lead the Death Commandos out for the uprising, and how in all that time he had only told her to "take care." Did he have any regrets? What had been accomplished by destroying the Shan? The enemy was now staging a comeback. Huhui history never changed; the outcome was always the same, over and over again. But nothing had come of their love.

The purple sun rose higher. Miss Qi and Ah Two ascended a small hill and gazed off into the distance. The forbidding golden plains stretched out all around them. A few purple clouds floated in the sky. It was autumn on the Huhui planet. That old purple sun seemed a little larger, which seemed to indicate that one day the Huhui planet would have an end. But when the sun died, what would happen to all the people? Would the Huhui, the Shan, the Feathered, Serpent, and Leopard peoples still be fighting? What would Sunlon City be like the day the sun died?

"Be careful, someone's coming."

Miss Qi looked in the direction Ah Two pointed and saw about ten Leopard people in the distance. Each led a string of prisoners that consisted of only four or five people. She knew that the others had been eaten, and she felt sad. The Leopard people were moving slowly, as if they were tracking something. Miss Qi whispered to Ah Two, "They might be looking for Commander Hua and us. Let's not hang around."

"It's too late," said Ah Two. "The Leopard people have extremely acute senses. If we run now, we'll be spotted at once."

They hid in the clumps of grass. As the Leopard people got closer, Miss Qi and Ah Two broke into a cold sweat. At that moment war drums were heard in the distance. The Leopard people halted and started talking among themselves. The sound of drums drew nearer, and Miss Qi lifted her head for a look. She saw more than a hundred cavalrymen with spears gradually closing in on the Leopard people.

"It's General Shi's cavalry!" shouted Miss Qi excitedly. "I've found him."

The ten Leopard people were soon surrounded by the cavalrymen. Both sides seemed at a standoff, then the Leopard people howled and shot off in all directions in an effort to break out. But the cavalrymen were just as quick, adroitly falling into ten small squads, each of which went after one Leopard person. Fierce as they were, they were no match for seven or eight spears. One by one they were pinned to the ground. Those who had not been killed roared, and some tried to pull the spears out of their bodies; but before they could, they succumbed to their wounds. The prisoners who had been freed by the horsemen surrounded the Leopard people and sucked up their blood. The Leopard people who were still alive screamed pitifully. Shocked, Miss Qi went pale and asked Ah Two what was going on. Ah Two shook his head and said, "Huhui legend has it that if you drink the blood of a Leopard person, you can live long without aging."

"Really?" said Miss Qi. "What makes that any different from Leopard people eating human flesh? This is too much!"

"Yesterday the Leopard people ate Huhui flesh; today the Huhui drink Leopard blood. This is attacking ▣ (du) with ▣ (du). I'm a butcher, and I've seen my share of this sort of thing. Let's go see the cavalry commander."

The commander was a young officer. He listened carefully to Miss Qi's account as he nodded his head.

"Good. Good. You'll have no problem seeing General Shi; he'll be here sooner or later. I'm in charge of mopping up enemy troops along the Jinsuo rail line. You can come with me."

The cavalry troops stacked the corpses of the Leopard people in a pile, then proceeded to skin each one of them. The prisoners who had drunk their fill of Leopard blood stood by watching with satisfaction, blood still staining their mouths. Miss Qi felt nothing but disgust. "Though the Leopard people are cruel, they are still people. Why must they be treated this way?"

The young officer seemed very embarrassed, and, blushing, said, "In the past, the Leopard people were not the enemies of the Leopard Brotherhood, but recently they have organized and invaded the plains. They have attacked several trains and killed a lot of passengers. That's why we have started to fight back. I don't necessarily approve of the skinning and the blood drinking, but they have eaten lots of people. They're making trouble for themselves, right?"

Miss Qi had no reply. She felt confused. Fortunately the skinning was performed quickly, and the Huhui who had survived the disaster were escorted away from that bloody pile of corpses.

The small squad approached the rail line, where a number of Huhui engineers were using a crane to set the toppled train upright again. Several hundred cavalrymen were gathered on both sides of the tracks. Seeing them, Miss Qi's heart beat with excitement. Who said General Shi's cavalry was done for?

"And General Shi?" asked Miss Qi, looking up as the young officer rode up beside her. "Is he here?"

"The general. . . ."

The young officer was interrupted by the loud, rhythmic chanting of the cavalry:

"Gen—er—al!"

"Gen—er—al!"

"Gen—er—al!"

Suddenly, countless horsemen advanced from all sides, their chanting echoing to the clouds. A flag bearer carried a large yellow banner embroidered with a leopard and the general's name. When the Leopard Brotherhood members saw the banner, they shouted with joy. Surrounded by cavalrymen, an awe-inspiring old warrior with white hair, dressed in golden armor, riding on a white steed, slowly advanced.

11

The Leopard-skin drums resounded. The Royalist cavalry passed in rows of ten, their eyes fixed respectfully on the general's banner—the Valiant cavalry with their scimitars; the Dragon cavalry with their long spears; the Routing cavalry with their pistols. General Shi's crack troops were the proudest of the Royalist contingent. It was they who had carried out the final charge against the Shan occupation army during the uprising. They did not fear death; they had earned the undying respect of the Huhui planet in exchange for seven thousand lives. It was they who struck terror in the Shan; it was they who kept Sunlon City children from crying at night. It was they who, like the phoenix, had been reborn in fire, having completely recovered their past splendor in only one year.

When the remnants of General Shi's cavalry had sorrowfully withdrawn from Sunlon City the previous year, only eight hundred warriors accompanied the general back to Golden Goose Fort. But as soon as word got out that the Leopard Brotherhood Cavalry was re-forming, every young Royalist swordsman ready for a fight bought a war horse and weapons and made their way from all parts of the Huhui planet to Golden Goose Fort. Everyone was aware of the fate of those seven thousand cavalrymen, but what was life worth? The Royalist swordsmen preferred death in battle to living in ignominy. The death of seven thousand swordsmen actually brought widespread fame and prestige to the Royalist party. General Shi's cavalry quickly recruited eight thousand men. After a year of rigorous training, the army was set to carry on its glorious tradition. It was at that time that the Leopard people had begun their harassment on the plains, and attacks by small bands of them on Huhui villages became a common occurrence. When a large force of Leopard people began openly to attack the Jinsuo rail line, General Shi, his patience at an end, ordered his troops to leave the training grounds at Golden Goose Fort and proceed to Jinjiakou.

The Leopard-skin drums sounded, and the warriors cheered. Astride his horse, the white-haired general inspected the precision military formation. Ah Two couldn't help cheering and said to Miss Qi, "No wonder the Leopard people are no match for the cavalry. With the cavalry and the Green Snake Brotherhood, Sunlon City will be impregnable."

"That's right," said Miss Qi. "Thank goodness we were hijacked by the Leopard people; otherwise we wouldn't have found General Shi. We should thank them."

The general had completed the inspection of the cavalry. Seven Leopard prisoners were brought before him and told to kneel. Knowing that disaster was approaching, they refused. A Valiant cavalryman spurred his horse forward and brought down his scimitar, killing one of the Leopard people. The other Leopard people, their eyes large with anger, howled, "Long live the Leopard People's Revolutionary Army!"

A Dragon cavalryman then spurred his horse forward and thrust his spear through the heart of another Leopard person, pinning him to the ground. The Leopard person ranted and cursed as before until he spit up blood and expired. Shaking with fear, Miss Qi observed the proceedings. Then, with total disregard for the situation, she ran forward, blocking the horsemen, and said, "No more killing! Aren't you ashamed of yourselves?"

The horsemen reined in their mounts and looked at each other. The general, who had heard this, asked, "Why do you want to save the Leopard people? Do you know how many Huhui travelers they have harmed?"

"The Leopard people should be punished for their crimes," said Miss Qi. "But for the world-famous cavalry to use Leopard people as living targets is just too cruel."

The general carefully looked over Miss Qi.

"I think we've met. You delivered a message from the cult leader prior to the uprising last year, didn't you?"

"That's correct," said Miss Qi. "I'm not here this time to deliver anything from the cult leader. I am here with a message from Yu Fang, leader of the Green Snake Brotherhood. You must lead your army in the defense of Sunlon City at once."

Hearing this, the white-haired general remained silent. Miss Qi had expected him to agree with alacrity to send troops, but instead he was silent for a long time. Miss Qi grew anxious.

"General, the Shan are staging a comeback. They have been inciting the Feathered, Serpent, and Leopard peoples to rebel. By staying here to fight the Leopard people, you are conforming to Shan plans. If the Shan take Sunlon City, it will be too late."

"Sunlon City, Sunlon City," repeated the general as if hypnotized. "Seven thousand of my soldiers died there. Sunlon City is a city of sorrow; I'll not go there."

"You have to go . . ." said Miss Qi. The general paid her no more attention. He motioned to his bodyguards. In twos they dispatched the remaining Leopard prisoners. One horseman raised the general's banner, which was greeted with thunderous cheering, after which the bodyguards surrounded the general and set off toward the north. The thousands of cavalrymen fell in behind. Miss Qi stood stunned beside the pile of corpses, unsure what to do next. Ah Two tried to console her. "General Shi has his hands full with fighting the Leopard people; that's why he can't go to Sunlon City. That's all right, the days of the aggressive Leopard people are numbered."

"I don't believe it," said Miss Qi. "I thought it was the general who most cherished the city. Why won't he send troops to save it? What are we going to do?"

Ah Two was a simple man. When asked this by Miss Qi, he scratched his head but could not come up with any plan. By then, the engineers had repositioned the train on the tracks, and the steam whistle on the engine tooted. The freed Huhui prisoners once again boarded the train.

"Why don't we go to Jinjiakou," suggested Ah Two. "When we arrive there, we'll decide on our next step."

With no definite idea, Miss Qi reboarded the train with the other passengers. On board, everyone recounted with excitement their experience of being hijacked by the Leopard people. Some had cut off pieces of Leopard hide and now showed the others, letting them admire the spoils of war. Those who had been lucky enough to drink Leopard blood told about its tonifying properties, how drinking it proved supremely efficacious for soothing their nerves. In utter disgust, Miss Qi turned to look out the window, leaving Ah Two to handle the Huhui men and women who thought they would enjoy a long life free from aging.

Miss Qi watched as the landscape gradually changed: the vast green plain gave way to rows of olive trees, and then flowers planted along the roads. She remembered reading in a geography book when she was a child that Jinjiakou was the biggest oasis on the plains. And now, even before they had arrived, the landscape had already changed so much. In the carriage, several children clapped their hands and sang:

> *The train flies*
> *The train flies*
> *Speeding through the mountains*
> *Over small streams*
> *Across how many miles?*
> *We're almost home*
> *We're almost home*
> *Mother will be so happy to see us.*

The train gradually slowed. In the distance a city was visible; Miss Qi knew that they had arrived in Jinjiakou. In spite of the noise in the carriage, Miss Qi could hear a humming sound from outside. In a short while, the other Huhui passengers heard it too. They all grew quiet. The humming grew ever louder; it seemed to be composed of countless human voices. Perplexed, Miss Qi asked Ah Two, "What is that sound?"

"I never expected that we would see this," replied Ah Two. "It's the Sacrificial Offerings for Transmigration, a great event held only once every seventeen years. What you hear is the Transmigration Prayer."

By the time the train pulled into the Jinjiakou Station, the chanting had become deafening. Covering their ears, the Huhui passengers all quickly got off the train. Ah Two led Miss Qi out of the station. Rows of purple banners lined both sides of the avenue in front and ran from the city gate all the way to the central square before the station. Huge crowds of people stood beneath the banners, leaving a route open. They were waiting for the arrival of the priest.

"It's not yet time. Let's go to my elder sister's house and have a rest," said Ah Two, leading Miss Qi through the bustling crowd.

"Time for what?" asked Miss Qi, her curiosity piqued. "What are they chanting?"

"I'll tell you when we get to my sister's house."

Ah Two's relatives lived at the mouth of a nearby street. His brother-in-law was also a butcher. His sister and her husband were kneeling and chanting in the small back room of their shop. Ah Two didn't want to disturb them, so he took Miss Qi to the second floor of the stone building and sat down by the window.

"From here we can watch the Transmigration Sacrifices," said Ah Two. "You can't see it any better than this and you don't have to push and shove to get a place. I remember that I watched the ceremony from this very place with my sister seventeen years ago."

"What is it that they are chanting?" asked Miss Qi.

"The Transmigration Prayer," replied Ah Two. "Jinjiakou is one of the few cities on the Huhui planet that still preserves the transmigration system. On the occasion of the sacrifices, everyone chants the prayer, celebrating the eternal nature of transmigration. It takes from early in the morning to afternoon to chant the entire prayer."

At that point, the tone of the chanting changed as everyone began the rhythmic recitation of a series of names.

"They have finished chanting the prayer," said Ah Two. "Now they are reciting the names of the dead. Through transmigration, life goes on even though the dead never come back. This recitation of the names of the dead is the way the living remember and express their regrets to the dead prior to transmigration."

Miss Qi watched from the window. It was almost noon, and the purple sun seemed brighter than usual. Countless purple banners flapped in the wind. The people standing beneath the flags looked hungry and thirsty as they chanted the names of the dead as they were broadcasted by the public address system. The meaningless sounds struck the eardrums like drops of water.

"Aside from a minority of families that have retained the privilege to transmigrate," continued Ah Two, "most of the people of Jinjiakou have no such right. Most people can only look on with envy at those few who can experience the miracle of rebirth. Everyone is especially enthusiastic when it comes to reciting the names of the dead because they all know that one day others will be reciting their names. That is the only thing that people can look forward to with any certainty."

"That's an unreasonable system," said Miss Qi. "I remember that our history teacher told us that the system was done away with after a large-scale armed rebellion by troops garrisoned at Jinjiakou. I never dreamed that such a vulgar custom still existed in your hometown."

Somewhat embarrassed, Ah Two hastened to explain. "Jinjiakou is a small place; popular customs are simple and conservative. While only about thirty families actually have the privilege to transmigrate, the Trans-

migration Sacrifices have actually become the one folk custom that the local people are most proud of. It's not that easy to do away with. See! The
priest is coming, and behind him are those who are going to transmigrate
this time."

The rows of people beneath the purple banners surged forward to get a
better glimpse of the cortège that had just entered the city gate. Miss Qi
observed the chief priest, four assistants, and twenty or so transmigrators
all in purple robes. Behind them followed the families and relatives of the
transmigrators. As the cortège slowly made its way to the square in front
of the station, the public address system went silent. The chief priest led
those assembled in a chant:

屮甼 *(chu-ru)*

屮甼 *(chu-ru)*

-ロ- -ロ- *(lu-mu lu-mu)*

ロ-ロ ロ-ロ *(mu-lu mu-lu)*

⊡ □ *(du-wu)*

⊡ □ *(du-wu)*

屮甼 *(chu-ru)*

屮甼 *(chu-ru)*

Then the transmigrators dressed in purple bowed to those assembled
and indicated their gratitude. The transmigrators were all around fifty
years of age; some had white hair, while others still looked young.

"They are all the most respected people in Jinjiakou," said Ah Two, as
he pointed out various people. "The man with the beard is the only sage
in Jinjiakou; the fat guy is the owner of the Golden Goose Fort Hotel; that
skinny woman is the president of the evening paper."

Miss Qi felt that one of the transmigrators looked familiar. Looking at
his face, she trembled.

"Yu Jin!"

Ah Two was startled when he heard Miss Qi shout. He too closely examined the transmigrators congregated in the square.

"Is that Yu Jin? How is that possible? True, the face is similar, but it
can't be him. Why is he here in Jinjiakou to transmigrate?"

"That's definitely him!" said Miss Qi, standing up. "Let's take a closer
look. What's he doing here? It's really strange."

They rushed downstairs. Ah Two's sister and brother-in-law were still
chanting. Miss Qi and Ah Two pushed their way into the crowd and with

difficulty made their way to the square. The transmigrators had already filed into a windowless building. The high priest and the four assistants slowly closed the large door. The chief priest turned around and made a singular awareness gesture. Everyone began reciting the final part of the Transmigration Prayer.

"They've all entered the Transmigration Center," said Ah Two. "In a moment, they'll all come out as seventeen-year-old boys and girls. This is the miracle of transmigration. Every seventeen years a group of fifty-one-year-olds transmigrates and returns to their youth of seventeen. They really are to be envied!"

The chanting grew ever louder, and Miss Qi was forced to cover her ears. Finally the chanting stopped. The high priest and the four assistants walked over to the door of the Transmigration Center and together performed a singular awareness gesture. Then they slowly opened the big door. Some time went by, and still no one emerged.

At first the spectators were silent; then they grew anxious and began to whisper among themselves. The crowd grew louder and louder. The high priest—a tall, thin man with a black face and long beard—was at a loss as to what he should do. After some consideration, he decided to enter the Transmigration Center. As he entered, he was pushed by someone and fell to the ground. The spectators were stunned. A man dressed entirely in black emerged from the center. He wore a black mask, and on his chest gleamed a small bronze statue. Seeing this, Miss Qi shouted, "It's the cult leader!"

The cult leader lifted his hands and the crowd grew silent. Laughing, the man in black said, "People of Jinjiakou! What time is this? The Shan bastards are planning to attack the Huhui planet. The Serpent people and the Leopard people have already risen in rebellion. You know that the Leopard people are engaging in all sorts of cruelties on the plains. What time is it? You're still playing the transmigration game. Aren't you ashamed?

"People of Jinjiakou! Transmigration is the most backward of systems and should have been done away with a long time ago. Since you are unwilling to do so, I've come to get rid of this unreasonable system for you. Today, I have taken away the twenty-one transmigrators. You need not concern yourselves with where they have gone. Henceforth, there is no transmigration system in Jinjiakou. I urge all of you quickly to convert to the Bronze Statue Cult. The Bronze Statue is the only true god that can rescue the Huhui planet.

"People of Jinjiakou! Please keep in mind that though flowers and fruit must fall, scattered by the wind, Sunlon City will be reborn!"

So speaking, the Stranger in Black stretched out his arms, and as his robe billowed, he suddenly vanished. The families of the transmigrators screamed sadly and rushed into the center. All twenty-one transmigrators had vanished without a trace, leaving the room empty, its walls covered with mirrors. The sadness of the family members turned to anger, and they turned on the high priest and the four assistants, nearly beating them to death. They then joined together and pulled down the center. The people of Jinjiakou, who were jealous and envious of the transmigrators, not only did nothing when they saw the center being pulled down, but actually applauded and cheered.

"If things go on like this," said Ah Two, sighing, "it will be the end of the Jinjiakou transmigration system like the cult leader said."

Miss Qi hung her head without saying a word. Ah Two knew who Miss Qi was missing and tried to console her.

"You must have been mistaken. The transmigrators are from Jinjiakou. How could Yu Jin be among them?"

"I wasn't mistaken," Miss Qi maintained. "He really was there. He was taken away by the cult leader. The cult leader. . . ."

As Miss Qi spoke, she broke into tears. It was difficult for Ah Two to convince her to return to his sister's house. His sister and her husband had finished chanting, and they were standing in a neighbor's doorway discussing the strange events that had just occurred. Ah Two introduced Miss Qi to everyone. Everyone was curious about the young lady from Sunlon City and looked her over closely; she just lowered her head to avoid everyone's inquiring gazes. Ah Two was afraid that Miss Qi was too tired, and asked his sister to prepare a bed for her upstairs so that she could get some rest. He then accompanied his sister to visit with the neighbors and chat. It had been several years since Ah Two last visited Jinjiakou, and he was in the mood to enjoy himself. He took out the sea serpent meat and roast chicken and shared it with the neighbors. Although Jinjiakou was a small town, it was a pretty good-sized city for the plains. The city had become quieter since the Leopard people began their activities. Ah Two then recounted what had happened to him over the last two days. They were elated to hear that General Shi had pursued the Leopard people northward. Some said that General Shi should annihilate them for all the cruelties they had perpetrated. Others didn't think the cavalry was a match for the Leopard people. Some were of the opinion that the cult leader had appeared at the ceremonies because he wanted to have his cut of the plains. No one knew who would control the plains in the future.

Although Miss Qi was resting upstairs, she clearly heard everything that was said downstairs. But her thoughts were turned solely to the one whom she had briefly seen at the ceremony. She was positive it was Yu Jin. Why had he become a transmigrator? Where had the cult leader taken them? Who was it who had ordered Gai Bao to come for her the day before in his Froghopper?

At dusk, Miss Qi heard the sound of hooves approaching like rain from the distance. Soon the street was filled with the clip-clop of horses' hooves. Miss Qi leaped out of bed, opened the shutters, and saw the Royalist cavalry returning.

"The cavalry is back!" reported Ah Two, running upstairs. Miss Qi nodded. Of course she had seen them, but the real question was, why were they returning so early to Jinjiakou? Had they been unable to defeat the Leopard people? Had they already wiped out the enemy? Or was there some other reason?

Miss Qi and Ah Two stood at the window watching the rows of horsemen pass. Then she saw three horsemen pass riding side by side. She gasped, unable to believe her eyes.

12

The first of the three horsemen wasn't really riding a horse—he himself looked more like a small horse, trotting along on all fours. He held his leopard head high, a smile on his round face.

"It's Commander Hua!" said Ah Two with surprise. "How did he get here? Didn't we shaft him?"

Having acute senses, he immediately turned his head toward the two people upstairs and laughed.

"My two Huhui compatriots, your exquisite plan forced me to wander far and wide. If I hadn't run into two other Huhui compatriots, I'd still be wandering in the Silurian Epoch."

Commander Hua pointed to the two other horsemen. One was a repellent green Serpent person, his tail dragging on the ground. He was so heavy that he seemed to crush his mount. The other was a short, fat 出 person. Miss Qi first greeted him. "How did you get here, Ah 出 (chu)?"

Ah 出 (chu) was overjoyed at seeing Miss Qi and Ah Two. "出-叮叮叮 (chu-lu-ru-mu), Ah Two, what are you two doing at Jinjiakou?" The three of them stopped, and the soldiers behind them were also forced to halt. The neighbors all came out to have a look. When they saw the Serpent person and the frightful visage of the Leopard person, they all fled back into their houses. Commander Hua laughed and said, "Since we have run into old friends, perhaps we should go inside and chat so as not to hold up the rest of the troops."

Hearing this, Miss Qi and Ah Two hurriedly came down. Ah Two's sister, brother-in-law, and several neighbors huddled fearfully in one corner. Commander Hua was invited to sit on the floor, but his head nearly hit the ceiling. Only by stooping was the vile Serpent person able to squeeze in as well, but his tail hung out the door. Ah 凷 (chu) bowed deeply to Miss Qi and Ah Two and said, "Allow me to introduce two friends of mine. This is Commander Hua, who was once a battlefront commander in the Leopard People's Revolutionary Army."

Miss Qi and Commander Hua spoke at the same time, saying, "We've met." Ah 凷 (chu) was very pleased. Then he pointed out the giant Serpent person and said, "This is Mr. Zhi-Hu; he is the general who guards 凷叴 (chu-ru) Pass, the Number One Underground Pass. He is a Serpent elder, and the number one warrior of the underground world."

"Mistaken is my brother 凷 (chu)," said Zhi-Hu Zhe. "This young maid be none other than Maistre 凷 (chu)'s precious pearl? Certes she be of much wit and pure of hart. And the other person is?"

"He is my servant," said Miss Qi. "Ah 凷 (chu), how did you escape from the Serpent people's cave? What about Yu Kui and the other Green Snake Brotherhood soldiers?"

"They are all okay," replied Ah 凷 (chu). "Yu Kui is already on his way to Hehe Village to meet up with Yu Fang's main force. We owe it to Mr. Zhi-Hu's mercy that we managed to escape from the cave. Not only did he not ⊡ (du) us, but he bravely led us back. He has helped us in our misfortune to stand on our own feet again; his goodness has made a new man of me, and his high morality reaches to the clouds!"

As Ah 凷 (chu) praised Zhi-Hu to the limits, the huge Serpent's tail swung back and forth outside the door. Miss Qi was confused. The Serpent and Leopard peoples were rebels, but Ah 凷 (chu) was their friend and they had all accompanied General Shi back to Jinjiakou. What was going on?

"Ah 凷 (chu)," asked Miss Qi cautiously, for fear of upsetting his two friends, "you probably don't know how serious the situation at Sunlon City is. Yu Fang is waiting there with the Green Snake Brotherhood for General Shi to come to the aid of the city. The Snake and Leopard peoples have taken the opportunity to invade. How at this time can you . . ."

Miss Qi found it difficult to continue. Zhi-Hu Zhe laughed heartily, shaking the entire room and making dust fall from the ceiling, frightening Ah Two and the other Huhui people so much that they huddled even closer together. After he finished laughing, Zhi-Hu Zhe shook his head and said, "Miss, thou art bold in thy open rebuke of the Serpent and

Leopard peoples. No common Serpent am I. Thou art oblyged to know that the Serpent people are restrained by the Shan and in their subiection, and lack libertie. Rescued I Ah 出 (chu) and Yu Kui to aide the Huhui gain victorie 'gainst the Shan and to yield the Serpent people libertie from their sore travaile. A greater good there be none."

"So that's the case," said Miss Qi. "But what about the commander? He hijacked a train last night, and killed defenseless Huhui women and children. You mean he already has seen the light? Isn't that a little too fast for a change of heart?"

"No, not at all," said Commander Hua, laughing, his face as round as the purple sun. "I was wrong last night to frighten you so. But you are not defenseless. You actually sent me to the end of the Silurian Epoch. I was there for twenty hard years. Fortunately I ran into Ah 出 (chu) and the reverend Zhi-Hu Zhe, who brought me back. What for you has been one night has been twenty years for me. In that time, I had the chance to read many ancient Huhui books, and I diligently studied the singular awareness philosophy. Owing to this, I underwent a great change and will never be the cruel person I was of yesteryear. It's been ten years since I have eaten any meat, much less human flesh."

Miss Qi didn't know if she should believe him or not. She asked Ah 出 (chu): "Ah 出 (chu), how did you manage to join General Shi's cavalry?"

"I am a Huhui historian. How could I not be concerned about the rise and fall, victory and defeat of the Huhui? Sunlon City's fate hangs in the balance and only General Shi can make the difference. That's why I've brought my two friends along to help the general."

"But the general is unwilling to send troops," said Miss Qi anxiously. "Can you convince him?"

"Fear not, I'll take care of it," said Ah 出 (chu) as if he were in control. "If he sends troops tonight, they will arrive at Sunlon City day after tomorrow."

When Commander Hua and Zhi-Hu Zhe heard this, one laughed and the other swung his tail. Miss Qi still had her doubts, and just as she was about to pursue the matter, in ran a hairy-faced cavalry officer, huffing and puffing. He stood at attention and saluted Ah 出 (chu).

"Mr. Ah 出 (chu), the general requests your presence. He would like for you, Commander Hua, and Mr. Zhi-Hu to proceed to headquarters at once."

"I understand," said Ah 出 (chu), obviously pleased with himself. "Miss, come with me to see the general and watch me convince him to send troops with my eloquence."

General Shi's temporary headquarters was set up inside the station. The purple banners along the avenue had not been removed and seemed to match the purple clouds in the evening sky. Miss Qi couldn't help but recall the grand occasion of the day's Transmigration Sacrifices and the surging throngs of people beneath the banners. Now a dense mass of cavalrymen stood in the same place, holding the reins of their war steeds, quietly waiting. There was a nip in the autumn air on the plains. The wind did not rage the way it did in Sunlon City, nor did it carry dust. Miss Qi understood then that that was why Jinjiakou had become an oasis on the plains.

Ah 出 (chu), Miss Qi, Ah Two, Commander Hua, and Zhi-Hu Zhe entered the station together. The aged, white-haired general was already seated in the center of the main waiting room. He wore reading glasses and held a book in his hand. He was absorbed in his reading. Ah 出 (chu) and the others entered without the general being aware. Ah 出 (chu) stepped forward, bowed deeply, and said, "General, we are here."

The general put aside his book and took off his glasses, examining the group carefully. He nodded ever so slightly to the Serpent person and said, "Was it Mr. Zhi-Hu who swept away the Leopard troops with his long tail this afternoon?"

"None other," said the huge Serpent person, raising four of his limbs. "Of time I have lacked to inquire of the general if thou hast comment or suggestioun for me."

"Hmmm . . ." said the general, looking at Commander Hua. "Although the Leopard troops were defeated by the reverend Zhi-Hu, your own contributions were in no way insignificant. Commander Hua and Ah 出 (chu) were able to convince many Leopard soldiers to throw down their weapons and surrender, thereby decreasing the casualties to my own troops. No small accomplishment."

The Leopard person shook his head and laughed. Based on what General Shi said, the outstanding contributions in that day's skirmish with the Leopard troops could be attributed to the three strange people. No wonder the cavalry had returned in victory so quickly. The three of them were overjoyed at General Shi's praise. Zhi-Hu Zhe swung his tail and mumbled to himself; Commander Hua smiled foolishly; Ah 出 (chu), his hands behind his back and his eyes to the ceiling, heaved a sigh of relief. Miss Qi could not suppress a smile. Suddenly the general spoke to her: "What are you doing here again? Who are you delivering messages for this time?"

Miss Qi rolled her eyes.

"I'm not delivering messages for anyone," she said charmingly. "I'm delivering one of my own. Is that okay?"

"Delivering one of your own? Goodness, can you talk." The general laughed. He was probably in a good mood, what with just having won a battle. He stroked his beard and said, "Well, what have you got to say? Speak up."

Miss Qi was about to speak when Ah 凸 (chu) interrupted. "General, Miss Qi is the daughter of my master Qi Mingzhong, sage of Sunlon City. Mr. Qi died heroically during the great uprising. If Mr. Qi had not solved the riddle of the five jade disks, enabling us to save the Death Commandos, the Shan warship would not have been destroyed, and the great uprising would have come to naught."

"I know," said General Shi, smiling at Miss Qi. "Miss, the last two times we met you were carrying messages requesting that I send troops to Sunlon City. I'm afraid you still want me to send troops, right?"

"You're entirely correct," replied Miss Qi, laughing. "You've already destroyed the Leopard troops, and there is no trace of the enemy on the plains. There is no need to worry about your rear. It's the right time to advance your troops on Sunlon City to defend it against a Shan attack."

The old general sighed and stood up. The book on his knees fell to the ground. Ah 凸 (chu) quickly retrieved it for him, and sneaking a glance, he saw that it was the ⼌⼍ (man-qia) *Art of War*. Originally, the ⼌⼍ (man-qia) Sage practiced the Way on Mount Huihui during the Anliu Era. He made an intensive study of the du-wu philosophy, and wrote numerous works including *Meditations on* ▣□ (du-wu) and ⼌⼍ *(man-qia) Art of War*, which all had an immense influence on later generations. Although the ⼌⼍ (man-qia) Sage wasn't a warrior, his *Art of War*, which he wrote as a consummately cultivated philosopher, became an invaluable book read by all Huhui strategists. Ah 凸 (chu) figured that General Shi, who had lived on the plains for decades, must have read the ⼌⼍ *(man-qia) Art of War* more times than he could count, and he still persevered in studying the essence of the work. Ah 凸 (chu) couldn't help but feel a great respect for him. The general paced back and forth through the main hall of the station mumbling to himself:

Mind is called ▣ *(du)*
Nonmind is called □ *(wu)*
Transform ▣ *(du) into* □ *(wu)*
Subdue □ *(wu) with* ▣ *(du).*

He repeated the verse, then turned to Miss Qi and said, "It's not that I'm unwilling to help the city. My best troops died there during the uprising, something that pained me more deeply than I could bear. After my return to Golden Goose Fort, I made up my mind to study the *Art of War*. According to the 凸·凸 *(man-qia) Art of War*, one must 'transform ▣ (du) into □ (wu), and subdue □ (wu) with ▣ (du).' For this reason, Sunlon City cannot be defended. Obstinately defending the city is like being a turtle caught in a jar—the Shan will be able to achieve victory at one go. If the Green Snake Brotherhood enters the city, the misfortune will be theirs; if the cavalry enters the city, we will fall into the same trap and again be subject to heavy attack. This being the case, I would be better off staying on the plains, maintaining a □ (wu) position, and working in concert with the troops defending the city. This is the best policy."

Miss Qi remembered that Ah 凸 (chu) had arrived at a similar view when he analyzed the Green Snake Brotherhood strategy while they were in the Serpent lair under the copper fields. Hearing the same thing now, she felt it hard to dispute. Ah 凸 (chu) bowed deeply to the general and said, "What you say is true. It is unsuitable to obstinately defend the city. And the 凸·凸 (man-qia) Sage did say 'Mind is ▣ (du), nonmind is □ (wu).' The difference between ▣ (du) and □ (wu) resides in the difference between mind and nonmind. An old saying puts it best: 'When you put your mind to planting a tree, it won't grow; but if you carelessly stick a willow twig in the ground, it will grow.' If you put your mind to defending the city to the end, you will find yourself in a ▣ (du) position of being passively attacked, which, of course, is dangerous. But if you can maintain a flexible □ (wu) position, taking the initiative to overcome the enemy, you will achieve your goal of defending the city by not defending it. In ancient Tai Nan, there was a strategist by the name of Captain Lichahate, who studied the art of war for several decades and came up with the principle of 'indirectness.' He believed that every successful strategy adopted an indirect approach to achieve precisely what a direct approach could not. The 凸·凸 (man-qia) Sage brought Lichahate's principle into play. The indirect approach is the same as his nonmind, or □ (wu). The direct approach is what the 凸·凸 (man-qia) Sage called mind, or ▣ (du). So when the 凸·凸 (man-qia) Sage said, 'transform ▣ (du) into □ (wu), and subdue □ (wu) with ▣ (du),' what he meant was to transform the direct approach into an indirect one, and use an indirect approach to subdue a direct one!"

Once Ah 凸 (chu) started lecturing, he danced for joy like a child who has just received his favorite candy. But those listening weren't necessarily interested. Though he was the eldest, General Shi listened patiently to Ah 凸 (chu)'s point of view. But Zhi-Hu Zhe swung his tail impatiently, and blinking his three eyes said, "Brother Ah 凸 (chu), ⊡ (du) is singular; □ (wu) is awareness. ⊡□ (du-wu) is of great use. The marvelle of singular awareness be in one mind. Need more be said? What might the purple heavens say?"

Ah 凸 (chu) hastened to bow, and said, "Mr. Zhi-Hu, what you are talking about is different. We want to ask General Shi to save the city. First we must be clear. Can the city be saved or not?"

Commander Hua laughed and said, "Ah 凸 (chu), you went on and on about direct and indirect approaches. May I ask if sending troops to Sunlon City is a direct or indirect approach?"

Ah 凸 (chu) was pleased as punch. He loved it when people asked him questions. But he didn't forget to bow to Commander Hua as he spoke. "Excellent question. If General Shi sends troops to defend Sunlon City to the end, that is the direct approach. But if he sends troops to Sunlon City with the aim of luring the Shan to attack and then annihilating the Shan force by taking them by surprise, that would be the indirect approach. Thus the direct approach can be transformed into an indirect one, but by the same token the indirect approach can be transformed into a direct one. It depends on whether you have mind or nonmind. If the Shan cannot guess which it is, success will be ours."

"I understand what you are saying," said the general. "You want me to send troops to Sunlon City as if I were going to defend it to the end, while keeping my main force outside to ambush the invading Shan. Not a bad plan."

"Then you agree to send troops?" asked Miss Qi excitedly. "You agree?"

"Young lady, if I don't send troops, you will never rest. My granddaughter is about your age, and she is demanding as well. But she has never asked me to mobilize thousands of troops."

"This is for the people and the nation," said Miss Qi, "and there is nothing wrong with that. So, do you agree?"

"The cavalry has scored a number of victories on the plains," said the general, sighing, "and the youngsters are itching for a fight. But sending troops this time will mean that many of them never will see Golden Goose Fort again."

At that moment a number of young soldiers who were acting as bodyguards spoke in unison: "We can die in the defense of Sunlon City; nothing could be more glorious, and we would die with no regrets. Though flowers and fruit must fall, scattered by the wind, Sunlon City will be reborn."

"I know how you feel." The general sighed again. "My aspirations are as yet unrealized. I have suffered much already, and the Huhui planet is full of tears and scars. Sunlon City is in a precarious situation. Even if we want to stay aloof, I'm afraid we won't be able to. Children, issue orders for the troops to march at once eastward along the Jinsuo rail line to mop up the remnants of the enemy force, and then on to Sunlon City."

Elated, the officers received the order and departed. Shortly, there was an uproar outside the station, and the soldiers began to chant rhythmically:

"Gen—er—al!"

"Gen—er—al!"

Hearing this, Miss Qi, Ah Two, and the three strange people were visibly moved. Zhi-Hu Zhe said, "The men are hartie, and can warre make 'gainst all foes."

Ah 屮 (chu) bowed to the general and said, "Not only do your troops not fear death, they actually look upon death in battle as a glory. With such troops, victory is assured. Let me be the first to congratulate you."

The general seemed not to hear Zhi-Hu Zhe and Ah 屮's (chu) praise. Miss Qi watched as he strode shakily from the station and mounted his war horse. Although everyone cheered, the general seemed to force himself to wave, as if he had nothing to do with victory and glory. Miss Qi immediately felt deep sympathy for the old man. Such a heavy burden rested on his shoulders. Miss Qi could surmise what was on his mind. So many young swordsmen would not hesitate to accompany him and sacrifice themselves in the defense of Sunlon City. To them it was a romantic sacrifice; to the general it had become a perpetual weight on his conscience. Of what use was victory? Wasn't the ultimate fate of the Huhui planet, like that of the purple sun, to die out?

The general departed, surrounded by his guards. The rows of cavalrymen under the purple banners clutched their spears and cheered. The sound moved heaven and earth. Although the people of Jinjiakou had been awakened earlier, they all remained inside their homes. They exhibited none of the excitement they had evinced during the day at the Transmigration Sacrifices. Only the refugees who had recently arrived from Sunlon City came out of their tents to cheer for the cavalry. They gasped aloud when they saw Zhi-Hu Zhe the giant Serpent person and Commander Hua the huge Leopard person among the troops.

Commander Hua laughed, and addressed the waving multitudes: "Huhui compatriots! Don't worry; you'll soon be able to return to Sunlon City."

On horseback, Miss Qi, Ah 出 (chu), and Ah Two followed the two strange figures. The procession soon exited the city gate. A long file of troops stretched to the horizon, which was covered with purple clouds. The banners waved; the wind blew. The neighing of war horses occasionally wafted through the air. The mighty cavalry had once again set out to do battle.

13

———

At the same time General Shi's cavalry set out in formidable array, something strange occurred at the camp of the Green Snake Brotherhood outside Sunlon City. The story goes that after the main force of the Green Snake Brotherhood withdrew from the copper fields at Five Phoenixes Mountain, Yu Fang ordered that troops be garrisoned along the West Hu River and the Hu River and guardposts be established from Red Iron Village in the north to River Mouth City in the south. The armored barges that came and went on the Hu River also received secret orders to stay on the lookout for any suspicious troop activities.

Autumn was the rainy season on the Huhui planet. Lightning storms often occurred over the western plains on autumn nights. To the east, in the Hu River Basin and in the region around Mount Huihui, rain fell continuously. When rainy season arrived, the river rose rapidly. The russet-colored water flowed quietly, often carrying a floating corpse down from the headwaters. The bargemen in the lower reaches of the river shook their heads at the sight of the corpses: a boat certainly had encountered trouble in the red sandy gorges where the water flowed quickly.

The rainy season that year had just started. Corpses floated downriver one after another. Most were soldiers in uniform, but there were also the corpses of Feathered people. Immersed in the river, the feathers on their wings took on the ashen color of death, making them look like huge drowned birds. The bargemen had never seen so many corpses floating in the river, especially those of Feathered people. This unusual situation was reported to the Green Snake Brotherhood. When Yu Fang heard the news, he immediately took Yu Kui, Liu Qi, and Wang Liu to have a look. They traveled by horse to the wharf on the Hu River at Hehe Village, a key military position.

On the wharf there were around ten corpses that the bargemen had fished out of the river. After carefully examining them, Wang Liu turned to Yu Fang and said, "Brotherhood Leader, although these soldiers are wearing the uniforms of frontier defense troops, they are not Huhui people. Just look at the proportions of their arms to their legs, and you'll see that beyond a shadow of a doubt they are Shan dressed that way."

The Shan had very long arms but relatively short legs. Wang Liu had noticed this special trait at once. Yu Kui couldn't help performing a singular awareness gesture as he said, "Brilliant; I think it's 㑒 (ru). Then what about the corpses of the Feathered people? Is there anything unusual about them?"

Wang Liu then examined the corpses of the Feathered people, most of which had been partly eaten by fish, and said, "This one is not very old, about two hundred years. He'd be considered a young warrior by the Feathered people. His torso shows signs of firearm wounds, and a good part of the feathers on his wings has been burned away. Looking at his face, it is clear that he died an agonizing death."

After hearing Wang Liu's autopsy report, Yu Fang said, "The Shan are extremely clever. By disguising themselves as Huhui frontier defense soldiers, they were clearly hoping to catch the Feathered people off guard. Given the look of things, it didn't come off the way they planned. If the Feathered people are being controlled by the Shan, that would really spell trouble. Wang Liu, Liu Qi—in your opinion, how should we handle this?"

As Wang Liu scratched his head and gave the matter some thought, Liu Qi replied at once. "We can't lose any time. Since the Shan have launched a surprise attack on the Feathered people, we should send troops to their aid."

Yu Fang nodded and asked Wang Liu, "What do you think?"

"I agree," said Wang Liu. "It looks as if for the moment we won't be entering Sunlon City. It might be better if Liu Qi and I see what is going on at Fort Ever Peaceful, and act as the situation dictates."

Yu Fang accepted their advice and ordered them to take three hundred warriors north to reinforce Fort Ever Peaceful, while he left Yu Kui to guard Hehe Village. He himself would return and take personal command of the Green Snake Brotherhood camp outside of Sunlon City.

Seeing Sunlon City so close but being unable to enter it made for a very unstable mood among the Green Snake troops. Mayor Ma had personally come to reward them, and later sent soul touchers and entertainers from the skyvision company to erect a theater tent and give grand performances as well as hand out gifts to keep the men distracted. By the time Yu Fang hurried back to camp on horseback from Hehe Village, it was already close to dusk. The song and dance show in the theater tent was approaching its climax. Outside the tent sat large groups of people who frequently applauded and cheered. When Yu Fang entered the camp, there wasn't a sentry to be seen; no one was there to stop him. Yu Fang was furious and upon entering his tent, called for cadres of all ranks and soundly reprimanded them. He ordered them to sound the snake whistles and have the men fall in, including the performers on the stage, to wait and be dealt with.

The poor soul touchers. Right in the middle of singing and dancing, they were dragged off the stage by the military police without any explanation. The head of the entertainment troupe was furious and demanded an explanation from the commanding officer. After a short while, the group was brought before Yu Fang. The troupe leader was a good-looking young artist. He angrily protested to Yu Fang: "We have come to entertain the troops. Though our contributions are small, we do work hard. Why have you arrested us like common criminals? I protest! I must protest!"

"You dare protest?" said Yu Fang angrily. "We are facing a formidable foe, and you come and disturb the troops, lessening their will to fight. I'm ready to have you all executed as spies."

When the lovely soul touchers heard this, they went pale and began to weep, and rebuked the troupe leader for tricking them into leaving the city to entertain the troops. The good-looking young leader was at a loss; he nearly jumped out of his skin. He dropped to his knees. "You see those soul touchers? Which of them is not a skyvision star? Out of a sense of patriotism they willingly accepted the hardship of coming to entertain the troops. Killing us is no big deal, but I'm afraid that the people of Sunlon City would be disappointed in the Green Snake Brotherhood."

Yu Fang saw the reason in what he said, and had to find a way out of the situation. Suddenly, snake whistles were heard from all around. His staff officer, who was bathed in sweat, rushed in to report, "It's bad. Troops from Sunlon City have come out and surrounded us. Mayor Ma is shouting at the gate of our camp."

Yu Fang was startled. He ordered that the entertainment troupe be detained and kept under guard while he hurried to the camp gate. Zhihuang Ma was in full military dress; in his left hand he held a laser gun and in his right a bullhorn. He was calling for the surrender of the Green Snake Brotherhood.

"Brothers of the Green Snake Brotherhood, you are surrounded. Throw down your weapons. You are part of us; put down your weapons and talk things over."

Yu Fang was so angry he nearly fell over. Pointing at Zhihuang Ma, he began to revile him. "You ungrateful wretch! I bring the Green Snake Brotherhood here to save Sunlon City, and you not only close the gates, denying us entry, you even want us to throw down our weapons! Do you think that's right?"

"You are wrong," said Zhihuang Ma, laughing grimly. "I urged you to return to Hehe Village a long time ago. But you chose to ignore me. You stationed your troops outside the city to hatch some sinister plot. For this reason, the nine bulu lords have authorized me to act as I see fit. Hurry up and throw down your weapons, and I might consider leaving you a way out; otherwise, don't blame me for my cruelty."

Yu Fang saw that Zhihuang Ma was backed by a large number of troops and had surrounded the Green Snake Brotherhood camp. But he couldn't believe his luck. Fortunately he had returned in time to muster his troops. And although Zhihuang Ma had more men, they were just rabble, no match for Yu Fang's experienced soldiers. Yu Fang had to laugh to himself.

"Yellow Ma, do you think that having more men gives you the advantage over the Green Snake Brotherhood? Let me tell you that since the brotherhood was founded, we have been through countless battles, and never once did we give up without a fight! It's no problem for me to surrender: all you have to do is convince my men and I'll do as you wish."

Hearing this, Zhihuang Ma was elated, and said, "Isn't what you're saying ■□ (woo-wu)? If I am able to convince your men to throw down their weapons, you must surrender at once. You can't go back on your word."

Yu Fang was amused. The thousands of Green Snake Brotherhood warriors had been trained since childhood. Zhihuang Ma was dreaming if he thought they would voluntarily throw down their weapons. Yu Fang took out his snake whistle and said, "Yellow Ma, Green Snake Brotherhood warriors fight, they don't capitulate. If you can convince even one of them, I'll surrender."

He then blew his snake whistle, which was immediately echoed on all sides by other whistles in response to their leader's call. Putting away his whistle, Yu Fang said, "Yellow Ma, being the mayor of Sunlon City, you had better hurry back. Otherwise I will give the order to attack. At that time, I may recognize you, but my snake blade won't."

Zhihuang Ma's smile disappeared and he grew composed at once. He motioned, and two men stepped forward. When Yu Fang saw them, he gasped. One of them was none other than an old man, the lord of the Sungood bulu and the spiritual leader of its 170,000 inhabitants, better known as the Old Do-Gooder. Behind him stood his chamberlain Lai Fu.

"I've always believed that one should not fight his own people," said Zhihuang Ma, smiling. "For that reason, I asked Bulu Lord Wu himself to come and ask you to surrender."

Yu Fang was furious, but he was a loyal and worthy man. He respectfully addressed the old man: "My respects to my lord. ᠴᠤᠯᠤᠷᠤᠮᠤ (chu-lu-ru-mu) to you."

"Well, well, well. No need for ceremony," said the Old Do-Gooder, smiling broadly and laughing. "Your loyalty is commendable for leading your troops here to defend Sunlon City. But the city is being protected by Mayor Ma's army of volunteers, and there is no threat at present. I think you should listen to Mayor Ma and withdraw your forces."

Only then did Yu Fang realize that the army surrounding the Green Snake Brotherhood was a volunteer army that Zhihuang Ma had just recently raised. How could such an army fight? In light of this, Yu Fang became even angrier.

"M'Lord, a volunteer army is certainly no match for Shan regulars. M'Lord, if you err in believing Zhihuang Ma's honeyed words and order us to leave, who will defend Sunlon City? Please carefully consider what you do."

The old man muttered and nodded his head, and then muttered and shook his head. With a fawning smile, Lai Fu, standing behind his master, said, "Yu Fang, we are aware of your perfect loyalty. But perfect loyalty demands perfect obedience. Obedience is the root of loyalty. Our lord wishes you to withdraw, and you should obey."

Grasping his sword, Yu Fang replied angrily, "M'Lord is surrounded by base people; I cannot obey such an order."

Lai Fu pointed at Yu Fang, and throwing a glance at the Old Do-Gooder, said, "You dare to rebel?"

"That is not so," said Yu Fang, unyieldingly. "A general in the field does not have to obey his master's order. Since the survival of Sunlon City is at stake, I will not withdraw."

Hearing this, the Old Do-Gooder said to Zhihuang Ma, "Well, well, Mayor Ma. Since Yu Fang is so resolute and his intentions are good, I see nothing wrong in letting him stay."

Lai Fu and Zhihuang Ma looked at each other. Lai Fu then said, "M'Lord, didn't you just hear Yu Fang say that if Mayor Ma was able to convince just one of his soldiers to lay down their arms that he would surrender? Why not let Mayor Ma give it a try?"

The Old Do-Gooder laughed and said, "We're all one big family. What is all this talk about surrendering? Okay. Mayor Ma, go ahead and try. But I think you lack my eloquence."

Hearing this, Yu Fang surmised that the bulu lord was muddle-headed. The Green Snake Brotherhood was unswervingly loyal to him, but he was willing to let Zhihuang Ma try to convince them to surrender. It was the first time that this loyal man had doubts about his spiritual leader. But Yu Fang was still very sincere. The Old Do-Gooder was right: how could Zhihuang Ma sway the Green Snake Brotherhood with his eloquence?

Zhihuang Ma raised his bullhorn and addressed the Green Snake warriors: "Brothers of the Green Snake Brotherhood! Your spiritual leader is here; throw down your weapons."

Zhihuang Ma repeated himself several times, but the warriors remained unmoved. At that moment a metallic sound arose all around. Yu Fang knew that Zhihuang Ma was up to something, but he knew that it wouldn't frighten his men. Just as he was about to ridicule him, something strange happened: several warriors threw down their laser guns and slowly walked toward the enemy. Yu Fang was startled and ordered the turncoats to halt. But they turned a deaf ear and continued on as if bewitched. Yu Fang was startled and angered. He took a gun from the guard beside him, intending to kill the traitors. Who would have expected that the guard himself would mechanically set off toward Zhihuang Ma? Yu Fang looked around and saw that about half his troops were laying down their weapons and starting toward the enemy. Yu Fang shot several of them, but the others remain unfazed, as if they had long since decided to surrender. Then Zhihuang Ma shouted at him, "Your men are smarter than you. Hurry up and surrender too."

Although Yu Fang wasn't the brightest person, he saw that something was not right, and that perhaps the sound of clashing metal could affect people's minds. He hastened to order the troops that hadn't been affected to plug their ears, fall back to the center of camp, and prepare for a bloody fight with the enemy. After about half the Green Snake Brotherhood troops had surrendered and Zhihuang Ma was certain that Yu Fang's actual strength was sufficiently reduced, making it only a matter of time before he himself surrendered, he ordered his troops to tighten the noose encircling the Green Snake Brotherhood. After the Green Snake warriors plugged their ears, there were no more surrenders. Zhihuang Ma's volunteer troops attacked several times, but each time they were repelled. That night they fought to a stalemate.

When the purple sun rose again, Yu Fang led the Death Commandos on a surprise attack to the west. The Death Commandos were able to breach the enemy's encirclement because the volunteers were unprepared and had the light of the purple sun in their eyes. The volunteer force really was a mob, for once they suffered a defeat, they were thrown into a panic. The Green Snake Brotherhood, taking advantage of the situation, launched a full-scale counterattack. The warriors fought courageously, each trying to outdo the others. The poor volunteer army—all they could do was regret that they hadn't been born with four legs so that they might flee all the more quickly. Their resistance was broken. Yu Fang led his troops in pursuit all the way to the city. Zhihuang Ma had long since fled back there. He stood atop the city wall shouting at the Green Snake Brotherhood with Lai Fu and the Old Do-Gooder, who was held against his will. Although Yu Fang hated Zhihuang Ma's guts, he had to be careful that he didn't harm the Old Do-Gooder. He stopped at the foot of the wall but would not attack the city. He regrouped outside. Nearly half of the five thousand volunteer troops were prisoners of the Green Snake Brotherhood.

The fierce battle outside at dawn alarmed the residents of Sunlon City. The people in the eastern part of the city mistakenly thought that it was a Shan attack and fled to the west with their children, immediately throwing the city center into chaos. The nine bulu lords were forced to order the gates to each bulu closed. Only skyvision reporters and residents with first-class privileges could move about freely. It had been a long time since the reporters had had anything newsworthy to report; they were like flies on dog shit as they swarmed to the eastern part of the city for news. Zhihuang Ma was prepared and held a press conference, accusing the Green Snake Brotherhood of launching an unprovoked attack against the volunteer army when they left the city on maneuvers, forcing the volunteers to defend themselves. As Zhihuang Ma held his press conference on the city wall, down below in the streets, the volunteers paraded their Green Snake Brotherhood prisoners. The prisoners were as impassive as clay idols. Seeing them, the Huhui people sighed. Some people were sorry that the Green Snake Brotherhood had turned traitor; others worried that the situation of the city might become even more difficult. The skyvision portrayed Zhihuang Ma as a man of wisdom and courage who had used his wits to break the Green Snake Brotherhood.

Yu Fang watched the skyvision in his tent. Seeing Zhihuang Ma, he was so angry that he could scarcely keep from smashing the skyvision set. At that moment it was reported that cavalry troops were rapidly approaching the Green Snake Brotherhood position. Yu Fang assumed that Zhihuang Ma was again trying to launch a surprise attack. He laughed coldly and said, "I'm not going to let you off this time, Yellow Ma. All right, guys, listen to me. I'll give a huge reward to anyone who can catch Yellow Ma alive. Who will go?"

Yu Fang shouted his offer several times, but had no takers. He thought it most strange until he remembered that his soldiers had all plugged their ears and couldn't hear him. Yu Fang leaped on his steed and unsheathed his snake blade. Seeing him unsheathe his sword, the soldiers shouted and fell in behind their leader to meet the enemy. On his horse, Yu Fang slashed his way through the enemy troops. The enemy soldiers gave way, and he found himself alone and in the open. While he was in his vainglory, a Leopard person shot out from the crowd and caught him unawares, knocking him and his horse to the ground. Yu Fang leaped up and was about to deal the Leopard person a death blow when he heard a charming voice shouting from afar, "Yu Fang! Don't hit him. We're all one family!"

Hearing Miss Qi's voice, he was overjoyed. The Leopard person who had knocked him to the ground walked over and offered his hand and said, "I am pleased to meet you, warrior Yu. I am Battlefront Commander Hua of the Leopard Army, and a good friend of Miss Qi's."

Yu Fang saw the round face and large ears of the Leopard person and his sweet smile as he proffered his hand. He knew that the sweeter the smile, the more vicious the leopard, and so he kept his guard up. Seeing him so wary, Commander Hua laughed and said, "Don't measure the mind of a Leopard person by the yardstick of a Green Snake. We are comrades. I won't eat you. You see, isn't that your good friend?"

Dressed entirely in white, Miss Qi rode up on a horse. Behind came Ah 出 (chu) and Zhi-Hu Zhe. Yu Fang recognized Ah 出 but had no idea who the Serpent person was. Ah 出 (chu) hastened to introduce them. In a short while, General Shi arrived, surrounded by his troops. After exchanging greetings, Ah 出 (chu) bowed to everyone there and, smiling, said, "The Green Snake Brotherhood and the Leopard Brotherhood are nearly all present; the people of Sunlon City can now sleep in peace. Will the heroes of the two brotherhoods be entering the city at once?"

"No," said the general, stroking his beard. "We must first locate the leader of the Bronze Statue Cult. We will enter the city only after our three groups put all their cards on the table."

"We can't wait any longer!" said Yu Fang, gnashing his teeth in anger. "Yellow Ma is on a rampage in the city. He is tyrannically oppressing the people. He has more than a thousand of our men in his clutches, and will kill them sooner or later. I have decided to attack the city at once; it is critical that we save the men."

Yu Fang then told them how Zhihuang Ma and his volunteer army had launched a surprise attack on them the previous night. Miss Qi suddenly recalled how she had seen all those expressionless people wearing bronze statues. She couldn't help but ask, "You said that they seemed entranced after hearing a metallic sound. Were they wearing little Bronze Statues?"

Yu Fang shook his head and said, "The Green Snake Brotherhood does not believe in the Bronze Statue Cult. Why would they be wearing Bronze Statues?"

"If they weren't wearing Bronze Statues, perhaps they were holding the bronze privilege cards handed out by Zhihuang Ma. Was there perhaps a badge of some kind?"

Then something suddenly dawned on Yu Fang. "Damn it! That entertainment troupe was handing out souvenirs all over the place. Many of the men took them. I'm sure that they were secretly involved in this."

Yu Fang immediately sent someone back to camp and had the troupe leader and the soul touchers brought to him. The troupe members thought that they were going to be executed; they were frightened out of their wits and wept. One of the soul touchers recognized Miss Qi and called to her, pleading with her, "You too are a soul toucher from Sunlon City. We share the same profession. Please, I beg you, let the great warrior Yu spare us."

Unable to bear it, Miss Qi turned to Yu Fang and said, "Do you really want to kill them?"

"Why not? Would that be letting them off too lightly?" said Yu Fang angrily. To the prisoners he said, "Under the pretext of being an entertainment troupe, you came with the intention of doing my soldiers harm. I might be able to spare you, but the souls of my dead brothers in heaven won't spare me. Prepare to die."

The good-looking troupe leader fell to his knees and pleaded, "We have no idea who is plotting against the good men of the Green Snake Brotherhood. How could poor artists like ourselves ever dream of working against the awesome Green Snake Brotherhood? Please spare us."

"That's easy," said Yu Fang. "Bring me one of the souvenirs and let me see it."

Hearing things take a turn for the better, the troupe leader with the pretty face took out a souvenir and respectfully presented it to Yu Fang, saying, "Such a small souvenir cannot convey our true esteem. Let me offer you this as a small token of the esteem of the residents of Sunlon City."

Yu Fang took the souvenir in his hand and examined it closely. "What is this thing for?" he asked.

"It's a pocket-size skyvision," replied the troupe leader. "It's to provide your soldiers with a little diversion on lonely nights."

"Damn!" swore Yu Fang. "The soldiers are on duty at night. How can they watch skyvision? Does it have some other trick inside? Ah 凸 (chu), you take a look."

Ah 凸 (chu) opened up the pocket-size skyvision. Being a smart 凸 (chu) person, he quickly found a pale green crystal.

"So there is a trick. This circuit puts out a high-frequency signal that can alter a person's mind. Zhihuang Ma must have been using the metallic sound to activate the signal that bewitched the soldiers."

"That treacherous Yellow Ma!" shouted Yu Fang, furious. "We will attack the city at once. I'll kill that Yellow Ma, or I'm not a man!"

"Take it easy," said Ah 凸 (chu). "Everyone understands your wish for revenge. But Sunlon City is more than just Zhihuang Ma. If the Green Snake Brotherhood attacks, the defenders will have to fight, and the people will suffer. We're facing a strong enemy. If we fight one another, won't we be playing into their hands?"

"Brotherhood Leader Yu," said General Shi, "I don't think we should be in a hurry to enter the city. It would be better to ask the nine bulu lords to open the city and let us enter in the name of the United Army against the Shan. At the same time, we can send someone to inform the cult leader that the Green Snake Brotherhood and the Leopard Brotherhood have joined forces to protect the city."

Miss Qi clapped and laughed charmingly. "That's wonderful! Since General Shi is the leader of the Royalist faction, the nine bulu lords will naturally accept his suggestion; and since General Shi's cavalry spilled their blood for the city, the people revere him. If the cavalry enters the city, Zhihuang Ma will not be able to carry out any plot, even if he has one."

After hearing this, Yu Fang no longer insisted that the Green Snake Brotherhood act unilaterally. Now that they had all agreed on a strategy, Ah 出 (chu) was to draft a letter and General Shi write it. It would request that the nine bulu lords open the city to the United Army. The letter was sent posthaste to the city. With the Green Snake Brotherhood in the middle and the cavalry taking up both flanks, the formidable joint force set off. Yu Fang and General Shi were at the head, and were closely followed by Zhi-Hu Zhe, Commander Hua, and Ah 出 (chu) as well as Miss Qi. Behind them followed the entertainment troupe that had handed out the souvenirs to the Green Snake Brotherhood, causing so much trouble. The force was huge, and the residents of the city were startled even though it was two miles away. The people were overjoyed to learn that General Shi himself was leading the cavalry that was coming to protect them. The nine bulu lords, led by the Old Do-Gooder of Sungood bulu, raced out of the East Gate to meet them. The Old Do-Gooder was all smiles when he saw General Shi and Yu Fang, and opened his arms and said, "You have finally arrived! I am here to welcome you warmly into the city on behalf of the residents."

Yu Fang thought to himself, "Yesterday m'Lord said that Mayor Ma's volunteer army would protect the city and that I should withdraw at once. Today he is actually welcoming us. That sort of switch leaves a person cold." He was now thoroughly disgusted by the old hypocrite, and therefore said coldly, "And where is Mayor Ma? Why didn't he bring his volunteer army to prevent us from entering the city?"

The Old Do-Gooder laughed and said, "Well, well, well, there was a big misunderstanding last night. Mayor Ma shouldn't have acted on his own and led his troops out to demand that you give up your arms. For this reason the nine bulu lords just held a meeting and decided to strip Zhihuang Ma of his title of mayor. Zhihuang Ma knows that he was wrong, and that's why he is not here to see his former master General Shi. He has already fled Sunlon City."

"He was such an intelligent person." General Shi sighed. "It's a shame that fame and wealth went to his head. Things have turned out so badly. It's too bad."

"Well, well, he is but reaping the fruit of his own actions," said the Old Do-Gooder. "General Shi, Yu Fang, the nine bulu lords welcome your immediate entry into the city."

"That's not possible," said the general, shaking his head. "The cult leader is not here yet. We must all agree before we enter the city."

The nine bulu lords were all shocked by the general's words. Secretly they were happy, because they didn't relish the idea of having the army in the city. The bulu lords formed a circle and discussed the matter in hushed tones. Then the Old Do-Gooder spoke for them, smiling broadly. "Well, well, you two are men of your word. We will welcome the United Army of the Leopard and Green Snake brotherhoods whenever it enters the city. We will also contact the cult members in the city and ask them to have the cult leader meet with you. We are releasing the Green Snake Brotherhood prisoners taken by Zhihuang Ma yesterday. Each man is to be given ten ⊡ (du) in compensation. If any Green Snake Brotherhood member wishes to take R & R in the city, all that we ask is that all weapons be left outside the walls. The residents of the city are grateful to see the cavalry here after having journeyed so far. We should send a troupe out to entertain them. Troupe Leader Li, your group has another mission."

Hearing this, the good-looking troupe leader went pale and shook his head, saying, "No way. If we entertain the troops we'll be lucky to stay alive. All the troupe members are asking for early retirement."

"No way. We don't want to do it," said all the gorgeous soul touchers in unison.

"Well, well," said the Old Do-Gooder, laughing, "what's done is done. You were used by Zhihuang Ma. It's not your fault. What if we give each troupe member and additional twenty ⊡ (du) as well as a first-class special privilege card?"

The soul touchers were wavering, but the troupe leader insisted. "Even if they are willing, I'm not going. I've got my old mother and my children to think of, and I can't risk my life for a little money."

"Well, well, Troupe Leader Li, you have the toughest job. What if we give you another thirty ⊡ (du) as well as a super-class special privilege card?"

Hearing this, the troupe leader smiled without saying a word. On the sly, Ah 凸 (chu) asked Miss Qi, "What's a super-class special privilege card? What is so magical about it?"

Laughing, Miss Qi whispered, "SPCs are something that Zhihuang Ma invented. Even though he is no longer in office, they are still being used. He is clearly a man of unique vision."

"Zhihuang Ma will go down in history for this," said Ah 出 (chu), the historian, excitedly. "I didn't realize he had it in him. Even we 出 (chu) make mistakes."

The Old Do-Gooder was still bargaining with the troupe leader and the soul touchers when General Shi and Yu Fang began issuing orders for their troops to pitch camp outside Sunlon City. At that moment, swarms of reporters and skyvision cameramen arrived to get the scoop. Zhi-Hu Zhe and Commander Hua became the focus of their efforts. As everyone was thus busily engaged, Ah Two suddenly shouted, "Oh no, the Shan are coming!"

Everyone was startled. Miss Qi looked where Ah Two pointed. There, to the southeast, smoke and dust rose as a column of horsemen charged toward Sunlon City.

14

"The Shan bastards are coming!" screamed the good-looking troupe leader at the top of his lungs. "Run for your lives!"

His piercing cry made the soul touchers scream. The reporters scurried here and there, unsure whether to flee or take advantage of the situation and gather the news. Led by the Old Do-Gooder, the nine bulu lords ran for the East Gate. Suddenly the camp of the United Army was thrown into chaos. The warriors had been pitching camp separately, but suddenly they had to assemble. Seeing his troops in disarray, Yu Fang leaped from his steed and shouted to the Death Commandos under his command, "Come with me. We'll block the Shan advance for a while."

More than twenty Death Commandos followed Yu Fang closely in a charge against the enemy. Seeing this, Zhi-Hu Zhe and Commander Hua laughed strangely, set off in pursuit, and soon caught up with Yu Fang. The three of them led the charge. When they were about to make contact with the enemy, a huge fellow stepped out of the ranks and shouted: "Brother!"

Overjoyed, Yu Fang reined in his horse. It was Yu Kui. He was wounded in his right shoulder and was covered with blood. He nodded and said, "I should be punished because I was unable to hold Hehe Village. Last night, a huge force of Shan bastards and Serpent people crossed the river. We fought bitterly all night, but by daybreak we could no longer hold out. I had no choice but to give the order to break ranks. The west bank of the river already has fallen into their hands. And at this very moment, enemy troops are marching toward Sunlon City."

Yu Fang looked up and saw that most of Yu Kui's troops had been wounded, and that they were only about a thousand men or a little more. Weeping, he said, "There were more than ten thousand men at Hehe Village, and only these few have survived?"

Ashamed, Yu Kui replied, "Their force is huge. Fully five or six thousand Serpent people turned out, and there were several hundred Shan warriors. We were no match for them."

Yu Fang knew this for the truth. One cruel, ferocious Serpent person was equal to ten Huhui people. And the Shan warriors were all battle-tested. Although there had been a lot of Green Snake Brotherhood troops at Hehe Village, only about two or three thousand were experienced fighters. He sighed and said, "The Shan are cunning. They don't just cross the West Hu River, they force their way across at Hehe Village, where our troop strength is greatest. Now that the west bank has fallen into their clutches, we will have to prepare for the decisive battle."

"Not so!" said Zhi-Hu Zhe, shaking his head. "Hest by the Shan, the Serpent people attacked Hehe Village. Happie certes they are not, but plaine they will not. The Shan must ward lest the Serpent people turn again them. Methinks that after subdewing Hehe Village, pause they will to regroup, and make no hastie batteil on Sunlon City."

As they were discussing the matter, General Shi arrived, leading two thousand crack troops. Yu Fang informed him that Hehe Village had been taken by the Shan and the Serpent people. The general was silent for a while, then said, "That's okay; at least we know what they are doing. After this defeat, I think it would be best if all the Green Snake Brotherhood troops remained here and were reorganized for the protection of Sunlon City. I'll lead the cavalry at once in a counterattack on Hehe Village."

Although the general was well intentioned, his suggestion was extremely unpleasant to the ears of Yu Fang and Yu Kui. Yu Kui was the first to lose his self-restraint. "Brother," he said to Yu Fang, "I lost Hehe Village. I have to recover it even if it costs me my life. Let me lead the men back to fight."

Zhi-Hu Zhe laughed and said, "A dismayed general should speak not of corage. Your force will bootlesse prove."

Yu Kui was furious. But he couldn't lose his temper, since Zhi-Hu Zhe had spared his life underground.

Stroking his white beard, General Shi said, "Zhi-Hu Zhe is right. The task of attacking Hehe Village rests with the cavalry."

"No," said Yu Fang in opposition. "General, I must decline your generous offer. Hehe Village is a base of the Green Snake Brotherhood and should not involve any other parties. It would be better if the general were to stay and protect Sunlon City while I lead the entire Green Snake Brotherhood force in an attack on Hehe Village."

"Great indeed!" said Zhi-Hu, clapping his claws. "Compete the Green Snake Brotherhood and the Leopard Brotherhood to die and in death be dismayed. Great indeed!"

Hearing Zhi-Hu Zhe's words, the Yu brothers and General Shi stopped bickering. In their hearts, they all knew that what the old Serpent person said was true. Alone, neither the Green Snake Brotherhood nor the Leopard Brotherhood was a match for the Shan. Even together, they might not defeat the Shan and the Serpent people. That is, unless a third force were to join—the Bronze Statue Cult. There was a thread of hope for the three forces together. But the cult leader had not yet appeared. Where could he be?

"Yu Fang," said General Shi, who was the first to regain some calm, "the Shan already have crossed the river. We are facing a formidable opponent and must be cautious. Let's first return to Sunlon City to mobilize the entire populace, and then make a plan."

Yu Fang had to agree with the general's suggestion. When everyone returned to the city, they found Miss Qi and Ah 出 (chu) sorely distressed and standing outside the East Gate. Miss Qi said, "It looks bad. When the bulu lords returned to the city, they barred the gates."

No one said a word. "What's the meaning of this?" asked Yu Kui angrily. "We risk our lives to come and protect the city, and they close the gates. That's too much."

Yu Fang reproached his brother. "They closed the gates for the safety of the people, not because they don't care about us."

"That being the case, they should still allow the wounded in to be treated," said Yu Kui, urging his horse forward. Then he shouted up at the gate tower, "□ (wu) the guard. Hurry and open the gate, and let the wounded in."

He shouted several times, but there was no response from the gate tower. Yu Kui's temper grew and he said to the men beside him, "Brothers, if they don't open the gate, we'll have to knock it down."

Yu Kui ordered his men to take a battering ram and smash the gates. This had an effect. After they rammed the door a couple of times, several men appeared on the gate tower. Yu Fang halted the soldiers. The nine hulu lords lined up atop the tower. The Old Do-Gooder smiled broadly and said, "General Shi, Yu Fang, and men of the Leopard and Green Snake brotherhoods, you are working hard. The Shan are approaching the city; that's why we have been forced to shut the gates. We hope you understand and can work with us on this."

"M'Lord," said Yu Fang, trying to restrain his anger, "the Shan have taken Hehe Village, and in the short run will not be attacking Sunlon City. We hope that you will allow those wounded at Hehe Village to enter the city to recuperate."

Hearing this, the Old Do-Gooder and the other bulu lords withdrew to discuss the matter. He returned and said to those outside the city, "Well, well, we'll send a medical team to have a look at the wounded. The entertainment troupe will also be sent. Don't be nervous; just concentrate on fighting the enemy outside the gate. We promise to back you up."

Yu Fang almost keeled over with rage.

"Why are you trying to reason with the jerk?" asked Yu Kui. "Let's force our way into the city."

"No," said the general sternly. "I came to save Sunlon City. How can I attack it? We brought troops to protect the millions of people in the city; there's no need to waste your breath arguing with the nine bulu lords."

Yu Fang was a loyal soldier and replied, "Okay, you won't let us in and we won't come in. Brothers, we are still committed to defending the city. We'll make a final stand here and shame the ingrates."

Although the soldiers were angry, they nonetheless obeyed and began to construct defensive fortifications around the city. General Shi ordered the Routing and Valiant cavalries to push southward to keep an eye on the enemy at Hehe Village; he ordered the Dragon cavalry to remain in the vicinity of Sunlon City, ready to aid the other two cavalries at a moment's notice. The deployments decided upon, the Green Snake and Leopard Brotherhood soldiers took up their assigned positions, ready to sacrifice themselves in protecting Sunlon City.

Once the Green Snake Brotherhood and the Leopard Brotherhood troops had deployed outside the city, the people inside also busied themselves. News of the fall of Hehe Village to the Shan and Serpent people spread, quickly filling the people with fear. Soon another group with first-class SPCs was rushing to flee. The courageous and upright Huhui youth directed their anger at the Serpent people, falling upon and killing the □ (wu) Serpent peddlers inside the city. Rumor had it that the □ (wu) Serpent people and the Gaiwenese were all spies for the Shan. The mob went to smash the Gaiwenese Drifters' Club, and the Gaiwenese shops were all looted. Strangely, the Gaiwenese had disappeared, and although the mob had stolen a lot of valuables, they didn't catch a single one. The angry mob then focused on the bulu lords. The nine lords had intentionally allowed the Gaiwenese to flee and had removed Mayor Ma from his position. Now they were refusing to let the Green Snake Brotherhood and the Leopard Brotherhood into the city. What were their true intentions? Were they selling out Sunlon City? The people recalled how the nine bulu lords closely cooperated with the Shan rulers when the Shan occupation army ruled the city. Perhaps they were once again leaning toward the Shan. How disgraceful!

The angry mob broke up and began rioting in each bulu, burning down the palaces of the bulu lords. Their lives threatened, the bulu lords had to flee to the Golden Palace in the city center, where they positioned guards without. The mob soon discovered their whereabouts and swarmed to the Central Station. Those who were holding SPCs and planning to flee the city by train became the target of the mob's fury. The people shouted the slogan: "Get rid of special privileges inside the city; fight the Shan outside the city!" and killed about half the SPC holders. The poor privilege holders! They regretted wearing their bronze tags around their necks, which marked them for a beating. Besides angry youths, the mob was composed of militiamen. They were the volunteer soldiers trained by Zhihuang Ma, and while they were impotent against the Shan, they were quite effective at causing trouble. They burned the bulu palaces, beat the SPC holders at the Central Station, and then surrounded the Golden Palace. The guards of the various bulu joined together to hold them off. They shot several hundred people. Although the guards were outnumbered, the mob was just rabble who no longer dared attack the palace; they just surrounded it. The chaos lasted from noon to dusk. Countless numbers died.

The nine besieged bulu lords who were in the Audience Hall of the Golden Palace knew that the guards couldn't hold out forever against the huge, angry mob. They paced nervously around the room. The lords of the Sundragon and Sunwork bulu complained to the Old Do-Gooder in one voice, saying, "It was you who said we should remove Zhihuang Ma from his job and oppose the United Army entering the city. Now look at the mess—the army is outside the city while Zhihuang Ma's militia is rebelling inside, and the Shan are on their way. What are we going to do? It's just 口中口山 (mu-ru-lu-chu)."

The Old Do-Gooder was himself secretly worried. He blamed his chamberlain Lai Fu for all the bad suggestions. Now he was in a terrible fix. Maintaining an outward appearance that nothing was wrong, he smiled broadly and said, "Well, well, a just cause enjoys abundant support. We all agreed to sack Zhihuang Ma; we all agreed that the army should not enter the city. The rioters are rioters, but just wait till the sand rains down and the heavenly shafts of light appear. They will leave of their own accord."

The Old Do-Gooder was doing his best to vindicate himself, but the other bulu lords wouldn't let him off. Pointing at him, the lord of the Sundragon bulu reviled him, saying, "You're still trying to justify yourself. Our palaces have been burned down. How humiliating. Do you expect us to take responsibility when you yourself won't?"

"You are famous throughout the city for your benevolence," said the lord of the Sunevil bulu. "You might as well do another good deed now and throw in your life. We'll hand you over to the mob and let them take care of you. Seeing you dead might appease them."

The seven other bulu lords clapped and praised this suggestion. The Old Do-Gooder had never dreamed that the other bulu lords would want to make him a scapegoat. He laughed, his eyes forming narrow slits, and said, "Well, well, well, a reasonable man is bold. Even if you kill me, the mob might not let you off. After I'm dead, the Green Snake Brotherhood will avenge me. It's a small matter to kill me, but no small matter to anger the Green Snake Brotherhood."

"Pay him no heed," said the Sunwork bulu lord. "Let's kill him first to help us out of our present predicament. Then we'll make other plans."

Some of the bulu lords nodded in agreement while others unsheathed their swords. The Old Do-Gooder broke into a cold sweat and shouted, "Lai Fu! Sungood guards, save your lord!"

"No one can save you," said the Sunevil bulu lord, pointing his sword at the Old Do-Gooder. "You've lived a life of hypocrisy. Finally, you'll do a good deed before you die. Prepare yourself."

The Old Do-Gooder's legs gave way and he collapsed on the ground. The Sunevil bulu lord was about to strike and the Old Do-Gooder was about to scream when a deep voice was heard.

"Stop!"

Startled, the bulu lords turned around. A man dressed in black and wearing a black mask said, "The twenty-seventh Supreme One, Paramita Hare Krishna Holy Holy Holy Law of Moses, Below the Honored Bronze

Statue Never Sinking Dharmapala Mountain God 7113218, greets you one and all. ▫ □ ▫ □ (du-wu du-wu), ⼧-◻⼧◻ (chu-lu-ru-mu)."

"Cult leader!" said the Old Do-Gooder, overjoyed. He picked himself up off the floor and said, "Cult leader, you arrived just in time. We've been looking for you. General Shi and his cavalry and Yu Fang and the Green Snake Brotherhood are all here. They await your word to enter and defend the city."

A cold snort was heard from behind the mask of the Stranger in Black. "How could those worthless people protect the city? All they will do is die at the hands of the Shan and the Serpent people."

The Old Do-Gooder hastened to trim his sails. "Well, well, well. Sunlon City is indeed favored. Fortunately in this time of darkness we have the cult leader to protect us. We're counting on you since the Green Snake and Leopard brotherhoods are worthless."

"Good," said the Stranger in Black, "you should have realized a long time ago that the cult is your only salvation. All you need do is respect me as your superior, and I will mobilize the cult followers to protect the city. That mob outside won't be able to do anything to you."

The nine bulu lords looked at one another. Some hesitated, but the Old Do-Gooder dropped to his knees and said, "The Sungood bulu voluntarily recognizes you as lord, and the 170,000 people will convert."

When the other bulu lords saw the Old Do-Gooder convert to the Bronze Statue Cult, none dared be remiss and all quickly fell to their knees. The cult leader laughed. "The nine bulu lords have all converted to the Bronze Statue Cult. Sunlon City is now in the hands of the cult. This has long been the case; I just wanted to hear it from your own lips. I wanted you all to voluntarily join us, you see."

"Well, well, well. Those who find the Way prosper; those who go against heaven perish," said the Old Do-Gooder. "From now on, you are the ruler of Sunlon City. Of this we all are convinced."

"I have led the cult through twenty years of bitter struggle to arrive at this day," said the cult leader, secretly happy. "There is now hope that the Bronze Statue of Sunlon City will make a comeback."

He then spoke to someone outside the Audience Hall. "Zhihuang Ma, you lead the troops out and tell the people to go home and rest."

Outside, Zhihuang Ma was heard to assent. Only then did the people in the hall realize that Zhihuang Ma hadn't fled the city but had temporarily gone into hiding. The Old Do-Gooder smiled broadly, then laughed drily and said, "So Zhihuang Ma . . . Mayor Ma was your subordinate. We treated him unfairly. My fellow bulu lords, I suggest that we reinstate Mayor Ma so that he can take control and calm the people."

The eight other lords assented as one. A short while later, Mayor Ma returned, saluted the man in black, and said, "The people outside have all departed. The volunteer soldiers have resumed their positions."

"Great!" said the Stranger in Black, nodding. He then turned to the nine bulu lords and said, "Since you have all come over and pledged allegiance to me, you must read my book, listen to what I say, and follow my directives. There must be no disloyalty. Do you understand?"

"Yes!" said the nine bulu lords together. "From now on we will read your book, listen to what you say, and follow your directives. If we are disloyal, may we immediately be shafted."

Hearing these words, the Stranger in Black raised his head, laughed madly, and said, "From now on the Bronze Statue Cult will be the state religion of the Huhui planet! Unfortunately, the true spirit of the Bronze Statue cannot reveal itself for the moment. But don't worry, with firm faith we can defeat the Shan and rebuild the statue." Then he added, "Since you have all converted to the cult, I will look upon you with my true visage."

As he spoke, he slowly removed his mask. The Old Do-Gooder was startled by what he saw. He blurted out, "Lai Fu . . . you are the leader of the Bronze Statue Cult?"

"Right. It is I," replied Lai Fu. "Old Do-Gooder, I want to thank you for looking after me for so many years. Thanks to the cover of the Sungood bulu, the Bronze Statue Cult was able to grow. But starting today, you are no longer our masters; now you must call me master."

"Old Do-Gooder," said Zhihuang Ma, "this is true democracy. Sometimes I am the people and you are the master; sometimes you are the people and I am the master."

The Old Do-Gooder appeared crestfallen. He was unable get hold of himself for a long time. His chamberlain Lai Fu had actually become his master. That man in black—Lai Fu—was very happy and asked Zhihuang Ma to lead the nine bulu lords in singing the "Song of Unity":

> Unite, unite
> Huhui boys and girls
> We will build a new Sunlon City
> With our flesh and blood
> Unite, unite

Huhui boys and girls
If you play no tricks
I won't have to be cruel
Unite, unite
Huhui boys and girls
Sing the song of unity together
Fill the land with happy sounds.

As the people in the Golden Palace sang the "Song of Unity," Sunlon City was shrouded by the night. The spike-shaped purple clouds gradually dispersed, forming a solid purple carpet. The yellow sand covered everything. Between the yellow firmament and the purple empyrean stretched the shafts of blue light. The shafts slowly changed position, forming a colonnade around Sunlon City, blocking all passage to the outside.

Naturally, the warriors of the Green Snake Brotherhood and the Leopard Brotherhood could not hear the singing inside the Golden Palace. Watching the blue shafts of light gradually close in, they felt oppressed. For they knew that when the purple sun rose again, the Huhui planet's greatest enemy would attack.

15

Dawn in Sunlon City.

The heavenly shafts of blue light enclosing Sunlon City disappeared one by one. The giant purple sun slowly rose above the distant mountains. Once again, Sunlon City was set free from the prison of the night.

The early rising residents of the city swept the streets clean of the sand that had accumulated the night before. People from all bulu headed for work, toward the city center. Passing the Golden Palace, they turned a blind eye to the corpses piled beside it. The previous day, when the nine bulu lords were besieged, the guards opened fire, killing many residents. By closing time, the police and militia were suddenly dispatched, scattering the demonstrators. Those who resisted were forcibly hauled away by men in black wearing Bronze Statues. The sensitive Huhui people knew that the situation had changed and no longer dared loiter on the streets. Word spread that the cult members had finally seized power.

The huge purple sun shone indolently over Sunlon City at dawn. The residents acted as if everything were the same, calmly going to work. But everyone had to glance around the streets to see if they were being observed by people in black. These people were everywhere, patrolling the streets in pairs; on their chests hung fist-size Bronze Statues. In one night, the cult members had taken complete control of the city. Everyone wondered if Mayor Ma had been a cult puppet all along. On the skyvision, he continued to call for the residents to support the city government, remain calm, and go to work. But behind him stood a row of cult members. Zhihuang Ma's militia had disappeared; the people guessed that the volunteer army had already donned black robes. The older residents sighed to themselves, because they remembered that it was the fanatical cult members who had brought about the fall of the Huhui empire during the Fourth Interstellar War. And now, unexpectedly, twenty-four years later, they had staged a comeback. But this time, the city's plight looked much more grim. The Shan and the Serpent people were on the border, and instead of cooperating with the Green Snake and Leopard brotherhoods to fight the enemy, the cult had taken advantage of the situation to seize power. The city was headed for disaster, unless . . . unless the army outside could halt the enemy advance. But lacking the protection of the city wall and the assistance of the cult, could General Shi and Yu Fang stop such a ferocious foe?

The Huhui people inside the city were worried; the army outside the city waited with apprehension. Shortly after the purple sun had risen, the Green Snake Brotherhood scouts returned to report that the Shan and the Serpent people already had left Hehe Village and were marching on Sunlon City in three columns. After consulting with each other, General Shi and Yu Fang decided that inaction would dominate action and the two armies would take up position and wait to fight the decisive battle.

The purple sun rose gradually, and the troops in the trenches began to sweat. Scouts kept arriving to report on the enemy's activities: forty kilometers away, thirty kilometers, twenty-eight kilometers, twenty-four kilometers . . . soon the scouts no longer had to report. The Huhui soldiers already could make out the three columns of men and horses sending up a huge dust cloud as they charged toward the city. The Serpent warriors held half pikes in their claws and shouted as they advanced at a run. Behind them followed Shan warriors in their scarlet uniforms. Every few steps, the Serpent warriors would raise their half pikes and give a strange shout. Hearing this at Green Snake Brotherhood headquarters, they couldn't help but feeling panicky. Miss Qi whispered to Zhi-Hu Zhe, "Are they trying to frighten us?"

"No, no," replied the old Serpent person, laughing, "before battle, the Serpent people eat to satietie. Their roares aide digestion as much as fryght the foe. Their shouts tell mee of their penurie. As the ancient *Serpent Classic* says: 'Examine their bellies; harken to their shouts. How can a Serpent conceal its heart?' "

Ah 出 (chu) bowed and said, "Is that so? Mr. Zhi-Hu Zhe is wise, indeed. You have my admiration. Where will the Serpent people attack first?"

Pleased with himself, Zhi-Hu Zhe swung his tail and said, "Hark! Dost thou hear that sound? The Serpents speak one to the other their plan of batteil. Intend they to feign left, then with their mightie force to breach the right flank, thereby thrusting a wedge between the two brotherhoods. Then will they proceed to devour one army at a time."

Angered, Yu Kui said, "Do they think it's that easy to eat up the Green Snake Brotherhood? Let me attack them by surprise first; I'll charge out and show them who is boss."

Yu Fang denied his request. The Serpent army was getting closer. Row after row of the strange green, long-tailed people were shouting and running back and forth on the field, challenging the Green Snake Brotherhood to battle. Yu Kui could not restrain himself and again asked to be allowed to answer the challenge. As Yu Fang was considering the matter, Zhi-Hu Zhe said, "I a Serpent person am. Better that I through suasion urge them to quit the field."

Zhi-Hu Zhe did not wait for Yu Fang to respond; flexing his tail, he sprang into the air. The Serpent people were startled to see him. Zhi-Hu Zhe shouted, "Precious children and grandchildren, warder am I of the Number One Underground Pass. Urge you I to cease from this strife, for kenest ye one and all that the five peoples are from single linyage come. The Shan be the foe of the Huhui planet and none other. And you they do employ ill-fauoredly."

Hearing this, the Serpent people began to put down their half pikes. Behind them, the Shan officers who were directing the fighting shouted, "Brothers, don't listen to his nonsense. That crafty old Serpent is a traitor. Down with the rulers of Sunlon City. SPRA, the Huhui planet is yours. Brothers, kill him!"

A number of Serpent people rushed toward Zhi-Hu Zhe and threw their pikes at him. The old Serpent laughed and, with a twist, knocked them to the ground with his tail. The Shan commanders ordered the Serpent warriors to launch a rain of pikes. Zhi-Hu Zhe was hard pressed to handle the situation. Suddenly, at the height of the danger, a gigantic yellow figure landed beside him and helped him knock aside the spears. Happily, Zhi-Hu Zhe said, "Be thou welcome, Commander Hua."

Laughing, the Leopard person said, "If we join hands, no one can get the better of us."

More pikes started to rain down on them. The old Serpent flicked the pikes away with his tail, and the Leopard person leaped into the air and knocked them to the ground with his paws. Both were exhilarated, one twisting about on the ground, one leaping in the air. Together they sang:

> *One Serpent,*
> *One Leopard,*
> *One after the other leaps.*
> *One tail swipes,*
> *Two paws smack,*
> *Crazily they fight the rascals.*
> *One, two, three,*
> *Three, two, one,*
> *Who will take up the challenge?*

Seeing the extraordinary bravery of Zhi-Hu Zhe and Commander Hua, the Serpent people couldn't help feeling useless. The Serpent warriors began to cheer. Beaming, Commander Hua said to the Serpent people, "My fellow countrymen! The five peoples—the Serpent people, the Leopard people, the Feathered people, the Huhui, and the 凸 (chu)—have a common origin. We shouldn't be fighting each other. Please hurry away."

Still they hesitated. Then Zhi-Hu Zhe flicked his tail and said, "Children and grandchildren, will you never understand? Then I'll help you. 凸冂 (chu-ru) Pass, the Number One Underground Pass, has been warded by my family for generations. True knights be those who enter and exit againe; he who quailes is of manhood fraile. Let he who has ⊡ (du) go one round with me. Who dares?"

Zhi-Hu Zhe shouted his challenge three times, and the thousands of Serpent people, as well as the Shan officers, all turned tail and ran. The Green Snake Brotherhood gained the victory without a fight. The battlefield was rocked with cheering. Miss Qi was clapping and cheering for the two of them when Ah 凸 (chu) suddenly shouted, "Oh no, General Shi is threatened!"

Everyone at headquarters hastened to look to the Leopard Brotherhood defenses on the right flank. Gunsmoke rose into the air as the cavalry fought bitterly. The crack troops of the Serpent people led by the Shan had already overrun the Leopard Brotherhood positions. The cavalry were masters of fighting on horseback, but in a battle like this they found themselves threatened again and again. Seeing the situation, Yu Fang was pleased and said, "The main force of the Shan has been sent into battle.

We have to beat them back; this is a heaven-sent opportunity. The purple sun is overhead! Brothers, let us fight!"

He took out his snake whistle and blew. The soldiers of the Green Snake Brotherhood responded to their leader's call by unsheathing their snake blades and charging from their defensive positions. Yu Kui led on horseback. He charged the rear of the Shan and Serpent force. Unprepared, they found themselves besieged in front and behind. The Dragon cavalry, which had been held in reserve, joined the fray at General Shi's orders. Caught in the pincer movement, the Shan and Serpent people lost more than one thousand dead. Defeated, they retreated. In their first joint fight, the Green Snake and Leopard brotherhoods had completely routed the enemy.

Morale was given a huge boost, and the battlefield erupted with cheers. The Huhui who had climbed up on the city wall to observe the fighting were overjoyed when they saw the enemy flee in defeat. Among those watching was the good-looking troupe leader. He burned with righteous indignation and said to those around him, "The Green Snake and Leopard brotherhoods risked their lives for us. We should be ashamed. The enemy is on the run; we should go and bring in the wounded and look after them, and let them feel the warmth of Sunlon City."

Everyone responded to the troupe leader's words. He led a group of people to the East Gate but was stopped by Mayor Ma's people, who wore bronze statues. In full armor, Zhihuang Ma smiled and said, "What you saw was just a show. Yu Fang and General Shi have conspired with foreigners. The purpose behind this show is to fool you. Don't fall for their evil plans. For the safety of the residents of Sunlon City, I cannot allow you to open the gates."

Some of the people believed him, but most did not. Some silently reviled Zhihuang Ma as shameless. More and more people gathered at the gate, and they grew increasingly excited and indignant. Someone began to sing, and the voices swelled. Pretty soon everyone was singing:

> *Yellow Ma,*
> *Yellow Ma,*
> *Has no love for his dad,*
> *Has no love for his mom.*
> *Receiving a little favor from others,*
> *He forgets his own home.*
> *Ha ha ha,*

Ha ha ha,
He forgets his own home!

When he heard this ditty, Zhihuang Ma was so furious he went black. As he motioned with his eyes, the cult followers advanced into the crowd and dragged a guy out. It was none other than the good-looking troupe leader. He was brought before Zhihuang Ma, who laughed coldly and said, "Such a patriotic singer. I'm convinced. If you want to revile me, I'll help you today. I'll let you go outside and entertain the troops."

The troupe leader knew he couldn't avoid it, so he steeled himself and sang:

Yellow Ma,
Yellow Ma,
Has no love for his dad,
Has no love for his mom.
Receiving a little favor from others,
He forgets his own home.
Ha ha ha,
Ha ha ha,
He forgets his own home!

The men in black detained him on the gate tower, but he continued to sing. Zhihuang Ma motioned, and a cult follower shoved the troupe leader off the tower. Seeing this, the people all wept and the soul touchers all cried. The men in black brutally dispersed the crowd, and their anger rose to the sky.

Yu Fang was directing his troops mopping up the battlefield when they heard a cry from the tower at East Gate. Startled, they watched as a man fell. They ran and saw that it was the troupe leader. His face was pale and he was scarcely breathing, but he managed to say, "Yellow Ma . . . colluded with the cult members to seize Sunlon City. . . . You heroes . . . must save the city."

So saying, he passed away. With anger, Yu Kui said, "That lousy Yellow Ma. If we don't kill him, we're not men. What are we waiting for? Let's fight our way into the city and kill the conspirator."

His face black with rage, Yu Fang ground his teeth and said, "Okay. The time of that ⊡ (du) man's death has arrived. Brothers, prepare to lay siege to the city."

He took out his snake whistle and blew several times. The Green Snake Brotherhood swarmed like ants to the East Gate. Under the direction of Yu Fang, Yu Kui, Zhi-Hu Zhe, and Commander Hua, the men were ordered to smash down the gate with a battering ram. Seeing that the Green Snake Brotherhood would soon knock down the gate, the white-haired general galloped over on his white steed. From his horse, the general shouted, "You can't do this, friends. We are here to protect the city. Why lay siege to it?"

"It's no concern of yours," said Yu Kui, holding the battering ram. "One of your men has colluded with the cult members to seize the city. How do you have the gall to say anything? Brothers, one, two, three, heave!"

The general leaped off his horse to stop them. "Although the Shan and the Serpent people have been defeated, they could still come back. Isn't it crazy to be at one another's throats instead of making ready?"

Regardless of his patient and earnest entreaties, the Green Snake Brotherhood simply ignored him and pushed him aside. Commander Hua laughed at him and said, "The closer the flesh and blood, the more they will eat each other. Otherwise, how could they be of close flesh and blood?"

The general was on the point of trying to persuade them again when Yu Kui shouted and took up the battering ram with Zhi-Hu Zhe, and knocked a hole in the gate. The Death Commandos rushed through the opening and unbarred the gate. The warriors outside unsheathed their snake blades and with a shout rushed through East Gate into the city. They were soon locked in combat with the cult members and their recently arrived reinforcements.

The purple sun continued to rise; its light poured over the buildings and the blood-soaked bodies of the warriors. From the Green Snake Brotherhood position on the battlefield, Miss Qi and Ah 亾 (chu) saw billows of smoke and flames rise from the direction of the Sungood bulu. Miss Qi gasped and began to weep. Ah 亾 (chu) nodded and sighed. "Sunlon City was fated for such a disaster. Although the Green Snake Brotherhood warriors are brave, they will never be able to kill all the die-hard cult members. And even if the cult leader can annihilate the Green Snake Brotherhood, he won't be able to save the city."

"Why?" asked Miss Qi, sobbing. "Why is that?"

Ah 亾 (chu) said, "The Bronze Statue . . . it is indeed the original sin of the city."

Miss Qi didn't understand what he was saying. She saw the white-haired general approach from East Gate, leading his horse by the reins. Behind him, the city was in flames. The general reached them and, giving a bitter laugh, said, "Miss, I'm sure you want me to lead the cavalry to save the city. That's the city you want to save. What more can I say?"

Ah 出 (chu) bowed to the general and said, "The fate of the city is in your hands."

The general shook his head. As he was about to speak, the sound of battle drums was heard in the distance. An officer from the Dragon cavalry galloped up and said, "General, the Shan and the Serpent people are back!"

"I know," said the general, standing up straight. "Raise the banner and sound the drums. Ready the cavalry to charge. Tell the troops that the very survival of the city will be determined by this battle."

"As you order," said the young officer with a look of determination. "Please mount your steed, Sir. We are already prepared. We await you to lead us to exterminate the Shan bastards."

The general mounted his horse. Awe-inspiring, he set off in the direction of the enemy. Immediately the Leopard Brotherhood cavalry raised a shout, chanting rhythmically,

"Gen-er-al!"

"Gen-er-al!"

"Gen-er-al!"

The eight thousand cavalrymen then spurred their horses forward, following their beloved leader to meet the attack of the Shan and Serpent people.

Miss Qi and Ah 出 (chu) watched the general and the eight thousand soldiers depart. Miss Qi turned around and, startled, shouted, "What's that?"

Ah 出 (chu) turned and looked in the direction of the city. Out of the thick smoke and flames, an incomparably large shape slowly rose. The weak light of the purple sun shone on the object. Its head began to emit a strange light.

"It's the Bronze Statue of Sunlon City!" said Ah 出 (chu), unable to believe his own eyes. "The Bronze Statue has returned!"

Shocked, the two of them watched as the huge shape rose ever higher. Miss Qi could not make out the statue's expression for the smoke, but she felt it was smiling malignantly. The Bronze Statue continued to grow, making the city at its feet look ever smaller and less significant. When the purple sun reached its zenith, the Bronze Statue also attained its past majestic size. It looked over the Huhui planet and the warriors fighting below. A peculiar smile spread over the bronze visage as if to encourage the antlike Huhui people fighting at its feet to sacrifice themselves for its sake.

Miss Qi looked up at the huge statue. She then realized that Sunlon City was facing yet another great catastrophe.

THREE

TALE OF A FEATHER

1

Dusk in Sunlon City.

The purple sun of the Huhui planet seemed to have increased in size; it took up nearly half the sky. The other half appeared to be occupied by the Bronze Statue. The remainder of the sky was nothing more than patches of thick, purple-colored smoke. The people fought, hacking one another to death on the streets of the city. The dead and wounded were piled by the roadside. Sundragon and Sungood bulu were already a sea of flames. Row after row of wooden houses were consumed in the conflagration. The people of the eastern part of the city—male and female, old and young—all wept, fleeing for their lives. The lords of the Sunnew and Sunold bulu in the western part of the city ordered that the gates be closed for protection, but they were burst asunder by those fleeing. The lord of the Sunold bulu personally led the troops under his command to seal the gates, but was killed by the refugees from the Sunevil bulu. The western part of the city was in chaos and people beyond number lost their lives.

The cult members who guarded the city did not disperse. Even after they lost Sundragon and Sungood bulu, they merely retreated to the city center and with their combined strength protected the Golden Palace and the Bronze Statue. Although the Green Snake Brotherhood had been able to occupy Sundragon, Sungood, and Sunevil bulu in the eastern part of the city, they were unable to fight their way into the city center. After the statue reappeared, it grew ever larger. All anyone had to do was glance up to see its fierce mien laughing malignantly at the Huhui people at its feet.

Seeing the size of the thing, the Green Snake Brotherhood warriors lost all will to fight. Despite the repeated urgings of Yu Fang and Yu Kui, they refused to advance. In anger, Yu Kui killed a number of the warriors under his command, but still to no avail. Seeing how things stood, Yu Fang said, "Yu Kui, don't blame them. Most of the Green Snake warriors are Sungood people, and seeing the bulu in flames and fearing revenge from the resurrected statue, they naturally are reluctant to fight. It will be dark soon; we won't be able to take the Golden Palace tonight. It would be better if we sent the men to fight the fires and first secure Sungood bulu. Tomorrow morning we will again attack the cult leader's final stronghold."

"Long delays cause lots of hitches," said Yu Kui. "We should press on without letting up and annihilate all the remaining evildoers. We don't know if General Shi can hold off the joint force of the Shan and Serpent people. The city will be put in a dangerous situation if we don't deal with the cult and if by some chance the Leopard Brotherhood is overcome by the Shan and the Serpent people."

Yu Fang knew that his brother was not exaggerating the gravity of the situation. Contrary to General Shi's advice that morning, Yu Fang had decided to attack the city. It was true, he was angry with the cult leader and wanted nothing more than to take this opportunity to destroy the cult and secure his rear. Otherwise, if the Green Snake and Leopard brotherhoods found themselves between the enemy and the city wall, they would be annihilated. Unexpectedly, the cult members had fought and died all day long, but the cult was still intact. Although the Green Snake Brotherhood had occupied one third of the city, if the Leopard cavalry were overrun by the enemy, the Green Snake Brotherhood would find itself beset from the front and the rear. Yu Fang pondered the situation, but couldn't come up with a strategy. Seeing how exhausted the Green Snake warriors were, he knew he couldn't order them to continue the attack. But if he missed this opportunity and didn't destroy the cult that night, he might suffer a crushing defeat the next day.

"We have to keep fighting," urged Yu Kui. "There is no other choice."

"Attack? How?" replied Yu Fang anxiously. "Look how tired the men are. Do you think they can keep fighting?"

Yu Kui unsheathed his snake blade and shouted to the warriors resting on the ground, "Brothers, come with me! Let's capture Yellow Ma and the cult leader alive!"

He shouted several times, but no one rose. Furious, Yu Kui was about to run the nearest warrior through with his blade when someone behind him forcefully restrained his arm and said, "You can't do that. How can compatriots kill one another?"

Restraining Yu Kui was none other than Commander Hua. When he stood fully upright he was half again as tall as the average man. He was spattered with blood, and a considerable part of his right arm had been burned. In spite of his ferocious looks, by temperament he was focused, and a smile spread over his large, round face. Zhi-Hu Zhe, the giant Serpent person who had returned with Commander Hua, was wounded more severely. One of his front limbs had been slashed, and a large piece of green skin hung loose on his back. Without the least show of heroics, he simply shook his head, swung his tail, and said, "Harken to me, be not life a blessing? Be not killing wrong? Should they die? No."

Yu Fang was overjoyed at seeing the two of them. When the Green Snake Brotherhood stormed the eastern gate that morning, no one knew where they had gone. Yu Fang had assumed that they had both been killed and never expected to see them return at dusk.

"Commander Hua, Mr. Zhi-Hu Zhe, you are just in time," said Yu Kui. "I'm organizing a suicide squad to capture Yellow Ma and the cult leader alive. Would you be willing to join us?"

"Can't you see that they are both wounded?" shouted Yu Fang, cutting off his brother.

"It doesn't matter,' said Commander Hua, smiling. "Capturing them alive is a good idea. But with that thing here, who will dare attack?"

Commander Hua pointed at the Bronze Statue. Shining in the fading purple light, it already appeared larger than it had a half hour before. Its eyes in particular looked cruel, and regardless of where one walked, they seemed to follow. It was no wonder the Huhui people of Sunlon City were scared out of their wits.

"Strange," said Yu Fang, sighing. "The statue didn't even exist yesterday, but now it's growing larger by the minute. I wonder what sort of supernatural powers the cult leader possesses that he can create such a huge statue in a single day?"

"Yeah," said Commander Hua, laughing, "if he can create such an enormous statue in one day, he should have been able to beat us long ago. We shouldn't wait for him to come evangelizing; we should convert to the cult immediately."

"Commander Hua," queried Yu Kui, "do you think the Statue is a fake?"

Commander Hua and Zhi-Hu Zhe looked at each other and laughed. Zhi-Hu Zhe, unable to stand the pain in his back, flicked his tail and shot up into the air, spun around, and said, "At which time when falsity is turned to truth, and truth to falsity; when nothingness becomes something, something reverts to nothingness. The cult leader's hocus-pocus can fool some of the people, but not us."

"Yeah." Commander Hua smiled. "Who can pull the wool over our eyes? When the army attacked the city, the statue suddenly appeared, taking the wind out of our sails. At the time I suspected some sort of trickery. Then Brother Zhi-Hu Zhe and I fought our way to the city center to see what was afoot. And just as I suspected, the statue is a fake!"

"The Bronze Statue is fake?" asked Yu Fang happily. "How did you determine that?"

"The real Bronze Statue is a huge metallic object; the fake is all smoke and mirrors, a machine-generated illusion," replied Commander Hua. "Take a look. As the sun sets, the statue starts to change."

Yu Fang and Yu Kui found this hard to believe. They watched as the huge purple sun set almost imperceptibly. As the burning eastern part of the city was tinged with the final glow of the sun, the Bronze Statue appeared more ferocious and fearsome than ever. The moment the sun sank below the horizon, the statue suddenly vanished. After a few seconds, it reappeared again, but with its color greatly altered.

"I get it!" said Yu Kui, jumping. "When the sun sets, the cult leader has to readjust the light source for his laser projector in order to produce a convincing illusion at night. The cult leader is a really cunning character. Fortunately, the two of you saw through it; otherwise we would have fallen for his tricks."

So saying, Yu Kui turned to the warriors and shouted, "Do you see that? The Bronze Statue is an illusion. What are you afraid of? Get up and let's catch the old guy!"

The warriors had no choice but to stand up and follow Yu Kui to the city center, in the direction of the Bronze Statue. Yu Kui signaled and began to sing hoarsely:

> *Army of singular awareness, army of singular awareness, army of singular awareness,*
> *We are the army of singular awareness of the Huhui planet*
> *Singularly aware and strong-willed*
> *Army of singular awareness, army of singular awareness, army of singular awareness,*
> 凸-凹凸-凹凸 *(chu-lu-ru-mu) the army of singular awareness. . . .*

The Green Snake Brotherhood warriors rushed to the foot of the Bronze Statue, but not without some misgivings. Wielding his snake blade, Yu Kui shouted, "Brothers, have no fear. The statue is an illusion. Watch me destroy it."

Yu Kui stepped forward and disappeared into the statue. The warriors then became believers and charged into the illusion. In the middle, a number of cult members clad in black stood guard around a laser projector. Seeing Yu Kui and the others burst in, they scattered in all directions with a shout. Yu Kui unholstered his laser pistol and destroyed the projector. The huge statue, which was nothing more than a projection, suddenly vanished, and the spiked purple clouds filling the sky gradually reappeared.

"Cult Leader, Yellow Ma, you're finished," said Yu Kui, laughing.

"Not necessarily," came a voice laughing coldly. "You overestimate yourselves."

The Stranger in Black speaking was none other than the cult leader, the Supreme One. Behind him stood Mayor Ma, dressed in a military uniform, and a large group of cult followers in black. At that moment Yu Fang, Zhi-Hu Zhe, and Commander Hua arrived at the ruins where the statue had just stood. Upon seeing Zhihuang Ma, Yu Fang was enraged. He pointed at him and reviled him: "Have you no shame, Yellow Ma? Your lord, General Shi, is fighting at this very moment against the Shan bastards outside the city, but you exploit the situation to join the cult leader and seize the city. General Shi might spare you, but I won't."

Zhihuang Ma shrank back behind the cult leader, who raised the bronze statue in his hands and said in a clear and ringing voice, "Yu Fang, there's no need to be angry. Zhihuang Ma is the true patriot, a man of ideals and integrity. In order to save the city, he willingly took it upon himself to bear the infamy of betraying his lord. He realized that if the Huhui people didn't join together and convert to the one true spirit of the Bronze Statue, Sunlon City would be entirely without hope. If you are patriots, you too should convert to our religion."

"Enough of your snake oil," replied Yu Kui, "your true spirit of the Bronze Statue is nothing but an illusion. I've already destroyed your projector, so what other tricks have you got?"

The cult leader made no reply. Instead he raised his bronze statue and chanted, then placed it on the ground. Strangely, the statue began to glow ever more brightly until it was a body of light. Then it began to flash, emitting beams of light. Then above the shining statue appeared a Bronze

Statue equal in height to three men. Watching, the warriors and cult members shouted and applauded.

"That's just one more of your stage tricks," said Yu Kui, unwilling to back down. "It doesn't amount to a hill of beans. If Ah 出 (chu) were here, he would tell you that he could he could make the same sort of pocket-size projector."

"Huhui people of little faith," said the cult leader, shaking his head, "the Bronze Statue is not an illusion; it is the revelation of the true spirit in your heart and mine. It really doesn't matter by what mechanical means it is made manifest. What matters is that our hearts are filled with the Bronze Statue; it is not something external to us."

"Nonsense," replied Yu Kui. "In my belly there are only roundworms, no Bronze Statue."

"Nor do I have anything of the sort," said Yu Fang.

"Me neither," said Commander Hua.

"Nor do I. Do I? No," said Zhi-Hu Zhe, swinging his tail.

The cult leader snorted coldly. Then he produced a bronze tag and pointed it at the green Serpent person's belly, which immediately began to glow until it looked like a lantern, clear and bright, inside of which could vaguely be seen a small bronze statue. Startled, Zhi-Hu Zhe mounted the air with a flick of his tail. Falling back to the ground, he rolled around. But regardless of how he rolled, his belly continued to glow. Sitting on the ground, he rubbed his light-producing belly and couldn't help but say, "Terrible, eaten have I of a thing disagreeable."

The cult leader laughed coldly, then pointed the bronze tag at Commander Hua. The Leopard was scared out of his wits; he hit the ground with all four legs and with his tail tucked, fled as fast as he could. The cult leader roared with laughter. Zhihuang Ma and the cult followers nearly doubled over in fits of laughter. Seeing the leader's display of supernatural powers, Zhihuang Ma took courage and said to Yu Fang, "I suggest that you take what's left of the Green Snake warriors and leave Sunlon City. To hesitate would anger the cult leader and cost you your lives."

"What a joke!" replied Yu Fang angrily. "I'm not afraid of death. The cult leader's power is gone. No evil magic he can show us will save you. Yu Kui, together."

Yu Kui could scarcely wait for Yu Fang to give the order. Immediately, he motioned to the warriors and said, "Attack! A huge reward to whoever captures the cult leader and Yellow Ma alive."

"Not so fast," the cult leader suddenly said. "The cult does not fear the Green Snake Brotherhood, but this encounter could cost us both dearly. Outside the city, the Leopard cavalry is collapsing and the Shan bastards are nearly upon us. If we kill one another, it will be difficult to defend the city."

"Who said the Leopard cavalry is collapsing?" asked Yu Fang, startled.

"Don't listen to the old thief's lies," said Yu Kui. "He's finished and just wants to stall for time."

"As I said," replied the cult leader angrily, "the cult is not afraid of you. We've already lost ten thousand followers, and another ten thousand will be just a drop in the bucket. But it would be unfortunate if the Shan bastards were to reconquer the city on account of this."

When Yu Fang heard that the city was going to fall into the hands of the Shan, he looked apprehensive. Unable to restrain himself, Yu Kui grasped his sword and shouted, "Shut your mouth, you old thief. Let's stamp out the cult first, then fight the Shan. Let's get rid of the thieves within the country and then fight against the foreign power."

"Don't be so rash," said Yu Fang, restraining his brother. He then turned to the cult leader and said, "You said that General Shi's cavalry was on the point of collapse. What proof do you have?"

"Why would I lie?" countered the cult leader. "The cult has never been soft-spoken nor submissive. I wouldn't reveal our weaknesses if the city's very survival hadn't reached a critical juncture. You know that whether we exterminate you or you us, the cost will be considerable. Therefore, as cult leader, I extend to you the hand of friendship so that we might join together to fight the Shan. Once the enemy withdraws, we'll still have time to settle old scores."

As Yu Fang hesitated, Yu Kui shouted, "No way! You killed my brother; you instigated Yellow Ma's surprise attack on us the day before yesterday. What is there to argue about?"

"Yu Jin gave his life to destroy the Shan warship," replied the cult leader. "He sought and found ▣ ▢ (du-wu). I can't be responsible for that. And as for Yellow Ma's attack, he was wrong. I was out of the loop on that. I tell you what, I'll hand Yellow Ma over to you to deal with as you will. Kill him or torture him; do as you see fit. How's that?"

Hearing this, Yu Fang and Yu Kui had nothing to say. Zhihuang Ma was scared out of his wits; he fell to his knees before the cult leader and pleaded, "Supreme One, won't handing me over to the Green Snake Brotherhood mean my measly little life? Please remember how I have served you. Even if I haven't contributed much, I have slaved for you. Spare me."

Zhihuang Ma pleaded and began to weep, but the cult leader was unmoved and said sternly, "Cult Member 888205, have you forgotten the oath you took upon entering the cult? If Sunlon City is destroyed, the cult will not be able to grow and prosper. As a cult member, you should take dying for the faith as the ultimate glory. If through your sacrifice, the Green Snake Brotherhood and the cult are able to cooperate in the defense of the city, then your death will be reckoned to be as weighty as Mount Huihui. You know that though flowers and fruit must fall, scattered by the wind, Sunlon City will be reborn!"

The cult leader spoke with the force of justice. Poor Zhihuang Ma had nothing to say; he lay on the ground trembling.

"Perhaps now," said the cult leader, addressing Yu Fang and Yu Kui, "you might be inclined to believe my sincerity."

"I believe," replied Yu Fang stroking his beard, "that everything must be sacrificed to protect the city; I can't believe anything else."

Yu Kui was visibly dissatisfied. Not waiting for him to speak, the cult leader pointed his bronze tag at Zhi-Hu Zhe's belly. Slowly it returned to normal.

"Marvelous," said Zhi-Hu Zhe happily. "My stomach does not ache. Where is the pain? It exists not."

The cult leader submissively cupped one hand in the other and said to the people standing around him, "I wholeheartedly welcome you heroic warriors of the Green Snake Brotherhood to join together with us to fight the Shan. Recall that yours truly was supreme commander of the United Army during the great uprising. At present, General Shi's cavalry is unfortunately on the verge of collapse; therefore, the difficult mission of defending Sunlon City has fallen on our shoulders. The Serpent people and the Shan will surely launch an attack against the city tomorrow morning. I suggest that everyone get some rest and prepare for tomorrow's fierce fight. Please remember, though flowers and fruit must fall, scattered by the wind, Sunlon City will be reborn!"

As the cult leader finished speaking, his robes began to billow, and in an instant he vanished. As soon as he had disappeared, the cult followers faded into the darkness. Only Zhihuang Ma remained kneeling on the ground, trembling. Yu Kui walked over and gave him a kick, spit on him, and said, "So, your day has come."

"I know," said Zhihuang Ma, sniveling, "that I must die for my crimes. But before that I have one request. When I heard the cult leader say that General Shi's cavalry was on the verge of collapse, it was like a knife in my heart. General Shi was my beneficent lord. I would be grateful if you would take me to where the general met defeat and sacrifice me to him."

Yu Fang was a just man, and hearing Zhihuang Ma's words, he nodded and sighed. "Rare, indeed, that you should be willing to sacrifice yourself for General Shi. I therefore grant you your request." He then turned to Yu Kui and Zhi-Hu Zhe and said, "I am greatly disturbed by what the cult leader said about the Leopard cavalry being on the verge of collapse. If they are unable to withstand the fierce attack of the Shan and the Serpent people, we bear some of the responsibility. Let's take advantage of the darkness of night and sacrifice Zhihuang Ma outside the city walls to pay respects to the general. Let everyone else get some rest."

No one had a different idea. Yu Kui bound Zhihuang Ma so tightly with sea serpent sinew that he shouted with pain. Laughing, Zhi-Hu Zhe said, "Yu Kui, why squander so much vital force? Hand him over to me and let him venture to escape as his luck permits."

"That would be too good for him," said Yu Kui, and spat. "He's too tricky. If we don't tie him up, he might get away."

Zhihuang Ma moaned. After tying him up, Yu Kui grabbed him and pulled him along, stumbling at a jog. Yu Fang and Zhi-Hu Zhe followed. When Zhihuang Ma fell, they would kick him to his feet again. Accustomed to being an official, Zhihuang Ma had never been treated so harshly. Weeping, he secretly cursed the cult leader for cruelly handing him over to placate the Green Snake Brotherhood, all the while trying to figure out some way of escape.

The four of them passed still-smoldering houses. Weeping with her head lowered, a young girl covered with blood sat beside her dead parents. Saddened, Yu Fang sighed and said, "Look what has become of our wonderful Huhui planet. If the Shan take the city tomorrow, who knows how many people will pay with their lives? The cult will harm so many people."

Yu Fang turned around and to his surprise saw yet another illusory Bronze Statue rising silently in the blowing sand to smile malignantly upon them.

"The cult leader never gives up," said Yu Fang angrily. "After we fend off the Shan attack tomorrow, the first thing we must do is round up the evil cult followers."

"I told you a long time ago that we should have killed the cult leader," said Yu Kui, "but you wouldn't listen."

They passed through ruins and piles of rubble to the eastern gate. The warriors who were supposed to be guarding it dozed beside the wall. Yu Fang couldn't bear to wake them. Quietly, they climbed through the break in the wall. Outside, a gust of wind howled, and cries were heard in the dark. Blue shafts of light lingered over the wilds, vaguely illuminating the countless corpses scattered over the ground. It was clear that both sides had suffered enormous casualties during the day's engagement. Stepping over the body of a Shan warrior, Yu Fang said to Yu Kui and Zhi-Hu Zhe, "General Shi must have fought with everything he had; the ground is covered with Shan and Serpent corpses. The cavalrymen fought without mercy."

With tears falling from two of his three eyes, Zhi-Hu Zhe couldn't help but say, "The unfortunate Serpent people, deceived, undone, and murdered by the Shan. Such a waste. The SPRA was but Shan trickery, and duped were these fools one and all."

Seeing the corpses of the Huhui and Serpent people littering the ground, Yu Fang and Yu Kui couldn't help but feel sad. Yu Kui kicked Zhihuang Ma to the ground, unsheathed his snake blade, and said, "This is the fault of you and the cult leader. You've done so much evil, I should have killed you a long time ago to atone for the deaths of so many."

Zhihuang Ma pissed and shit his pants in fear. Lying on the ground, he pleaded, "Please don't raise your hand yet. Though my death won't be atonement enough, we still haven't found the general. Why are you so anxious? Killing me, you will lose a sacrifice."

"I can't wait," said Yu Kui with a thrust of his sword. Zhihuang Ma rolled around to escape him. Yu Kui stepped on Zhihuang Ma's neck; he shouted out in pain.

"You deserve to die today." Yu Kui laughed. "Prepare to exercise your ⊡ ☐ (du-wu) spirit."

"Someone's coming," said Yu Fang, stopping Yu Kui before he could kill Zhihuang Ma.

Yu Kui was quick to ⊣⊡⊢ (lu-mu) as a group of soldiers slowly approached from the distance. When Zhihuang Ma heard Yu Fang say that someone was coming, he suddenly shouted, "Help, help, the Green Snake Brotherhood is trying to kill me!"

2

Fearing lest Zhihuang Ma alert the enemy, Yu Kui knocked him senseless, reviling him: "So you want to cry for help, you piece of trash."

But the soldiers clearly had heard him and surrounded them. Yu Fang motioned for Yu Kui and Zhi-Hu Zhe to crouch down, and whispered, "There are not many of them. Let's attack individually, capture a couple, and take them back for interrogation."

"You forget," said Zhi-Hu Zhe, "a Serpent person's weaknesse is the darknesse. Although fine is my hearing, the night circumscribes my actions. Let me ward Zhihuang Ma and the two of you try to make the enemy turn face."

Yu Fang and Yu Kui went to meet the enemy's attack, one to the left and one to the right. After going a short distance, Yu Kui was stopped by three swordsmen. "Green Snake Brotherhood friend," said the first one, "we are a Leopard Brotherhood patrol. What are you doing here?"

Learning that the Leopard cavalry had not collapsed, Yu Kui was overjoyed. He sheathed his snake blade and said, "I am Yu Kui, third in command of the Green Snake Brotherhood. We are looking for General Shi. You've come at the right time. Please take me to see him."

The three swordsmen looked at each other. "The general has been wounded and is in hiding," said the first one. "If you wish to see him, you must abide by our conditions."

"What conditions?"

The swordsmen drew their laser pistols and in one voice said, "Throw down your weapons, 凸-口-叶 (chu-lu-ru-mu)."

Yu Kui knew he had fallen into a trap, and it was too late for any regrets. The three swordsmen were actually Shan warriors disguised as Leopard Brotherhood members. One disarmed him; another struck him several times and asked in a shrill voice, "Whom did you just kill? Was it a wounded Shan warrior?"

"I didn't kill anyone," said Yu Kui, shaking his head.

"Nonsense," said the leader. "I clearly heard someone calling for help. It must have been a Shan warrior. Hurry and confess, or I'll get nasty."

"It wasn't a wounded Shan warrior." Yu Kui laughed. "The Green Snake Brotherhood is not in the habit of indiscriminately killing unarmed enemy soldiers."

Unconvinced, the Shan squad leader beat Yu Kui till he saw stars. In a short while, four other Shan warriors returned with Yu Fang and Yellow Ma. After working over Yu Kui, the squad leader turned to Yu Fang. Both were beaten black and blue, but revealed nothing. The Shan squad leader had no choice but to order that the men be escorted back to the Shan and Serpent encampment.

The army of the Shan and Serpent people had fought with General Shi's cavalry the entire day and casualties had been heavy. Some of the Serpent people had lost their tails, some had lost three of their six limbs, others had lost two of their three eyes. They lay moaning in the dark beside the Hu River. Yu Fang and Yu Kui could see that there were three or four thousand Serpent people lying on the riverbank, their half pikes beside them. Both men were alarmed. "Before the fight with the Leopard cavalry, "whispered Yu Fang to Yu Kui, "it was estimated that there were a little more than five thousand Serpent people. There must be three or four thousand of them here. I never expected them to be such brave and hardy fighters. They are indeed worthy adversaries."

Before Yu Kui could reply, the Shan soldier escort lashed out at them and shouted, "No talking!"

Serpent people liked living out under the open sky; they had no need for tents and slept beside the river. The Shan, by contrast, had pitched their tents in neat rows on high ground. Yu Fang counted more than seventy tents, indicating that there were seven or eight hundred Shan. Yu Fang couldn't help feeling heavy of heart. It appeared that the enemy army was still a formidable force, and that the Green Snake Brotherhood and the cult followers would have a hard time defending the city against attack the following day. And since Yu Fang and Yu Kui unfortunately had been captured, the Green Snake Brotherhood, finding itself leaderless, would have an even more difficult time.

Yu Fang and his brother were escorted to a tent. The soldier escorting them shouted that they should enter it, and then he began to rain blows on them with his stick. They staggered forward, stumbling into the tent, where Yu Kui chanced to fall on someone lying on the ground. That person shouted in complaint, "Hey, watch where you're going. My neck is ready to snap as it is. 卟哻卟凷 (mu-ru-lu-chu)."[1]

Yu Kui quickly got to his feet. Then from the side someone was heard to shout in surprise, "How were you two captured?"

Yu Fang was overjoyed when he saw Miss Qi, and immediately clasped her hand and said, "Thank goodness, you're all right, 凷卟哻卟 (chu-lu-ru-mu). And what about Ah 凷 (chu)?"

"I'm over here," said Ah 凷 (chu), getting to his feet. Bowing deeply to Yu Fang and Yu Kui, he said, "I am grateful beyond words that you have rushed here to rescue Miss Qi. Am I correct in assuming that the Green Snake Brotherhood has already eliminated the Bronze Statue Cult in Sunlon City?"

Somewhat ashamed, Yu Fang proceeded to narrate what had happened in the city. Hearing his account, Miss Qi and Ah 凷 (chu) gasped repeatedly. Ah 凷 (chu) rubbed the red nose on top of his head and said, "The cult leader created the illusionary Bronze Statue in order to frighten the city residents. Who could have foreseen that he would be able to frighten the Green Snake Brotherhood as well? It is clear that the cult leader's magic is very powerful."

Miss Qi's eyes grew red as she listen to Yu Fang tell about the conflagration inside the city and how the homes of the Sungood people were destroyed by the fire. She was concerned and wondered what had happened to Ah Wen, Ah Three, and Ah Four. Then she began to weep as she thought of how Sunlon City was still facing catastrophe. Knowing that she was concerned for the members of her household, Ah 凷 (chu) tried to console her, saying, "Don't worry. Ah Wen most certainly was able to lead Ah Three and Ah Four to safety. Though destroyed by fire, houses can be rebuilt. All we have to do is beat the Shan bastards and then we can return and rebuild."

"But can the Huhui people beat the Shan bastards?" asked Miss Qi, brushing her tears away. "Today we witnessed the Shan destroy General

---

[1] 卟哻卟凷 is a Huhui imprecation meaning "unfortunate," and is the opposite of 凷卟哻卟 .

Shi's cavalry; braver Huhui warriors would not be able to withstand them." Yu Fang and Yu Kui then asked about the fighting outside the city. Miss Qi gave them a detailed account of what had transpired.

———

Not long after the Green Snake Brotherhood had stormed the eastern gate, the enemy troops attacked again en masse. Without a sign of fear, the general had taken up his sword, mounted his horse, and led his eight thousand cavalrymen into battle. But the Serpent attack that time was different: more than five thousand Serpent people had formed five large regiments and arrayed themselves in a rectangular formation, five deep. The three front rows carried long spears, while the two rows bringing up the rear were armed with javelins. In strict formation, they advanced. Miss Qi and Ah 出 (chu) had observed the fighting from a hill outside the city. When Ah 出 (chu) saw their formation, he shouted that things looked bad and then rolled all the way down the hill. Miss Qi was right behind to help him up, for he had taken a hard fall. Fortunately his sense organs were located on top of his head; if not, they might have been battered and bruised like the rest of his body. Miss Qi couldn't help scolding him: "Ah 出 (chu), what are you doing? You should be more careful."

"It doesn't look good," said Ah 出 (chu), his eyes wide open. "The Serpents always have lacked organization and discipline, so how can they now array themselves in a Five Tigers Seizing a Sheep Formation? I'm afraid that General Shi's cavalry is going to suffer great losses. Wait here, Miss, and I'll go warn him." He then struggled to his feet.

"I'll go with you," said Miss Qi, unwilling to let him go alone.

"The battlefield is a dangerous place," protested Ah 出 (chu).

But Miss Qi walked faster than he did. Ah 出 (chu) had to run to catch up with his headstrong mistress. It was hilly east of Sunlon City, and the two of them crossed a level valley; all they could hear from behind the hills was the sound of the slaughter. Ah 出 (chu) kept insisting that they hurry, but he couldn't go any faster, and Miss Qi had to drag him along. They easily climbed to the top of one hill when they heard the buglers sounding the charge. Panting, Ah 出 (chu) said, "Can't go on. . . ." The two of them lay down on the slope to watch the charge.

In the cavalry, four squads of ten horsemen formed a company; four companies formed a battalion; four battalions formed a regiment; and four regiments formed a brigade. The Dragon cavalry brigade was to lead a frontal attack. The Dragon cavalry soldiers, clad in white with white helmets, were armed with long lances. Row after row charged the Serpent regiments. The Serpents formed a square; the front row of soldiers armed with long lances knelt, while the two rows behind dipped their long lances, forming a triple line of defense. The two rear rows threw their javelins when the chance presented itself. The two thousand horsemen of the Dragon cavalry charged the first line of Serpent defense and quickly found themselves in a bitter struggle. Although one regiment of Serpent troops on the right flank was scattered, the other two regiments successfully checked the cavalry attack.

At that moment the order to charge was sounded again. The Routing cavalry brigade suddenly appeared on the left flank. The black-clad horsemen fired their pistols in unison on the enemy, breaching the Serpent formation from the side. The two rows of the first line of Serpent defense were scattered, leaving the center in a critical situation. Gratified watching the battle from the hillside, Ah 出 (chu) folded his hands across his forehead and said to Miss Qi, "For being able to break the Five Tigers Seize a Sheep Formation, General Shi is worthy of his reputation. It will be hard for the enemy to regroup. For the Shan to train the Serpent rabble to array in such a formation is no mean feat; but to regroup is impossible."

But before Ah 出 (chu) had finished speaking, the first line of Serpents had run to the rear, and the two rows that had been in the rear quickly combined to form a hexagonal array. The erstwhile defeated Serpents regrouped in the middle. Curious, Miss Qi asked, "What kind of formation is that?"

"I can't believe my eyes," gasped Ah 出 (chu). "That's the Six Gate Golden Lock Formation, which disappeared a long time ago. I never would have dreamed that the Serpents would be so quick to employ it. One of the Shan is extremely competent. But General Shi is by no means weak; let's see how he breaks this formation."

The bugles were heard again, and the Dragon and Routing cavalry brigades retreated, disappearing without a trace behind the hill, leaving the Serpents in their strange hexagonal formation. It was already noon and the purple sun was intolerably hot. On the slope, Miss Qi and Ah 出 (chu) could hardly stand the oppressive heat. In the valley, the Serpents held up scarcely better under the sun, and the formation began to fall apart. Suddenly, the call to charge was heard from three hills. The three cavalries charged from three different directions. The white-clad Dragon cavalry were armed with long lances; the black-clad Routing cavalry fired their pistols; and the purple-clad Valiant cavalry attacked with their scimitars. Together they attacked the enemy position. Full of praise, Ah 出 (chu) shouted, "The Triple Talent Formation breaks the Six Gate Golden Lock Formation. Marvelous! General Shi is a superior strategist. The Serpents are finished. Let's go down and join the excitement."

Ah 出 (chu), who was as round as a winter melon, was so excited that he took off for the valley without waiting for Miss Qi to agree. Miss Qi had no alternative but to stick close to him. By the time they were halfway down the slope, the two armies were fighting fiercely, and the sound of killing filled the air. Miss Qi glanced up and noticed that the hills were covered with row upon row of soldiers clad in scarlet. Startled, she grabbed Ah 出 (chu) and said, "Look!"

When Ah 出 (chu) saw the surrounding hills covered with Shan warriors, his expression changed, and he said, "This is bad. That's the Ten-Sided Ambush Formation. The Ten-Sided Ambush captures the flood dragon; the Leopard Brotherhood soldiers are sitting ducks."

But even at that critical juncture, Miss Qi had to laugh. The commanding officer of the Shan no doubt thoroughly understood General Shi. He let the Serpents array themselves in some old formations on purpose so that General Shi, who was fond of the art of war, would be anxious to demonstrate his skills, forgetting that the Shan were his real enemies. She wanted to say something, but Ah 出 (chu) paid her no heed; instead, as he looked skyward, he mumbled to himself, "Ten-Sided Ambush, Ten-Sided Ambush. How can that be overcome?"

"Don't bother thinking about how to overcome it; let's get out of here."

But they were too late—several Shan warriors appeared and took them prisoner. From their vantage point on the surrounding hills, the Shan swept the valley floor with their laser guns, killing many Serpents along with the cavalrymen. Only a few horsemen were able to escape the crossfire. There in the bottom of the valley, most of the eight thousand poor Leopard Brotherhood cavalrymen—the awe of the Huhui planet—were reduced to ghosts.

———

Yu Fang and Yu Kui were in tears by the time Miss Qi finished her story. Yu Fang sighed and said, "I expected that the cavalry would not be able to fend off the relentless attack of the combined force of the Shan and Serpents. The eight thousand warriors are to be admired for giving their lives in defense of the city. Tomorrow, the Green Snake Brotherhood will also have to exercise its singular awareness spirit. We cannot allow the praise to go the Leopard Brotherhood alone."

"The Shan bastards are despicable," said Yu Kui. "What are we doing waiting around here? We should hurry up and think of a way to escape. I'll cover your escape; it doesn't matter if I die. Hurry back to Sunlon City and lead our brothers in a fight to the end!"

Ah 出 (chu) stood up, bowed deeply to the two brothers, and said, "I'm willing to sacrifice myself. Please take Miss Qi and flee; I'll run first to draw the attention of the guards, and then you run the opposite direction. We'll meet again, Miss."

So saying, Ah 出 (chu) swaggered toward the tent door. But before reaching it, he was hurled through the air, landing heavily on the ground. Two people then entered the tent. When Yu Fang saw the leader, he went black with rage, and pointing at him reviled him: "Yellow Ma, you collaborated with the Bronze Statue Cult, framing the loyal and honest, plunging the people of Sunlon City into the abyss of misery. And now you turn coat and surrender to the Shan. You have no shame!"

"As the saying goes: ⊡ (du) is the mark of a truly great man," Zhihuang Ma said, laughing coldly. "The cult leader, that old creep, was ready to sell me for nothing just for his own advantage, and you were going to sacrifice me to General Shi. If I don't settle accounts with you now, when should I?" He then turned to the masked Shan officer, and with great respect said, "Sir, Yu Fang and Yu Kui are the brains behind the Green Snake Brotherhood; it is they who lead the resistance against the Shan. Execute them and the Green Snake Brotherhood, being without a leader, will fall apart, and the city will be yours for the plucking."

Outraged, Yu Kui leaped and grabbed Zhihuang Ma by the throat. Zhihuang Ma struggled, and the two rolled across the ground. The masked officer pointed his electric pistol at Yu Kui and fired, stunning him. Overjoyed, Zhihuang Ma faced the officer and kowtowed, saying, "Sir, thank you for saving my life. You see how violent he is. Have done with him at once to avoid problems later."

Before the officer could respond, Ah 出 (chu) stood up and bowed deeply to the Shan officer and said, "Article 24512 of the Interstellar Public Code stipulates that when two planets are at war, they are obliged to treat their prisoners well. After hostilities have ended, prisoners must be exchanged under the supervision of the Interstellar Peace Tribunal. Planets violating the Interstellar Public Code can be vaporized. The Shan are a people with a golden civilization and are incapable of uncivilized behavior such as murdering prisoners in cold blood."

The masked officer nodded and said to Zhihuang Ma, "The 出 (chu) person is correct. The Shan do not kill prisoners. Keep your thoughts to yourself."

Miss Qi found the officer's voice very familiar. Then it came to her. Staring at her, the officer said, "Miss, I must ask you a few questions. Please come with me."

This startled Ah 凸 (chu). He stepped in front of Miss Qi and said, "If you have anything to ask, then ask me. Out of curiosity we came to observe the battle between the joint force of the Shan and Serpents and the cavalry when we were captured by your patrol. According to the Interstellar Public Code, noncombatants are to be treated as prisoners of war."

"Sir," said Zhihuang Ma in a persuasive tone of voice, "I know this girl and this 凸 (chu) person. They run a tavern in the Sungood bulu of the city. They often pass information to the Green Snake Brotherhood and are not to be trusted. Sir, do not be taken in and tricked by the artful words of these two spies."

"I understand," replied the officer somewhat impatiently. "Didn't you say that the old Serpent watching you was able to flee after you wounded him? I'll send a group of warriors to accompany you to the battlefield to look for him. He has a lot of influence among the Serpents, and must be apprehended. Send for some men."

Seeing that the officer was not going to accept his advice regardless of what he said, Zhihuang Ma couldn't help feeling that it was all a waste of time. He mumbled to himself, "Sincere advice is often grating to the ear; often grating to the ear is sincere advice. Too bad."

"You're wrong, Mayor Ma," said Ah 凸 (chu), bowing deeply. "You are a traitor, so you should say traitorous advice is often grating to the ear; often grating to the ear is traitorous advice. So it was you who wounded my dear Serpent friend Zhi-Hu Zhe; you really are evil. He is the brave guardian of the Number One Underground Pass of the Serpent people. You will not be spared. May you 卟-哻-叫凸 (mu-ru-lu-chu)."

After the masked officer had called some men to lead Zhihuang Ma away, he turned to Miss Qi and said, "Miss, it is now our turn to chat."

Ah 凸 (chu) was about to protest when Yu Fang and Yu Kui both stood up to block their way. But Miss Qi said, "Don't worry. I'm not afraid of him."

She followed the masked officer out of the tent. It was already late at night, and the Hu River could be heard flowing in the dark. The countless Serpent people gathered along the riverbank hissed strangely. Far away, a solitary shaft of blue light suddenly blazed with a white light, as if someone had mistakenly stumbled into it, to be hurled to another time and place in the history of the Huhui planet. The masked officer sighed and said as if to himself, "It's a strange planet. I never thought I'd spend my whole life here. I've never liked night on the Huhui planet. What about you, Miss?"

Miss Qi sighed as well. Only one other person she knew disliked night on the Huhui planet. But she knew that the masked officer in front of her wasn't that person. Softly she said, "Captain Mai, I don't like it either."

The masked officer's frame seem to tremble, and in a quavering voice, he said, "So you do remember me, Miss Qi."

"Of course I do; I'm not that forgetful." Miss Qi laughed. "Why are you wearing that mask? Are you trying to copy the cult leader?"

Captain Mai made no direct reply but, pointing at the golden-red shaft of light rapidly receding into the purple clouds, said, "At last I have come to know the source of the cult leader's power. Zhihuang Ma has got it wrong. The Green Snake Brotherhood is not our adversary, nor is the Leopard Brotherhood. The Bronze Statue Cult is not the real enemy of the Shan either. Our real enemy is the history of the Huhui planet. The cult leader simply understands how to manipulate that history. But if his powers were greater still, yet he would not be able to hold out against the final general offensive of the Serpents and the Shan."

By that time, some of the Serpent people were beginning to climb into the Hu River, where they swam like four-legged sea serpents. Those who remained on the riverbank played their flutes, which sounded so sorrowful. Miss Qi recalled the first time she was taken prisoner by Captain Mai and escorted to the Shan warship. She couldn't help asking him, "What about your warship? Why not attack Sunlon City with your warship?"

"Warship . . . even if the warship could be flown," said Captain Mai, sighing, "there is no need for it since the Shan and the Serpents have joined forces."

Miss Qi was happy to hear this. Hastily, she asked, "Then are Yu Jin and Gai Bo your prisoners?"

"Miss Qi," said Captain Mai, unable to keep from laughing, "*you* are my prisoner; I should be the one doing the interrogation. How did you manage to switch roles? I can see you're still quick tongued. You and Ah 凸 (chu) came secretly to collect military intelligence and were captured. Yu Fang and Yu Kui came personally to rescue you. What are you up to?"

"Nothing," said Miss Qi, "we just came to join the excitement. How were we to know that unfortunately you would scatter the Leopard cavalry?"

"They were routed, not scattered," said Captain Mai, immediately correcting her. "Given the antiquated way of fighting and General Shi's inability to change, we would still have routed them even if they had ten divisions of cavalry."

"No way," said Miss Qi, not backing down for one second. "You relied on the tough Serpent troops. You used them as bait, and when the cavalry attacked them with everything, you were able to succeed by luck. Otherwise you Shan would be no match for a hero like the general and troops so willing to sacrifice themselves."

Captain Mai gazed at her with his bright, piercing eyes. After a while he said, as if to himself, "You're right. General Shi is a hero. Even though he was defeated, the Huhui people will always remember him. But what about us? We're just a bunch of homeless refugees. Even if the Death Commandos hadn't destroyed our warship, still we wouldn't be able to go home. We were forgotten a long time ago by the empire. It doesn't matter in the least to the empire if we quell the Huhui rebellion or die heroically trying. Look at this sky—there's not a single star. Where I come from, the sky is filled with shining stars when night falls. I still remember how many nights I spent with friends, drinking and singing under the stars. I never expected to spend my life fighting such a meaningless war on the loneliest, most forsaken planet in this corner of the Milky Way galaxy."

As Captain Mai spoke, the Serpent people on the riverbank stopped playing their flutes, and all those in the river had climbed out of the water. Countless numbers of them lay curled up in the dark, hissing continuously, as if thousands of rattlesnakes had slithered onto the riverbank. Miss Qi couldn't help but shudder.

"Don't be afraid," said Captain Mai. "It's just their habit. On the night before battle, the elders choose the first line of soldiers who must be prepared to die. They enter the river to wash away their sins, while those on the riverbank play their flutes as a way of seeing them off. They really are not that willing to fight, but we have promised them complete autonomy once Sunlon City is retaken. For the freedom of their descendants, they have to cooperate with us."

"Then are the Leopard people and the Feathered people also cooperating with you under the same terms?" asked Miss Qi.

"Perhaps," said the tall Shan officer. "Miss Qi, you really like to ask questions. Fortunately for you, you ran into me. If someone else had taken you captive, you would have been charged with spying and called to account. Do you think they would have let you ask so many questions?"

"Who told you to let me ask questions? And who said you had to answer?" asked Miss Qi. "Anyway, there is only one way left open for us Huhui people, and that is to fight you Shan to the bitter end. You are free to choose how you dispose of me."

Miss Qi's display of awe-inspiring righteousness only served to elicit laughter from Captain Mai. "Miss Qi, you are one of a kind," he said. "Don't worry, I'm not going to do anything to you. You and I didn't start this war. When it's over, we'll go on living, right? I don't care what others think; I don't consider you an enemy. I hope you feel the same about me."

"Since you keep saying that I'm not an enemy and this war is meaningless, why do you keep on killing my compatriots?" The words were scarcely out of her mouth when she regretted her own stupidity. Almost at once she added, "I know the Shan occupation forces aren't going home, but if you are willing to live at peace with the Huhui people, we certainly would accept you and allow you to live and work in peace and contentment."

"Is that really possible?" asked Captain Mai, shaking his head. "The Huhui people are ready to kill one another, so how could you live at peace with a foreign race? Soon we will attack Sunlon City, and the Green Snake Brotherhood and the cult are still bickering. But that's okay; casualties will perhaps be lessened on both sides. I hope you understand that all of this is destined by fate, and no one can do anything to change it."

Miss Qi couldn't help blushing when her eyes met the fiery gaze of the Shan officer. She knew that he was afraid she would blame him for whatever happened. Although he was concerned about her opinion of him, he had already decided that the Shan would conquer the city and she was fated once again to be a slave. No, she couldn't accept the idea that Sunlon City was to be destroyed. There had to be a way to deliver her people.

"Casualties will be heavy if the Shan attack the city. . . ."

Miss Qi was cut off by an argument that had broken out among the Serpent people on the bank of the Hu River. Those who had been hissing suddenly began to coo like pigeons, but a thousand times louder. It went on for a matter of moments, growing ever louder.

"Wu. . . ."

"Wu. . . ."

"Wu. . . ."

Captain Mai and Miss Qi were frightened by the sound. A Shan warrior clad in scarlet hastened along the riverbank to report to Captain Mai, "Captain, the situation looks bad. The Serpent people are on the verge of rebellion!"

3

Countless Serpent people were gathered on the banks of the Hu River. Their green scales flashed in the weak light, and they brandished their half pikes at the sky. Suddenly a group of them stood up, their eyes wide open, shouting: "Wu . . . Wu . . . Wu. . . ."

As this group sat down, another group stood up, brandishing their lances and shouting. Miss Qi trembled with fear. Although unfamiliar with the customs of the Serpent people, she guessed that it was a war dance performed before going into battle. Captain Mai took out his pistol and handed it to Miss Qi.

"Hurry up and get to the other side of the hill and watch the excitement from there, but whatever you do, don't show yourself."

Miss Qi was touched to realize that he really was concerned about her. Captain Mai motioned with his hands and then led the hundred or so Shan warriors in scarlet who had hastily assembled to the riverbank in the midst of the Serpent people. But Miss Qi didn't pay attention to what the captain had told her; instead, she followed the Shan at a distance. Captain Mai led the Shan warriors to the heart of the Serpent people's position and there directed his men to array themselves in a Diamond Formation. Standing at the crown of the formation, Captain Mai shouted to the Serpent people around him, "Men of the SPRA, the time for the decisive battle with the Huhui people has not yet arrived. Please remain calm, and do not get excited."

Captain Mai shouted, repeating himself several times. The Serpent people indeed calmed down and began to disperse. Three green Serpent elders, their tails coiled, approached the Shan force. Seeing them, Captain Mai bowed and politely said, "Can I be of service, gentlemen?"

The leader of the three grasped his tail in one claw and covered his middle eye with another. His other two front claws were folded in a prayerful gesture. Solemnly he said to Captain Mai, "Please allow me to pay my respects."

The attitude of the green-skinned elder indicated to Captain Mai that he was observing the highest Serpent etiquette, and he was touched. Serpent people were fierce and fought bravely and, generally, didn't set much store in etiquette, save for a few of the elders. Serpent society consisted of two classes: the nobility and the commoners. The elders were of the hereditary nobility. Long ago, the oviparous Serpent people had devised a unique system of inheritance: the year before they died, they went to the copper fields and selected an egg. In the dark, they would leave a special mark on the egg, and the young that hatched from these specially marked eggs would be part of the nobility. The Serpent elders had a method of transmitting their knowledge to these hatchlings, after which they would go to the lair beneath the copper fields to die. At death, the elder would be laid out so that he held his tail in one hand and covered his middle eye with another. The other two front claws would be folded in a prayerful gesture. This was the highest form of Serpent etiquette and wasn't used lightly—only at death, at funerals, or when friends broke with one another. Although Serpent people were by nature fierce and didn't like to make friends, when they did so, it was for life. This concept of loyalty was unique to the Serpent people. Since it was considered extremely serious when friends broke, the etiquette used for death was adopted.

Captain Mai knew that the elder's attitude did not bode well. "Esteemed elder Zhi-Zhi Gong, what is this? Haven't the Shan and the Serpents concluded a mutual defense pact? Why all the formality?"

"Zhi-Zhi Nan, Zhi-Zhi Yi, and myself have talked things over. Since the joint Shan-Serpent force began this operation, and after a number of battles, the Shan have suffered few casualties, while our best troops have been decimated. We cannot but begin to wonder if the Shan aren't using a Serpent-wave strategy while biding their time, waiting for the chance to eliminate us. Now you are asking us to attack Sunlon City. I'm afraid that by the time the city is taken, there won't be any Serpent people left. Therefore, we have decided that we will not be used any longer by the Shan, and that *you* should attack the city."

Suddenly, Zhi-Zhi Gong's tail came down on the ground with a whack. The other two elders did likewise. Observing this, the other Serpent people standing around began to strike the ground with their tails and shout: "Wu . . . Wu . . . Wu. . . ."

Concealed among some trees close by, Miss Qi watched as the Serpent uproar grew. She couldn't help but be concerned for Captain Mai. But good Captain Mai knew no fear in the face of danger. Instead, he stretched out both arms and said, "Men of the SPRA, please hear me. It has been an easy fight getting to the city, and it rests there for us to reach out and take. If you withdraw now, we will fall short of success for lack of a final effort, and do you think that in future the Huhui people will spare you? Men of the SPRA, please carefully consider the possible implications. Since the Shan and the Serpents have formed an alliance, naturally we will share alike in good fortune and in adversity. In the attack on Sunlon City, the Shan are duty-bound to be in the van and would not think of asking you to fall first."

The Serpents nodded in agreement with Captain Mai. Zhi-Zhi Gong's three eyes blinked, and he said, "I have always respected you as a real Shan man, but does the Shan command hold a view different from your own? Even if you had no intention to betray us, can you guarantee that the Shan commander won't sell us out?"

Before Captain Mai could reply, several flares appeared above a nearby hill. At that moment, about a thousand soldiers clad in scarlet came down over the hill, laser guns blazing at the Serpent people on the riverbank. The flares blinded the Serpents, who had poor night vision, and they began to scream.

"Serpent people," shouted someone from the slope, "lay down your weapons at once. Resistance is futile, and all traitors will be dealt with with utmost severity. Serpent people, lay down your weapons at once."

"The Shan are cunning," said Zhi-Zhi Gong, angrily. "This old Serpent will fight you to the end!"

Wielding his tail, the serpent elder swept at Captain Mai but was shot down by the men to the right and left of him. Given the situation, Zhi-Zhi Nan and Zhi-Zhi Yi knew that resistance was pointless. They blew their whistles and the Serpent people put down their weapons. Half the Shan warriors remained on the slope as a precaution while the other half descended the hill, herding the Serpents together. The six limbs of the two green-skinned elders were bound and their tails pinned to the ground. The two elders figured they were done for and with their eyes wide open, they shouted, "Serpents, we have been betrayed by the Shan. Sons and grandsons, swear that you will avenge us!"

Squatting on the ground, the Serpents once again began to hiss. Some took out their flutes and began to play a sorrowful tune. Unable to restrain himself, Captain Mai said to the Shan commander who was descending the hillside with an armed escort, "Commander, the Serpent people are our allies. They can be forgiven their mutinous behavior just prior to battle. Please consider giving them a special amnesty."

Peeking from among the trees, Miss Qi recognized the Shan commander as the short, bald-headed guy she had seen on the Shan warship. So he hadn't died!

"Captain Mai," he said in a high-pitched voice, "how can mutinous soldiers be pardoned? If they go unpunished, how will we be able to maintain military discipline? You mustn't be soft on them."

Hearing this, the two Serpent elders shouted, "You bald soprano! If you want to kill us, just kill us; if you want to ⊡ (du) us, just ⊡ (du) us. If we as much as bat an eye, we are not Serpent heroes!"

Nothing angered the Shan commander more than having his baldness and his high-pitched voice pointed out. So when two Serpent people used his nickname, he was fit to be tied. He jumped to his feet and cursed. "Captain Mai, shoot these Serpents at once! I can't stand to see them alive! Shoot them! Shoot them at once!"

"Commander," replied Captain Mai coolly, "if we kill them, can we still expect the Serpents to fight for us? Please reconsider."

The commander did cool off. Lying on the ground, Zhi-Zhi Nan and Zhi-Zhi Yi shouted: "Don't think you can trick us, you bald soprano. Even if you don't kill us, the Serpents will never be used by you again."

"Don't anger me," replied the commander, laughing coldly. "I know you have no desire to live, so I'll let you go on living. Serpents talk too much. I'll just take what you say as nonsense. If you convince the Serpents to help us attack the city, I'll pardon you for all crimes."

"Not a chance!" said Zhi-Zhi Nan. "To know is difficult; to do, easy. It has taken us a little while to learn your true colors, and we won't be duped again."

"Not a chance!" said Zhi-Zhi Yi. "To know is easy; to do, difficult. We knew you were tricky, and no matter how you threaten or cajole, we will maintain a policy of noncooperation, no matter what."

Seeing their unanimity, the commander at once changed his tune and said, angrily, "I don't care whether it's easier to know than to do or easier to do than to know. Today I demand unity of knowing and doing. I'm going to teach you a lesson. Someone come and cut the tails off these two traitors!"

He shouted his orders. Captain Mai was on the point of interceding when the Shan warriors on the hillside began to shout, grouping together chaotically. When Captain Mai turned to look, he saw the Shan tents in flames. The commander also saw it, and shouted: "Spies! Captain Mai, send someone to put out the fire."

Taking advantage of the situation, the two aged Serpents who had been pinned to the ground shouted: "Serpent sons and grandsons, fight your way out!"

Hearing this, the Serpents began to shout strangely. Some soared into the air with a flick of their long tails; climbing and rolling, others rushed the nearest Shan warriors and began to fight hand to hand. The Serpents fought for all they were worth, and not only were the Shan unable to hold them off, they found themselves pinned down by the Serpent people. Seeing this, Miss Qi, who had been hiding among the trees, couldn't help but applaud and cheer. Someone tugged at her clothes from behind.

"Don't stand there watching the excitement; get out of here quickly."

Turning around, she saw Ah 凸 (chu), who looked to the left and right, -凸 (lu-mu), and said, "Zhi-Hu Zhe did a good job of creating a disturbance by setting the fire. The Shan will pay dearly. Let's take advantage of the chaos and get out of here!"

Miss Qi was worried about Captain Mai; she didn't know where he was. She wondered if he had fallen to the Serpents or had managed to flee. After repeated urgings from Ah 凸 (chu), Miss Qi had no alternative but to follow him at a run along the Hu River toward Sunlon City.

The sky was gradually growing light; the river slowly turned purple. Flocks of ducks flew by, hugging the water's surface. One after another, they dropped into the water. As she ran, Miss Qi asked, "Was it Zhi-Hu Zhe who saved your lives?"

"No, it was Commander Hua," replied Ah 凸 (chu), panting. "Thank goodness he arrived in time, otherwise we would have been done for. Zhihuang Ma is such a treacherous fellow. After the Shan officer took you away, he came back with the intention of killing us. But he had no idea that Commander Hua had long been following him in secret. The Leopard people are, after all, very strong. With just a few blows he was able to knock Zhihuang Ma and the two Shan sentries unconscious. Then Zhi-Hu Zhe went around creating disturbances, toying with the Shan until their heads spun. If he had not done so, do you think the Serpents would have been able to break out?"

"What about Yu Fang and Yu Kui?"

"They were uneasy and returned at once to Sunlon City. It was a close shave, but the Serpents were able to free themselves from Shan control, and Sunlon City is now no longer facing a crisis. If the Shan attack the city, they won't succeed without the support of their warship."

They ran to the riverbank. Ah 出 (chu) sat down and, panting, said, "Let's rest a bit. I can't run anymore. Why must we run so hard if the enemy is not chasing us?"

Miss Qi couldn't help but laugh.

"I'm not forcing you to run; you were the one running for your life. Okay, let's take a rest."

Ah 出 (chu) lay down on the sandy shore to rest. Miss Qi stood and looked around. Quietly flowed the Hu River, enveloped in a bluish fog. Through the mist she could make out a huge grayish shape that seemed to rise gradually, but despite the nearness of the battle, the fighting could not be heard. The gray shape seemed to increase in size, its face ever clearer. Miss Qi shuddered at the sight of the Bronze Statue's cruel smiling face. Seeing the statue, Ah 出 (chu) rolled over, got to his feet, and said, "This is bad. The statue looks more and more hideous. Disaster is looming over the city. Hurry up, let's go."

Leaving the riverbank, Miss Qi and Ah 出 (chu) headed toward Sunlon City. As the fog thinned, the expression on the statue's face grew clearer. Occasionally it bared its teeth in a malignant smile; occasionally it looked distressed. Feeling ever more ill at ease, Miss Qi asked Ah 出 (chu), "Why does the statue's face change like that of a living person? I seem to have seen that face before."

"You're right," said Ah 出 (chu), looking skyward. "It seems to be ever more alive. But that just means more Huhui people will die. I remember that at the end of the Fourth Interstellar War, the Bronze Statue's face changed every day. Each time the cult followers went out to do battle, the statue would smile broadly as if self-contented. I saw it cry only once, and that was just before it was vaporized. That was the only time I saw it filled with regret. On account of this, your dada and I went to the Huhui History Archives to read how the statue was described through history. We discovered that that was the only time the statue ever showed any sign of repentance."

"I'm afraid you can't call it repentance," said Miss Qi. "On the verge of death, a person's words will be □ (wu); on the verge of death, a horse's neigh will be sad. The evil statue knew that it was about to be vaporized; it cried for itself, not for having sent so many Huhui people to their deaths."

Sighing, Ah 凸 (chu) replied, "You don't understand, Miss. The Huhui people willingly died for the Bronze Statue. You can't blame it. It is the soul of the Huhui people. You say it is evil, which amounts to saying that we ourselves are evil."

"But the statue has already been vaporized—how could it reappear to control our lives? I don't think this statue is real, but rather an instrument used by some evil people. If the Huhui again fail to see the light, it could spell their end."

Ah 凸 (chu) made no reply. Miss Qi knew that he was sometimes very obstinate. She was just about to scold him when he suddenly screamed. The strange sight before her left her speechless.

They were not far from Sunlon City, but from their vantage point on a hill, there was no trace of it. All that stood on the site of the city was that incomparably large Bronze Statue. But it already looked different than it had just a few minutes ago: it had lifted its arms and raised its head toward the sky, as if challenging the purple sun of the Huhui planet or imploring the gods to descend from heaven. All around the statue, the purple clouds were dispersed, as if scattered by some powerful energy emanating from it. The base of the statue was concealed in a rolling sea of mist. The statue seemed to struggle as it grew, but the mist spread ever more quickly. In a short time, the lower half of the statue was entirely concealed in the mist, and from a distance the sound of thunder was heard, much like the rumble of cannon fire. The statue reached into the mists, pulled something out, and then thrust it into its mouth. Miss Qi saw the squirming object and shouted, "It's eating people! Ah 凸 (chu), it's eating people!"

In that moment of terror, the mist spread toward them, obscuring the earth and heaven until they could no longer see their hands in front of their faces. Miss Qi heard Ah 凸 (chu) shout, "Miss, where are you?"

She groped her way in the direction of his voice while calling his name. Ah 凸 (chu) shouted in response several times, then abruptly fell silent. She knew something was amiss. Unsheathing the snake blade at her waist, she proceeded forward cautiously into the dark mist. She felt the moisture against her face, the cold prickling her skin. Recalling how she had seen the statue eating people, she began to cry. She had never hated the statue more than at that moment; nor had she ever despised the backwardness of the Huhui people more than then. Why had they been unable to rid themselves of the Bronze Statue, generation after generation? Why had they believed all the lies of the cult, generation after generation? How many patriotic and honorable Huhui people had ended up as sacrifices in the mouth of the statue? If she hadn't seen it with her own eyes, she never would have believed that the statue could eat people. But if that poor squirming object wasn't a Huhui person, what was it?

Suddenly, a strong wind whipped up in the dark, scattering the mist above her head. Miss Qi looked up and broke into a cold sweat. A huge hand descended toward her out of the clouds. As if immobilized by a spell, she couldn't even shout, much less move. Just as the hand was about to touch her, she rolled to one side with all the strength she could muster. With a deafening roar, the hand struck the ground, sending sand and rock flying. Miss Qi continued to roll away, and without meaning to, fell into a deep hole. She fell to the bottom, where she lay dazed. Having come up empty, the giant hand slowly withdrew and disappeared into the black mist. Miss Qi knew that she had been lucky, and that she had been saved by falling into the hole. She groped around looking for her snake blade but encountered a warm head. Terrified, she was about to scream when she heard the head speak. "Don't be frightened, it's me."

"You nearly scared me to death," she said as if to rebuke him, but her heart was already at ease. "Did you see that hand?"

"Yes," said Ah 凷 (chu). "Strange, strange. I don't understand it."

"What's so strange? You still don't believe that the statue eats people?" asked Miss Qi angrily. "Aren't you being a bit of a pedant?"

"It's not that I don't believe it," said Ah 凷 (chu), getting to his feet, "but the statue is not alive; it doesn't need to eat people. Moreover, the real Bronze Statue was vaporized a long time ago. I'm afraid that what we have seen is not the Bronze Statue of Sunlon City."

"If it's not the Bronze Statue, what is it?"

"凷-凵凸凵- (chu-lu-ru-mu), ▣□ ▣□ (du-wu du-wu)," replied Ah 凷 (chu) seriously. "The Evil Spirit of the Huhui planet has unexpectedly come to haunt us at this moment. Let's get out of here."

"What evil spirit? What evil spirit?"

Without replying, he mumbled to himself, and set off at a brisk pace. Miss Qi had no alternative but to follow. She kept her eyes fixed on the dark mist for fear the hand would reappear. Ah 凷 (chu) seemed to have completely forgotten the recent danger and continued ahead. Miss Qi was just about to caution him when the strange scene repeated itself: the black mist surrounding them suddenly parted, even more rapidly than the last time. Miss Qi didn't even have enough time to utter a sound before the mist had entirely disappeared. There in front of her stood a gleaming golden city.

"It's Sunlon City!" shouted Miss Qi, in surprise. "Sunlon City has reappeared!"

Panting, Ah 出 (chu) halted. That awe-inspiring, eternal city stood proudly on the open plain, shining under the purple sun. Miss Qi couldn't believe her eyes. A moment ago, all she had seen was the Bronze Statue and not a trace of the city. But now, Sunlon City had reappeared and the statue had vanished!

"Where is the statue?"

"It was right here!" said Ah 出 (chu). "Fortunately we ran, otherwise I wouldn't want to think about what might have happened. I hope I'm right."

"Right about what? What are you talking about? One minute you're talking about some evil spirit, the next minute you're telling me to run. What's going on?"

"Miss," replied Ah 出 (chu), laughing, "if we had been but a moment slower, we would not have seen anyone. I was right. That black mist was the Evil Spirit released at the destruction of the Huhui planet and the breaking apart of the heavenly shafts at the end of the Anliu Era. The relationship of time and space was altered with the appearance of the mist. If we had been a little slower, who knows into what corner of the Huhui planet the mist might have cast us. It's all right. Sunlon City is still here, so the mist didn't remove us too far from our original time and place."

"But the statue is gone," said Miss Qi, realizing why Ah 出 (chu), who was normally so lethargic, ran like hell. Still somewhat worried, she continued, "Space might not have changed, but time certainly could have. Could we be at some other point in time in the history of the Huhui planet?"

"That's hard to say," said Ah 出 (chu), shaking his head. "Let's go. Let's venture into the city and have a look."

This time, Miss Qi ran faster than Ah 出 (chu). Panting heavily, Ah 出 (chu) said, "The black mist has vanished. Why run so fast? Sunlon City is right in front of us, and it's not going anyplace."

Miss Qi slowed down and waited for him to catch up. Then she was overcome by another doubt.

"Was that strange hand in the dark mist part of the Evil Spirit?"

"Perhaps, perhaps not. The 出 (chu) sages throughout history have speculated, based on the results of manipulating the wisdom beads, that an evil spirit would be unleashed at the end of the Huhui planet, but no one has actually seen the Evil Spirit of time and space. But today our eyes have been opened."

"But didn't we see a man-eating Bronze Statue? Then isn't it part of the evil spirit? When the statue was eating people, and just before it was covered by the mist, you could see that it wasn't the Evil Spirit of time and space. Then where did the statue go?"

"How many times do I have to tell you that the Bronze Statue doesn't eat people?" said Ah 出 (chu), upset. "Didn't Yu Fang and Yu Kui tell you that the Bronze Statue was an illusion created by the cult leader? How can an illusion eat people?"

"But I clearly saw it."

"That perhaps was the Evil Spirit of time and space causing trouble; or perhaps it was a trick of the cult leader's. Since he can create the illusion of a Bronze Statue, why can't he create the illusion of the Bronze Statue eating people?"

Miss Qi didn't want to argue with him anymore. She knew that Ah 出 (chu) would never accept the fact that the Bronze Statue ate people, but she wasn't going to give in. She had just seen the statue reach into the mist, pull something out, and thrust it into its mouth. And when the hand had tried to catch her, it had struck the ground, sending sand and rocks flying into the air. Was that an illusion? She didn't believe so.

But that golden city, standing there before her as if in relief, seemed real enough. How beautiful the purple sun was, rising slowly, shining over the Huhui planet. Miss Qi sighed. Who cared about an Evil Spirit of time and space or if the Bronze Statue ate people? As long as the city continued to exist, there was hope.

The closer they got to the city, the stranger they felt. The open-air market outside it seemed much larger. Small stalls had been erected where peddlers sold all sorts of dry goods, grain, and fruit and vegetables. The place was crowded and bustling with people as if no fighting had broken out just the day before. The eastern gate, which had been breached by the Green Snake Brotherhood the day before, had been completely repaired. Miss Qi stopped a peddler; he thought she wanted to buy something. Pointing at the basket on his back, he said, "Fresh sea serpent meat, twenty-five ▣ (du) a kilo. You want some?"

"I don't want to buy anything," said Miss Qi. "I just want to ask you how the situation is. What about the Shan bastards?"

"Shan bastards? What Shan bastards?" said the peddler, smiling. "Would the Shan be allowed to create a disturbance on the most excellent Huhui planet? Do you see any Shan here?"

"But the Shan were attacking the city just yesterday. How can they be gone now?"

Taken aback, the peddler looked Miss Qi over and said, "Miss, that happened three years ago. Didn't you know that?"

"We just got back from picking medicinal herbs on Mount Huihui," Ah 凵 (chu) replied hastily. "We haven't had any news of the world in many years. Then has the Shan Occupation Army been routed?"

"Haven't you heard?" said the man with a shrug of his shoulders. "If the bastards hadn't been defeated, do you think we could live and work in peace and contentment? If you're not going to buy anything, I don't have any time to stand around and chit-chat. Sorry, 凵-凵句凵- (chu-lu-ru-mu)."

"凵-凵句凵- (chu-lu-ru-mu)," replied Ah 凵 (chu), bowing. "Sorry, but just one more question. Who is ruling the city now?"

"Who else?" replied the peddler setting off, fearing lest they detain him any longer. "Who else but Mayor Ma?"

"Zhihuang Ma?" asked Miss Qi and Ah 凵 (chu), looking at each another.

"Him again!" said Miss Qi, laughing. "There's no getting the better of him. Come on, let's go pay the mayor a visit."

4

The first city wall of Sunlon City was built by the nine immigrant families from outer space. The only remaining portion of that original wall was near the Golden Palace, and it surrounded 3,500 square meters. Of course, when it was built, there was no Golden Palace; it was, on a reduced scale, a model of what would come later. Over thousands of years, the city wall had expanded just like annual rings on a tree to its present size. The outermost layer did not change much during the Anliu Era. There was an inner and an outer wall, and the space inside the inner wall wasn't much larger than what was contained within the original wall, including the Golden Palace and the site of the Bronze Statue. After the city was occupied by the Shan, they demolished the inner wall. The outer wall was composed of from one to three layers. The part around Sunwork, Sunbright, Sunnew, and Sunold bulu was of at least two layers, and that was because most of the attacks on the city came from the plains. The city wall around the other five bulu—Sunart, Sundark, Sundragon, Sungood, and Sunevil—were composed of a single layer of simple construction and appeared very weak. The Green Snake Brotherhood had entered the city through a breach in the eastern gate and, in the fierce fighting, damage had been greatest in Sundragon bulu and neighboring Sungood bulu, nearly half of which had been destroyed by fire.

When Miss Qi and Ah 出 (chu) entered Sunlon City, not only had the eastern gate been repaired, but Sundragon and Sungood bulu looked much as they always had. As they walked, they looked and marveled. After three short years, Sunlon City appeared as prosperous as it had in the past. Looking and laughing, Ah 出 (chu) said, "The Evil Spirit of time and space actually did us a favor. If I didn't see this with my own eyes, I never would have believed that Sunlon City could be reborn. 出-口-口-口- (chu-lu-ru-mu)! There's no underestimating the Huhui spirit of singular awareness."

Miss Qi was also secretly pleased. She noticed that among all the pedestrians there wasn't a single cult follower, which seemed odd to her. Could the power of the cult have declined so rapidly? Then she recalled the sight of the Bronze Statue eating Huhui people. Even if it were a deception of the Evil Spirit of time and space, she still trembled. Not only were there no cult followers sporting little Bronze Statues, but there were no Green Snake Brotherhood members armed with snake blades either. There weren't any Serpent people, no Gaiwenese. . . . All the passersby were ruddy complected and looked satisfied, but . . . .

"Look at the . . ."

"I know," replied Ah 出 (chu) in a whisper. "Don't be alarmed. Let's go back to the eastern gate."

The moment they turned around, the street vanished, as did the buildings. They found themselves once again in the black mist, so thick they couldn't see their hands in front of their faces.

Miss Qi was terrified. Beside her, Ah 出 (chu) said, "Remain calm, and turn around."

Turning around, once again they were confronted with the bustling streets. No one in the thronging crowd paid them any mind.

"What's going on?"

"I don't know. The Evil Spirit of time and space doesn't want us to go back, so we won't go back."

"Is the Evil Spirit still playing games? Is this really Sunlon City?"

"Shhh . . . hurry, let's go."

Having learned their lesson, Miss Qi and Ah 出 (chu) didn't turn around. They followed the street in the direction of the Golden Palace at the city center. The street became ever more crowded. Arriving at the square, they saw that it was a mass of people, all healthy and all smiling. But there wasn't a single Gaiwenese, Serpent person, Green Snake Brotherhood member, or cult member to be seen, just thousands of ruddy Huhui people, all expectant, all looking at the Golden Palace.

"What are they doing? So many strong young Huhui people. It's strange. . . ."

Before Ah 出 (chu) had finished speaking, the people began to shout with joy. Their right fists upraised, they faced the Golden Palace and shouted, "Field Marshal Ma! Field Marshal Ma!"

Miss Qi stood on tiptoe in the crowd, trying to see what was happening. Out of the palace walked a man sporting the golden cape of a land, sea, and air field marshal. With his left hand, he waved in response to the crowd. Seeing him, the crowd became very excited and shouted, "The people's planet! Field Marshal Ma! Field Marshal Ma!"

One young girl fainted as the crowd continued to chant, "Huhui hero! Field Marshal Ma! Field Marshal Ma!"

When the field marshal raised both arms, the crowd grew silent. In a clear voice, he said, "Huhui youth! Today we celebrate the anniversary of our resistance against the Shan. Deeply saddened, we remember those who sacrificed themselves three years ago. Three years ago today, I led the soldiers and the populace and with one stroke defeated the joint Shan and Serpent force, delivering the city from danger and bringing peace. Since that time, the people have lived in peace and prosperity. . . ."

"Long live Field Marshal Ma!"

"But Huhui people of idealism and integrity paid a heavy price in their fight against the Shan. We thank those who gave their lives for the Huhui planet. The brothers Yu, General Shi, the cult leader, and thousands of his followers all died protecting Sunlon City. Today is a national day of mourning. Let us honor these fallen heroes with a minute of silence."

Tugging at Ah 出 (chu)'s clothes, Miss Qi said, "Zhihuang Ma said that Yu Fang, Yu Kui, General Shi, and the cult leader were all killed. I don't believe it!"

"Only if all the heroes were no more," snorted Ah 出 (chu) coldly, "would Yellow Ma be allowed to bray without restraint. Field marshal, indeed. A field marshal of his own making. What a joke!"

"How dare you insult our leader!" A young man behind them wearing a yellow scarf grabbed Ah 出 (chu) and shouted, "I caught someone insulting our leader!"

At once, another ten young people with identical yellow scarves were there, pressing in on Ah 出 (chu) until he could scarcely breathe. He pleaded repeatedly, "Please, 出-叻叻-叻 (chu-lu-ru-mu). Give me some room to breathe."

Miss Qi attempted to mediate, and she too found herself held. The two of them were escorted before the palace. The moment he laid eyes on them, the field marshal recognized them. He laughed and ordered the yellow-scarved youths to escort them into the Audience Hall. Ascending the throne, he said, "Miss Qi, Ah 丑 (chu), it's been a long time. Fate is capricious; fate is capricious. You probably never expected to see me again, did you?"

"Mayor Ma," said Miss Qi, laughing, "every time I see you, you seem to have risen even higher. That's no mean feat."

Zhihuang Ma stroked the rows of medals on his dress uniform and replied with satisfaction, "You flatter me. Since I was of age, I have fought for the country and the people. Over and over again, I have performed deeds of merit. I have won the love and respect of the people, and naturally have risen ever higher."

"Yellow Ma," said Ah 丑 (chu), bowing deeply, "that should come as no surprise, seeing how you promoted yourself. What is surprising is how the people of Sunlon City have permitted it. Don't you think it's extremely funny that you should be field marshal of the land, sea, and air when Sunlon City has no navy or air force?"

"Who says I have no navy or air force?" Zhihuang Ma laughed. "Tomorrow I am going to Hehe Village to give a pep talk; my fleet of armored barges will be transporting the marines to New Menghan City. Our airships will set off at the same time to gain dominance over the Gaiwenese Froghoppers. This march on New Menghan City is being undertaken by the three branches of the armed forces—the army, air force, and navy—and it is nothing to scoff at. I have acceded to the position of field marshal to personally direct the three branches in mounting this punitive expedition against the Gaiwenese wanderers."

Miss Qi and Ah 丑 (chu) looked at each other. Scratching his head, Ah 丑 (chu) said, "Why would you want to send troops against New Menghan City before having done everything in your power to deal with the Shan and Serpent people?"

"There is nothing to be concerned about: the Shan were annihilated a long time ago, the remnants of the Serpent people have returned to their lair beneath the copper fields, and the Feathered people are a long way off on Mount Huihui. In all the Huhui planet, the only ones who oppose me are the Gaiwenese, and they are entrenched in New Menghan City. After I have dealt with New Menghan City, the entire Huhui planet will be united!"

The more Miss Qi heard, the stranger it all sounded. Although the Gaiwenese did congregate in New Menghan City, she had never heard of them raising an armed insurrection. Now Yellow Ma was saying he wanted to subjugate them. Had the Shan really been annihilated by Zhihuang Ma? And what of the Yu brothers, General Shi, and the cult leader? Had they really died fighting, as Zhihuang Ma said?

Before she could pursue the matter, Zhihuang Ma stood up and, straightening his uniform, said, "You were disrespectful to me during that moment of silence, a crime for which you deserve death. We'll just forget the incident for old time's sake, since you are both old friends. Not only will I not give you a hard time, but I'll ask you to join me in the campaign. And as Ah 屮 (chu) is a Huhui historian, I'll ask you to record my deeds once I have completed the grand task of unifying the Huhui planet. And you, Miss Qi, since you have always underestimated me, I'll ask you to observe what an outstanding military commander I am. Our crack troops are setting off tonight. You might as well accompany the first dispatch of troops. Take them to Army headquarters and hand them over to Commander Liu to look after."

Without a word, the yellow-scarved youths who had captured Ah 屮 (chu) and Miss Qi pushed the two of them out the main gate of the palace. Outside, on the square, thousands of Huhui youths waved their left hands as they fervently sang the "Army of Singular Awareness Song." It was a huge spectacle. Ah 屮 (chu) couldn't help but sigh and shake his head.

"A bunch of dummies! A real bunch of ninnies! As if the Huhui hadn't done enough killing. Now, tricked by Yellow Ma, even more people will die for no reason!"

"Nonsense!" shouted the youth escorting Ah 屮 (chu), as he gave him a slap on his smooth, shining neck. "The Gaiwenese are not Huhui people. Field Marshal Ma is leading us to attack them because only by exterminating the foreigners can the Huhui planet be united."

"The Gaiwenese have lived here for generations and have become Huhui people. How can you say otherwise?" asked Miss Qi. "Are you saying that the Serpent people, Leopard people, Feathered people, and 屮 (chu) people are not Huhui?"

The young man looked at Miss Qi angrily but said no more. Not yet twenty, he was tall and thin, and wore a bronze tag on his chest. Miss Qi recognized it immediately as one of those SPCs invented by Zhihuang Ma or the cult leader.

"Are you still using SPCs?"

"What SPCs?" asked the young man. "I don't know what you are talking about."

"That thing around your neck; that's an SPC."

The young man suddenly understood, and proudly replied: "This is a ⊡ □ (du-wu) medal given by Field Marshal Ma himself to loyal yellow scarves. It's not an SPC, as you call it. Lofty Huhui youths who exercise the ⊡ □ (du-wu) spirit must go through a rigorous examination before they are allowed to join the yellow scarves. And only the most loyal are given bronze medals. Not everyone gets one."

Miss Qi knew that it was yet another of Zhihuang Ma's tricks to control the Huhui youth and couldn't help laughing. He devoted so much effort to devising these, and every time, the Huhui were taken in. The young man was clearly loyal and devoted to Zhihuang Ma. She tried a different approach: "What's your name?"

"I am Yellow Scarf #56!" said the young man proudly. "Only the first ninety-nine Yellow Scarves have bronze medals. Do you understand?"

"Tell me, #56, how could the Gaiwenese start an armed rebellion? They've always lived in New Menghan City. They do business everywhere and have never had a quarrel with the Huhui. Why would they suddenly rebel?"

"You're wrong. Field Marshal Ma told us that they are a cannibalistic race, and their language is full of hidden references to cannibalism.[1] Every year many Huhui children disappear from Sunlon City. They are kidnapped by the Gaiwenese, then taken away and eaten."

"Don't be ridiculous." Ah ⊥ (chu) laughed. "It's true that on their old planet, they were a race of man-eaters, but after their home was vaporized, in their pain, they swore an oath not to eat people. Instead they decided to devote their cannibalistic talents to doing business. That's why this wandering people have become the best businessmen among the stars."

"Field Marshal Ma was right," said #56 volubly. "The Gaiwenese do nothing but exploit us, and their behavior is about the same as it was back in their cannibal days. Each day we pass without exterminating them means one more day that we lack power and prosperity."

They were already at the barge wharf outside Sunlon City's southern gate. Troops had been deployed all around the wharf, and the ten or so barges all flew banners with the surname Ma. The soldiers busied themselves loading machinery and food onto the boats. #56 led them to the first barge moored at the wharf, where a group of soldiers stood around an officer, who was 270 centimeters tall and was arguing vociferously as

---

[1] On the Gaiwenese language, see "The Translation of a Poetic Masterpiece" in the *Nebula Suite*.

he pointed at a military map. The young Yellow Scarf raised his left hand and, performing a lovely salute, said, "Commander Liu, Field Marshal Ma ordered me to escort these two criminals here and hand them over to you. He asks that you watch them and take them on the campaign."

Without looking up, he replied angrily, "When? I don't have time to watch criminals."

"Field Marshal Ma said . . ."

"卄-口-乜出 (mu-ru-lu-chu), take them back to Field Marshal Ma, and tell him that we're not running a detention center here. All the barges are filled with troops, and two less means that much less trouble!"

Miss Qi seemed to recognize his voice, when Ah 出 (chu) suddenly shouted: "Liu Qi! It's you!"

Startled, he looked up and saw Miss Qi and Ah 出 (chu). His anger melted into a smile, and he said, "Well, it's none other than Miss Qi and old Ah 出 (chu). So we meet again."

It was Sharp Knives Liu of the Green Snake Brotherhood, one of the Yu brothers' most beloved subordinates. But he seemed to have transformed himself into the commander of the Sunlon City Marine Corps. With the wave of a hand, he said to #56, "Okay. You go back and report to Field Marshal Ma that you have turned the two of them over to me. Wait a minute," barked Liu Qi, just as the young Yellow Scarf was about to leave. "Tell Field Marshal Ma that the first dispatch is taking a one-month supply of food. If we can't take New Menghan City within thirty days, we'll come back."

"Commander Liu," replied the young man, somewhat surprised, "if you fail to complete your mission of taking the city, you should exercise your ▣ ▢ (du-wu) spirit and commit suicide. How could you even think about running back?"

"出 (chu) this suicide shit!" barked Commander Liu. "If Field Marshal Ma wants to commit suicide, he's welcome to lead you Yellow Scarf ignoramuses and do so. There's no way I'm going to sacrifice myself for him. Now get the hell out of here!"

After sending #56 away, Liu Qi escorted Miss Qi and Ah 出 (chu) aboard ship. He was still cursing. "The reason for sending us in the van is to knock us off. Zhihuang Ma can't deceive me that easily!"

Bowing deeply, Ah 出 (chu) said, "You were one of the good men of the Green Snake Brotherhood. How is it that you are now one of Yellow Ma's subordinates, slaving away for him?"

Taking them into the cabin, he shut the door and said, sighing, "You think I want to? But after Yu Fang and Yu Kui died in battle. . . ."

"They both died?" gasped Miss Qi, tears welling from her eyes. "How can that be?"

"It's been three years. I never would have thought you didn't know." Liu Qi sighed. "The year the Shan and Serpent people attacked Sunlon City, General Shi led his cavalry in an oath to die defending the city. They heroically kept their word. Fortunately the Serpent people couldn't stand the Shan oppression and revolted just prior to the attack. Taking advantage of the Shan weakness, Yu Fang, Yu Kui, and I led an attack from the city. The cult leader and the cult followers joined with us in a bitter fight against the Shan on the banks of the Hu River. And though we thoroughly routed the enemy, our losses were heavy, and even the Serpent people were nearly exterminated. . . ."

"So taking advantage of the situation, Zhihuang Ma again took possession of the city!" Ah 出 (chu) seldom got angry, but at the mere mention of Zhihuang Ma he ground his teeth. "Yellow Ma is the number one enemy of the Huhui."

"In order to preserve what was left of the brotherhood," Liu Qi continued, "I had no alternative but to cooperate with Zhihuang Ma. Now he's come up with this evil plot of sending us in the van to attack New Menghan City. His goal is to finish off the Green Snake Brotherhood."

Miss Qi wept as Liu Qi spoke. So they all had died! Yu Fang, Yu Kui, the cult leader, Captain Mai, all dead! Miss Qi denied this brute fact. Ever since her father had passed away, seldom had she cried. She had accepted the fate of the Huhui people, and as a Huhui, she could not escape this tragedy. But in the face of yet another tragedy, she couldn't help being sad. Ah 出 (chu) tried to comfort her. "The Yu brothers and General Shi sought ▣ ▢, and they found ▣ ▢ (du-wu). Don't be sad. What's important is that their sacrifice has preserved Sunlon City."

"To what end?" said Miss Qi, crying. "The city did not fall into the hands of the Shan, but it is now in Zhihuang Ma's clutches. Is he any better than the Shan?"

"You can't look at it that way. After all, the Shan are foreigners; they are not one of us, and their hearts are ▢ (wu)."

"For brothers to kill one another," replied Miss Qi angrily, "is much worse than foreign subjugation. I have no respect for the Huhui!"

"Miss Qi is right," said Liu Qi. "I don't want to attack New Menghan City, but I have no other plan. Zhihuang Ma is a tough customer, and many members of the Green Snake Brotherhood have been tortured to death by him. Attacking New Menghan City will be the same—many will die fighting the Gaiwenese. I really don't know what to do."

"There's always a way," said Ah 凸 (chu). "Just take it one step at a time."

At that moment, one of Liu Qi's subordinates entered and said they were prepared to get under way. Liu Qi acknowledged him with a wave of his hand. Then he spoke to Miss Qi and Ah 凸 (chu), saying, "You're right. As for today's plan, all we can do is take it one step at a time. Let's get going."

They exited the cabin to watch. The entire Marine Corps battalion boarded the barges. Yellow flags were hoisted above the sixteen barges. In single file, they left the wharf gate and entered the canal. The inhabitants of Sundragon bulu stood along both banks, watching and waving to the marines. The canal water was filthy and smelly. As the ships passed, roiling the water, the stench increased. Miss Qi knew that this was due to the fact that all the fish for the city were transported via the eastern wharf gate at Sundragon bulu. The fish were cleaned at the wharf, and one could well imagine the accumulated stink with the passage of years. Soon the flotilla entered the West Hu River. The banks opened up and the turbid yellow water became brownish in color. The sixteen barges adopted a V formation and, with flags whipping in the breeze, set a course south to Hehe Village. Liu Qi's command ship took up position in the center. Proud and satisfied, Liu Qi 呂呂 (lu-mu) around him. Then, turning to Miss Qi and Ah 凸 (chu), he said, "This corps of marines is composed of the Green Snake Brotherhood's crack troops. Three years ago, before the Shan and Serpent people launched their attack on the city, Yu Fang ordered Wang Liu and me to take three hundred warriors north to reinforce Fort Ever Peaceful. Unexpectedly, even before we reached Red Iron Village, Hehe Village had been captured by the enemy. By the time we heard the news and hastened to Sunlon City, the fighting was over. Sorely grieved, Wang Liu and I, after discussing the matter, decided to retreat to our lair in Hehe Village to recuperate and protect what was left of the brotherhood forces."

"What happened to Wang Liu?" asked Miss Qi. She recalled how Liu Qi and Wang Liu, who was so smart, had nearly lost their lives in a surprise attack beneath the copper fields.

"Isn't that him approaching?" said Liu Qi, pointing at the river in front of them. Three barges displaying green flags were coming. Standing at the bow of the lead ship was the old warrior, Wang Liu; his head was bald and he sported a heavy beard. He was looking directly at Liu Qi's boat. Soon, the two barges pulled alongside each other. Wang Liu laughed and greeted Miss Qi and Ah 凸 (chu): "How have you been since we last parted? From a distance, I thought it was you, and sure enough, I was right!"

"Wang Liu," said Liu Qi, "Zhihuang Ma sent Miss Qi and Ah 凸 (chu) to join the van. He wants to finish off all of us."

"Great," replied Wang Liu, pointing at Ah 凸 (chu). "No one has got more stratagems than old Ah 凸 (chu). He can help us out."

"You flatter me. Zhihuang Ma wants us to go to New Menghan City, ostensibly to finish us off. I don't know if that will provide us with a golden opportunity to revolt or not."

"Revolt?" said Liu Qi. "All together we have but three hundred men, and some of them probably are informers working for Zhihuang Ma. We'll be finished off before we have a chance to rebel, as well as be accused unjustly of being traitors."

"A perfect time to exercise the ▣□ (du-wu) spirit." Ah 凸 (chu) laughed. "The ancient 中□ (man-qia) Sage said it best: 'mind is ▣ (du); nonmind is □ (wu). Transform ▣ (du) into □ (wu); subdue □ (wu) with ▣ (du).' Zhihuang Ma intends to lead us into injustice. That's the perfect time for us to transform ▣ (du) into □ (wu) and subdue □ (wu) with ▣ (du)."

"How can ▣ (du) be subdued?" asked Miss Qi. "Don't go boasting now, Ah 凸 (chu)."

"I'm not boasting," said Ah 凸 (chu) in all seriousness. "The Gaiwenese have always been on friendly terms with the Huhui, but Zhihuang Ma wants to send a punitive expedition against them now. People are going to wonder. We should play it by ear. If Zhihuang Ma has forced them to rebel, we can expose his tricks for what they are; then the field marshal won't be able to carry out his plan."

"But what if they really are rebelling?" asked Miss Qi. "Don't forget that Gai Bo might have been a Shan spy. It is quite possible that the Gaiwenese might secretly have been in league with the Shan."

"Don't worry," said Ah 凸 (chu). "Gai Bo was a double agent clandestinely working for the cult leader. He wouldn't join the Shan."

At first Miss Qi was going to disagree, but then she thought better of it, deciding it wasn't worth arguing about. The more a person argued with Ah 凸 (chu), who was so conceited and arrogant, the more obstinate he became. Miss Qi stood at the side of the vessel and looked toward the shore; there she saw the layered crags and the mountain range that included Five Phoenixes Mountain winding away to the south, where it was lost in the mist of dusk. She recalled the year Yu Fang and Yu Kui led their troops in search of the Serpent lair beneath the copper fields. And now, Yu Fang and Yu Kui were no longer among the living, and the surviving members of the Green Snake Brotherhood were facing extinction. What did the future hold for this isolated but loyal and righteous force filling nineteen barges? For the moment the Huhui planet was at peace, but would it last?

Thinking of her dada, Yu Jin, and Captain Mai, Miss Qi wept. Those who had loved her most were gone. What point was there in living? She stared blankly at the reddish water. Behind her she heard Ah 出 (chu).

"Night has brought a chill. Go into the cabin."

She nodded, but didn't budge. Another Huhui night, and once again she was leaving Sunlon City. She had become a stranger there; in three short years, she no longer recognized the place. Had the city changed, or was it her?

"Go inside."

Ah 出 (chu) continued to urge her. Miss Qi wiped away her tears. Just as she was about to go in, Ah 出 (chu) and a number of soldiers appeared startled.

"What's wrong?"

She looked into the distance where Ah 出 (chu) pointed. A huge beast floated in the middle of the river ahead of them. Its head rose like that of an agitated snake; it opened its mouth and emitted a mournful cry.

5

There are many legends concerning the sea serpents of the Huhui planet. Some say the huge beast and the Tai Nan dinosaur had the same origins. Why the Tai Nan dinosaur became extinct at the end of the Cretaceous age is a riddle that Tai Nan scientists have never solved. The Huhui believe that the dinosaur and the sea serpent were both introduced by the Interstellar Livestock Company. The company had intended to use Tai Nan and the Huhui planet as pasture. They never expected that the herbosaur, after being exposed to radiation, would mutate into so many different varieties, such as the tyrannosaurus, hadrosaur, triceratops, pterodactyl, dromaeosaur, and stegosaurus. But the small-boned, meaty herbosaur was all but eliminated by the mutations. When the Interstellar Livestock Company returned to harvest the herbosaur and discovered that the they had become extinct and that none of the mutations was edible, they destroyed them all in anger. But because the company was unable to supply the goods as promised, they went bankrupt and left the sea serpents on the Huhui planet, where they continued to reproduce.

The sea serpent of the Huhui planet was most like the Tai Nan Liang dragon, which was closest to the herbosaur introduced by the Interstellar Livestock Company. And in spite of its large size, its meat was tender and juicy, and much tastier than beef, lamb, or pork. Although of frightening aspect, it was actually quite gentle, and would dive underwater and flee upon contact with people. There had never been a case of one harming a person. Every part could be used. The Huhui fishermen, after sailing out to sea, had only to catch one and they would have food for a year. Thus the old Huhui saying: "One sea serpent is worth more than a mountain of gold or silver."

The sea serpent was a warm-blooded aquatic animal. It had a small head, a long neck, smooth skin, and a row of blowholes along its back. A mature sea serpent weighed about sixty metric tons, making it the largest creature on the Huhui planet. Fortunately, they were not too bright, and when they met a hunter, they always fled without fighting. Although they couldn't fight, they did have another instinct—they could foresee the time of their own deaths. Prior to death, they would emit a sad cry. Their low and deep calls could be heard over great distances.

"凸 (chu) . . . . . . oh"

"刁 (lu) . . . . oh"

"吇 (ru) . . . . oh"

"叮 (mu) . . . . . . oh"

Hearing a sea serpent, Huhui fishermen would set out to catch it by following its sad cry because it wouldn't bother to dive and flee but would allow itself to be cut to pieces. That is why 凸刁吇叮 (chu-lu-ru-mu), those auspicious Huhui words, were an imitation of the sea serpent's sad cry. The misfortune of the sea serpent was good luck for the fisherman. But as it was known that luck and misfortune were two sides of the same coin, the word for "misfortune" in the Huhui tongue was 叮吇刁凸 (mu-ru-lu-chu), or the reverse of the auspicious words.

The strange behavior of the sea serpent was something that Huhui scientists never tired of discussing. Could the beasts really foresee the time of their death, or were they just weary of life and committing suicide? If the latter, then clearly the sea serpent contemplated the meaning of life, and animals that could contemplate the meaning of life were not stupid. If the former, then clearly they had an unusual ability or a special intelligence. Regardless of which it was, they should have been fairly intelligent. However, based on their observations of young sea serpents in captivity, Huhui scientists discovered that they were quite stupid. How could such a stupid animal know when it was going to die? Huhui scientists could not solve the riddle of the sea serpent just as Tai Nan scientists could find no solution for the riddle of why the dinosaurs died.

Owing to their great size, most sea serpents lived in the Xinsu Sea and rarely entered the Hu River. Occasionally one would swim upriver by mistake, where it would either beach itself or be discovered and captured by fishermen. That is why when the Green Snake Brotherhood flotilla encountered one in the river, everyone was startled and crowded along the sides of the ships for a look.

Miss Qi had never seen a sea serpent before and was frightened by its size. It was as long as two barges, and its neck was the height of three men. The blowholes opened and closed, spraying a fine mist. The beast seemed not to be aware of the existence of the barges. It looked toward the sky, emitting its sad cry.

"凸 (chu) . . . . . . oh"

"凵 (lu) . . . . oh"

"凸 (ru) . . . . . . oh"

"凸 (mu) . . . . . . oh"

Everyone just stared blankly at the huge creature. It cried out sadly before sinking slowly beneath the water. Only then did people seem to wake up. Liu Qi shouted, "One sea serpent is worth a mountain of gold or silver. Luck is with us, brothers. When it surfaces again, we'll kill it."

"You can't," said Miss Qi. "The poor thing. If we kill it, can we bring it on board? What good is killing it if we can't take it with us?"

"She's right," said Ah 凸 (chu). "It's wishing us good luck. It swam upriver especially to wish us happiness—a rare occurrence. We shouldn't do it any harm."

Liu Qi agreed. He motioned for his men to lower their weapons. In the amount of time it takes to drink a half cup of tea, the sea serpent resurfaced, blowing mist. It had swum to within fifty meters of the barges. Turning, it cried to the flotilla several times, then disappeared beneath the water.

Ah 凸 (chu) said in surprise, "It seems to be showing us the way."

"That's impossible," said Liu Qi, shaking his head. "Sea serpents are not that intelligent. Besides, who could have sent it?"

He ordered the barges to halt. A short time later, the sea serpent thrust its head and neck out of the water. When it saw that the flotilla had halted, it cried out anxiously.

"It's true," said Liu Qi, surprised. "All right! Let's see where it leads us."

The sea serpent kept a distance of 165 meters between itself and the boats. It would dive below the water, then resurface and give a couple of cries. Night had fallen, and Liu Qi ordered the men to take turns standing watch on deck. Miss Qi wanted to help out but was prevented from doing so by Liu Qi. He asked her to go below and get some rest. Although she was unwilling, she was tired. In the hold, she flopped down on some sacks of grain and listened to the pulsing engine until she fell asleep.

Miss Qi was awakened when the barge rolled. She got up and almost stumbled into the engine. The hatch opened and Ah 凸 (chu) peered in.

"Are you awake? Did you sleep well?"

"Why is the boat rolling so? Where are we?"

"Come up and see for yourself."

Up on deck, Miss Qi couldn't help but gasp. No wonder the boat was rolling so much. They were on the open, wave-filled sea. In the distance, the shore was visible, as were some square buildings.

"Where are we?"

"At sea," said Liu Qi, pointing to a row of gray buildings on shore. "We just passed the big city of River Mouth. These waves are huge. Our boats weren't designed for the open ocean. It's going to be rough."

"To sail the open ocean, we'll have to rely on the helmsman." Ah 凸 (chu) laughed. "But what is there to fear with a sea serpent to guide us?"

"Where is it?" asked Miss Qi.

Liu Qi pointed ahead of them. It just dived beneath the water, maintaining a distance of 165 meters. The sea serpent looked much smaller in the open water. Only its long neck could be seen; its back was scarcely visible.

"凸 (chu) . . . . . . oh"

"凹 (ru) . . . . oh"

"凸 (chu) . . . . . . oh"

"凹 (ru) . . . . oh"

Miss Qi felt something was strange. Ah 凸 (chu) nodded and said, "You're right. It has changed its tune. This sea serpent is really intelligent. Right now, it's singing about how tough its life is. All day long it surfaces and dives, resurfaces and dives. . . . 凸 (chu) oh, 凹 (ru) oh, 凸 (chu) oh, 凹 (ru) oh. That's the sad song of the sea serpent."

"Are you just pulling my leg again?" asked Miss Qi, laughing.

"You've hit the nail on the head," said Liu Qi, laughing. "Old Ah 凸 (chu) just likes to tell tall tales."

"No, I don't," said Ah 凸 (chu), looking up at the sky. "That's the way it is. If the sea serpents didn't sigh over their own hard fate, would they commit suicide?"

"Who knows if they commit suicide?" said Liu Qi, shrugging his shoulders. "But this sea serpent is really behaving strangely. Instead of heading out to sea, it keeps following the shore. It's as if it knew the boats can't sail the deep sea. If it were to set out to sea, we would have to give up following it."

"Where is it leading us? To New Menghan City?"

"It's heading in that direction," said Liu Qi. "We were on the way there ourselves, so there is no need for a sea serpent to guide us."

"Look! It has turned about," shouted Miss Qi and Ah 凸 (chu). Its long neck appeared and disappeared amid the waves, but it was heading for open water.

"I just said this one was smart," said Liu Qi, "and it heads for deep water. We can't follow it."

"We've already followed it this long," said Ah 凸 (chu). "Lay your fears aside and follow it a while."

But the waves increased in size, and the boats were more like matchboxes amid the swells. Many of the warriors began getting seasick. Ah 凸 (chu) vomited and was overcome with nausea. He lay on deck gasping.

"Now I understand their 凸ㅁ 凸ㅁ (chu-ru chu-ru) lament," said Ah 凸 (chu). "I can't take this constant rolling."

In response to Ah 凸 (chu)'s lament, the sea serpent cried out sadly:

"凵 (mu) . . . . . . oh"

"ㅁ (ru) . . . . . . oh"

"凹 (lu) . . . . . . oh"

"凸 (chu) . . . . . . oh"

"It has changed its tune again!" said Ah 凸 (chu), lying on deck. "This sea serpent is harboring evil intentions. It's cursing us. 凵ㅁ凹凸 (mu-ru-lu-chu). Oh no! Why didn't I see it sooner? This beast might have misled us intentionally."

"Turn about 180 degrees and head for shore!" ordered Liu Qi hastily. But he was too late. A large wave rose, overturning two barges, which sank in a matter of seconds. Liu Qi cried out and, beating his breast, cursed himself and then Ah 凸 (chu). "It's your fault. To sail the open ocean, we have to rely on the helmsman. That's what you said. Now we've lost Wang Liu and dozens of warriors in the sea, with no bodies to recover. Who said 凸 (chu) people are wise? You're useless; you ought to change your name to ㅁ (ru) person, scorned alike by yourself and others!"

Embarrassed, Ah 凸 (chu) accepted Liu Qi's insults in silence. As they neared the shore, the waves grew smaller. Unexpectedly, the sea serpent was right behind them, calling sadly:

"凹 (lu) . . . . . . oh"

"凹 (lu) . . . . . . oh"

"凹 (lu) . . . . . . oh"

"凹 (lu) . . . . . . oh"

"Do you think you can trick us again?" shouted Liu Qi. "Prepare your weapons, men. Let's kill the thing."

The sea serpent approached even nearer. Liu Qi motioned for the boats to surround it and for the men to fire at its head. The creature didn't flee, but stretched out its neck to give the warriors a better target. Still it cried sadly:

"凶 (chu) . . . . . . oh"

"口 (lu) . . . . oh"

"卪 (ru) . . . . oh"

"屮 (mu) . . . . . oh"

The sea serpent's head was severed. Liu Qi ordered the boats to approach the body. He fished the strange creature's head out of the water. Its eyes were wide open and its mouth opened and closed, as if to continue its cry: "凶卪 凶卪 (chu-ru chu-ru)."

"It knew it was time to die," said Ah 凶 (chu), sighing. "It was saying a prayer for itself."

Ah 凶 (chu) squatted to inspect the severed head of the sea serpent. Never did he expect that it was capable of movement. Suddenly it stretched and recoiled, swallowing fully half of Ah 凶 (chu). Everyone gasped and immediately set about to rescue him. Fortunately, swallowing Ah 凶 (chu) was the sea serpent's last act before death. They pried open the beast's mouth and pulled Ah 凶 (chu) out. Since his sense organs were on top of his head, he didn't lose anything as they pulled him from the sea serpent's mouth. Once out, he struggled back for another look. In light of the situation, Liu Qi laughed and said, "Being swallowed once by a sea serpent is not enough? You want to try it again?"

Ah 凶 (chu) paid no attention to Liu Qi and climbed back in the sea serpent's mouth. Soon, he climbed out again carrying a light green sphere studded with needles.

"I was right. Zhihuang Ma was behind this. This control was stuck in the sea serpent's mouth. Without a doubt, this beast was tricked by Zhihuang Ma into taking the bait and then controlled by him to deceive us and lead us to our deaths in the open sea."

"Zhihuang Ma is so tricky," said Miss Qi, rolling her eyes. "Unfortunately, since he can control one sea serpent, he can control them all. From here on out, it's going to get more dangerous."

But before she had finished speaking, the sea seemed to boil, and countless sea serpents, large and small, appeared.

"Get ashore!" shouted Liu Qi. "Hurry up and get ashore."

The ten-plus barges set off toward the shore at full speed, pursued by the group of sea serpents. Together they called out:

"凸 (chu) . . . . . . oh"

"𠃊 (lu) . . . . . . oh"

"卐 (ru) . . . . . . oh"

"𠂊 (mu) . . . . . oh"

Fortunately, the barges were amphibious and equipped with rubber tires below. One after another, they rolled onto the beach. Unable to leave the water, the sea serpents roared for a while before diving beneath the surface.

"That's simply amazing!" said Miss Qi. "Zhihuang Ma can control all the sea serpents in the Xinsu Sea. Who'll ever go in the water again? Now we'll never get to New Menghan City."

"We can't get there by sea," said Liu Qi, "but we can still get there by land. New Menghan City isn't too far from here. If we follow the coast, the sea serpents won't be able to do us any harm."

Although the progress of the barges on land was slow, it was steady. The barges had been specially designed for transporting cargo in the Hu River basin, whence their low speed on land and in the water. On two amphibious vehicles, everyone set off along the beach. Occasionally, the long snakelike neck of a sea serpent came out of the water and looked around before dipping below the water's surface again. Knowing that they were still being observed by the sea serpents, Miss Qi felt 凸卐 (chu-ru). She said to Ah 凸 (chu), "The barges are too slow; the sea serpents can swim faster. This is not the way to do things."

"What are you afraid of?" asked Ah 凸 (chu). "口口 (qia-xia)[1] the sea serpents can't leave the water. They are no threat to us. If they want to accompany us to New Menghan City, that's their business."

Suddenly the barges came to a halt. The helmsman pointed ahead and said, "We can't go this way."

They all sighed when they saw that they had reached the end of the beach. A black precipice reared up before them. To continue, the two amphibious craft would have to enter the water. Seeming to know what the Green Snake Brotherhood members had in mind, the sea serpents all came out of the water, crying:

"卐 (ru) . . . . . . oh"

---

[1] Qia-xia is close to 横豎 (literally, "horizontal and perpendicular") in classical Chinese, meaning "anyhow."

"屮 (ru) . . . . . . oh"

"屮 (chu) . . . . . . oh"

"屮 (chu) . . . . . . oh"

"They want us to surrender," said Ah 屮 (chu). "屮屮屮屮 (ru-ru chu-chu), kneel down and surrender or hands up and surrender."

"We're not going to surrender. Whoever heard of the Green Snake Brotherhood surrendering to a bunch of sea serpents?" asked Liu Qi, scratching his head. "What are we going to do? We can't go this way, so we'll have to go around."

But that was easier said than done. The black precipice was actually part of a rocky mountain that extended into the sea. The two amphibious craft made their way along the foot of the mountain for a while, but the terrain became ever more rugged and soon the cumbersome craft had to stop. With no other plan, Liu Qi ordered everyone to set off on foot to find a way over the mountain. The mountain seemed to be no more than a huge pile of square, black stones. There was no way over. The Green Snake Brotherhood members took out their mountaineering ropes and, one tied to another, they began the unusually difficult ascent. Fortunately for them, the mountain wasn't that high, and after climbing the height of thirty blocks of stone, they reached the summit, a huge black stone that could hold several hundred men. The Green Snake Brotherhood task force didn't cover the stone. Miss Qi looked to the west and saw a small bay at the foot of the mountain. Along the shore of the bay stood small, round, rainbow-colored dwellings. There was a foreign quality about the place. Miss Qi gasped as she realized that it must be New Menghan City, where the Gaiwenese dwelled.

"The Gaiwenese wandered everywhere after their planet was vaporized," said Ah 屮 (chu), standing behind Miss Qi. "Knowing that the Gaiwenese previously had been cannibals, many people would not accept them. Only the Huhui were magnanimous enough to permit them to settle here and allowed them to freely engage in business. The Gaiwenese rebuilt their old capital on the shores of the Xinsu Sea. That's New Menghan City."

Miss Qi knew that Ah 屮 (chu) was scared of standing at the edge of the black stone and tugged at him on purpose.

"Look at those houses. Why are the roofs the color of the rainbow?"

"Don't push me!" said Ah 屮 (chu), hurriedly dropping to the ground. "The Gaiwenese believe that a synthesis of all contradictions is possible, and the rainbow-colored, domed roofs of their dwellings are an expression of that philosophy."

"Delightful. I remember Gai Bo saying 'life is death; death is life.' I hope that I can be that philosophical."

Miss Qi couldn't help sighing as she recalled the world-weary sea serpents. If even the sea serpents of the Huhui planet were weary of life, how much more so the people of the planet? Then she noticed several dozen black specks appear on the sea beyond the harbor. They were making their way for the bay, and left huge white wakes.

"Sea serpents!"

Seeing them, Liu Qi ordered the resting men to stand up.

"The object of the surprise attack was no doubt New Menghan City. Brothers, let's go down and help the Gaiwenese fight the sea serpents."

"We won't make it in time," said Ah 出 (chu), laughing. "By the time we get down there, the sea serpents will be in the harbor. We'd be better off just enjoying the spectacle of the Gaiwenese fighting the beasts from up here. It's not something you're going to see every day."

"It's not right to gloat over someone else's misfortunes!" said Miss Qi angrily. "If by some chance the Gaiwenese are defeated by Zhihuang Ma's puppet sea serpents, it'll be a disaster for the Huhui planet. We have to warn them."

"I know how." Liu Qi pulled out a flare gun and shot a signal flare in the direction of New Menghan City. They didn't know if Liu Qi's signal flare had been effective or if the Gaiwenese already had been prepared, but multicolored bursts broke the water's surface, and the black specks disappeared one after another.

"I was right," said Ah 出 (chu), clapping his hands. "This is not a sight you are going to see every day. 出咕呼母 (chu-lu-ru-mu), the Contradiction Torpedoes of the Gaiwenese are really effective against the sea serpents."

Despite the fact that half the black specks had vanished, the remaining sea serpents continued to head toward the harbor. The number of explosions increased until all the specks had disappeared. Miss Qi breathed a sigh of relief.

"Fortunately, you were able to warn them," said Miss Qi to Liu Qi. "Zhihuang Ma's sea serpent suicide corps has been wiped out."

"Don't forget that we were the task force sent here by Zhihuang Ma," said Liu Qi, smiling bitterly. "We've already revealed our position. Once the Gaiwenese are finished with the sea serpents, they'll turn their sights on us. Look!"

Several dozen black specks appeared in the air above New Menghan City, then fell to the ground beyond the city before leaping into the air again. The bounding objects were heading straight for the mountain.

"Gaiwenese Froghoppers!" gasped Ah 出 (chu). "It's the Gaiwenese air force. Froghoppers are effective on marshy ground, but I've never seen them jump to the top of a mountain."

But Ah 出 (chu)'s concerns were unjustified. The first Froghopper reached the foot of the mountain and gave another leap. It made it halfway up the slope. It seemed to rouse itself again and leaped to the next stone. It did this three or four times before alighting gently atop the mountain among the Green Snake Brotherhood warriors. Its engine was shut off; the cockpit hood was thrown open, and out leaped the Gaiwenese pilot. He saluted the warriors and said, "Let's be friends."

"Gai Bao!" shouted Miss Qi, suddenly recognizing the big blue-skinned fellow. Gai Bao was delighted to see her and made a singular awareness salute.

"Right," he said. "That's me. So you remember me. Wonderful. Let's be friends."

"Gai Bao," said Miss Qi, overjoyed at meeting an old friend, "did you see our signal flare?"

"Of course," replied Gai Bao. "We had been observing your every move. If you hadn't shot the signal flare demonstrating your friendship, you already would have been decimated by the Gaiwenese. I'm here to welcome ambassadors of peace, am I not?"

"Lucky, lucky," said Ah 出 (chu), bowing deeply. "Those who come don't come to fight; and those looking for a fight don't come. Our intentions are friendly, as you can obviously see."

"There's no need to speak of such things." Gai Bao laughed. "Fortunately, the Great Spy is as omniscient as a god. We were able to annihilate Zhihuang Ma's sea serpent suicide corps. Zhihuang Ma's Marine Corps were stuck on the mountain. No trick of his will be missed by the Great Spy."

"Great Spy?" Miss Qi asked inquisitively. "Who is the Great Spy?"

Big, blue-skinned Gai Bao smiled and pointed at the Froghopper.

"The Great Spy is the one," he said, "who would like to invite you, Miss, to New Menghan City for a good talk."

6

The Green Snake Brotherhood had climbed to the summit of Black Stone Mountain with some difficulty. From their vantage there they had watched the suicidal attack of the sea serpents on New Menghan City and their subsequent annihilation by Gaiwenese Contradiction Torpedoes. Not only had the brotherhood been unable to offer any assistance, but the Gaiwenese had dispatched Froghoppers to Black Stone Mountain to pick them up. In addition to the pilot, a Froghopper could accommodate only one other person, so the thirty Froghoppers used for military purposes made repeated trips to transport the Green Snake warriors to the square next to the New Menghan City wharf. Since Miss Qi was the first to be transported down off the mountain by Gai Bao, she had ample time to inspect the surroundings as she waited for the rest of the warriors to arrive.

Surveying New Menghan City from the distant vantage of Black Stone Mountain, one could see the charming and exquisite, rainbow-colored round houses lining the shore of the harbor. But up close they were, in fact, found to be large, two-storied, cone-shaped structures. Small lanes paved with green cobbles ran between the buildings, and exotic flowers and plants grew around the houses. The Gaiwenese were great lovers of flowers. Although they were careful and frugal businesspeople, when they returned home they knew how to enjoy the finer things in life. Vehicles were prohibited on the green cobbled lanes where entire families were seen strolling together. Miss Qi heard the engine of a Froghopper start; then one of the dome-shaped houses slowly split open, after which a Froghopper shot into the air. Since private Froghoppers were not permitted to alight within the city, they were used only when residents had business outside the city. In this way, New Menghan City preserved the ancient elegance of Old Menghan City.

The Gaiwenese had evolved from frogs, and for this reason the shore was lined with outdoor baths. But the outdoor baths did not have sandy beaches; instead, they were lined with steep and precipitous rocky cliffs. In imitation of the forebears, bathing Gaiwenese were in the habit of squatting on the rocks and croaking. They would then leap into the water, where they would swim and croak. But on this day, having knowledge of the coming surprise attack by the sea serpents, not one Gaiwenese *gaibao* or *gaisong*[1] was sporting in the water. A single sailboat was seen setting out to sea from the wharf to retrieve the dozens of sea serpent corpses.

Miss Qi walked to the wharf to watch the ship. The strong wind filled the golden sail and the boat cut through the water. Upon reaching the farthest buoy, the boat changed tack and entered the open sea beyond the breakwater. The Gaiwenese soldiers continued vigilantly to man their posts next to the torpedo launchers on the breakwater in the event that the sea serpents launched another attack. In New Menghan City, the Gaiwenese went about their business as usual but were very curious about the Green Snake Brotherhood warriors on the square because they were seldom visited by Huhui people. The sudden appearance of so many warriors had drawn a crowd of onlookers. They were especially curious about Ah 凸 (chu), who found himself surrounded by a horde of children. Using threats and cajolery, Gai Bao asked the onlookers to make way for them. Then he ran over to the wharf for Miss Qi.

"Miss Qi, the Great Spy is waiting for you. Please come this way."

"Who is this Great Spy?"

"Come along and you'll find out."

Gai Bao led them in single file to a house near the square. From outside, the house didn't look very large, but once inside, they discovered a stairway that led to a large underground passageway. The Gaiwenese had long been prepared for war, which perhaps was the result of the painful lesson still etched in their memory of when the Gaiwen planet had been vaporized. New Menghan City was, in fact, actually an underground city; the structures below ground were far more imposing than those above. Af-

---

[1] *Gaibao* is Gaiwenese for "wife"; *gaisong* is Gaiwenese for "child."

ter years of construction, a reproduction of Old Menghan City had been built above ground, while New Menghan City was in fact located below. The Green Snake warriors sighed with amazement as they followed the wide avenue to the municipal government building at the center of town. Stone statues of famous Gaiwenese historical figures lined both sides of the broad avenue; some sat magnificently atop stones while others looked angrily, frogwise, toward the sky. The newest statue, which happened to be the last, caught Miss Qi's attention. She paused for a closer look and was joined by Ah 凵 (chu) and Liu Qi. The statue was especially lifelike; even the skin color and clothes were no different from those of a living person. Ah 凵 (chu), who was able to read Gaiwenese, stooped down to read the inscription below the statue, which read:

SHRINE OF GAI BO, THE 7,856,324,451ST GREAT SPY

"I thought the statue looked familiar, and it turns out to be Gai Bo!" Miss Qi sighed. "Too bad he's dead, and now an immortal."

"Life is death; death is life," suddenly spoke the statue. "Just as to be born is to die, so to die is still to live. To risk one's life is to bring the dead back to life. Life and death; death and life. Let's be friends. It has been a long time."

The statue turned and stepped down off its pedestal. The 240-centimeter-tall, blue-skinned Gaiwenese wore a seven-pointed hat with an orange tassel dangling from each point, and a deep yellow raincoat with the collar turned up. Miss Qi was both curious and amused by the nondescript ceremonial dress of the spy.

"So you're still alive! You even sent Gai Bao to tell me you had become an immortal. Aren't you ashamed of yourself?"

"I didn't lie to you," interrupted Gai Bao. "Following the uprising against the Shan, Gai Bo disappeared. We thought he had died when the Shan warship was destroyed. We erected this stone statue in memory of his meritorious service, never dreaming that he would show up two years later as alive as ever."

Bowing deeply, Ah 凵 (chu) addressed Gai Bo: "In life you were a famous spy; in death an immortal. No wonder you are called the Great Spy. The honor fits the achievement. You have my admiration."

"It's only Ah 凵 (chu) who knows me and can rebuke me, isn't it?" said Gai Bo, proudly. "It is my greatest honor to be revered as a Great Spy by my compatriots. That's why when I returned to New Menghan City, I removed my statue. When I have nothing to do, I stand on the pedestal myself to give the Gaiwenese children the chance to see a dashing spy."

As they were talking, several Gaiwenese children arrived, and Gai Bo immediately took his place once again upon the pedestal. Smiling, he stooped down to sign autographs for the children and pose for photos with them.

"This is the first time I've ever seen a living statue," said Liu Qi, laughing. "You really have patience."

After the Gaiwenese children had departed, Gai Bo once again stepped down from his pedestal. "In life it's the daily grind; a reputation comes after death," he said. "The time I spend as a living immortal is an investment that will produce returns. It is because the Gaiwenese see me as a living immortal that they have elected me as mayor."

"You're also the mayor here?" asked Miss Qi, surprised. "Power corrupts, so it won't be long until you become another rotten apple like Zhihuang Ma."

Gai Bo again took his place on the pedestal so that some tourists could take photos.

"We can't stand around all day watching you play the immortal," said Liu Qi impatiently. "Why did you ask us here?"

"This is the last group of tourists. Let's go inside the municipal building and talk." Gai Bo led the warriors into the municipal building. Gai Bao stood by the door, handing out bags of food to the warriors. They were then entertained in the main auditorium with Gaiwenese song and dance as well as the special Gaiwenese skill of spraying water, much to the delight of the Green Snake Brotherhood warriors.

Addressing Miss Qi, Ah 凵 (chu), and Liu Qi, Gai Bo said, "The hospitality of New Menghan City has always been enthusiastically warm. Let's go to my office to discuss matters of fundamental importance while the warriors enjoy themselves."

Several questions had been gnawing at Miss Qi for some time. Upon entering Gai Bo's office, she could no longer restrain herself. "That year when you acted as a counterespionage agent for the cult leader, you managed to get on board the Shan warship and destroy it. How was it that you survived? Did any of the Green Snake Brotherhood members in the demolition squad return alive? Was the warship entirely destroyed, or did the Shan manage to secure it in some remote corner of the Huhui mountains? Do they have the strength to fight again? Where were you three years ago when the combined Serpent-Shan Army attacked Sunlon City?"

With a wave of his hand, Gai Bo laughed and said, "My dear young lady, if you have questions, please ask them one at a time. How can I answer such a string of queries? Please, all of you have a seat and I'll tell you."

The mayor's office was underground. One wall was of thick glass that opened to the sea. All sorts of fish as well as Gaiwenese divers could be seen. Pointing at the sea beyond the glass wall, Gai Bo said, "What you see before you is the undersea landscape of the harbor. You can see how many hard-working Gaiwenese are laboring beneath the water to strengthen our defenses. But you'd never notice it in New Menghan City.

"We Gaiwenese are the only people in the universe who have had their home vaporized by the Shan. Since then we have been forced to wander the universe. Our bitterness at this is not easily understood by outsiders. We have been able to reestablish our home with ease on the Huhui planet, and we cherish it deeply. We never imagined that the Shan would take advantage of the chaos created by the Bronze Statue Cult and occupy Sunlon City. There is a profound enmity between the Gaiwenese and the Shan, but we are profoundly grateful to the Huhui people for allowing us to reside here, and that's why we decided to do everything in our power to help the Huhui in their fight against Shan rule. We were clear that the cult was the most fanatical and unified of organizations on the planet, and the cult leader was a talented man of vision. That's why we decided to work closely with the cult. I don't seem to be giving your brotherhood the respect you deserve, but given the situation at the time, our decision to cooperate with the cult seemed the most reasonable choice. The Council of Gaiwenese Elders decided to send me to infiltrate the Shan organization because of my counterespionage training. At the same time, and under the direction of the cult leader, I did counterintelligence work for the army.

"I suffered a lot on your account, but the job demanded it, and I don't blame anyone. But I was able to win the confidence of the Shan and to freely come and go from the warship. On the day of the uprising, I seized the opportunity and eliminated the guards at the side door, allowing Yu Jin and the demolition squad to slip into the ship. Without me working from the inside, there is no way that the demolition squad could have succeeded."

Miss Qi no longer sounded so excited. "And later? What happened to him?"

"After Yu Jin led the demolition squad onto the ship, we discussed the matter and decided to blow up the ship after it had taken off. Although the squad could have escaped on the ground, our main reason for not blowing up the ship there was that the Shan might have been able to repair it, something that would have been impossible to do if it were blown up in the sky. The valiant members of the squad were all prepared to die; even I thought I was destined for immortality. But I never expected that our plan would actually work to save the Shan. Of the ten small groups that were to destroy the ship, five were annihilated by the Shan before we took to the air. That left only five small groups to finish the mission. Although the ship was severely damaged, it did not crash immediately. Under the leadership of the commander, the ship set down in the widest part of the East Hu River."

"No wonder some people said that the ship went down on Five Phoenixes Mountain," said Ah 出 (chu), as if he suddenly understood. "Actually, it flew over Five Phoenixes Mountain and went down in the East Hu River. No wonder we couldn't find it under the copper fields: it was hidden at the bottom of the river!"

"You can't say that it was hidden at the bottom of the river," continued Gai Bo, "because after it sank there was no way to repair it. But the ship going down in the river allowed the Shan soldiers on board to escape. Later the Shan were able to rally their forces because the officers had been able to swim to safety and hide in the vicinity of Five Phoenixes Mountain."

"What about the demolition squad?" asked Miss Qi anxiously. "What about Yu Jin?"

"Every member of the squad was loaded with explosives. All of them, including Yu Jin, took their own lives. They were truly saviors of the Huhui planet."

Unable to retrain herself any longer, Miss Qi began to cry. Although Miss Qi knew that Yu Jin probably had come to such an end, she had never given up hope. Now Gai Bo's account had dashed all her hopes. Gai Bo also found it hard to bear and, sighing, said, "Yu Jin sought and found ⊡ □ (du-wu). Since death is like life, don't be grieved, don't cry."

"There's no bringing Yu Jin back, but how did you manage to escape death?" interjected Liu Qi. "Why didn't you die?"

"You must be kidding. I'm a spy, not a demolitionist. We Gaiwenese aren't much interested in exercising the singular awareness spirit, so there was no reason for me to blow myself up. Besides, when the ship was exploded in midair, I figured I was done for; I never expected that we would put down in the river and that I'd be given a second chance. After I escaped, I returned to the South Gate of Heaven and made my report to the cult leader. I never dreamed that he would ask me to hide and not allow me to return to New Menghan City or Sunlon City. His reason for this was that if the common people knew that the Shan hadn't been destroyed they would cause a disturbance, affecting social stability."

"The cult leader really is a rotten guy!" said Miss Qi, angrily. "So he knew all along that the Shan had not been destroyed, and he used this to wipe out the Green Snake and Leopard brotherhoods. He has brought so much suffering to the Huhui people."

"He also made me suffer by making me hide in Fort Ever Peaceful for nothing for more than a year," said Gai Bo. "Only when I received news of the Green Snake attack on the Shan and Serpent people at the copper fields did I understand how the cult leader had fooled me. He was intent upon uniting the Huhui planet and exterminating the Gaiwenese, who are unbelievers. So I hurried back to New Menghan City and convinced the elders to repair the undersea defenses. It was a good thing I did so, otherwise we would have been conquered by the cult. At the time, I considered contacting Miss Qi but was unsuccessful."

Ah 㕚 (chu) stood up, bowed deeply, and addressed Gai Bo: "You are a man of some foresight. You have my admiration. But the cult leader was already dead three years ago when the Shan and Serpent people attacked Sunlon City. Now it is Zhihuang Ma who is vainly trying to unify the Huhui planet and not the cult leader."

Gai Bo laughed. "Old friend, I'm a Gaiwenese immortal, and you are more astute than I. Zhihuang Ma is simply one of the cult leader's running dogs. The cult leader manipulates him the way he did the Old Do-Gooder. Otherwise, how could Zhihuang Ma ever be so ambitious as to try to take over the whole planet?"

Miss Qi thought he had a point, but Ah 㕚 (chu) couldn't believe it. "I'm a Huhui historian. It is clearly recorded that the Huhui planet's best died in the fight against the Shan and Serpent people. Not only did General Shi, Yu Fang, and Yu Kui die, but so did the cult leader and the nine bulu lords. That's what the historical records say, and they can't be wrong. I shouldn't be forgetting my responsibility as a historian and revealing the secrets of our history, but I have to correct your mistaken notion that the cult leader is still alive. 㕚㔫㕦㕥 (chu-lu-ru-mu)."

"All right, I don't know if he is dead or not, but one hero is still alive, so the records occasionally are wrong," Gai Bo replied.

Hearing this, Ah 㕚 (chu) leaped to his feet. "I have utmost respect for you; I never expected that you would requite □ (wu) with ■ (woo).[2]

---

[2] Requite □ with ■ means "requite kindness with enmity."

How can you say that the historical records are wrong? What do you think we Huhui historians do? You must know that the histories were compiled with the concerted cooperation of the Huhui historians and the historians of the universe, and it is a painstaking work with a profound grasp of the torrent of time. How can you utter such foolishness that the histories are mistaken?"

"I'm sorry. I meant no disrespect for the Huhui historians, but General Shi is still very much alive and living here in New Menghan City."

Liu Qi, Ah 出 (chu), and Miss Qi were all startled. "General Shi, here in New Menghan City?"

"Right. His cavalry was annihilated in the fight against the Shan and Serpent people, and he was severely wounded. Fortunately, two people helped him flee the battlefield. They walked for seven days in the desert and were saved by Gaiwenese traders who met them on the road."

"Can we see him?" asked Miss Qi.

Gai Bo nodded. At that moment, Gai Bao rushed in, desperate and low-spirited. He reported: "It looks bad. Zhihuang Ma's army has surrounded the city."

"That was quicker than I expected," said Gai Bo. "I would like to continue talking with you about the general, but we now find ourselves in a tight situation. Let's first figure out a way to repulse the enemy, then discuss other things."

They quickly returned to the square near the wharf. Miss Qi looked around and saw that the hills around New Menghan City were full of yellow banners, but she had no idea how many enemy soldiers there were. Three airships were passing back and forth, dropping bombs on the city. The Gaiwenese set out in Froghoppers to engage the enemy, but they couldn't jump high enough to meet the airships. They jumped here and there, but to little effect. Liu Qi had assembled the Green Snake officers on the square and, after a short exhortation, was about to lead them out to fight the enemy when Gai Bo stopped him.

"Hold on. Where are you going?"

"Out to fight Zhihuang Ma!" replied Liu Qi. "Although there are only two hundred of us, we're going to fight for all we're worth today. Thanks for your hospitality. We can't repay you, so we'll kill some of the enemy for you."

"There's no need!" Gai Bo hastily replied in all sincerity. "The troops Zhihuang Ma has sent to attack us are not his trusted troops. It's just a way for him to get rid of all his detractors. First he sent you, then he sent the sea serpents in a surprise attack. And although the hills are now covered with yellow banners, it's all just a bit of swashbuckling show as far as I can tell. It's the airships that are the real problem. If we could knock them out of the sky, the siege would be lifted."

Ah 出 (chu) looked up and knit his brows. Then he came up with a strategy. "Zhihuang Ma calls himself the field marshal of the combined forces. His navy was nothing more than a few Green Snake Brotherhood barges; his air force must be these three airships, and they can do nothing but drop a few bombs. I'd just like to implement a little plan to deprive Zhihuang Ma of his title."

Ah 出 (chu) then outlined his plan. Liu Qi and Gai Bo were overjoyed. They immediately called together the Froghopper pilots and the Green Snake warriors and gave them a briefing. The thirty-plus military Froghoppers were readied at once on the square; in each sat a Green Snake warrior waiting to take off.

The three airships went out over the harbor, bombing the defending soldiers on the breakwater and sinking the sailing ships on the sea. They then turned about to bomb the city. At Gai Bo's command, a pair of Froghoppers took to the air, leaping outside the city. The Green Snake warriors each held one end of a metal cable. In this way, the two Froghoppers were as one, a taut umbilical cord strung between them. Soon the two Froghoppers headed back toward the city again. Another Froghopper quickly took to the air, jumping onto the cable between them. The spring in the cable catapulted the one Froghopper to the same altitude as the airships. The Green Snake warrior on board was armed with a hand-held rocket launcher. The moment the Froghopper neared the airship, he fired the rocket, blowing the airship out of the sky. The whole operation was performed with the brilliant precision of trapeze artists in the circus. The Gaiwenese and the Green Snake warriors on the ground applauded enthusiastically.

But the second group was not so lucky. One of the Froghoppers became entangled in the cable and fell straight to the ground, killing pilot and warrior. The third group was successful acrobatically, but the rocket missed its target. At that time, the remaining two airships seemed to sense something was amiss, so they turned and fled beyond the city while ascending to a higher altitude. At Gai Bao's command, the fourth and fifth groups went into action: two pairs of Froghoppers leaped beyond the city and as they leaped back, the other pair sprang, and landing lightly on the metal cables found themselves right on the tails of the fleeing airships. The warriors launched their rockets, and the two airships exploded at the same time and fell as balls of fire outside the city.

"Bravo! What shooting! Bravo! What shooting!" said Gai Bo as he stretched out his nine-fingered hand to shake hands with Liu Qi. "The Green Snake rockets were right on target!"

"It was the skillful maneuvering of the Gaiwenese pilots!" said Ah 出 (chu), smiling broadly at seeing his strategy a success. "Zhihuang Ma's air force is finished."

As the Gaiwenese and the Green Snake warriors celebrated their victory, the thousands of yellow banners suddenly vanished, and by the time Liu Qi led his troops out in pursuit, there wasn't an enemy soldier to be seen on the hills. They captured just a few soldiers with yellow scarves and returned triumphant.

After their victory, Ah 出 (chu)'s elation suddenly vanished. Miss Qi had never seen him so worried. She hastily tried to comfort him. "Even if the histories contain a few errors, why should you be so upset?"

With a good deal of emotion, Ah 出 (chu) looked at Miss Qi as if he were looking at a ghost.

"How could there be errors? How could there be mistakes in the complete histories? If there are errors, then we historians should commit suicide. The whole unique time-space continuum of the Huhui planet will collapse! The heavenly shafts, the heavenly colonnade, the pivots of time will all collapse. That's too frightening to contemplate." Ah 出 (chu) couldn't help but wipe his sweat away and mumble, "It's too frightening. What are we going to do? What are we going to do?"

"I don't understand why you are so nervous," said Miss Qi. "In everything there are errors, and the histories are no exception. Unless, that is, you remembered them incorrectly."

"Impossible. I've already contacted the other 出 (chu) people on the Huhui planet telepathically, and they confirm that I am correct. According to the histories, General Shi died fighting the Shan and Serpent people. The cult leader also died in the fighting at Sunlon City. How can the histories be wrong if all 出 (chu) have read the same passage?"

"Then the histories are incorrect."

"Impossible!"

There was nothing Miss Qi could do about Ah 出 (chu)'s stubborn temper, except to say, "Well, since the histories are not wrong, then perhaps Gai Bo is mistaken. Perhaps it is an imposter calling himself General Shi. Perhaps the Evil Spirit of time and space is behind this."

"Oh!" gasped Ah 凸 (chu), turning white with fear. "Let's not mention it. This is no time for jokes."

Recalling that black fog and the hideous-looking Bronze Statue, Miss Qi said no more.

"You're right. Perhaps Gai Bo is mistaken," said Ah 凸 (chu), grasping at his last hope. "There is no way that General Shi could still be alive."

"Let's be friends, let's be friends," said Gai Bo, who happened to catch what Ah 凸 (chu) said. "Could I fool you? I'll take you to see the general right now."

Gai Bo led Ah 凸 (chu) and Miss Qi to the underground city, but not to the government building. Instead, he turned right on the main thoroughfare and entered the Gaiwen hospital. As he walked, he said, "Since the general arrived here, he has been very depressed. He is unwilling to return to the plains and has been unwilling to see anyone. In order to preserve his good name, I have told no one that he is still alive."

"Then why tell us?" asked Miss Qi.

"For two reasons," confessed Gai Bo. "First, I'm doing it for him. If you can encourage him by telling him that the Green Snake Brotherhood will see him back to the plains, he might be able to assemble his old supporters and reestablish his great name. Second, I'm doing it for the Gaiwenese. Although we repulsed Zhihuang Ma's attack today, he might return again tomorrow. When I was a counteragent for the cult leader, I developed a clear understanding of him. If one day goes by and he can't take New Menghan City, he won't rest a day until he does. If the cavalry can be rallied again and return to Sunlon City with the Green Snake Brotherhood, then Zhihuang Ma will be forced to leave us alone."

"Leave it to the Gaiwenese to see all the angles." Miss Qi laughed. "If it's good for the Huhui planet, then we'll be more than happy to cooperate. What do you say, Ah 凸 (chu)?"

Ah 凸 (chu) looked toward the sky, lost in his own thoughts. Gai Bo paused outside a sickroom. Whispering, he warned the two of them, "General Shi has changed. When you see him, control your emotions so as not to break his heart."

Gai Bo opened the door. Miss Qi was the first to enter. In the dim lamplight, she saw a man sitting in a chair. Moaning to herself, she felt her eyes fill with tears.

7
——

Seeing the old man in his chair, Miss Qi couldn't believe her eyes. How could that thin, dry man, his face all wrinkles, be the world-famous General Shi? She remembered him as an awe-inspiring general clad in gold armor, sitting astride a white charger, surrounded by his cavalry. One shout from the general would be met with a hundred cries in response. Could that old man sitting in the chair, his blanket slipped down, really be him?

"General?"

He didn't look up. Perhaps he was asleep, or deaf. Sadly, Miss Qi approached the old man to cover him again with his blanket. When she touched him, she realized that beneath the blanket the lower half of his body was gone. She nearly cried out in fear.

"The old general lost both his legs," said Gai Bo behind her with a sigh. "By the time we got him back to New Menghan City, it was already too late. Fortunately, we were able to operate; otherwise he might have died."

"But what's the difference between his present state and being dead?" asked Miss Qi, unable to keep from crying out. "It's too much!"

"You're right." Gai Bo sighed. "The general thought about taking his own life a number of times but fortunately was discovered by his nurses. The Gaiwenese elders have discussed it several times but have never arrived at a solution. We can't send him back to the plains, nor can we bear to sit by and watch him fade this way. After all, he is a Huhui hero, respected by one and all."

Ah 凸 (chu), who all along had been silent, suddenly fell to his knees with a thud. Kowtowing repeatedly, he murmured:

Winds arise
Valiant warriors gather
The general gives his orders
Their duty is but to obey!

Ah 凸 (chu) wept as he recited the lines. Miss Qi also cried, and the big blue-skinned Gaiwenese wept and his skin turned green.[1] The old man in the chair apparently heard the three of them weeping. He raised his head and, perplexed, asked, "What time is it?"

"It's time to eat," replied Miss Qi, wiping her tears away. "You're awake."

The old man's eyes searched her face for a long time; then suddenly he smiled like a child.

"Oh, so it's you, Miss."

"Yes. So you still remember me?"

"I remember. . . . Every time I see you it means going to war. You're the goddess of war, right?"

Miss Qi hastily nodded. "Right, I'm the goddess of war, and I've come especially to ask you to go into battle."

The old man slowly shook his head. "I can't. My boys have all died. Of the entire cavalry, only I am left. And . . . I'm . . . not much . . . good."

He lowered his head as he spoke and drifted off to sleep once more. Miss Qi couldn't help but cry again. Gai Bo urged her out of the room, rebuking her: "Why are you so *gai-skinned*?[2] I wanted you to comfort the general, but instead you cry your head off. Your weeping will put everyone in the grave."

Ah 凸 (chu) spoke on her behalf. "Don't be angry, my friend. When the general saw Miss Qi he saw the goddess of war. That's actually a good sign. Only the goddess of war can reawaken a cavalryman's fighting soul."

Gai Bo's skin gradually returned to its normal hue. "My friends, in order to save the Huhui planet, we must bring the general around. If you have any ideas, let's hear them."

---

[1] The skin color of the Gaiwenese changes with their mood. When they are happy, their skin becomes red; when sad, it turns green.

[2] Gai-skinned means "weak and useless."

"▣ ☐ (du-wu) pills!" shouted Ah 凸 (chu). "That's what we need right now."

"They are poisonous," replied Miss Qi, startled, "and they are addictive if used for any length of time. How could you think of giving them to the general?"

"They are also an antidepressant," said Ah 凸 (chu). "The general would be better off dead rather than prolonging his life this way. If we can rally his spirits by using the pills, then any possible addiction is a small matter."

He immediately removed a small bottle from his pocket and handed it to Gai Bo.

"Have the nurse give him two pills every three hours. The effects should be noticeable within one day."

Miss Qi began crying yet again. Gai Bo hurriedly escorted her away from the hospital to the quarters that had been arranged for her and Ah 凸 (chu). The small dome-shaped building was located on a low hill by the sea overlooking New Menghan City harbor. In spite of having been busy all day long, Miss Qi did not feel at all tired. She stood gazing out the window. The sea shimmered as countless heavenly shafts of blue light moved across the surface of the water. Miss Qi pushed open the window; a cold breeze blew in. From afar, Miss Qi could hear the sadly resonant cry of a sea serpent:

"凸 (chu) . . . . . . oh"

"口 (lu) . . . . oh"

"口 (ru) . . . . oh"

"口 (mu) . . . . . . oh"

Was another sea serpent about to meet its death? Or was it bemoaning the misfortunes of its own kind? Miss Qi shivered and closed the window. She felt more alone than ever. The world seemed more foreign to her since the deaths of her dada and Yu Jin. She didn't know how much longer she could go on, and somehow the reason for doing so was lost to her. She recalled the general, his legs amputated, in the Gaiwenese hospital. Had he too lost the will to live? Was it perhaps all predestined? She remembered Ah 凸 (chu) said that according to the histories, Sunlon City would be reborn. But the histories might also contain errors. Was Sunlon City forever doomed?

"Ah 凸 (chu)," shouted Miss Qi. "Ah 凸 (chu)!"

Ah 凸 (chu) came running up the stairs, panting. "What is it, Miss?"

"What are you up to? I call and you don't respond!" said Miss Qi. But seeing the wisdom beads in his hand, she suddenly understood. He too was uneasy and was trying to resolve his doubts by manipulating the beads. "You've been at it half the day. Any answers?"

"No," replied Ah 凸 (chu) in all frankness. "It's too bad your dada isn't here; it would make all the difference. Your father was the wisest Huhui sage. I can only come up with vague probabilities. Profound manipulations are beyond me."

"Do the complete histories contain errors?" she asked, interrupting him.

"Impossible," he replied. "There are no errors in the complete histories. But . . . if under certain circumstances . . ."

"What circumstances?"

"The Evil Spirit of time and space . . ." muttered Ah 凸 (chu). "After billions of years, when heaven and earth are nearly spent and the Huhui planet is on the verge of destruction, the heavenly shafts might break, releasing the Evil Spirit of time and space. Time and space for the Huhui planet would break down and, since time would no longer exist, neither of course would history. There can be no errors in the complete histories, but history could have a stop. It could fall away, layer by layer, twisted into a different form, and be reduced to ashes. . . ."

"We've seen the Evil Spirit of space and time with our own eyes," said Miss Qi, unable to control her fear. "Then what you're saying is that the whole planet is on the verge of collapse. How frightening!"

"That's why I wanted to carefully manipulate the beads," said Ah 凸 (chu), breaking into a sweat. "Perhaps it's not so serious if the heavenly shafts break apart; perhaps the Evil Spirit of time and space is not that terrible and cannot utterly destroy the past, present, and future of the Huhui planet but rather just disintegrate part of it. Unfortunately, I'm not that proficient with the beads and can't come up with an answer."

But Miss Qi's alarm gave way to a shred of hope.

"According to the histories, General Shi should have perished, but he is still alive. Wouldn't that seem to imply that our present part of history has disintegrated? Then isn't it possible that my dada, Yu Jin, and the others are also alive? Then perhaps isn't there a chance that I'll see them again?"

"Don't get carried away," said Ah 凸 (chu) tenderly. "Nothing that has existed can be entirely extinguished. Somewhere in time and space, you'll always be able to encounter them once again. We will always exist. Do you understand?"

"But I'll never see them again," said Miss Qi, her tears falling.

"In the time and space of now, you won't; but they still exist. We'll be as one in the entirety of Huhui time and space. That is, unless the Evil Spirit of time and space . . ."

As Ah 凸 (chu) spoke, Miss Qi gasped. The harbor beyond the window suddenly vanished, leaving their domed house deathly silent and shrouded in utter blackness. But in a moment it all reappeared, the sea still glimmering, the sea serpent still crying sadly, all as if nothing had happened.

"What's the matter?"

Ah 凸 (chu) was silent for a time and then said, "Go to bed, Miss."

Miss Qi knew that the planet was collapsing, but strangely she was not afraid. She couldn't care less—it had to come apart someday. Perhaps Ah 凸 (chu) was right and in the end, they would all be one: Dada, Yu Jin, she herself, Ah 凸 (chu), Ah Wen, Ah Two, Ah Three, and Ah Four. . . .

It was Gai Bo who woke them. The morning found him in an exceptionally good mood. Standing outside Miss Qi's window, he shouted: "Miss Qi! It's late; it's time to get up."

Miss Qi pushed open the window, and Gai Bo hastily gave her a deep bow.

"Good morning! Did you sleep well?"

Miss Qi smiled captivatingly. New Menghan City was quite lovely in the morning. The vapors of the previous night had disappeared, and the flowers and plants, so pretty and fresh, were covered with dew. It was impossible to make a connection between the inauspicious scene of the night before and the peaceful scene then before her eyes. Miss Qi laughed, seeing Gai Bo's skin suffused with a reddish glow.

"Are you in such a good mood that even your skin has changed color?"

"The general is feeling better, so I'm feeling better."

"Really?" said Miss Qi, delighted. "Is he awake?"

"I kid you not. Hurry, come with me and see for yourself."

Miss Qi bounded down the stairs. Ah 凸 (chu) was sleeping soundly and blocking the door. Miss Qi knew that he was trying to protect her with his own body. Her eyes tingled. She called to him softly.

"The general is awake!"

"I know," said Ah 凸 (chu), blinking. "The ⊡ ▢ (du-wu) pills never fail. He is bound to improve."

Upon leaving the domed house, Gai Bo sang and danced with a group of Gaiwenese children in the cobblestone lane. They sang the "Song of the Gaiwenese":

The cannibal opens his mouth and bites
Bites, bites, bites!
The cannibalized opens his mouth and screams
Screams, screams, screams!
The person standing by and watching opens his mouth and laughs
He ha ha
Gai, Oh! Gai, Oh!
Gai, Yo! Gai, Yo!
Whether you bite, scream, or laugh
Bite! Scream! Laugh!
Don't forget to
Gai, Yo! Gai, Yo!

Gai Bo grew more excited as he sang. He leaped up on a large green stone beside the road, howled at the sky, and began to sing:

By the blue sea
Appears the purple sun
New Menghan City produces a living immortal
He seeks happiness for the Gaiwenese
Hey ho!
The best sword on the Huhui planet
A living immortal
Like a swing
Swing back and forth without touching the edge
There is the living immortal
Hey ho!
There the Gaiwenese never rest.

"Enough singing," said Miss Qi. "If you keep it up, the whole city will come to see the Great Spy."

"You are much too kind," said Gai Bo, leaping off the stone. "Let's go see the general."

Before reaching the hospital, they ran into Liu Qi, who was pushing the general in a wheelchair. They were out for a leisurely stroll on the broad avenue. The general's complexion was ruddy and he sat bolt upright in his chair. Before Miss Qi could say a word, the general raised his right hand and, pointing at Miss Qi, said, "The two times I came to the aid of Sunlon City, it was at your bidding. What advice do you have this time?"

"This time I'm not bidding you to lead your troops to Sunlon City, but to return to the plains."

"The . . . plains . . ." muttered the general. "That's where I was born and grew up. And that's where I'll be buried."

"No," said Ah 凸 (chu), "the plains is where your lifetime of exploits began. It's also the base where you rally your forces. Zhihuang Ma has usurped power in Sunlon City, enraging men and gods. The Huhui people need you. If you return to the plains, the valiant warriors of the Huhui planet will rise again and make their way to join you. Soon the cavalry will be as it was of old. Soon, order will return out of chaos to Sunlon City!"

"So many Huhui youngsters lost their lives on my account," said the general, sighing. "I can't bear to sacrifice their precious lives again."

"You are mistaken, general," said Ah 凸 (chu). "Though flowers and fruit must fall, scattered by the wind, Sunlon City will be reborn."

The old general's eyes sparkled and, nodding his head, he said, "Right. Though flowers and fruit must fall, scattered by the wind, Sunlon City will be reborn. Unfortunately, my troops have all been killed or scattered. Going back to the plains, I'm afraid, won't be all that easy to manage."

Hearing the general, Liu Qi was overjoyed and quickly fell to his knees. "General," he said, "I, Liu Qi, and two hundred members of the Green Snake Brotherhood are willing to follow you to the plains. As long as we intend to annihilate Zhihuang Ma and his henchmen and deliver Sunlon City from oppression, I'd go through fire and water without so much as a peep."

Miss Qi clapped her hands and laughed. "We'll all follow you to the plains, general. You can't decline. Isn't that right, Gai Bo?"

She repeated herself several times, but Gai Bo didn't answer. He had seen a number of tourists and hastened to climb atop a large stone to pose for photos. Unexpectedly, they turned out not to be tourists at all. Instead they knelt before him and in tears pleaded: "Save us, Great Spy. Save us, Living Immortal."

Gai Bo just as hastily climbed down off the stone and addressed them: "Let's be friends. What seems to be the problem?"

"Zhihuang Ma's army from Sunlon City has returned and surrounded New Menghan City. We are frightened that the Gaiwenese will again be slaughtered. Please, lead us out of here."

Laughing, Gai Bo said, "Friends and countrymen, arise. As the old saying puts it: 'When soldiers arrive, we use a general to keep them away; when water rises, we use earth to keep it at bay.' I have my own way; there is no need for fear."

He proceeded to take out a small, folded-up piece of paper, much like a dry, square tofu cake. Unfolding it, he spread it out on the stone. From his breast pocket, he took out a small disk with an arrow painted on it and placed it face down on the paper. Ah 出 (chu) asked, "Can you also manipulate a great plate?"

"Is there a great spy who can't?" asked Gai Bo sternly. "It was a required course at the counterintelligence school."

"Great!" said Ah 出 (chu) ecstatically. "Miss Qi and I will help you ask the great plate."

"That won't be necessary," replied Gai Bo, with one hand covering the plate. "I can handle it by myself. The Great Spy is also a great great plate manipulator."

He extended one blue finger and pressed down on the plate. The plate began to spin and fly about the paper and then suddenly came to a halt. Gai Bo mumbled, "Will Zhihuang Ma's army take New Menghan City? The plate says impossible. How should we deal with the enemy? The plate says go underground for safety. Is that clear?"

The people prostrated themselves before Gai Bo and in unison said, "The Great Spy and Great Plater are greatness unparalleled. We will no longer fear Zhihuang Ma."

Gai Bo put away the paper and the small plate. He commanded those present to relay the order to all quarters that the old and the weak and the women and children were to take shelter in the underground city. The young and fit were to defend the city by taking up position at various strong points. About one third of the rainbow-colored domed buildings were actually blockhouses, but externally were indistinguishable from the other homes. The blockhouses were all connected underground. In this way any fortified point that was hard pressed could be swiftly reinforced.

After deploying his defenses, Gai Bo said to the others, "If Zhihuang Ma has the audacity to attack, we'll be ready. It is secure here; protect the general, break out, and make for the plains."

"Gai Bo," replied Liu Qi ardently, "the Green Snake Brotherhood does not cower in the face of death. We'll stay here and fight with you. After we have pushed Zhihuang Ma back, we'll have plenty of time to escort the general back to the plains."

Gai Bo looked all around to make sure there were no Gaiwenese nearby, then whispered, "If you don't leave now, you'll never leave. Zhihuang Ma's army will soon surround us. I know very well that we can hold New Menghan City, but with just a few thousand men, we won't be able to break out. It would be better for you to break through now, protect the general until he can rebuild his cavalry, and then return to rescue us."

Miss Qi knew that Gai Bo was too proud ever to acknowledge the danger that was clearly confronting New Menghan City.

Ah 凸 (chu) bowed and said, "Take care of yourself, Gai Bo. 凸-ᠯ-ᠴᠣ- (chu-lu-ru-mu). And please, by all means, do not seriously consider joining the immortals."

"Life is death; death is life." Gai Bo laughed. "We Gaiwenese have always taken death lightly. But you have to break through with the general—the very safety of the Huhui planet depends on all of you. Let's be friends. Let's all be friends!"

They all knew that what Gai Bo said was true, so they hesitated no longer. At that moment, from above the underground city, they could hear the sound of cannon fire. Zhihuang Ma's army had begun its attack on the city. Gai Bo shouted for Gai Bao to lead the way. The Green Snake Brotherhood escorted the general quickly through the tunnel. The tunnel went deeper and deeper, until surely they must have been under the harbor. Ah 凸 (chu) sighed as he marveled over how much thought had gone into the construction—the Gaiwenese had already built an escape route. They walked for a long time and the tunnel began to ascend, apparently as it departed from the harbor. Upon reaching the exit, Gai Bao said, "I'm seeing you off on your long journey; we'll be sure to meet again. Through this door you'll return to the Huhui planet. To the north lies the great desert. 凸-ᠯ-ᠴᠣ- (chu-lu-ru-mu), let's be friends."

He opened an iron door and again exhorted them, "Once outside, get away from here as quickly as possible. I'm going to destroy this exit to prevent someone from stumbling upon the tunnel or any spies among you from revealing the secret."

"But," said Miss Qi, "that means that no one from New Menghan City will be able to escape."

"Don't worry, Miss," said Gai Bao, laughing. "Although the Gaiwenese aren't too particular about the singular awareness spirit, when danger strikes, people will be willing to join the immortals. You Huhui people are the same when it comes to Sunlon City. We will not lightly abandon New Menghan City, our second home. Good-bye, one and all."

Gai Bao waited until all the Green Snake Brotherhood warriors were out before closing the door. The door was quite ingenious because it was perfectly camouflaged to match the soil of the hill. They now found themselves atop a small hill on the opposite side of the harbor. Across the water, they could see that Zhihuang Ma's army had already penetrated the southwest corner of the city and was fighting the Gaiwenese street by street. Not only were the Gaiwenese offering stiff resistance on the streets, but they had also launched all the Froghoppers, which were jumping about the city dropping bombs on Zhihuang Ma's troops. Occasionally a Froghopper was hit and fell smoking to the ground. In the face of death, the Gaiwenese pilots yelled, "Let's be immortal!" Although the fighting was fierce, Zhihuang Ma's forces had not gained the upper hand. Reassured, the group set off from the hill. They hadn't gone very far when the earth shook beneath their feet and the entire hill collapsed, sending up a cloud of dust. It was leveled in a matter of moments. They knew that Gai Bao had destroyed the door and they were filled with regret.

General Shi was carried on a litter by two warriors. But now he struggled to sit up. Miss Qi hurried over to comfort him. "We're outside New Menghan City now, and soon we'll be in the desert. The plains lie across the desert. Please rest."

"We can't enter the desert," said the general, struggling, his face darkening. "We'll be done for if we enter the desert."

"Why?" asked Liu Qi. "Your home lies across the desert. Although the Green Snake Brotherhood warriors cannot compare with your cavalry, they are not afraid of the desert. We've got seven days of food and water, and we'll be across in three."

In an attempt to show off in front of the general, Liu Qi addressed the warriors, "Brothers, sound off!"

Stirred to the quick, the men shouted in unison:

"One, two, three, four!"

ㄔㄌㄖㄇ (chu-lu-ru-mu)!

One, two three, four!

ㄔㄌㄖㄇ (chu-lu-ru-mu)!"

General Shi shook his head and sighed. "I don't doubt that the Green Snake Brotherhood will brave the desert, but we can't go there. If we do, we're done for!"

Miss Qi wondered why such a brave general would suddenly be afraid of the desert. She halted and spoke to Liu Qi. "The general has said repeatedly that we should not enter the desert. There must be a reason. Let's not be hasty."

Liu Qi nodded and immediately ordered everyone to halt. Before them stretched the sandy yellow ground. Liu Qi ordered his men to stand guard and then sent out a small reconnaissance party. The nine men hadn't gone very far, they hadn't even reached the sand, when suddenly they vanished from sight. Startled, Liu Qi sent out another party. They too vanished. Everyone watched with eyes wide open. One moment they were there advancing, the next moment they were gone. Miss Qi recalled how the harbor had vanished the night before and said to Ah 凵 (chu), "Do you think it's the Evil Spirit?"

Frightened, Ah 凵 (chu) trembled and was unable to speak. Liu Qi quickly asked Miss Qi, "Who? Who are you talking about?"

Before Miss Qi could explain, something strange happened. The ground split open and a wide chasm full of black mist appeared. They couldn't tell how deep it was. Ah 凵 (chu) fainted, and Liu Qi asked again, "Who is it? Who has such powers?"

"The Evil Spirit of time and space."

It was not Miss Qi or Ah 凵 (chu) who had spoken. The two of them were quite startled. The general struggled to sit up on his stretcher. Pointing into the chasm, he said, "Right. That weird spirit is behind this. This chasm is its doing."

"Have you seen the Evil Spirit of time and space?" asked Miss Qi.

The old general made no reply.

"We can't enter the desert," said Liu Qi. "Let's head west through Xin-su Village and make our way around the desert to get to Golden Goose Fort."

Liu Qi ordered his men to withdraw to the left. Just as they were about to march, the chasm disappeared and the eighteen missing warriors reappeared nearby, still inching forward. Liu Qi pulled out his serpent whistle and blew several times. The warriors heard and returned at a run. Liu Qi asked them where they had gone. They didn't know what he was talking about and said that they had been advancing as ordered until they heard his whistle. They hadn't been slacking. Nodding, Ah 凵 (chu) said, "The fissure in time and space is becoming increasingly evident. It's my guess that a nearby passage through time and space has collapsed but has been repaired by people in the future. That's why the chasm disappeared and the warriors reappeared. The general is right, we can't cross the desert. Going around is a good idea. General!"

The general had collapsed on his stretcher. His eyes were tightly shut and his expression one of intense pain. Ah 凵 (chu) took out some pills. He forced open the general's mouth and gave him the medicine and some water. Miss Qi knew that once the general started taking the medicine, he wouldn't be able to stop, otherwise his entire body would feel as if it were being crushed under a lead weight. But even if he did take the medicine without stopping, the pain would continue to grow. Ultimately, he would become paralyzed, and his bones would disintegrate. Once a person began taking the medicine, they had only seven or eight months to live. Would they make it?

"Ah 出 (chu) . . ." Miss Qi sobbed.

"He's better," said Ah 出 (chu), nodding. "Let's be on our way."

8

Vast are the heavens and the earth. The purple clouds filling the sky were like hanging spikes. They spread, melting together into a solid purple carpet. There seemed to be fewer heavenly shafts of blue light than usual; occasionally one even would appear to be missing. On the flat expanse of the yellow desert, a small troop slowly inched along. They had traveled for three days and three nights without resting, marching to deliver Sunlon City. The robust warriors of the Green Snake Brotherhood took turns carrying the general's stretcher. The legless general lay there gritting his teeth, bearing the pain. Only occasionally did he let a groan escape. Anxiously, Miss Qi walked beside the stretcher looking after this hero of the Huhui planet. But her efforts were limited: he used the strength born of his own will to combat his misery as the pills tore his bones apart. Although the medicine had returned his mind to its normal state, it was destroying him physically. When the pain became almost unbearable, he would sit up and scream: "Are we almost there?"

"Almost," replied Miss Qi to comfort him each time. "We're almost to Golden Goose Fort."

Golden Goose Fort was General Shi's training camp; it was also the ancient site of a battlefield from the last war of restoration. After the great uprising against the Shan, General Shi restored the prestige of the army there. When he marched his troops east, Sunlon City trembled. But the cavalry had been obliterated save for the general himself. The Huhui planet was about to fall into Zhihuang Ma's hands. Miss Qi kept wondering how much time they would have if New Menghan City were taken by Zhihuang Ma. But she acted unconcerned as she walked alongside the general.

Although night had long since fallen, Liu Qi kept urging everyone forward. At times he was seen at the head of the column; at other times he halted and waited for every last man and horse to pass before he picked up his pace and headed on. From the way he busied himself like a mother hen with her chicks, Miss Qi knew he was worried that the Evil Spirit of time and space might reappear. Miss Qi was touched. Then she remembered something and asked the general, "How do you know when the Evil Spirit of time and space is here to make trouble?"

The general closed his eyes and did not reply immediately. Miss Qi assumed he was asleep until she heard him sigh a short while later.

"Near the end of the Huhui planet, the Evil Spirit will manifest itself. I'm an old man and no longer know if I will live to see Sunlon City reborn. Even if we do make it back to Golden Goose Fort, that doesn't mean we'll be able to raise an army. It worries me that the Evil Spirit will become ever more savage."

"Ah 出 (chu) says that the Evil Spirit is a demon released when the Huhui planet collapses, rupturing the heavenly shafts of light. I think that the Bronze Statue is the Evil Spirit." Miss Qi tucked in the general's blanket and asked, "What do you think?"

Once again the general sighed.

"I lost my legs to the Evil Spirit of time and space, and it crushed the two guards who saved me to a pulp in its hand. I know it is hiding there in the desert, waiting to make its move. The two hundred Green Snake Brotherhood warriors are no match for it."

Miss Qi wanted to pursue the matter further when the column suddenly came to a halt. Liu Qi ran back along the column whispering, "Something's happening. Spread out! Don't fire unless you hear my snake whistle."

Everyone took cover wherever they could. They waited for a while, but still nothing happened ahead of them; nor did Liu Qi appear. The sky gradually grew light as the purple sun slowly rose above the horizon. The sun, which appeared even larger above the flat land, seemed to occupy half the sky. Their surroundings became very clear. They had already reached the outer wall of Golden Goose Fort. No more than a kilometer away, several columns of black smoke rose from a tumbled-down wall. Perhaps the sentries were preparing the morning cookfires. After a moment, the sound of gunfire was heard coming from the direction of the fallen wall. After another moment, Liu Qi and two warriors appeared on the wall and motioned for the rest of them to follow.

The seven soldiers guarding the toppled wall had been killed. The remainder had been disarmed by Liu Qi's assault troops. The breakfast they had just prepared was consumed by the Green Snake Brotherhood warriors. Liu Qi posted sentries in the four directions on the toppled wall and then gave the order for everyone to rest. He approached General Shi and said, "We are less than sixteen kilometers from Golden Goose Fort proper. Unexpectedly, Zhihuang Ma had deployed a line of scouts to keep a lookout. According to the prisoners, two regiments are guarding Golden Goose Fort. He obviously took precautions. It will be impossible to attack the fort by day, so we might as well take a breather here and launch a surprise attack tonight."

The general had just taken the singular awareness medicine that Ah 出 (chu) had prepared for him and was in good spirits. He asked Miss Qi to help him sit up. He spoke to Liu Qi: "I trained Zhihuang Ma. In marching his troops and arraying them for battle; he is following the rules. Even if you launch a surprise attack under cover of darkness, I'm afraid the Green Snake Brotherhood will still suffer heavy casualties. But most of the troops he has sent to Golden Goose Fort have deep ties with the plains. It would be better if I went and convinced them to surrender."

Hearing this, Liu Qi appeared reluctant. Ah 出 (chu) bowed and spoke to the elderly general, "Brave is the general! Zhihuang Ma is a profound schemer. Even if there are a lot of people from the plains in the two regiments, Zhihuang Ma certainly mixed them with his own trusted subordinates and members of the cult. If you approach them about surrender, you might end up being harmed."

The general lifted his head and laughed. "I have conducted war over thousands of kilometers, and my one sword has been equal to that of thousands. Now I'm nearing the end of my road, and all I've got is this sword in my hand. If I can't convince Zhihuang Ma's men to come over and follow me, how will I ever form a new cavalry? This plain is where I will be buried! I've made up my mind. There's no need to say anything more."

Without hesitating, Miss Qi said, "The general wants to go, but he can't go alone. It'll just have to be arranged. If the soldiers defending Golden Goose Fort think they are surrounded by the enemy, they'll be more likely to listen to the general when he tries to persuade them to surrender."

"You're right," Ah 出 (chu) hastily added. "This is one hundred percent in accord with the 㔾口 (man-qia) *Art of War* and the principle of subduing

□ (wu) with ⊡ (du). If by deception we can strike fear in their hearts so they don't know what to believe, they won't dare hold out."

"All right." The general nodded. "Liu Qi, we'll stick with your original plan and let the young men rest for half a day. We'll wait till dusk before moving out and arraying for battle."

Miss Qi knew that the old general liked deploying for battle more than anything else, and it had caused him a good deal of suffering. She had to smile seeing that he hadn't changed. Fortunately, she had spoken as she did and thereby dispelled the general's intention to singlehandedly talk the enemy into surrendering, at least for the time being. The Green Snake Brotherhood members, including Liu Qi, had not rested for three days and three nights. Now they all looked for a place beneath the wall to lie down. Miss Qi attended the general until he was asleep; Ah 凸 (chu), who was lying nearby, was soon snoring loudly. Although she was exhausted, she had no desire to sleep and so, having nothing better to do, she walked beyond the wall. The Green Snake sentries warned her not to wander too far. She nodded and strolled out onto the plains.

The purple sun of the Huhui planet seemed to have increased in diameter, but it shone with less intensity. It was more like a warm purple sea pulling the Huhui planet to its breast than a shining sun. Sometimes the sight of the purple sun filled Miss Qi with fear. But today the purple sea actually made her feel serene and peaceful. One day the planet again would sink into that sea to become one with the purple sun. After that, the sun would burn more brightly and with greater warmth and, bathed in fire, it would die, forming a black hole in the universe. But in another universe, the Huhui planet would be born anew, and everything would begin again. She was not afraid of this impending bath of fire but actually welcomed it. It would mean an end to everything. She would shed her skin like a cicada and soak her feet in the purple sea.

Strong gusts of wind blew over the plains. The wind whipped up the sand here earlier than in Sunlon City. By noon the yellow sand had risen to blot out the light of the purple sun. The particles of sand struck Miss Qi's face and bare arms, making them tingle with pain. She decided to go back. Just as she was about to turn around, she noticed a black mist rolling in from the northwest. It appeared as if there were a huge human form within the rolling black fog.

Her heart pounded as she realized what it was. The gigantic Bronze Statue faded in and out of view. She couldn't see its feet, but it was approaching steadily. Miss Qi was afraid of the trouble it might cause, but it strode southeast without pausing. Obviously it was headed toward Sun-lon City. It walked on, but amid the whirling sand, it vanished in an instant. It suddenly occurred to her that the fissure in time was widening, but someone was repairing it and that was why the Evil Spirit of time and space hadn't been able to work its will. Who in the future was laboring to repair the passage through time?

"Miss Qi!" shouted someone. Miss Qi turned around to see a young, blond-haired girl. She vaguely remembered having seen this historian from the future. That was at the South Gate of Heaven just prior to the great uprising against the Shan. "Do you remember me? It's Mei Xin."

"I remember you. You told the cult leader that he was the most unscrupulous schemer of the age."

The blond girl smiled, revealing her sparkling white teeth. "You have a good memory. By your calendar that was four years ago. I never expected you to remember so clearly."

"I suppose that for you it occurred just yesterday." Miss Qi felt that the girl's face hadn't changed in the least, while she herself had aged considerably. She felt a twinge of jealousy. "What are you doing here? Didn't the Evil Spirit of time and space try to prevent you?"

"Call me Mei Xin, okay?" requested the blond-haired girl. "So you know about the Evil Spirit of time and space too! Actually, it's not a monster; it's just that a passage through time is collapsing. Time and space are in chaos and different historical events and personages are getting mixed up. Fortunately they have repaired this section of the passage, allowing me to come back and collect some materials. Oh no," blurted out Mei Xin, grimacing, "I've already said too much."

"It doesn't matter. You won't destroy the comprehensiveness of Huhui history, because the Evil Spirit has all but done so," said Miss Qi, taking Mei Xin's hand. "The wind is really blowing. Let's get inside the wall and talk."

"I can't stay too long," said Mei Xin, hesitating. "Actually, I'm looking for my boyfriend. His name is Wang Xin.[1] He's also a grad student in the Institute of Huhui History. He's tall and thin. Have you seen him?"

Miss Qi shook her head and burst out laughing. "There are so many tall, thin people, how would I know him if I saw him? And apart from you, I haven't met anybody else from the future. Why are you looking for your boyfriend on the Huhui planet?"

---

[1] On the story of Wang Xin and Mei Xin, see "A Love That Ruined the Nation" in the *Nebula Suite*.

"Because he has fallen in love with the place." Mei Xin sighed. "I've never met anyone so obsessed. It's a great taboo for any historian to develop deep feelings for the object of his research. But he loves only Sunlon City. The city does have its enchanting places, but after all, we are historians from the future and we shouldn't love a bygone world. I'm terribly sorry!"

"It's all right," said Miss Qi. She really liked this young girl who spoke what was on her mind. "I know our fate. If I happen to run into your boyfriend . . . his name is Wang Xin, right? If I happen to see Wang Xin, how shall I contact you?"

"You can't contact me, but you can tell him to go back to the future, where I'll be waiting for him. Also, but perhaps I shouldn't say . . ."—Miss Qi could feel her hand melting away—". . . be careful crossing the river. . . ."

The air around the blond-haired girl began to move rapidly, as if a transparent net were being pulled around her. Then she vanished. Miss Qi thought about what Mei Xin had said. "I'll be waiting for him in the future." She was so in love. Who was waiting for her in the future? Then she pondered for a while the last words Mei Xin had uttered: "Be careful crossing the river." What did they mean? Wasn't Mei Xin aware that no river ran through the plains?

The high wind was blowing more fiercely. Miss Qi could scarcely withstand it; she covered her face and ran for the fort. Everyone was still resting, but the general leaned against the wall, wide awake, clutching his precious sword with both hands. Miss Qi squatted beside him and said, "Won't you rest a bit?"

"There's no need," said the general, smiling bitterly. "These old bones are about done for. The pain is so bad that I can't sleep. But I am clear about one thing: we won't make it back to Golden Goose Fort."

"Why?" asked Miss Qi, looking at the general's weather-beaten face and snow-white hair, covered with yellow sand. His long suffering had made him look even older. "If we don't go to Golden Goose Fort, where will we go?"

"To the Great Plains to the north," replied the general. "Zhihuang Ma has not necessarily stationed troops at Golden Goose Fort to guard against me. The entire Huhui planet thinks I'm dead. Only two hundred Green Snake Brotherhood troops are left, and if by some chance the soldiers guarding Golden Goose Fort don't surrender and we make a direct attack, our losses will be enormous, if not total. I figure Zhihuang Ma has posted soldiers at Golden Goose Fort to keep an eye on the Leopard people to the north. Obviously, he hasn't been successful in controlling them, and that being the case, Silverfield Village must be unguarded. For that reason I think it best to return to the plains up north and appeal to patriots there to join us. Once the cavalry has regained a bit of its original vigor, I'll move south to Jinjiakou, cutting the Jinsuo Line, forcing the soldiers guarding Golden Goose Fort to throw down their arms. Once the plains have been entirely recovered, I'll head east to Sunlon City."

"Great idea!" How long Ah 出 (chu) had been awake, no one could say. He stood up, bowed, and said, "Brilliant is the general. The 冖 口 (man-qia) Sage said it best. . . ."

"No more of the *Art of War*," said the general impatiently. "Speed is precious in war. Let's be on our way."

Miss Qi hurriedly awakened Liu Qi. Hearing the general's plan, Liu Qi added his approval as well. He was an excellent organizational officer: immediately, he had assigned the Green Snake warriors their tasks. Eighty of them were to escort the general around Golden Goose Fort to the Great Plains to the north. Another one hundred warriors were broken into pairs that were to spread the word all along the Jinsuo Line that the general was staging an uprising up north. At the same time, they were to sabotage the rail line and destroy military facilities there. The remaining twenty warriors were secretly to return to Sunlon City to mobilize what was left of the Green Snake Brotherhood to initiate a guerrilla war.

The plan set, the warriors moved out at dusk and soon crossed the Jinsuo rail line. There they parted with the warriors who were to return to Sunlon City and those who were to spread the word along the rail line. In single file, the two groups followed the line east for a distance. Every once in a while, two men would disappear into the darkness of the plains. The eighty remaining warriors who were to loyally protect the general continued northward. Miss Qi, Ah 出 (chu), and Liu Qi brought up the rear. Recalling the time she had taken the train with Ah Two, the butcher, to Jinjiakou and how they had been attacked by the LPRA, Miss Qi felt a twinge of fear.

"The general's decision not to make a frontal assault on Golden Goose Fort is no doubt wise," said Miss Qi to Ah 出 (chu). "But the northern plains are under the control of the Leopard people. In the past the general's cavalry cruelly suppressed the LPRA. Do you think they will let him off easy this time?"

"Hard to say," said Ah 出 (chu). "The Leopard people are cruel and cunning. In their eyes, the cavalry's suppression was a trivial matter and won't necessarily elicit much hatred. Don't forget that during the Snake and Leopard War the Royalists rose up in rebellion several times on the plains, and on each occasion they fought with the Leopard people, using them in the van. There is still a possibility that they will cooperate with the old general. Besides, with my eloquence I can probably convince some of them."

"There won't be a problem if Commander Hua is still around. According to the complete histories, were Commander Hua and Zhi-Hu Zhe both lost in the war against the Serpent people and the Shan?"

"It's not recorded. They weren't considered important enough to be included in the histories."

"Great!" replied Miss Qi. "If Commander Hua is still alive, then the Leopard people will help us."

As they were discussing the matter, the wind on the plains increased, whipping up the sand. Everyone lowered their heads and slowly advanced into the wind. That night, they were exhausted. Lightning flashed amid the purple clouds and large drops of rain began to fall. During the day, the plains were dry; the rainstorms, though brief but heavy, usually came at night. Everyone was soaked to the bone. When they seemed in dire straits, they fortunately came upon a walled village. Walls the height of two people were built around all villages on the plains to prevent incursions by bandits and the Leopard people. The Green Snake warriors gathered at the foot of the wall in an attempt to find shelter from the rain. The rain and lightning passed on over the plains and the wind rose again. Everyone was wet and cold and began sneezing.

A guard posted in a watchtower on the wall stuck his head out the window. Miss Qi saw him and gasped. He looked exactly like Ah 凸 (chu)—his head was like a meatball, with his five sense organs on his crown. Ah 凸 (chu) bowed with great formality. The guard in the watchtower vanished, and soon the heavy wooden gate to the village was slowly pushed open a crack. The 凸 (chu) person who had appeared in the watchtower window now came swaggering out of the gate. Liu Qi immediately performed a singular awareness salute and said, "My companions of the Green Snake Brotherhood happened upon your village, and we made so bold as to take shelter from the rain at the foot of your wall. 凸-叮呫叮- (chu-lu-ru-mu)!"

The 凸 (chu) person was of slighter physique than Ah 凸 (chu). He returned the salute and said, "Ah 凸 (chu) already told me. Please come in."

Miss Qi recalled that the 凸 (chu) people of the Huhui planet were all telepathic. No wonder the 凸 (chu) person had understood them without

Ah 凸 (chu) even opening his mouth. Only after they entered the village did they realize that it was entirely unlike any other Huhui shepherds' village. There were no houses inside the wall, just a huge square building with no windows. Seeing their confusion, the 凸 (chu) person laughed and said, "This is our 凸 secret. We never expected that you would chance upon it. My name is Ah 凹 (ru), and like Ah 凸 (chu) I was an official historian. After the Shan occupied Sunlon City, we slowly made off with the important Huhui histories and housed them here. What you see before you is the sole history library on the Huhui planet. You will never find a better base for the general to recuperate and rebuild the country."

"Right!" said Ah 凸 (chu). "The library can hold two or three hundred people. When Ah 凹 (ru) and I built this secret library, we looked for a place that would never interest the Shan. We never expected that it could be used as a base by the general."

"It is indeed admirable that the two of you would be willing to sacrifice your library to be used as a base by the general," said Liu Qi. "But if the flames of war happen to destroy the library, won't you be distraught?"

"Don't worry about that," replied Ah 凸 (chu) sternly. "With the appearance of the Evil Spirit of time and space, I realized that the Huhui planet is facing a disaster. The integrity of histories cannot be guaranteed, and time and space are on the verge of collapse. The historical facts contained in these books have been undermined by the Evil Spirit and have lost all value. Wouldn't you say so, Ah 凹 (ru)?"

"Inaccurate histories are garbage," added Ah 凹 (ru) sternly. "From now on, the complete Huhui histories are incomplete. This is an earth-shaking change for the Huhui planet. Ah 凸 (chu) and I as well as all other 凸 (chu) people must determine how to reestablish the Huhui histories. You can use the books in this library to build a fire."

The Green Snake warriors were overjoyed by what Ah 凸 (chu) and Ah 凹 (ru) said. They immediately took a pile of books and made a fire to warm themselves. Watching as the books they had so painstakingly stored away were reduced to ashes in the courtyard, fat Ah 凸 (chu) and skinny Ah 凹 (ru) couldn't help feeling sad. Hand in hand they circled the burning books, singing "The Song of the 凸 (chu)":

凸凹 *(chu-ru)*
凸凹 *(chu-ru)*
‐□□‐ ‐□□‐ *(lu-mu lu-mu)*
□‐□ □‐□ *(mu-lu mu-lu)*

⊡ □ *(du-wu)*
⊡ □ *(du-wu)*
凸叩 *(chu-ru)*
凸叩 *(chu-ru).* . . .

Finishing their song, the two of them buried their heads in their arms and wept. Liu Qi couldn't bear the sight and ordered his men to stop burning the books. But in the warmth of the fire, the warriors were able to dry their clothes, after which they each found a spot in the library and slept. Only General Shi, who was taking the pills, remained awake, moaning. Miss Qi and Ah 凸 (chu) knew that the general's bones were slowly coming apart, and there was nothing they could do about it.

Miss Qi vented her anger on Ah 凸 (chu). "The medicine is too deadly. It shouldn't have been given to him in the first place."

"What other choice was there?" Ah 凸 (chu) sighed. "Huhui history is coming apart at this very minute. Perhaps we'll all soon be destroyed. The general won't suffer much longer, whatever happens."

"Then what was the point of encouraging him to rebuild the cavalry? Why bother retaking Sunlon City? Why bother about anything, since Zhihuang Ma won't be around much longer and the city will soon be destroyed?"

Miss Qi's words left Ah 凸 (chu) speechless for some time. After a while, he said, "We can't just give up. We have to keep on fighting. I have always taught you that though flowers and fruit must fall, scattered by the wind . . ."

". . . Sunlon City will be reborn," continued Miss Qi angrily. "But what if this conviction is wrong? What if Sunlon City is never reborn? Then why have so many people sacrificed themselves?"

Ah 凸 (chu) couldn't answer her. All he could say was, "Miss, you should get some sleep. I may not be able do anything else, but your dada wanted me to look after you, and that I will do till the very end. Go get some sleep. If your dada were still alive, he would want you to rest. Don't think about it anymore."

Miss Qi wrapped herself in a blanket, tears streaming down her cheeks. But she did fall asleep. She dreamed of their noisy tavern. Ordered around by Ah Wen, Ah Two and Ah Three were bustling about busily. In the kitchen, Ah Four was humming and making snake soup. Her dada sat cross-legged on his bed, engrossed in manipulating the wisdom beads with Ah 凸 (chu). The three Yu brothers talked loudly and laughed with the other guests. Occasionally, Yu Jin would glance over at her as she played her piano. Blue-skinned Gai Bo stole a glance from the doorway. Outside, Captain Mai led his patrol. She smiled in her dream, suffused with satisfaction.

She was awakened by someone knocking at the door. All the Green Snake warriors in the library were also awakened. In the darkness, Liu Qi's voice was heard, calm and composed. "Don't panic. Check your weapons. Everyone outside and stand along the wall. Don't fire unless you hear my snake whistle."

9

<hr>

Without so much as a sound, the Green Snake warriors positioned themselves around the walled perimeter. The knocking from without was ever more urgent. Liu Qi motioned with his eyes, and Ah 出 (chu) clambered up the stairs to the watchtower. Opening the wooden window shutters, he shouted, "Who the □ (wu) is knocking on the gate so early in the morning?"

"Open up, 出 (chu)," came the shouted reply from outside. "We're followers of the general and have been riding all night to get here, and would like a bowl of water to quench our thirst. We'll pay you ten ⊡ (du) for your trouble."

Ah 出 (chu) closed the shutters and looked at Liu Qi. Liu Qi nodded. Ah 出 (chu) clambered down the watchtower stairs and opened the gate. About a dozen cavalrymen on their horses burst in. Only after they were inside did they notice that all around them stood Green Snake Brotherhood warriors aiming laser guns at them. All they could do was dismount and surrender. Their leader, not willing to give in, swore, "So, you evil remnants of the Green Snake Brotherhood are holed up here doing your dirty work. Do you think your lives will be worth anything when the general discovers you?"

"You claim to be followers of the general," said Liu Qi, "so don't you know that he is here?"

Startled, the horsemen wept tears of joy. "We're the guards at Golden Goose Fort. Last night we heard that the general was forming the cavalry, so we decided to desert our posts and come at once. We never thought we'd find him. It's really 凸-ᗡ凸- (chu-lu-ru-mu)."

Ah 凸 (chu) bowed and said, "It surely is 凸-ᗡ凸- (chu-lu-ru-mu). The general decided to launch an uprising on the northern plains, and here you are. Obviously the news has spread quickly over the plains and the general's name still retains something of its renown. There is still a hope of reestablishing the cavalry."

"If those fleeing to the general can find this place so quickly," said Liu Qi, shaking his head, "then Zhihuang Ma's troops will be here soon. Given the present situation, we must continue north."

"Not so," said Ah 凸 (chu). "Frightened by the general's renown, Zhihuang Ma's troops might be unwilling to move. Our present location is on the road to Silverfield Village north of Golden Goose Fort, and those fleeing to the general must come this way. If we stay here a few days longer, the ranks of those fleeing will swell and the cavalry will soon be what it once was."

As Liu Qi wavered, the cavalrymen spoke. "The 凸 (chu) person is right. Of the two regiments stationed at Golden Goose Fort, at least half are ready to desert. Perhaps others are like us and on the plains looking for the general at this very moment. And no matter what, those who do remain won't act rashly."

Liu Qi was a cautious person, and the words of the men stood for nothing. He went to ask the general's opinion. With Miss Qi's assistance, the general had put on his armor and was sitting upright in a chair and ordering four warriors to carry him outside. As soon as the cavalrymen saw the white-haired old general, they knelt down and shouted:

"Gen-er-al!"

"Gen-er-al!"

"Gen-er-al!"

The old general greeted them with a wave and said to Liu Qi, "We must raise our banner to protect the Huhui planet and retake Sunlon City."

Liu Qi bowed and said yes. The bannerman unfurled a good-sized yellow banner prepared by Gai Bo on which was embroidered a leopard and the general's surname. He climbed atop the watchtower and raised the banner. Those assembled roared with joy. Once raised atop the tower, the banner seemed to work its power, and there was a steady stream of people knocking at the gate. The walled compound couldn't contain all the Royalist swordsmen. Worried that there might be some bad apples in the bunch, Liu Qi decided to keep only the eighty Green Snake Brotherhood warriors within the walls to protect the general. Those coming to join him would for the moment form a company and be stationed outside. By dusk, more than two thousand had assembled outside the walls, and more kept coming.

Miss Qi had never seen anything like it, and was nearly moved to tears. But the general showed no signs of being excited. Each time his cavalry was annihilated, it reappeared as if by miracle, renewed by hot-blooded young men from all parts. Although the general didn't appear excited, Miss Qi felt that he was concealing a certain anxiety. Within the span of one day, he had fainted several times due to the pain, and he was growing ever weaker. The general's anxiety only increased as the ranks swelled. After the great uprising against the Shan, the remnants of the cavalry retreated to Golden Goose Fort where they trained for a full year. Could he now polish this rabble into a strong fighting force in such a short time?

Around dusk, the general once again regained consciousness after fainting from pain. He then asked that the warriors carry him outside the walls for an inspection. Miss Qi and Ah 出 (chu) followed close behind to make sure that nothing unexpected occurred. Groups of young swordsmen stood around bonfires, talking loudly and laughing. One person beat on a leopard-skin drum with the hilt of his sword and sang a Huhui folksong. The blue heavenly shafts moved slowly in the distance, and shortly after a burst of lightning a peal of thunder was heard as if echoing the drum. A firm and vigorous voice sang:

> *The purple sun sinks in the west*
> *The time for rest*
> *Has come again*
> *Turning round suddenly*
> *There I see*
> *That solitary city.*

The singer repeated the tune again and again. The general sighed deeply, and his tears fell, moistening his clothes. By way of encouragement, Ah 出 (chu) said, "In a few days there will be more than nine thousand horsemen, sufficient to strike terror in the hearts of the Leopard people to the north and to make Sunlon City to the east tremble. These young men are all willing to die for you. Zhihuang Ma can be annihilated with great ease; there is no reason to be worried."

"I'm already old, and the situation looks bad." The general sighed. "The Huhui planet won't be saved even if Zhihuang Ma is beaten."

Shocked, Ah 出 (chu) said, "Don't think that way, general. Only you can alter the fate of Sunlon City."

"You are an official historian," said the general, laughing bitterly. "Certainly you know that the history of the Huhui planet is written, and the fate of Sunlon City cannot be changed."

"Nothing is certain since the appearance of the Evil Spirit of time and space," replied Ah 出 (chu). "According to the histories, you should have died in the fight against the Serpent people and the Shan, but you're still here. So it is possible to change the fate of Sunlon City."

"The appearance of the Evil Spirit of time and space bodes ill," said the general, shaking his head. "It indicates that the Huhui planet is entering its final decline. I would rather have died fighting the Serpent people and the Shan than see the collapse of the Huhui planet."

Once again the general was overcome by the pain and fainted. Fighting to hold back their tears, Miss Qi and Ah 出 (chu) hastily took the general back inside the walls. After a short while, the wind whipped up and the rain poured down. Thinking about the thousands of swordsmen camped under the open sky, Miss Qi mobilized the warriors of the Green Snake Brotherhood to help her serve snake soup. Although the young men were soaked to the bone, their spirits remained high. Wherever Miss Qi went, she was greeted with jubilation. Fortunately, the storm soon let up and, with the permission of Ah 出 (chu) and Ah 卩 (ru), she had more books removed from the library and fires built to warm the swordsmen. In the span of a single night, the complete histories of the Huhui planet were reduced to ashes.

The next day, even more deserters arrived, including an entire cavalry battalion with officers who had ridden all night from Jinjiakou. That night, Liu Qi did a head count and ascertained that more than five thousand men had arrived. Such a large force couldn't continue to camp in the open outside. Fortunately, after the general took a larger dose of the medicine, his spirits improved. The following day, he decided to break camp and head north to Silverfield Village.

Although the cavalry still amounted to nothing more than rabble, they did look a formidable array under the yellow banner. The general ordered the cavalry battalion to take up the van, with all the others falling in behind. Liu Qi and the eighty Green Snake Brotherhood warriors took position to the left and right as guards. Miss Qi and Ah 出 (chu) urged Ah 卩

(ru) to accompany them, but he was determined to stay behind to look after the nearly empty library of Huhui history. Ah凸(chu), who wasn't normally very emotional, was in tears and could hardly bear to say good-bye to Ah凹(ru). After they had marched for about half a day, Ah凸(chu) suddenly screamed, "Oh, no!" and collapsed on the ground. Liu Qi and Miss Qi immediately came to his aid. Ah凸(chu) slowly came around and, crying, said, "Ah凹(ru) is dead! Zhihuang Ma's troops broke down the gate and destroyed the library with Ah凹(ru) inside."

Miss Qi knew that 凸(chu) people communicated telepathically. Ah凹(ru) had volunteered to remain behind in order to warn them, even at the cost of his own life. They both felt miserable.

"Zhihuang Ma has gone too far," said Liu Qi, beside himself with anger. "Once the cavalry has been trained, Ah凹(ru) will be avenged!"

"Before he died, Ah凹(ru) informed me that Zhihuang Ma has in excess of ten thousand troops," said Ah凸(chu) tearfully. "His airships are also patrolling the skies."

"It must be Ma's main force," said Liu Qi, both startled and angered. "Does that mean they have taken New Menghan City? I never expected them to move so quickly."

Liu Qi reported the news to the general immediately. Hearing it with a frown, the general said, "We have to get to Silverfield Village at once. If we can convince the Leopard people to cooperate with us, there will be no need to fear Zhihuang Ma."

Liu Qi gave orders to pick up the pace. Of the five thousand new recruits, only a little more than one thousand had horses. The remainder had to run. Fortunately, they were close to Silverfield Village. They would be at the foot of the mountains before dusk. Although Silverfield was called a village, it was actually a castle located at the edge of the Huihui mountain range. Because there were silver mines in the vicinity, Huhui troops had been stationed there since ancient times—not only to supervise the miners, most of whom were criminals, but also to defend the area against the Leopard people who would occasionally appear. In the time of the constitutional monarchy, Huhui government troops fought several times with the Leopard people near the silver mines. After the Fourth Interstellar War, the conquering Shan people dispatched interstellar warships to suppress the Leopard people, but to no avail. With the success of the great uprising against the Shan, a power struggle took place among the three factions. The government pulled its troops out of Silverfield Village, and the castle fell into the hands of the Leopard people. After Zhihuang

Ma usurped power, he busied himself with the south; he had not yet taken Silverfield Village in the north. By leading his cavalry north, the general was hoping to take advantage of the historical connections between the Royalists and the Leopard people and convince them to join in the fight against Zhihuang Ma, thus allowing his troops a respite.

When the cavalry division reached the foot of the mountains, they cheered upon seeing the castle. The mountain itself wasn't high, but it was craggy. The castle had been constructed in a depression in one of the crags as if it were a natural formation inlaid in the mountain itself. It was not easily attacked from below, and even if the peak were scaled, there was no way to attack the castle with rolling logs or scalding water. No wonder the Huhui people had been able to defend it for thousands of years with a minimum of troops. Even the fierce Leopard people had been powerless against the castle guards.

But the castle was now in the hands of the Leopard people, who stopped the general's troops at the foot of the mountain. Their numbers were not great—fewer than two hundred warriors arrayed in two defensive lines. Between the two lines paced a huge Leopard person—much like a male lion—on all fours. Observing him from a distance, Miss Qi asked Ah 凸 (chu), "Doesn't the commanding officer look like Commander Hua?"

"A little," replied Ah 凸 (chu). "I'll go have a word with him. Commander Hua! Commander Hua! Commander Hua!"

Ah 凸 (chu) shouted as he walked toward the Leopard lines. Having keen eyes and ears, the Leopard person stood upright and was fully twice as tall as the average Huhui person. Ah 凸 (chu) hastily bowed to the commander and said, "How have you been since we parted, Commander Hua? 凸-◻⊐◻- (chu-lu-ru-mu)."

The Leopard person smiled, revealing two rows of sharp teeth.

"I am Commander Hua, but I don't know you. I'm afraid you must be looking for my brother, who died two years ago in the war with the Serpent people and the Shan. I am now the commander of the LPRA."

"Old friends are passing away one by one," said Ah 凸 (chu), sighing. "It makes one feel so ◙ ◻ (du-wu). So, you're Commander Hua's younger brother—no wonder you look so much alike. My name is Ah 凸 (chu). I knew your brother well, you could say we were close friends. Your brother was so heroic. I remember that he and the Serpent elder Zhi-Hu Zhe warded off an attack by several thousand Serpent warriors. . . ."

"Do me a favor and don't mention my brother," said the Leopard commander angrily. "Isn't it enough that I've had to live my entire life in his shadow? Everyone knows what a hero my brother was, how great he was. It seems unfair to me. He's dead, but people only want to talk about him. My mother cries for him every day. It really gripes me."

Not having expected his fulsome praise to backfire, Ah 出 (chu) smiled broadly. "You look more stalwart than your brother, a born superman. It's only natural that you should take your brother's place as leader of the Leopard people. Congratulations!"

Unexpectedly, these words aroused Commander Hua's ire: "Are you making fun of me, you fatball? I'm a poet and I detest physical activity, but my mother insists that I take my brother's place. Other people may laugh at me, but you have no right to make fun of me!"

Only then did Ah 出 (chu) notice that although this commander was bigger and taller than his brother, he was actually thinner and less robust; by Leopard standards, he was a tall, thin youth. Fortunately, Ah 出 (chu) had a quick mind, and he hastily continued, "A poet and a soldier! The Leopard people have always been known for their martial prowess; now with a leader who is both a scholar and a warrior, they are to be admired even more!"

Hearing this, Commander Hua's anger turned to joy. "I hope to follow the example of the Tai Nan sage, Zhu Geliang, and become a scholar-general," said Commander Hua. "Would you care to hear some of my poetry?"

Before Ah 出 (chu) could reply, there was a commotion behind the Leopard lines. A squad had arrived as reinforcements from the castle at Silverfield. Seeing the fat Leopard woman in charge, Commander Hua let his arms fall to his sides and respectfully said, "Ma, this 出 (chu) person is an old friend of brother's."

Ah 出 (chu) hastened forward, bowed, and said, "Mrs. Hua, 出-卩呷卟 (chu-lu-ru-mu)."

Standing upright, the woman was as tall as her son, but much heavier. Coldly measuring Ah 出 (chu), she replied, "You were a friend of Dalang's?"

"That's right," Ah 出 (chu) replied hastily. "My name is Ah 出 (chu), and your son and I were bosom friends, as close as brothers. We both helped General Shi fight the Shan bastards. At present, the general is leading his cavalry north, and we were hoping that you might help us again to attack Sunlon City and topple Zhihuang Ma's hated regime."

Commander Hua smiled, exposing two rows of sharp teeth. "That's possible," he said. "We don't like Zhihuang Ma either."

"Control yourself!" shouted his mother angrily. Commander Hua immediately shut his mouth. Pointing at the cavalry at the foot of the mountain, she smiled coldly and said, "So the general wishes to cooperate with us? I'm not stupid enough to provide cannon fodder for the Huhui people again. If my oldest son hadn't gone to fight the Shan at Sunlon City, he wouldn't have lost his life in the Hu River. He was wronged!"

So saying, she began to weep. Her son hastily tried to wipe her tears away, but she pushed him away and continued her tirade. "So the general wishes to cooperate with us? Forget it! Every time that old guy goes to war, his horsemen all end up dead. The dead cannot speak, and the living continue to be deceived into thinking that following the general is the ultimate honor. My oldest son died on account of him, and now he's here to trick my second son. My son has never been even one tenth as nimble or fleet of foot as his brother. Since my oldest son couldn't take care of himself, do you think my second son can keep himself alive? Forget it! Forget it!"

Given the situation, Ah 凸 (chu) knew that it was pointless to say anything more. Her son had been humiliated in front of his troops. In an attempt to regain his dignity, he turned his anger on Ah 凸 (chu). As if snatching up a chicken, he grabbed Ah 凸 (chu) and said, "You also had a part in my brother's death. I should eat you so that you can join him."

"There's no need to harm him," shouted his mother. "Let him go. Ah 凸 (chu), go and tell General Shi that under no circumstances will we cooperate with him. As he come a long way, he has my permission to camp at the foot of the mountain tonight, but he must leave tomorrow morning!"

Ah 凸 (chu) had no alternative but to return to camp and report that the Leopard people were unwilling to cooperate. The old general was lying on his litter, mumbling. When he heard the news, he sighed and said, "Heaven has forsaken me." He was already weak, but after the news he fainted from the pain. Miss Qi, who had been looking after him, couldn't keep from weeping. It was Liu Qi who had an idea. He spoke to Miss Qi and Ah 凸 (chu), saying, "It doesn't look as if Silverfield will be able to hold out. Zhihuang Ma's main force is closing in. Ahead there is no way out for us; behind the army is bearing down on us. There's no way that this untrained mob will be able to defeat Zhihuang Ma's crack troops. We have to move, but where? To the north is Mount Huihui; to the west is Leopard territory; to the south is Zhihuang Ma. We can only head east."

"Going east is best," said a dispirited Ah 凸 (chu), suddenly growing excited. "Traditionally, both banks of the Hu River have been Green Snake Brotherhood territory. The Serpent people have also been active there. We can head east along Mount Huihui to the Red Sand River and from there cut south and go around Red Iron Village back to Green Snake Brotherhood territory! As long as we get support from the brotherhood, the cavalry will be able to catch Zhihuang Ma unawares and retake Sunlon City."

Miss Qi knew nothing about military matters, but hearing Ah 🀰 (chu), she at least felt that they had a chance. Liu Qi repeatedly mumbled to himself, saying, "Actually, there is nothing left of the Green Snake Brotherhood, so even if we return to the West Hu River basin, I'm afraid we won't be able to rally many troops. But if we have the support of the locals, we can increase our strength."

"There's still hope," said Miss Qi. "But can the old general hold on that long?"

"I'm not worried about the general," said Liu Qi. "He's a hero and can bear the pain. The question is, will the young people who have arrived stick with us?"

It was a question for which none of them had an answer. But the resonant singing of the young men seemed to answer for them. They didn't know that it had been decided that the cavalry would march east, but once they knew, perhaps they would have even more determination because it was a great opportunity to achieve immortal fame in battle. If the cavalry were able to take the city in one fell swoop after a long march, they would be more than willing, even if it meant their lives. Something then occurred to Miss Qi and she asked Ah 🀰 (chu), "How is it recorded in the complete histories? Does the cavalry stand a chance of succeeding?"

"You know I can't reveal that in advance," said Ah 🀰 (chu), a trifle upset. "I'm an official historian, and it's my responsibility to preserve the integrity of the histories. But even so, since the appearance of the Evil Spirit of time and space, anything is possible. No one knows how this period in history will play out."

Miss Qi recalled the sight of the huge Bronze Statue striding east across the desert. It too was headed for Sunlon City! But here in the mountains there wasn't a trace of the Evil Spirit. It was gradually growing dark and the blue shafts of heavenly light were appearing. The silver smelting furnaces stained the sky red to the northwest. The young cavalrymen had all disappeared into their tents to rest, and the Leopard sentries posted on the mountain to watch them had all withdrawn to the castle at Silverfield. After visiting the general, Miss Qi felt like returning to her own tent. She looked in the direction of the castle and saw a line of fireballs coming rapidly in their direction. She remembered when she last saw such fireballs and quickly wakened Liu Qi and Ah 出 (chu). Liu Qi summoned the cavalrymen with his snake whistle to meet the enemy. The approaching line of fireballs turned out to be a group of Leopard people running on all fours, clutching torches in their mouths. As they neared the cavalry encampment, about thirty of them stood up and took the torches in their right hands. They all shouldered bags. Seeing that they meant no harm, Liu Qi ordered the sentries to allow them in.

Seeing the leader of the Leopard people, Ah 出 (chu) hastened forward and with a deep bow, said, "Welcome, young Commander Hua."

"You're mistaken," replied a woman's voice. "My grandma feared that he might have a mishap on the road at night, so she sent me with some things."

"Then are you . . . old Commander Hua's daughter?" asked Ah 出 (chu), happily. "I'm happy to meet my old friend's daughter. What's your name?"

"My name is Hua Mulan. My grandma wanted me to bring these provisions to you, and she told me to wish you instant success and victory. 出-出-出-出 (chu-lu-ru-mu)."

Hua Mulan then ordered the Leopard people to put down their bags, which were soon piled in a heaping mound. Overjoyed, Liu Qi and Ah 出 (chu) thanked her over and over again. Seeing that she was an odd being with a human head and a leopard's body, but with the face of a lovely and charming young lady, Miss Qi took her by the hand to speak to her. Hua Mulan smiled cleverly and said, "Although my grandma told you to leave, she does sympathize with you. We Leopard people detest Zhihuang Ma, so take your time in leaving. I'll see that the LPRA secretly protects you."

"You're going to protect us?" asked Ah 出 (chu), surprised. "The young Commander Hua is not here, but you are? That's not good."

"My uncle is a poet. What does he know about military matters?" asked Hua Mulan, displeased. "We Leopard people—unlike you Huhui people—have never favored one sex over the other. If you don't appreciate our kindness, then forget it. Let's go!"

The young Leopard girl whistled, and the Leopard people took their torches in their mouths and departed with her in all haste. The line of fireballs meandered up the mountainside to the castle at Silverfield and disappeared. Ah 出 (chu) and Miss Qi couldn't help but heave a sigh. Liu Qi gave orders for the Green Snake warriors to gather up the provisions brought by the Leopard people and divide them among the cavalry officers and men. After each man received ten days' provisions, morale improved greatly and in spite of the darkness they once more began to sing, awakening the general. He asked some soldiers to help him outside for a look. Liu Qi reported that the Leopard people had delivered supplies; the general nodded and said, "I knew that the Leopard people would maintain the appearance of neutrality while secretly helping us. Now that we have sufficient provisions, I propose to lead the army east, training the men as we go. There's no way Zhihuang Ma would expect the cavalry to enter the mountains. Since we have more men than horses, it will actually be as easy to take the mountain road as a flat road. Once we take Fort Ever Peaceful, we'll have nothing to fear from Zhihuang Ma."

Hearing the general, Liu Qi was gladdened and said, "The general discerns things like a prophet. I believe our only road is to the east. We'd best leave early in the morning so that when Zhihuang Ma's troops arrive they will come up empty-handed."

Liu Qi was a gifted officer who did what he said. That very night he organized each cavalry company. When the purple sun rose slowly in the east beyond Mount Huihui, the cavalry was ready to enter the mountains.

Since the mountain road was narrow, Liu Qi positioned the men without horses in the center to proceed one by one, with the horsemen at both ends to protect them. The Green Snake Brotherhood warriors brought up the rear. The cavalry battalion from Jinjiakou followed the main force at some distance. As Liu Qi saw it, Zhihuang Ma's troops would come from the south and would meet with resistance from the cavalry battalion, allowing for the withdrawal of his main force.

Shortly after the troops entered the mountains, the situation took a turn for the worse. One of Zhihuang Ma's airships discovered their position and circled above them. It frequently dropped bombs, and although no men or animals were lost, the troops were forced to slow their pace. Liu Qi swore loudly, lamenting his lack of Gaiwenese Froghoppers and his inability to do anything about the airship.

The airship followed them the entire day and departed only at dusk. The general then ordered the men to quick march, making camp late at night. But on the following day the airship reappeared, dropping bombs to harass them, thereby ruining the general's plan to train the men as they marched. When night fell, they once again quick marched, but couldn't shake the airship. Men and beasts were exhausted, and as they marched through the night, some men fell and were killed. Morale started to decline and a few men ran away. Knowing that the situation was grave, Miss Qi urged the general to do something, saying, "You can't keep marching the troops every night. If you do, a lot of people won't be able to take it; they will become discouraged and run away."

"They joined me of their own free will," said the general with a bitter laugh. "I can't stop them if they want to leave. Marching by night is a form of training."

"It won't do," said Miss Qi, anxiously. "If you continue with this forced march, the army will scatter. Then how will you retake Sunlon City?"

"Young lady, you are always very opinionated. Okay, we'll stop. Do you have any good ideas?"

"Let's find a good place to hide," replied Miss Qi without stopping to think. "Since the airship is able to locate us each day, we must have a spy in our midst. Let the men rest a couple of days while we find and eliminate the spy. Then the airship won't be able to find us."

"Good idea! We'll do as you say."

That night the general halted the march and sent out a scouting party to locate a secluded valley where he concealed the army in a dense wood. Ah 出 (chu) did his utmost to help Liu Qi eliminate the spy. It didn't take him long to find a young man with a bronze tag in their midst. It was none other than #56 of the Yellow Scarves, whom they had seen once before in Sunlon City. Ah 出 (chu) snatched away the bronze tag, but even then the young man would not admit his guilt. Liu Qi wanted to execute him then and there, but Miss Qi intervened.

"Why kill him? Without his bronze tag, he has no way to contact the airship. And Zhihuang Ma has no way to locate him." Liu Qi saw that she was right. He spared #56 and released him in the dense wood.

The cavalry rested in the valley for three days, and the airship never was able to locate them. After rest, morale was improving. When the general felt well, he'd call together a number of swordsmen for some training. But his body grew weaker, and he fainted from the pain several times each day. No one knew the score except Miss Qi, Liu Qi, Ah 出 (chu), and a couple of trusted Green Snake warriors. Watching the general grow weaker, Miss Qi became very anxious. Having been with him for some time, she discovered that in many respects he was much like her dada. Although on the surface he was stubborn, she could easily talk him around. Both the general and her dada loved the Huhui planet and would sacrifice anything for it. In only one respect did they differ: the general was possessed of a deep sense of guilt. Since he had no children, he frequently felt despondent about himself. He treated Miss Qi like his own daughter. Even when he was in the worst pain, it only took a few words from Miss Qi to set him smiling like a child.

After their rest in the valley, the general decided to continue eastward. The men only had three or four days of provisions left and they were at least two days from Red Sand River, so they had to be on their way. Fortunately, they were not followed by the airship and the march proceeded smoothly. With Liu Qi leading the troops, they reached the river on the afternoon of the following day. He at once ordered the men to cut wood to make rafts with which to cross the river.

Miss Qi walked with the Green Snake warriors bringing up the rear, and they reached the river that evening. She saw that the river did in fact run red and rapid. She stood on the bank and gazed into the distance. Suddenly someone came up behind her and covered her mouth. She struggled with all her might. The person whispered to her, saying, "Don't panic, Miss Qi. I came especially to save you."

10

Mount Huihui was located 800 kilometers north of Sunlon City, and was the source of the East and West Hu rivers. It was rich in mineral deposits and timber, especially fir, juniper, and black wood. The largest iron mine on the Huhui planet was located near Red Iron Village. Red Iron Village had a population of 120,000 and was the economic center of the north.

North of Red Iron village, up the West Hu River, stood Mount Huihui. Fort Ever Peaceful was located 35 kilometers from the village. At that point, the river branched into two tributaries: the Red Sand River and the Huning River. The Red Sand River was so named because of the large amount of red sand it carried. The Huning River originated at the North Gate of Heaven and was the true source of the Hu River. Fort Ever Peaceful had a population slightly in excess of 10,000. It was situated on a hill overlooking the river. Farther north from the fort was the home of one of the Huhui planet's three indigenous peoples, the Feathered people. Historically, troops were always stationed at Fort Ever Peaceful to prevent their southward expansion. For this reason, it was a city of strategic importance in the north.

From Silverfield, General Shi's cavalry transversed Mount Huihui at great risk and difficulty to arrive at the western bank of the Red Sand River. Their aim was to force a crossing of the river and capture Fort Ever Peaceful. Once it was in the hands of the general, his cavalry could control the West Hu River Basin and be like a dagger at the throat of Sunlon

City. Even if the cavalry didn't immediately head south, they could entrench themselves at the fort, rest, and ready themselves for the enemy's attack and work in conjunction with the Leopard people to the west and the Gaiwenese to the south to keep Zhihuang Ma's troops constantly on the run.

Such was the general's ideal plan. Although they lost four days to the harassment by the airship on Mount Huihui, their massing on the western bank of the Red Sand River had come off rather smoothly. When they arrived at the riverbank in the evening, the eastern shore was quiet. Liu Qi ordered his men to cut trees along the river for the making of rafts to force a crossing of the river the following day. The soldiers cut down the trees, dragged them to the riverbank, and lashed them together with sea serpent sinew. By nightfall they had constructed sixty rafts.

Miss Qi stood gazing from a high point on the riverbank when someone covered her mouth with his left hand, held a knife to her heart with his right hand, and dragged her into the woods. She fell to the ground and was released. Miss Qi recognized him; it was none other than Yellow Scarf #56, the young man whose life she had saved just a few days earlier.

"Why have you come back, #56?"

"I've returned to save you," he replied, pointing at her chest with his knife. "You'll stay alive only if you come with me."

"Nonsense! Even if you killed me, I wouldn't go with you."

"Please don't choose your own destruction," implored the young man. "The cavalry is finished. Do you think they will get across the river? You have no idea how many men and horses are waiting on the other side to slaughter the cavalry. Wait and see. Tomorrow the river will flow red with blood and not sand."

Startled, Miss Qi struggled to her feet and said, "Kill me. If you don't I'll go warn everyone. You have to kill me."

She stood without fear of death. The young man hurled his knife to the ground and said, "You saved my life, so I'll spare you. ᠴᠠ ᠬᠠ (qia-xia) my bronze tag has been destroyed, so I won't be spared by Field Marshal Ma. I've got to run for my life to the farthest corner of the world. Take care of yourself. ᠴᠤ ᠯᠤ ᠷᠤ ᠮᠤ (chu-lu-ru-mu)!"

Without further ado, #56 took to his heels and fled into the wood. With scarcely a forethought, Miss Qi hurried to the riverbank and told Liu Qi what #56 had said. "The cavalry can't cross the river! It's too dangerous."

"It would be dangerous if there were troops waiting in ambush on the opposite shore," muttered Liu Qi. "But what if it's a plot on the part of

#56? He secretly tailed us and discovered our plan to cross the river but didn't have time to inform Zhihuang Ma. That's why he warned you."

"Then," replied Miss Qi, flushing, "I was taken in by him."

"Not necessarily," said Liu Qi. "We had best seek the opinion of the general and see what he has to say."

The general's tent, which was guarded by eight Green Snake warriors, had been pitched in a clearing by the wood. Ah 出 (chu) helped support the general as he sat in front of his tent. His eyes were closed; his face was pale and large beads of sweat stood out on his forehead.

"What's wrong?" asked Miss Qi, alarmed. "He was fine a moment ago, wasn't he?"

"He's not so good," said Ah 出 (chu), shaking his head. "The pain was coming every hour or so. Now it's continuous. Luckily, the old general can take it."

Miss Qi couldn't help but weep. The general opened his eyes and said, "It doesn't matter. Liu Qi, is everything ready?"

"Everything is ready, but something has happened." Liu Qi then related what #56 had told Miss Qi.

"Pay him no mind," said the general, smiling with his eyes closed. "There was once a military genius in Tai Nan by the name of Zhu Geliang who used an empty city strategy to frighten an enemy army into retreating. Young #56 wanted to trick us by using the same strategy, but I won't be taken in."

"With a word you have revealed his scheme!" said Liu Qi happily. "I had the same thought. Even with supernatural speed, Zhihuang Ma couldn't possibly send a huge army to reinforce Fort Ever Peaceful in two or three days. We'll stick to our original plan and cross the river tomorrow."

Miss Qi began to have doubts when she heard what the two of them had to say. She then questioned Ah 出 (chu).

"Ah 出 (chu), I know you are not willing to reveal the secrets of the complete histories, but can you tell me if the cavalry will be successful in crossing the river tomorrow? It's important. Don't lie to me. Will the cavalry be successful in crossing the river?"

"General Shi should have died in the war against the Shan and Serpent people, but he didn't. Once an error has crept into the histories, then all entries could be incorrect."

"I'm not concerned about erroneous entries," said Miss Qi unreasonably. "Just tell me and let me decide."

"Miss, I'm an official historian, I can't . . ."

"So what? Wasn't Dada your master? Didn't he put me in your care before he left us? Tomorrow the cavalry is going to cross the river, and I want to join them. If I die, it will be because you concealed the historical facts and prevented me from making the right decision. My death would be on your hands. Would that be any way to repay Dada?"

Miss Qi scared Ah 出 (chu) out of his wits. Hastily he knelt and said, "How can I forsake my master's last wish? You're putting me in a very difficult position; I don't deserve such responsibility."

"In that case, be quick about it and speak up."

"Okay, I'll tell you," said Ah 出 (chu), figuring he couldn't make any excuses. "Anyway, the complete histories are undone, so even if I do reveal heaven's design, I won't be breaking my oath as an official historian."

"No one is going to blame you," said Miss Qi. "Hurry up and tell me."

"There is no record in the histories of General Shi leading the cavalry across the river. This is only natural, because he was said to have perished in the war against the Serpent people and the Shan. So how could he lead the cavalry across the river? But someone else did."

"Really? Who?" asked Miss Qi and Liu Qi at the same time. Even General Shi opened his eyes a bit.

"Gai Bo."

"Gai Bo?" said Miss Qi, unable to keep from laughing. "Are you sure?"

"Yes, Gai Bo," said Ah 出 (chu) in all seriousness. "According to the histories, Zhihuang Ma sent troops to attack New Menghan City, killing nearly all the inhabitants. Led by Gai Bo, those who survived wandered west with Zhihuang Ma's troops in pursuit. Gai Bo fled to Mount Huihui and eventually to Red Sand River."

"So that's how it was," said Miss Qi. "Did he cross the river successfully?"

"Yes. He and the Gaiwenese occupied Fort Ever Peaceful. From there they sailed downriver and hooked up with the Serpent people and attacked Sunlon City. Gai Bo and most of the Gaiwenese died in battle, but the Serpent people finally captured the city. After the Serpent people massacred the inhabitants, the Anliu Era of Huhui civilization came to an end."

Everyone pondered Ah 出 (chu)'s words. Finally the general broke the silence. "I understand now. I'm taking Gai Bo's place. It's me that has been wandering and not Gai Bo; I'll be the one to cross the river, not

Gai Bo. That being the case, I'll be the one to retake the city and not Gai Bo." The general's voice trembled with excitement. "That means there is still hope for Huhui civilization. If I don't link up with the Serpent people, then it'll be the cavalry that attacks the city. It won't matter who is successful. Since both sides will be Huhui people, the massacre of the city inhabitants can be avoided. If we can succeed in overthrowing Zhihuang Ma's regime, the Huhui planet may again see halcyon days!"

The general grew more excited as he spoke. Infected by his enthusiasm, Ah 凸 (chu) stood up, bowed, and said, "General, I feel guilty for having revealed the secrets of the histories. Since history has unraveled, if the general can rewrite this stage, then the future of the Huhui planet can well be completely altered!"

"What's left to say?" asked Liu Qi. "The future of the Huhui planet rests with us! Though flowers and fruit must fall, scattered by the wind, Sunlon City will be reborn!"

Miss Qi was gladdened to see the three of them so happy. But she saw the general close his eyes and sweat break out on his forehead. She spoke hastily to Liu Qi and Ah 凸 (chu), saying, "The general is tired, let him rest."

She helped the general into his tent to lie down. His entire frame shuddered with pain, but he made not a sound. The sight saddened Miss Qi. She came out and said to Ah 凸 (chu), "Can you give him any medicine?"

Ah 凸 (chu) shook his head. "Once the poison from the pills takes effect, nothing can be done for it. The general only has about another month to live."

"By then, I hope we'll be in Sunlon City—then he can die in peace." Hearing Ah 凸 (chu)'s words, Miss Qi felt that there wouldn't be any problem in getting to the city. "Are you sad about the histories being destroyed?"

"Of course I am, but I also feel relieved," said Ah 凸 (chu) as he gave a pill to Miss Qi. "Tomorrow we're going to cross the river. It's cold by the waterside. Take one of these to ward off any illness."

Miss Qi took the pill as she was told and lay down outside the tent. The pill Ah 凸 (chu) gave her soon took effect, and her whole body felt hot, dispelling all cold. Miss Qi was lulled to sleep listening to the faint sound of the swiftly flowing Red Sand River.

It was already light when she awakened. She leaped up only to find that the general's tent was nowhere in sight, and the Green Snake Brotherhood guards were gone. She realized what Ah ㄓ (chu) had done. Surprised and angered in turn, she quickly made her way to the riverbank. All the rafts were gone. Then she heard shouts coming from the river.

The three thousand soldiers, fifty to a raft, were rowing across the river to the eastern shore. The two thousand horsemen rode their horses across. Miss Qi saw that Liu Qi and the general were on the lead raft directing the crossing. Beside them the drummer forcefully beat the war drum.

"Hey, wait for me!" shouted Miss Qi, waving vigorously to attract their attention.

"They can't hear you," came a voice from behind her. "Even if they could, they couldn't turn back for you."

"Ah ㄓ (chu), this is your doing!" said Miss Qi angrily. "Why did you do it?"

Miss Qi's rebuke inspired laughter rather than fear in Ah ㄓ (chu).

"Don't be angry. Once the soldiers have succeeded in crossing the river, they will immediately send a raft back for us. We won't have long to wait."

The horsemen who had swum the river with their mounts reached the eastern bank. Just as the first wave of cavalry reached the shore, gunfire broke out from the wood. The leading horsemen began to fall into the water.

At first, Miss Qi and Ah ㄓ (chu) didn't know why the soldiers were falling. A few seconds later they heard the gunfire. Miss Qi was stunned, but a moment later found her voice and shouted: "It's an ambush. There's an ambush in the woods. How are we going to get word to the general?"

Each succeeding wave of horsemen was mowed down by gunfire, with only a few retreating back into the river. By that time, the sixty rafts were nearing the shore. The soldiers began leaping into the water to avoid being hit. They swam to shore and crawled onto land. A group of soldiers charged into the wood and engaged the enemy. Others took advantage of the situation to haul the rafts up on the beach to serve as temporary cover. The horsemen, who had suffered the heaviest casualties, finally made it ashore and regrouped behind the rafts. Liu Qi carried the general ashore to the command post on the beach. One fearless Royalist raised a yellow banner with the general's name on it next to the command headquarters, greatly boosting morale.

Liu Qi unsheathed his sword and shouted, "Brothers, charge!"

The soldiers leaped from behind the barricade and, shouting, charged toward the wood. The remaining horsemen formed two groups, flanking left and right.

But it was only then that the enemy troops that lay in ambush showed their real strength. Nearly ten thousand fully armed troops from Zhihuang Ma's army came out of the wood to fight hand to hand. Suddenly, two airships appeared, coming along the Red Sand River. They dropped bombs on the beachhead. The cavalry fought with their backs to the water.

Their hearts burned as they watched the fighting from the opposite shore. Miss Qi wept profusely, regretting that #56's warning had not been heeded. She also rebuked Ah 凸 (chu) for saying that the river crossing had been successful and thus leading the old general and Liu Qi to underestimate the enemy and thereby do themselves harm.

Distraught, Ah 凸 (chu) sighed and said, "The complete histories said that only Gai Bo successfully crossed the river. They said nothing about the general. How was I supposed to know?"

"You've put them in grave danger!" said Miss Qi, giving Ah 凸 (chu) a shove. "What are we going to do? Can they get back?"

Before long, the outcome of the battle was clear: nearly all of the five thousand soldiers had been killed or wounded. A few had retreated to the beachhead position, swearing to defend the general unto death. But the two airships made a number of passes, dropping bombs. Unlike the wood, the beach provided no cover, and the soldiers were blown to bits. Gunfire ensued and the general's banner was toppled. One swordsman took up the flag and was immediately gunned down. Another took his place, only to meet the same fate. At that moment, a blood-soaked Liu Qi appeared. He hoisted the general on his back, took the flag, and, roaring, ran for the river and dove in. Seeing this, the other swordsmen knew that the tide had turned against them, and they too leaped into the river, ending their lives. Others ended their lives with their own guns. Soon the river ran red with blood. In less than two hours, the awe-inspiring cavalry had been annihilated on the banks of the Red Sand River.

Witnessing the demise of the cavalry, Miss Qi and Ah 凸 (chu) had no tears left to weep. They dropped to the ground. Shortly, Zhihuang Ma's army fell in and departed. The airships disappeared. The Red Sand River regained its peaceful calm.

"How could it have happened?" asked Miss Qi. "For the general to die that way and for the army to have vanished like mist and smoke. How is it possible?"

"According to the complete histories," said Ah 出 (chu), sighing, "the general should have died in the war with the Shan and Serpent people, but in fact, he died crossing the river. It seems that the errors in the histories are being corrected. Perhaps each generation thinks that it masters history, but each generation in fact rewrites history. One historical necessity is replaced by another, and thereby loses its necessity."

"I don't want to hear any more of your damned theories!" said Miss Qi angrily. "All theories are lies for fooling oneself and others."

"The general might still be alive in spite of having fallen in the river," said Ah 出 (chu) to comfort her. "Liu Qi jumped into the river with the general on his back. Given Liu Qi's ability to swim, they might very well be safe. The cavalry always rises from the ashes like a phoenix; only after they are destroyed can they rise again."

"What are we going to do?"

"Do?" muttered Ah 出 (chu). "Good question. Let's return to Sunlon City."

Back to Sunlon City, Miss Qi thought, back to her birthplace. Even if she were a complete stranger there, it was still home. Back to Sunlon City.

They looked once again at the Red Sand River. The gunsmoke was disappearing over the water; the blood had flowed away; and a single raft floated back toward them.

"This is the raft to carry us to Sunlon City," said Ah 出 (chu). "Let's go."

The pudgy 出 (chu) person leaped onto it. Miss Qi hesitated a moment and then followed suit.

They drifted downstream on the raft, soon passing Fort Ever Peaceful, where the soldiers were celebrating their victory over the cavalry by shooting off fireworks. Where the Red Sand River conjoined with the Huning River to form the Hu River, the water grew turbulent. The speed of the raft increased, and by dusk they had passed Red Iron Village. Miss Qi lay curled up on the raft, unable to speak for the loneliness she felt. Ah 出 (chu), who held an oar and stood at the prow of the raft, was also silent. The sky gradually grew dark and the raft sped on. The water splashed continuously on Miss Qi and, although she felt cold, she drifted off to sleep.

Vaguely she heard Ah 出 (chu) calling to her, "Wake up, wake up."

Startled, she awakened. The raft had become stuck amid reeds and had to be freed. Miss Qi thought that Ah 凸 (chu) had awakened her for that purpose, but he indicated that she should look off to her left.

In the weak light, a huge human form strode ahead of them.

"The Evil Spirit of time and space!" whispered Miss Qi. "Like us, he's hurrying to Sunlon City! How far are we?"

"We're on the tributary of the West Hu River, and can't be too far from Sunart bulu," said Ah 凸 (chu). "We literally returned over a thousand kilometers of river in one day. But the Evil Spirit is faster than we are."

"Don't you think that the Evil Spirit of time and space is the Bronze Statue?"

Ah 凸 (chu) didn't reply, but merely said, "Hurry up. The appearance of the evil spirit means that Sunlon City is in danger."

By the time they made their way through the reeds to the shore, they had no idea which way the evil spirit had gone. Ah 凸 (chu) anxiously urged Miss Qi to hurry on. They were in a rural area north of the city. It was harvest time, and the Huhui farmers labored in the fields under the purple sun. They sang folksongs as they loaded sheaves of wheat onto a large truck. Miss Qi and Ah 凸 (chu) walked on a small road through the fields. The farmers waved to them, and Miss Qi stopped to ask, "凸-口-凸 (chu-lu-ru-mu). Have you seen the Evil Spirit of time and space? Have you seen a giant come this way?"

The farmers nodded. A young woman stuck out her tongue and said, "He was huge and frightened us to death. But strangely, when he walked through the wheat fields, he didn't disturb a single grain."

"Which way did he go?" asked Ah 凸 (chu) hastily.

The farmers pointed in the direction of Sunlon City.

"Yesterday, the Serpent people came through here," said an old farmer. "And today it was the giant. Don't know what sort of trouble is brewing in the city."

"There were Serpent people here too?" asked Ah 凸 (chu) anxiously. "How many of them?"

The old farmer shook his head. "No idea. Never saw that many before. They all carried half pikes. If you two are thinking about going to the city, by all means be careful."

Miss Qi thanked the farmers, and the two of them continued on their way. The closer they got to the capital, the fewer the number of farmers in the fields. Some fields had only been half harvested, but not a soul was in sight. Miss Qi felt 凸 口 (chu-ru), and said to Ah 凸 (chu), "Huhui farmers are the most industrious. How could they just quit harvesting?"

"There are two possible explanations," said Ah 出 (chu). "First, they might have been pressed into service by Zhihuang Ma; or second, they might have been captured by the Serpent people. . . ."

Before Ah 出 (chu) had finished speaking, he cried out in alarm and fell into a trap in the field. Miss Qi tried to catch him, but she missed his hand. Anxiously, she called out to him over and over again.

11

Not a sound was heard after Ah 凸 (chu) fell into the trap.

"Are you okay?" Miss Qi shouted anxiously.

"Don't worry, Ah 凸 (chu) isn't seriously hurt. Let's be friends."

Miss Qi looked up and saw three big Gaiwenese, and gasped, saying, "Gai Bao, what are you doing here?"

Of course Gai Bao was the leader of the three, and he ordered the other two to pull the net up out of the trap in which Ah 凸 (chu) was entangled. It took Miss Qi and Gai Bao quite a bit of time to extricate him. Opening his eyes wide, Ah 凸 (chu) said, "Gai Bao, 凸-口ㅁ- (chu-lu-ru-mu). I presume Gai Bo is here too."

"Right," said Gai Bao. "Not only Gai Bo, but all the surviving Gaiwenese are here to avenge the massacred Gaiwenese."

"Avenge the massacred Gaiwenese?" asked Miss Qi. "Then Zhihuang Ma took New Menghan City?"

Gai Bao nodded as he wept, as did his two subordinates. "All our gaibao and gaisong were butchered by Zhihuang Ma," replied Gai Bao angrily. "This is the worst catastrophe to befall us since our planet was vaporized. But this time we have no place to flee to. This is it for us. Zhihuang Ma bathed New Menghan City in blood, so we'll do the same in Sunlon City!"

Miss Qi's heart was pounding. She knew this was the final vengeance of the Gaiwenese and was overcome with sadness. "The people of Sunlon

City are innocent; you should not vent your anger on them. The guilt is Zhihuang Ma's."

"The people of New Menghan City were innocent too, but they were all killed. What else can be said?" asked Gai Bao. "The Gaiwenese have been exterminated and are finished as a people. Even if all the Huhui people in Sunlon City were killed, it wouldn't mean the end of the Huhui. Is that fair?"

Miss Qi made no reply. Only after they arrived at the Gaiwenese camp outside the city did she understand what Gai Bao meant by the Gaiwenese being exterminated. Of the entire Gaiwenese army, fewer than two hundred soldiers remained, and they all looked sorely grieved. Twenty Froghoppers were parked in front of the camp, all that remained of the Gaiwenese air force. Gai Bo was talking with his soldiers when he saw them arrive. The three of them wept together. Wiping his tears away, Gai Bo said, "You're just in time. I'm sending the Froghoppers in to bomb Sunlon City, after which we'll attack. Please inform the general that it would be best if the cavalry attacked at the same time."

"I'm afraid that won't be possible," said Miss Qi, relating how the cavalry had been defeated by Zhihuang Ma's army after crossing the Red Sand River.

Everything suddenly became clear to Gai Bo. "No wonder Zhihuang Ma's army lost no time in leaving right after the massacre—they had to fight the general! Too bad New Menghan City couldn't hold out another two days; otherwise Zhihuang Ma wouldn't have had the time to move his troops and defeat us and the general. We'll deal with him as he has dealt with us. We're going to attack his old lair while his main force is still at Fort Ever Peaceful, and when he least expects it."

Ah 出 (chu) bowed and said, "Old Bo, I don't want to belittle the ambitions and dignity of others, but can you really hope to take Sunlon City with fewer than two hundred Gaiwenese?"

"We Gaiwenese are determined to die fighting," said Gai Bo angrily, his skin turning red. "Who can stop us? Besides, the Gaiwenese are not the only ones looking for revenge. Look."

He pointed to the open country to the south, where three thousand Serpent people swarmed, hissing. The leader, a huge green Serpent person, saw Gai Bo, Gai Bao, Miss Qi, and Ah 出 (chu), but paid no attention to any save Ah 出 (chu). "Ma!" he said.

Startled, Ah 出 (chu) gave the huge Serpent person the once over. The Serpent laughed and said, "Ma, don't you recognize me? It's me, Ah You."

"Ah You!" Ah 出 (chu) sighed. "I never dreamed you'd grow to be so big. As a mother, I'm quite embarrassed. Are you here for revenge too?"

"That's right," said Ah You. "After the Serpent elder Zhi-Hu Zhe died in the war against the Shan and Serpent people, Zhihuang Ma poisoned all the Serpent women and children in the name of entertaining the troops. He thought he could do away with the Serpent people once and for all. We've waited a long time for this day. We won't stop until we have Zhihuang Ma's head."

"Indignation and discontent with Zhihuang Ma are widespread," said Gai Bo, nodding. "His end is near, just wait and see."

He pointed to the north, where rows of Leopard people were approaching, strong and vigorous. At their head was Hua Mulan, the young woman Miss Qi had seen once at Silverfield.

"We said that we would secretly protect General Shi," said Hua Mulan to Miss Qi. "We never expected that he would cross the river and die in battle. I'm so ashamed that I've led the crack Leopard troops here to avenge the general. But that's not all—I've also enlisted another group of friends."

Hua Mulan pointed to a flock of rapidly flying eagles. Thirty-plus Feathered people alighted before them.

"Serpent, Leopard, Feathered peoples, and Gaiwenese are all here!" Gai Bo laughed. "Let's be friends. The indigenous peoples of the Huhui planet have been oppressed and used by the Huhui people for a long time. We should have awakened a long time ago. It is the day to right all wrongs and to wreak vengeance. Take Zhihuang Ma alive! Bathe Sunlon City in blood!"

Gai Bo raised his arms and shouted, and the two hundred Gaiwenese shouted with him; the Serpent, Leopard, and Feathered people joined in. Miss Qi had never seen so many of the odd peoples together, and she felt ill at ease.

Gai Bo continued to shout, "Friends, the decisive battle is at hand; the trumpet to counterattack has sounded! Let me now assign duties: the Serpent people will lead the main attack since their numbers are greatest; the Leopard people will be responsible for the right flank; and the Gaiwenese will assist from the left. The Feathered people and the squadron of Froghoppers will deal with Zhihuang Ma's airships. Forward! Forward!"

Tears streaming from his three eyes, Ah You said to Ah 出 (chu), "I'm going now, Ma. I planted a bomb at the mouth of the Serpent lair at the copper fields. If we all die in battle and anyone tries to enter the lair, they will be blown to bits and the world of the Serpent people will be closed forever."

"It has not been easy for us to meet, and now we must part again," said Ah 出 (chu) sadly. "Take care. 出-刂-卩-卟 (chu-lu-ru-mu)."

The huge Serpent person sobbed, as did his companions who followed him, as he rushed toward Sunlon City. Hua Mulan set off with the Leopard people, and Gai Bo prepared to lead the Gaiwenese.

"Gai Bo," said Miss Qi, "I have one request. Let Ah 出 (chu) and me take a Froghopper and return first to the city."

"Sunlon City is on the brink of disaster," replied Gai Bo, surprised. "What do you intend to do? Keep in mind that weapons don't have eyes and no one can guarantee your safety inside the city."

"I understand," said Miss Qi. "But Sunlon City is my home, and I must go back."

Miss Qi looked at Ah 出 (chu). He lowered his head but didn't offer any opposition.

"I know how you feel," said Gai Bo, sighing. "Even if the Serpent people and the Gaiwenese capture the city, there is no way to reverse our fate of extinction. I hope you understand our feelings as well."

Gai Bo then gave orders to the pilots, and Miss Qi and Ah 出 (chu) each boarded one Froghopper and set off with the rest of the squadron. As each Froghopper leaped away, the thirty Feathered people took to the air. As they neared Sunlon City, three airships suddenly appeared. The Froghoppers attracted the notice of the airships from the front while the Feathered people sneaked up behind, entered the cockpits, and hurled out the pilots. The poor Huhui people screamed as they fell to their bloody deaths. The Feathered people then steered the airships into the city wall, where they exploded, leaving three large gaps. The Serpent people, Leopard people, and Gaiwenese climbed in through the gaps and killed the guards.

In the chaos, the two Froghoppers carrying Ah 出 (chu) and Miss Qi leaped into the city, landing in the square before the Golden Palace. After leaving their cargo, the two Froghoppers hopped away. The huge square was empty and no one guarded the Golden Palace. Ah 出 (chu) and Miss Qi ascended the stone steps.

"Zhihuang Ma's troops have all run away," said Ah 出 (chu), panting. "So imposing yesterday, but besieged on all sides today. Indeed, the wheel of fortune turns from prosperity to decline."

They entered the broad Audience Hall. A solitary individual in full armor sat upright and solemn on the golden throne.

"Zhihuang Ma," shouted Miss Qi angrily. "What are you doing sitting here? The Serpent people, Leopard people, Feathered people, and Gaiwenese are attacking the city. This disaster is all your doing! Why don't you go and plead for peace? Do you want all the people of the city to sacrifice themselves for you?"

Regardless of how she reviled him, Zhihuang Ma made no reply. Approaching the throne, they saw that his eyes stared straight ahead and that he was pallid. Miss Qi gasped in alarm.

"Zhihuang Ma is already dead," said someone behind the throne. "He knew that the tide had changed, so he killed himself as a show of regret to the populace of the city."

"Supreme One," said Ah 出 (chu), bowing. "So it was you who was pulling the strings. I discovered that the complete histories had lost their validity when General Shi survived the war against the Serpent people and the Shan. I figured you were also still alive."

The cult leader appeared from behind the throne. "Could I die if the Huhui planet has yet to be united?" he said, laughing. Miss Qi found the cult leader's hideous face familiar, but for the moment couldn't say where she had seen it.

"You killed Zhihuang Ma, though he did deserve it," said Miss Qi angrily. "But the people of Sunlon City are innocent. Don't you see that they will certainly be massacred by the indigenous peoples?"

"What do you know?" snorted the cult leader contemptuously. "The Green Snake Brotherhood and the cavalry have been wiped out; the Serpent people and the Gaiwenese are as good as extinct; and the Leopard people and the Feathered people are no worry. This is the result of my clever tricks. This is the final struggle. The Huhui people will unite to win, and the cult will rule all under heaven and the history of the Huhui planet will be rewritten."

"Everyone will be dead," said Miss Qi. "What good will it do to rule all under heaven?"

"Fear only the unexpected. Follow me."

The cult leader strode out of the Golden Palace. Miss Qi and Ah 出 (chu) followed closely. There under the purple sun, in the middle of the square, stood a huge Bronze Statue, like some ancient buddha from time immemorial.

"Look, the Bronze Statue has at last returned." The cult leader laughed insanely. "This is not one of my tricks, an illusion from a projector. This is the Bronze Statue! The ancient prophecies were correct—the Bronze

Statue has indeed returned to lead the valiant soldiers in the Fifth Interstellar War!"

"Most honored cult leader," said Ah 凸 (chu) hastily, "don't be mistaken. This is not the real statue, this is the demonic image of the Evil Spirit of time and space."

This was the first time that Miss Qi ever heard Ah 凸 (chu) admit that the Bronze Statue was the Evil Spirit. She couldn't believe her ears.

"Oh man of little faith," said the cult leader, again laughing insanely, "the Bronze Statue exists beyond time and space. Some mistake it for the Evil Spirit. But the Bronze Statue is none other than the spirit of Sunlon City itself!" He strode toward the statue.

"The Bronze Statue is not the spirit of Sunlon City," called Ah 凸 (chu) behind him. "It's the original sin of the city."

The cult leader appeared not to hear. He walked before the statue and lifted his arms. The statue seemed to hear his prayer, for suddenly it reached out, grabbed the cult leader, and stuffed him into its mouth. The cult leader was not seen to struggle but was swallowed whole by the statue.

"Run, Miss!" Ah 凸 (chu) and Miss Qi turned and ran toward the Golden Palace. They could hear the insane laughter of the cult leader.

"Oh man of little faith, I am the spirit of Sunlon City, as well as its original sin. On account of me, the lives of the Huhui people have meaning. I will lead the Huhui people in conquest of the universe, and wash away all past shame. Though flowers and fruit must fall, scattered by the wind, Sunlon City will be reborn!"

"We don't need you!" shouted Miss Qi. "You are a lifeless thing; you never existed. Why do you want to control our lives? You are not the spirit of Sunlon City. We don't need you!"

The Evil Spirit of time and space roared in anger, and as it did so, the entire palace shook. It roared again, and the purple sun suddenly vanished and a black mist rolled in outside the palace.

"We don't need you!" shouted Miss Qi. "Be gone!"

A voice from within the mist seemed to reply, but vaguely and unclearly, "Although . . . flowers . . . and . . . fruit . . . must . . . fall . . . scattered . . . by . . . will . . . be . . . reborn."

The black mist began to vanish; the purple sun reappeared through the gray smoke and the ground ceased to tremble. Cautiously, Miss Qi and Ah 凸 (chu) came out of the palace. The square was empty, with no trace of the statue.

"It's gone," said Ah 出 (chu), scarcely able to believe it. "The Evil Spirit is really gone."

Miss Qi knew that if the Evil Spirit was gone, the Bronze Statue was gone for good, never to reappear on the Huhui planet. Ah 出 (chu) flopped down on the ground and slowly spoke. "The Evil Spirit really is gone."

"Of course it is," came a voice. "This passage through time and space has been repaired, at least for the moment. The fissure in time and space has been stopped up, and the Evil Spirit won't be coming back. At least not in this time and place in history."

Hearing the voice, Miss Qi knew at once that it belonged to Mei Xin. The blond-haired girl from the future smiled and walked toward them. "The Evil Spirit is a tough one. It nearly destroyed this part of history, changing the entire future of the Huhui planet. But it was defeated."

"Does its defeat mean the end of Sunlon City?" asked Miss Qi in spite of herself. Mei Xin hung her head and made no reply. Miss Qi asked once more.

"The Serpent people have already begun the attack, right?" she replied helplessly. "My boyfriend Wang Xin is also on the wall, taking part in the final defense. He plans to stay."

"What about you?"

"I'm staying too."

Miss Qi looked at this small woman and felt sorry for her. She took her by the hand and said, "Little fool. We were fated to be born in Sunlon City and can never escape. But why trouble yourself?"

"He is staying, so I am staying," said Mei Xin calmly. "At least if we are both here, no one can separate us."

Miss Qi wanted to ask Ah 出 (chu) again about the end of Sunlon City. He sat on the ground, staring blankly as if nothing mattered. She knew there was no point in asking him again.

Why bother? The end was already clear. The Gaiwenese Froghoppers were dropping bombs on the city, and many parts were already burning; the fire was spreading from roof to roof. Half the sky was red and people were crying, fleeing in all directions. Mei Xin let go of Miss Qi's hand and said, "It looks bad. The city will soon be destroyed. I have to go find Wang Xin."

The blond girl ran east. Miss Qi let her go in search of her love while she remained behind with Ah 出 (chu), who was sitting on the ground. She walked to the center of the square. Moments ago, the Bronze Statue had been there; now nothing remained but emptiness and loneliness. The old purple sun hung like a huge disk in the sky, shining on the soon-to-be-destroyed city. Miss Qi recalled how the cult leader had worn a mask. She at once knew that it was the face of the Evil Spirit. Perhaps millions of years from their present day, the Huhui planet was on the brink of dying, and the collective will of the Huhui people had taken shape as the Evil Spirit—no, as the Bronze Statue—to change fate. They tried and almost succeeded in altering history. Had they perhaps succeeded in some other part of history? Miss Qi didn't want to imagine what kind of place the Huhui planet would be if ruled again by the Bronze Statue. But was it not perhaps the only way for the Huhui people to save themselves?

Miss Qi looked all around one last time at the burning city, the place where she was born and grew up. The Serpent people would soon break through. What of Mei Xin and Wang Xin? Would they both die under the half pikes of the Serpent people? She should have been afraid, but she wasn't. She knew she had time. She stood on the very spot from where the Shan warship had lifted off for the last time. Yu Jin was on that warship, and calmly he had detonated the explosives on his back. She didn't know what he was thinking at that moment, but she knew what she was thinking. Yu Jin, Captain Mai, Dada . . . none of those whom she loved would ever die. Not forever. Everything that exists, exists forever; from time out of primordial chaos till the end of days, everything would exist forever. . . .

The buildings in the capital were burning; the flames leaped into the air. The golden flames looked as if they would burn for eternity. Miss Qi stood at the center of the square waiting for dusk to settle on the city.